MW00762653

The Long Man

Pauline Furey

To Eric & Kathy —

A learning experience for some —
Memories for others —

Pauline Furey.

© Copyright 2003 Pauline Furey. All rights reserved.

No part of this publication may be reproduced, stored in a retrieval system, or transmitted, in any form or by any means, electronic, mechanical, photocopying, recording, or otherwise, without the written prior permission of the author.

Printed in Victoria, Canada

National Library of Canada Cataloguing in Publication

Furey, Pauline
    The long man / Pauline Furey.

ISBN 1-55395-306-1

    I. Title.

PS3606.U74L65 2002   813'.6   C2002-905342-0

This book was published *on-demand* in cooperation with Trafford Publishing.
On-demand publishing is a unique process and service of making a book available for retail sale to the public taking advantage of on-demand manufacturing and Internet marketing.
On-demand publishing includes promotions, retail sales, manufacturing, order fulfilment, accounting and collecting royalties on behalf of the author.

Suite 6E, 2333 Government St., Victoria, B.C. V8T 4P4, CANADA

Phone	250-383-6864	Toll-free	1-888-232-4444 (Canada & US)
Fax	250-383-6804	E-mail	sales@trafford.com
Web site	www.trafford.com	TRAFFORD PUBLISHING IS A DIVISION OF TRAFFORD HOLDINGS LTD.	
Trafford Catalogue #02-[cccc]		www.trafford.com/robots/02-[cccc].html	

10   9   8   7   6   5   4   3   2   1

The Long Man is a work of fiction based on historic fact. Certain actual names and places are mentioned in the narrative and in conversation which are connected to relevant events occurring in World War Two, but these individuals and locations are included only to enhance the credibility of the story. The primary characters and the village of Long Bottom are purely fictional and any resemblance to any actual place or person is entirely coincidental.

**For the Guinea Pigs
With Gratitude**

Author's Note

Much has been written about World War Two and the events leading up to its onset in September, 1939, but the characters featured in The Long Man are so diversified they offer five entirely different aspects of similar events during that time.

As well, an intriguing tale is interworven with historic fact which presents excitement, humour, tragedy, and triumph. The reader will experience the constant fear of detection during clandestine operations; feel the thrill of aerial combat in the vulnerable cockpit of a Hurricane; empathise with the soldiers entrapped on the beaches of Dunkirk and understand their dreadful ordeal; laugh at the humorous misconceptions of a bewildered child, and feel the relief of victory--yet suffer the sense of loss as the war draws to its close.

This is a story that will bring back memories to some, and reveal the extraordinary conditions of that war both in combat and on the home front to others.

Acknowledgements

This story, which takes place during World War Two, could never have been written without the help of those people who so willingly responded to my interviews and research both in England and America. With this kind of valuable contribution, I was able to talk with Battle of Britain pilots, women pilots of the Air Transport Auxiliary, survivors of the Dunkirk ordeal and those who took part in that incredible rescue, members of the still-active Guinea Pig Club, and so many others who offered facts pertaining to personal experiences while clarifying dates and events, and who generally brought history back to life.

My profound thanks goes to them all.

Cover design by Merin Grellier

CHAPTER ONE

Paris, August, 1939

In an atmosphere fraught with tension and anger, a small group of military and civilian aides stood at a respectful distance from the British, French, Belgian and German dignitaries who were making their tight-lipped farewells. The Ritz foyer seemed to shimmer in the heat of summer adding to the already uncomfortable ambiance, yet Janine Parke appeared cool and decidedly collected. In spite of the serious distraction concerning potential war between Germany and Europe, appreciative looks in her direction assured her that her blond hair was in place and her choice of the slim green crêpe dress this afternoon had been a good one.

She looked across the foyer to the main salon and noted a few people continued to indulge in the food and drink while waiting for the illustrious group to leave. Others slowly drifted toward side doors anxious to make their hasty exits. She watched the high-ranking British military officers and members of Parliament, the European governmental representatives accompanied by their senior military advisors, and the British Ambassador to France with his counterpart to Belgium as their expressions of disgust subsided into sadness. Conversely, the Germans eyed each other with tight, smug little smiles as they began to move toward the main door. The façade of polite conversation was over and all present were anxious to learn the vital outcome.

Janine knew that social protocol suggested that the general body of guests remain as a gesture of courtesy until the last dignitary had left. Because of this, she continued to hover between the foyer and the salon and pretended to listen to her companion's comments. In truth, she absorbed the social interplay within the area with an expert eye, well aware that several others were doing the same thing. She watched as two well-known Hungarian film-makers moved ever closer to a Russian diplomat, surreptitiously eavesdropping on his conversation with a prominent Belgian businessman. Near the bar, a popular British actor appeared to be charming a young German countess. Janine could see that he had strategically positioned himself in order to easily watch the proceedings in the foyer and utilise his prowess in lipreading. A beloved composer of risqué songs leaned against the magnificent grand piano in a wide alcove, sipping wine. He pretended to exude utter boredom, but she knew he was making an uncannily accurate mental list of significant names that would be of interest to the British Government. All of these observations would be reported to British Intelligence within the hour.

She feigned interest, swirling the wine in her untouched glass, as Mrs. Clyde-Pruitt prattled on beside her and watched the florid mouth move like a red sea anemone as it alternately sucked in nourishment from offered refreshment trays, and spat out useless gossip between swallows. Janine continued to scan the room. Standing a little apart and concentrating on the contents of his wine glass, Claude Simone avoided her glance. She watched him take one quick sip and then place the glass on the tray of a passing waiter. Still deliberately ignoring her, he walked through the open French doors and out on to the terrace. Not until he had disappeared from sight did she allow herself to absorb Mrs. Clyde-Pruitt's remarks enough to make comment.

"Surely the establishment of the Maginot Line along the Franco-German frontier, and the acceleration of French armament production should indicate that Prime Minister Edouard Daladier is apprehensive?" she said, watching Mrs. Clyde-Pruitt's rhythmically clenching jaw.

An old waiter, who appeared intent on getting to the kitchen to relieve himself of an almost empty tray of hors d'oeuvres, looked surprised as Mrs. Clyde-Pruitt deftly lifted two delicacies from it and popped them both into her mouth at the same time. She chewed quickly with bulging cheeks obviously anxious to give her own opinion on the brewing war situation as soon as she had swallowed. Janine saw her chance to continue, uninterrupted for the moment.

"Doesn't the alliance with Britain and the promises of Anglo-French solidarity concerning the dismemberment of Czechoslovakia by the Germans, plus the promise to support Poland against German aggression, signify growing distrust?"

Mrs. Clyde-Pruitt swallowed too quickly and choked into her napkin. Again, Janine continued.

"Now that German involvement is no longer an issue in Spain since that civil war is over, isn't it general knowledge that German manpower resources have been built up and could immediately be drawn upon?"

Mrs. Clyde-Pruitt opened her mouth to speak as Janine looked at her watch.

"Oh, look at the time," she said, before the good lady

could say a word. "I have an early start scheduled in the morning in order to make the deadline for my magazine column."

"But you can't leave before they do," Mrs. Clyde-Pruitt gasped, glancing toward the dispersing group.

"Good night, Mrs. Clyde-Pruitt," Janine said loudly. Then moving closer she whispered "..... and if I were you, I would start packing.   I doubt that you will be allowed to maintain your residence in France after the Führer begins to execute his plans.   Isn't it obvious to you that Britain will declare war on Germany any minute?"

"What do you mean?" Mrs. Clyde-Pruitt whispered back. "Are you mad?   Are you not aware of the agreement at Munich?   Are you not aware that the weakened divided countries are in social and economic crisis? Nazism is merely offering to strengthen these weaknesses and to create order and social harmony, not to mention work for everyone.   There is to be large scale urbanisation and the availability of quality German products........" The voice faltered and faded.

Janine felt almost sorry for the silly woman. How could anyone so close to the British Ambassador to France be so easily hoodwinked?   How could anyone possibly observe the conversation that had just taken place amongst those in that illustrious circle at the bottom of the stairs and not detect the ominous overtones?

A general convergence of people toward the main entrance signified that the guests of honour were leaving at last and Janine hurried toward a side door where her driver waited. There was no sign of Claude. No matter. She would see him in the morning.

*   *   *

As Janine slid between the cool hotel sheets, she began to ponder her life and wondered how the war would affect it. She thought about her childhood in the serene environs of Provence and her happy youthful days at the Sorbonne where she read linguistics. She knew her talent for languages had resulted in an impeccable English vocabulary, although she still constantly fought with her French accent.

She thought about her parents, aging now yet still cultivating their vineyards and flower gardens in Aix-en-Provence. How would the war affect them? How lucky she was to have them--always understanding and willing to listen to her youthful whims during university days. Acknowledging her adventurous spirit, they had agreed to finance her further studies in aviation and ultimately the purchase of a Fox Moth.

She remembered that it was during one of her flights to England that she met Henry at a party in London. He was about to commence his internship at King's, having completed his studies in medicine at Cambridge, and mutual friends had insisted on a celebration. Her friends had urged her to speak to him since he was far too serious and shy, they said. Although the complete antithesis of one another, they were uncannily attracted and, to the surprise of everyone, later married. From the beginning, Henry had been understandably preoccupied with a rapidly growing list of prestigious patients and she remembered fondly how he condoned and even encouraged her to continue flying to France to frequently visit her parents and friends there. Yet she loved Flint House, too, which was Henry's small inherited estate in Sussex. When David was born a little over nineteen years ago, she was surprised and pleased when her interests in English country life flourished, and eventually her visits to France began to dwindle. Yet after Yvonne's arrival eighteen months later, Janine clearly remembered her renewed restlessness which led to her ultimately begin living an irrevocable lie.

My linguistic talents, she remembered, my social standing (which accessed me to both political and aristocratic social gatherings), a good working knowledge of European topography and an overall awareness of international politics formed, I suppose, the ideal synthesis for a clandestine listening post. Although the major issues of the Great War of 1914-1918 had been resolved, a loose network of intrigue undoubtedly continued to operate, focusing often in the capital cities of Europe and in North Africa. I suppose I was bound to be caught up in it.

She shut her eyes tightly, wishing sleep would come. But her mind was fired up from the disturbing afternoon's activities and continued to prod her awake.

She recalled that the prospect of spying did not appeal to her at first, yet as the bellicose overtones of Nazism began to creep into Europe, she knew that it would be just a matter of time before the smoldering black obsession would erupt and rapidly spread. The belatedly realised (although in some quarters accurately predicted) deceit attached to the Czechoslovakian and Polish issues, and the installation of Nazis in the Austrian cabinet were clear examples of this.

The opportunity to write the travel column for *Out And About* magazine created the perfect journalistic guise for a cover-up.   Claude Simone--she smiled as she remembered her initial thought that he was such an unlikely French anglophile and professional spy due to his strange idiosyncrasies--partnered her as they hovered at the edge of discussions, sorting out pertinent facts and general atmospheres and subsequently relaying them to the Secret Intelligence Service (SIS) recipients in London.   I've always hated consistently deceiving Henry and the children into thinking that I am merely fulfilling my restlessness while gathering material for my column, she thought.   Surely now all this will change. I know nothing about military intelligence and will probably be of no further use. With this comforting thought, sleep came to Janine at last.

*   *   *

The Fox Moth stood in silhouette the next morning against the first glimmer of dawn. Sprawling Orly airfield was uncannily quiet as Janine climbed into the cockpit. The aircraft seemed to exude its eagerness to be airborne as it waited on the tarmac beyond the dark bulk of a hangar. Hot air from the recent engine warm-up shimmered above the cowling and rose in faint undulating waves toward the night sky and a soft wispy mist hung over the field like a fading parade of nocturnal spirits.   It was the last day of August, 1939 and across the almost deserted aerodrome an aura of apprehension mingled with the cloying perfume of summer.

"We'll just make it," Claude said in English as opened

the door of the lower cabin.   Not without effort, he had perfected his articulation and passed easily as an Englishman. "All civilian aircraft are to be grounded in Britain tomorrow. German troops are preparing to march into Poland, in spite of Chamberlain's warning to Hitler."   He threw a small bag into the cabin.   "I understand the British Expeditionary Advanced Air Strike squadrons have already left for France."

"It's about to happen then?" Janine said, with a great sigh.

Claude nodded.   "The British will declare war and the French, of course, will immediately follow suit."

Although expected, the imminence of war shocked her. France would no doubt be one of the first to feel the impact due to its shared frontier with Germany.   Should she try to convince her elderly parents to leave their estate in southern France and flee to England?   She had noted the justified anxiety on her companion's face.   The son of Parisian Jewish intellectuals, he must know that his parents would be targeted first.

"Can you convince your parents to leave?" she asked.

He shook his head.   "In spite of German anti-Semitic feelings and their despicable solutions to the so-called problem now taking place in the occupied countries, my father remains adamant.   He'll never leave." He sprang easily into the cabin and closed the door.

Janine pulled on her goggles and helmet. The engine quickly sprang to life and she taxied the aircraft to the end of the runway and waited for permission to take off. Soon they were soaring into a sky streaked with the first insipid light of dawn and she banked and turned toward the west, away from the brightening horizon. As they gained altitude, she pondered over her own choices. Should she remain in England with her beloved husband and children, or return to Provence before it was too late?   As they passed the Kentish coastline her mind boiled in turmoil.   Unable to confer with anyone, it was essential that she weigh her priorities and make up her mind quickly.   Perhaps a posting in Britain in an advisory capacity using her invaluable knowledge of French terrain would be useful to secret operations should France be occupied; and yet this might also apply if she were in France advising the British of German military movements.   Either way, she must try to manipulate her parents away and bring them to the relative safety of England.   At least the Channel offered a bonus.   A defensive moat perhaps.

As she filed her arrival at the operations desk at Croydon aerodrome, she felt calmer but still undecided.   Claude's problem is far more vital, she thought.   Jews--especially those with public influence--were being rounded up in Poland. She wondered what she might do to help, and turned to speak to him. But the opportunity did not present itself since he had already left.   She knew, however, that he would see to it that a full report of their observations in Paris would be on record in London almost immediately.

*   *   *

Flint House, Long Bottom, East Sussex

Janine disliked wasting time but she nonetheless completed her travel article knowing that the likelihood of it being printed was remote.   It would be a moot point to advertise the pursuit of pleasure when such travel would now be prohibited. As it was, all civil aviation had been grounded the day after she returned from Paris and her aeroplane had gone into storage for the duration of the war.

She leaned back in her chair and stared pensively through the window. The grounds were already showing signs of autumn colour, in spite of the continuing hot weather. Perhaps she should think about having the flower beds removed to make way for vegetables. Now that war had officially been declared on this balmy Sunday afternoon, the threat of siege of the islands and the shortages that would undoubtedly follow, must be taken into consideration. A frown formed between the blue eyes as her thoughts turned to her family. Remembering the awful injuries sustained by troops who fought in the French trenches in the last war, she surmised that Henry would be involved with the returning wounded in this coming conflict. No doubt he would put the family town house in Bayswater to more use while working in the London hospitals.

Yvonne, not quite eighteen, was surely too young to be involved in spite of her energy and willfulness. Yet her determination and inherited love of aviation could possibly put her in harms way. But it was an inevitable fact that David would be called to service with his Oxford University reserve squadron, and this prospect frightened Janine.

Her son had grown from an untidy schoolboy into a good-looking young man who bore a remarkable physical likeness to his tall, gray-eyed and dark-haired father. But there the resemblance ended since David exuded the nonchalant enthusiasm of youth and made no secret of his obsession with flying. Only in countenance did he resemble his reserved and conservative father and there had been polite conflict over his lack of interest in the study of medicine, which was entirely

Henry's preference.

She looked up as a few turning leaves fluttered from the top of the great elm by the summer house. The wind had picked up, and clouds began to dim the mellow light of the afternoon, throwing the ancient phenomenal etched figure of the Long Man of Wilmington, outlined in chalk on the face of the South Downs, into its accustomed shadow. The foyer clock chimed three and by habit Janine synchronised her watch. David should be back from his walk soon. Perhaps this would be the last time she would see him out of uniform. Aware that her own activities abroad did not lack some risk, she was nonetheless not prepared for her son to face obvious dangers in a fast fighter aeroplane.

* * *

David

A billowing mass of grey cloud swelled over the crest of the South Downs. They encroached across the sun and passed undulating shadows over the two hundred and twenty-six foot outline of the Long Man of Wilmington. Ragged scraps of cirrus spume tore away and tumbled southward, racing along the course of the Ouse River toward Newhaven and the English Channel. The locals knew that the strange two-dimensional chalk giant, carved into the short turf to expose the distinct white outline, was thought to be of Roman origin since his motionless stride had spanned the slope for as long as anyone could remember. According to some speculation the Long

The Long Man of Wilmington
(Personal photograph)

Man resembled an outline depicted on ancient Roman coins, yet on the other hand it was also a consideration that Benedictine monks had put him there.   Pilots who flew over him saw a long, slim figure while observers on the ground, their visual aspect impaired by the slope and thus foreshortening the figure, saw him as squat and stocky.   He appeared to support himself on either side by two long poles.   If the intention was to view him in his long, slim form one might wonder if the Romans (or the Benedictine monks) had indeed developed the concept of aviation.

David Parke stood at the top of the hill above the mammoth faceless head with feet firmly planted to balance his six-foot height against the gusts.   He looked down at the solitary street that formed the ancient village of Wilmington, trailing like a kite tail until it halted abruptly at the juncture of the main Lewes road.   To the north, barely visible amongst the trees, he could see the neighbouring village of Long Bottom nestled in a hollow at the base of the downs.   Poplar trees, dim in the haze of flurrying blue smoke from a bonfire, obstructed a direct view of the big flint stone house that stood in its grounds on the edge of the village.   Flint House had been David's home since his birth, yet only now in his twentieth year, did he clearly appreciate the serene ambiance about the place.   He always loved the summers when it stood in a collar of riotous colour mingled with varied greens; and the autumns when brilliant golds and auburns prevailed; and the springs when the daffodils glowed in a moving pattern of light and shade. Even in winter the grounds were colourful with brilliant holly berries, evergreen privet, ivy, and pyracantha that softened the sharp outlines of the solidly square house.

He could remember no direct adversity ever threatening the tranquillity of life in the village or any possible obstacle arising to prevent him from pursuing his reluctant pre-med studies at Oxford. But, even as he looked across the hills and valleys of this green and pleasant land, he knew things were about to change. Now, at last, he would experience the speed of the new Spitfire fighter plane, or perhaps the older Hawker Hurricane.   His heart beat a little faster as he considered the limited amount of time he had to learn the complexities of these aircraft in order to compete with the battle-experienced Luftwaffe pilots, many of whom had gained successes during the Spanish civil war.

A sudden shaft of sunlight exploded from the edge of a cloud highlighting the black, bounding figure of his Scottish terrier running along the hedgerow at the base of the hill.

"Home, Charlie!" he shouted.   "I've a train to catch."

After a brisk walk back across the fields, he kicked off his Wellington boots at the scullery door and tried in vain to prevent Charlie from barging past him to drink from his water bowl.   He grimaced at the track of muddy footprints across the floor as Jenny, the housemaid, sullenly followed them with a wet mop.

"I'd like to stuff that little Scot into a Haggis one day," she muttered.   "Why can't he learn to wipe his feet?"

"He's a slow learner, Jenny.   He'll get the hang of it eventually.   After all, he's only two."

"He'll not see three if he keeps it up," she growled.

Mrs. Dougherty, the cook, frowned from behind the scrubbed kitchen table.   "That's enough, Jenny," she said. "You can take in the tea tray as soon as you're finished."

Jenny looked at David from under lowered lashes, suppressing a grin.   "Right away, Mrs. Dougherty."

David knew that Mrs. Dougherty despaired over Jenny's lack of respect yet knew that the traditional submissiveness of servants, especially the young ones of lower grade, had faded somewhat since the onset of the Flapper era in the 'twenties.

He found his mother in her sitting room flicking idly through a magazine. Her bright blond hair looked slightly tousled and she tapped one foot impatiently. He flopped into an armchair and stretched his long legs out in front, noting the usual hole in the toe of his sock.

"The weather's clearing," he said.

She looked up and smiled, continuing to idly fan the magazine pages. The absence of her usual vivacity and optimism, obviously subdued by the recent news of war, disturbed him and he did not know what to say to comfort her.

"I can't elaborate on the war situation, you know," she said suddenly, throwing the magazine down on the seat beside her.

"I don't expect you to," David said. "All I know is that my squadron will be called to service pretty quickly, and that I can't wait to get into action."

Janine studied his eager, young face and sighed. "It's a serious business, you know. You can't treat it as a lark."

"I know, but the thought of really flying......I mean....the Avro Tutors are nice, but....well.....you know......."

"I do understand that aspect of course, David. But the opposition is formidable.   There was much talk of it in Europe........"

"What were your observations in Paris?"

"Observations?   I was simply there on social and magazine business--completely irrelevant to war, of course. It's just that everyone knows that the Germans mean business.....nasty business."

"Well, they lost the last one, didn't they!"

"They're arrogant and extremely dangerous, David."

He did not like her tone or her unaccustomed agitation. Perhaps if he changed the subject........

"Would you talk to Father about a car?" he asked.   "I

quite enjoy gadding about in George Ravensbrook's MG, but I'd much rather have one of my own."

Janine rose to answer a light tap on the door . "Under the circumstances I think you should have some form of transportation," she said, as Jenny entered with the tea things. "You'll probably be stationed somewhere out in the country. But there'll be a petrol shortage, of course."

Jenny carried the tray to a side table and as she delicately stepped over David's legs, she offered him an ample view of her own shapely ones.

"The boys from the farm went into Eastbourne to join up," she said, putting the tray down. "They're mad! Can't wait to go out and get themselves killed!"

Janine winced. "Yes, Jenny. Thank you."

".........and Mr. Mallory's getting all the old men together in the village to defend us," Jenny went on. "He had them lined up with pitch forks and broom handles right after the announcement on the wireless."

"Thank you, Jenny!"

"Cook says you're going to close up Flint House and go and live in London. Is that what you're going to do, Mrs. Parke? Will you give me a good reference, if you do? Or perhaps I can go with you."

"Please, Jenny. Go and have your own tea, there's a good girl. We'll talk about all that later."

Jenny lifted her short skirt and stepped back over David's legs, who grinned appreciatively. Yet, in spite of her brashness, he saw that her hand trembled.

"Make the most of the biscuits," she said. "They're going to be rationed along with everything else."

"She's scared stiff, poor thing," he said after she had closed the door behind her. "Can't be much older than Yvonne, really. Where is my willful sister, anyway? I haven't seen her all weekend."

"She's been in London since she returned from school in France and claims that she's going to find a way to fly, regardless of the ban."

"She's dreaming, of course."

"At this moment, David, I wish I were dreaming."

*   *   *

Yvonne

By the time Yvonne Parke stepped from the train at Lewes, her anger had subsided.   How asinine, she thought, to think that women pilots are incapable of evading enemy aircraft should they cross our shorelines.   Comforted by the knowledge that her friends in the flying club at Croydon had concurred, she knew she was not alone in her indignation.   Only hours away from earning her mechanic's license for single-propeller aircraft, her aeroplane had been confiscated by the government and she was left literally holding the spanner.   Determined to keep her hand in any way she could, she decided to board the fifty-foot family river boat which they kept on the Ouse River at Lewes and practice on its big marine engine.

Having bicycled from the station she found *Summer Solstice* moored near the Lewes Rowing Club located off Cliffe main street, just a few yards from the Snowdrop Inn.   It would take only a couple of minutes to change into the old overalls she kept in the cabin, and put in a good hour or so before cycling home to see David off.   Although anxious to see her

The Long Man   Pauline Furey

Author's Rendition of *Summer Solstice*
(With kind permission of John Devereaux, Cdr.USN Ret)

brother, her pursuits in London were vital to her. She eyed her bicycle propped up by Ben Boniface's office, and felt a hint of guilt. Perhaps she should go home first. It would be some time before David would get leave once he was called to service. Obviously she should have rearranged her priorities. She looked at her watch, hesitating between the bicycle and the boat. Oh, surely a few minutes would not make that much difference would it?

But time passed far too rapidly, and as she replaced the last nut on the hatch, she realised that she had lingered much longer than intended. As she stood up, she felt the breeze stiffen and the boat shudder, protesting against the wavelets that slapped against the hull. Pressing her fingers into the small of her back to ease the stiffness, she looked across the narrow span of the river and saw the outlines of the town already fading in the dusk.

"She could use some paint."

The voice startled her and she spun around, narrowing her eyes to peer into the shadows along the bank.

"Ben?"

As he reached the boat in three easy strides and stepped aboard, she wondered how long he had been watching her.

"Not much chance of that now," she said. "Like everything else, paint will be scarce."

He perched on the gunwale, casting himself into silhouette against the backdrop of the town.

"The river barges are a priority, you know, and maintenance needs will always be provided for," he said. "I can always.....ensure..... that there's some paint left over."

"Thank you, but there's no hurry."

She looked at the black hulks of the barges, empty now and riding high in the water against the wharf on the opposite bank. Tomorrow, they would be reloaded and taken downriver to Newhaven. The barge men were no doubt in the Snowdrop Inn enjoying their beer and would soon be going home to hot baths and heavy meals. She wondered why Ben was not with them since he kept the barges in good repair and enjoyed a certain camaraderie with the men.

"What are you going to do now that war has been declared?" he asked.

"I want to fly if I can. There has to be some way."

"I thought all civil aviation had been grounded."

"It has. But perhaps there might be some form of ferrying service women could do."

He remained silent.

"What will you do, Ben? Join up?"

"Your brother's reserve squadron will go immediately I should think," he said, ignoring her question. "The British Expeditionary Force hasn't fared so well, you know. Some of them have been pretty badly shot up."

Was he being deliberately cruel? Although she had known him for two years, he was generally something of an enigma. She often wondered why he had rented a room at Mallory Cottage in Long Bottom village and yet owned several pieces of commercial property in Lewes. True, Doris Mallory was an excellent cook and since Ben often went out of town for days at a time, his somewhat transient arrangement made sense. He had no close friends that she knew of and seemed to quietly blend with people in all walks of life, listening to what they had to say, but saying little himself. To her he was an odd conglomeration of a salty reprobate and a man of letters. She guessed him to be in his late twenties and, in spite of the dilapidated, oversized fisherman's jumper he always wore, could see that he was in excellent physical condition. He kept the angular lines of his face, now obscured by shadow, clean shaven and the tight brown waves of his hair closely cropped.

She surmised that Ben Boniface was shy, yet he never failed to meet an eye.   In fact, his habit of staring a person down with his clear, hazel eyes had become a point of irritation with some.

Reeling from his remark, she turned toward the cabin.

"I must change and go home," she said, abruptly. "Good night, Ben."

He obediently left the boat and disappeared into the shadows.

As she mounted the bicycle, he appeared again and laid his hand across the handlebars, intentionally delaying her.

"I don't think it would be a good idea to fly," he said. "Civilian aviation has been grounded for good reason."

She shrugged and tried to push down on the pedal.

"They're sending children down this way from London, you know," he said, still firmly holding on to the bicycle. "Your family could open some of the vacant bedrooms at Flint House and you could take care of the evacuees instead."

"Perhaps Doris Mallory will open Mallory Cottage to some of them, too," she snapped.   "Then what will *you* do?" She eyed the strong shoulders and firm jaw line.   "Will you consider joining up then?"

Pushing down hard on the pedal she forced his hand away and spewing gravel, levered herself up the slope to the road with one foot. Ben Boniface remained on her mind as she rode along the darkened road toward Long Bottom. She had seen him recoil from the children who came down to the river in the summer and concluded that he was either intolerant of them, or simply bewildered by them. Doubtful that he would maintain his current living arrangements if London evacuees did intrude into his privacy, she wondered where he would go or what he would do if he chose to avoid serving in the military forces.

CHAPTER 2

December, 1939

The rich smell of cordovan leather surrounded David as George Ravensbrook's MG nosed its way southward through a blinding blizzard.   Events in general had happened in quick succession since the onset of the war and it seemed only yesterday that he and George were plodding their way through the rigors of the Initial Training Wing at Hastings.

The University Reserve Squadron had been called to service on the fifteenth of September, just a week after France declared war on Germany and on the same day that South Africa came into the war.   Only then did David and his university colleagues begin to really take notice of RAF activities on the Continent.   Early in September BEF support squadrons had made attacks on German warships at Wilhelmshaven and Brunsbüttel with some losses; and, only two days after he had been called to service, the British aircraft carrier, *HMS Courageous* was sunk with few survivors. The Whitley squadrons were dropping propaganda leaflets into enemy terrain while conducting reconnaissance and gathering intelligence.

At home, gas masks and food rationing were affecting

the daily lives of everyone. In anticipation of air raids the government had delivered corrugated Anderson shelters to civilians, and complete blackout had been enforced throughout the land after sunset. In October, *HMS Royal Oak* was torpedoed by the Germans at Scapa Flow, and an attempted assassination of Adolf Hitler had failed.

Now, a day before Christmas, he and George were halfway through a specially accelerated course at Cranwell RAF College in Lincolnshire and although they happily looked forward to the holiday leave, were most anxious to get into the action. Since The Honourable and Mrs. Richard Ravensbrook were on diplomatic service in India, an invitation had been extended by Janine for their son to join the Parke family for Christmas. David enjoyed George's company and was pleased when he accepted. They had met at Oxford while they were in their first year. Both were rummaging through one of the many book shops in the town and although their academic interests were dissimilar since George was reading law, they immediately became friends. It amused David then to watch his new friend's unconscious awkwardness as he knocked one book down and tripped over another. Without the slightest trace of consternation, he replaced the books and continued his conversation with enthusiasm and a ready wit. Of medium height with sandy hair and freckles, David soon learned that George had the fortunate knack of dispelling gloom in any given situation and his most attractive asset was a broad and genuine smile.

"Do you think we can make it through?" David asked, peering out into the swirling snow.

"Of course!"

David leaned forward a little to get a better view of the driver's face, and the spreading blot that burgeoned around his left eye.

"That eye is almost shut, you know. Are you sure I shouldn't take over the wheel?"

21

"Have no fear!"

"You suffer these ghastly injuries every week during rugby season and you've bruised, lacerated, twisted, and sprained almost every part of your body. Do you really expect to make any headway with my sister with a shiner like that?"

George growled appreciatively at the mention of Yvonne and smiled licentiously. He leaned forward against the steering wheel and wiped his gloved hand over the inside of the windscreen.

"Fogging up a bit," he muttered.

"Heavy breathing will do that," David said. "She'll talk about aeroplanes, you know."

"She can talk all she likes. I'll be more than glad to make observations about sleek and graceful lines. Especially hers."

"She's anxious to see if the Air Transport Auxiliary will take on women as ferry pilots."

"Is she now? It'll never happen, of course. Most of the squadrons are ferrying their own operational aircraft, plus trainers. Anyway, it would be sheer madness to allow women to fly in hostile conditions."

"If I were you, I wouldn't mention that," David cautioned. "She's a bit touchy on the subject."

"I'll try to remember, but I always seem to lose my faculties when I'm around her and end up colliding with the brunt of her sarcasm."

"Well, the quick temper seems to be inherent with red hair, you know."

George smiled again, and whistled long and low.

* * *

Janine surveyed the people around the dinner table with satisfaction. Mrs. Dougherty had done a splendid job with the food and Jenny spilled wine only once while serving David who had diverted an embarrassing situation by insisting that he could mop up his own lap.

The two young men in uniform appeared fresh and untried, yet Janine wondered how much experience with women, or life itself, either of them might have had. Judging from David's perfunctory reaction to Jenny's advances, perhaps there had been very little on his part. In any event, Jenny had been right about closing up Flint House and if she had any ulterior motives concerning David, they could go no further. George, on the other hand, seemed determined to progress as far as possible with Yvonne, and made no secret of his admiration. Janine smiled ruefully as he blundered his way out of her daughter's favour.

"......open cockpits in winter are sheer torture.   How will women manage?"

"The same way men do," Yvonne snapped.

"You could go in First Aid Nursing Yeomanry," George persisted.   "Much safer, and you wouldn't be depriving some poor chap of a job that way."

David's deliberate sleight of hand sent his second full wine glass crashing to the snowy tablecloth as a warning to his friend. Only then did George awaken to his clumsy choice of words.

It occurred to Janine that her daughter's preoccupation with her desire to fly might cause her to be largely unaware of the affect she had on men.   Tonight, she looked especially lovely in the candlelight as her hair fell in soft bronze waves about her face. The tawny eyes belied the mellifluous effect as they sparked with indignation. For all her schooling, she ignored the beneficial qualities of light social conversation and, to Janine's despair, often preferred to plunge into a good, solid

23

argument.   But Yvonne had always been difficult--headstrong, short tempered, and often surly as a child--she now displayed an unpopular trend toward superciliousness and an intolerance of the lesser classes.   Certainly, this was not condoned by anyone else in the family, and Janine had pointed this out directly upon Yvonne's return from France, with disastrous results.   Enraged, and hurling snide accusations of class indifference toward her mother, Yvonne had banged out of the house and gone to London.

Yvonne, however, was not the only problem Janine faced this evening. The enemy advancement continued in Europe and the French, strong in military numbers, tenaciously manned the length of the Maginot Line. But Hitler's intention to overrun France was quite obvious. Janine continued to receive uncensored letters from her parents in Provence which indicated that things seemed to be functioning normally. Even so, she felt uneasy. On the surface it appeared that only defensive preparations were evident in England, but she knew that many less obvious offensive strategies were in the planning stage; so unobtrusive in fact, that the Americans had named this period of waiting and watching the Phoney War. More disturbing was the lengthening lack of communication from Claude.

Since their last flight from Paris her coordinators at SIS had allowed her time to help with the incoming Czech and Polish refugees in London. Language barriers had hampered processing, but the authorities had found a few who spoke either broken English or, more often than not, French. But a massive roundup of Fifth Columnists, who were everywhere in southern England, went into operation and Janine was led to believe that Claude might be involved with this.   Yet, when they were pursuing different sources of information in the past, he had always kept in touch.

It occurred to her that he may have attempted to make personal contact with his parents in Paris. If this were the case and he had made an unofficial entry into France, he would be in considerable danger since two British MI6 agents had been kidnapped by the Germans only last month. If these men were known to the Abwehr, then the possibility of Claude being identified was highly likely.

Jenny brought in the dessert and George now turned his attention to Henry, asking him probing questions concerning wartime injuries. Henry spoke briefly on the subject, and quickly suggested an adjournment into the library. Janine did not miss the flash of concern that passed across her son's face. The squadrons in France were not faring well, and she knew that many pilots had been badly injured--or had not returned at all.

*   *   *

Late that night David lay in bed thinking about the conversation at dinner. How bad can these injuries be, he wondered? He had sprained his ankle once playing tennis and had inadvertently burned his hand on a hot iron in the laundry. But although both injuries had hurt like hell at the time, it had not taken long to recover. One's bound to get knocked about a bit in war, he thought.

He awoke the next morning to see a sprinkling of snow on the window sill glowing crystalline yellow in the early sun. The blizzard evidently stopped short of London and spilled only its dying edge toward the south. He got up and leaned his elbows against the sill and watched a robin flute the edge of the birdbath below with a rim of tiny asterisks. The last of the chrysanthemums under the great elm drooped under powdery white bonnets, and through the branches he could see the sun melting its liquid light into the snow up on Long Barrow. Somewhere behind the poplars, the Long Man slept beneath his white blanket.

After breakfast Janine suggested that everyone join her for a walk to Mallory Cottage.

"Doris and Toby took in two London evacuees in October, and I thought it might be nice to take gifts to them. I'm sure they must be very homesick."

Yvonne smirked, thinking of Ben Boniface. The arrival of children at Mallory Cottage must have been quite a shock to his need for quiet and privacy. She wondered if he might have yet considered joining one of the branches of the armed forces in order to serve his country--or at least give him an excuse to escape from two noisy London children.

As they walked through the village, Mallory Cottage looked sugar coated with a thin layer of snow on the thatched roof. Its latticed windows winked in the sun and appeared to be signaling to Arthur Banberry's tiny stationery shop on the opposite side of the narrow street. Doris Mallory answered their knock, wearing her customary porkpie hat with a wilted pheasant feather stuck in the brim. Her cheeks shone rosily from the warmth of the kitchen and her brown eyes twinkled with pleasure.

"Come in! Come in!" she beamed.

They ducked their heads to avoid colliding with the low dark beams and trooped into the front room where a fire crackled in the fieldstone fireplace. Toby Mallory half rose from his chair to welcome them and gestured to the various other armchairs about the room, inviting them to be seated. He and Doris exuded the similar attributes of contentment that stem from retirement and country life and he greeted his guests with genuine pleasure.

"David in uniform!" he said, shaking his head. "I still think of him as a little boy."

George placed a hand on David's shoulder and held him

at arms' length.   "And I always thought you were born grown up," he said.

Toby's chuckle faded and his expression changed to one of concern.

"I do wonder," he said, "if we aren't being a bit complacent about this war.   I mean, we have all our defences up along the coast--at least in this area we do.   But lack of any action has made people careless about carrying their gas masks. Mr. Banberry has had to warn quite a number of people in the village about chinks of light showing at night.   He's our local Air Raid Warden, you know."

He looked around his circle of guests as they murmured in agreement.

"Obviously the enemy has his sites set on other targets at the moment," George said.   "But, you're right, Toby, I think our turn might be coming before long."

"They won't let us civilians anywhere near all the gun batteries along the cliffs, but it would be impossible to hide those tall towers they've put up.   Something to do with the Air Ministry, I'm told.   Do you know what they are, chaps?"

David and George glanced at one another and shrugged, knowing full well that the three hundred foot structures were the new radio detection towers.

"AMES they call them," Toby went on.   "Air Ministry Experimental Stations.   Well, they're just some of many odd things going on around here."

Janine knew that several arrests had been made near the towers when the general roundup of Fifth Columnists was in operation.   Perhaps she should try to distract Toby from this touchy subject.

"Where are your evacuees, Doris?   We've brought presents for them."

"Nice children," Toby said.   "Even Ben gets along with the girl, you know."

Yvonne snickered.

27

Doris leaned against the door post and called for the children. "Unfortunately, Ben's not here. We're used to his absences, of course.   But I had hoped.......at least for Christmas..."

She turned her attention to the stairs as the children clattered down and shuffled shyly into the room.

"This is Kate Hawkins. She's just turned ten....." The girl moved behind Doris' skirt as all eyes turned toward her. ".....and her brother, Hugh who is twelve." Hugh stood his ground but looked decidedly uncomfortable.

In appearance there was little in common between the two children since Kate was small and dark with thin arms and legs, while her brother was stocky and fair. Janine had heard horror stories of the East London evacuees being infested with fleas and who had been sewn into their unwashed underwear, but these children were obviously not of that class or calibre. Although unsure of themselves at this moment, they appeared to be reasonably well-mannered. The girl surveyed the gathering of adults with large almond-shaped eyes, and upon seeing George's bruised eye she moved into the room and stood in front of him.

"Does it hurt?" she asked.

"Only when I blink."

Her mouth seemed to simultaneously pout and smile giving her an expression of quizzical amusement.

"Hugh had one like that once after a cricket game," she said. "He said the ball hit him, but I think someone socked him in the tea room."

Hugh came to his own rescue as colour heightened in his cheeks.

"It was the bail that hit me, not the ball," he muttered. "You never get anything right."

"Well, you did tell me that the Gestapo doesn't like little English girls, and I understood that all right."

"It was a joke," Hugh said, kicking at the edge of the

carpet.

Kate turned her attention toward David. "He also told me that the *Graf Spee* scuttled itself in Monti-something. Did you know that?"

David smiled. "Montevideo. Yes, I did know that actually."

Yvonne sat thinking about Ben. Doris had mentioned that there was a certain compatibility between him and the girl. Yet he chose not to be present for her on this Christmas morning. Surely barge business could not have called him away.

"Mrs. Mallory tells me that you and Ben have become friends," she said to Kate. "That's quite an accomplishment. Ben doesn't make friends easily, you know."

"Really? We don't talk very much, but we do have staring contests. Sometimes I win."

"Do you know where he is now? It's rather a shame that he isn't here to share in the Christmas festivities, don't you think?"

"Oh, I don't know." Kate said. "I expect he's enjoying himself in his own way. He's probably gone off somewhere with his girl friend."

"Girl friend?"

Kate nodded and eyed the table where Janine had laid the packages. "Yes. I saw them in the village once and drew a picture of them. I like to draw pictures, you know."

"These are for you," Janine said, getting to her feet. "Let's see what's inside, shall we? Toby tells me you draw quite well, Kate. I've brought you a sketch book and pencils. You will have to come to Flint House later on and show me what you've done."

Yvonne frowned and stared into the fire. In all the time she had known Ben there had never been any evidence of a woman in his life.

29

*   *   *

Claude Simone stood with his hands held high on either side of the warehouse window sash and closed his eyes. Before him the town of Lewes, crowned with the ruins of the old castle, looked like an earthbound Hades in the brilliant winter sunset. Below, the snow-covered river wharf was void of activity on this Christmas day, and his lonely footprints were the only evidence of mortal presence. A solitary seagull huddled on top of a bollard and mewed forlornly only once, then settled down again to doze.

Claude opened his eyes and looked at the crimson glow reflecting on his hands and felt a sudden compulsion to withdraw them. His fingers curled around a note in his jacket pocket and he thought again about the odd manner in which it had been delivered. Having completed his business in Banberry's post office several days ago, a woman he had never seen before approached and handed him the note without explanation or further communication. He had glanced quickly at her face, noting the sharp angular bones and, more noticeable, the cold, pale eyes, before she turned and hurried away.

It was a strange missive--uncoded and brief--indicating that he should meet her in his warehouse on Christmas day. Methods of contact from London headquarters often varied but were rarely this overt.

He looked down at the wharf and saw a slight, athletic figure walking toward the warehouse, leaving a trail of pointed footprints beside his in the snow. He pushed up the window and caught her attention, pointing toward a door at the side of the building. She raised her hand in acknowledgment and

30

disappeared into the doorway.

He could hear her running up the long stairway and waited at the top to greet her. As she mounted the last steps, she looked up at him without smiling.

"I am Beatrix Dierick," she said. There was no evidence of breathlessness after her long climb as he shook her outstretched hand. ".....and you are Claude Simone.....or should I say Ben Boniface?" Her mouth stretched into a feline smile that failed to reach her eyes.

He still had no idea who the woman was and disliked the advantage she held over him. Something about her made his skin creep and he sensed he should be careful.

"You were born and educated to a point in France," she went on.

"Yes," Claude said. "But before you go on, perhaps you would show me some kind of identification."

She narrowed her pale eyes and shook her head.

"I don't think that will be necessary," she said. "You'll understand why when I have finished."

She removed her gloves and he noticed that her hands were large and white and seemed out of proportion to the rest of her.

"You received a degree in International Law from Cambridge University," she went on. "and a second degree in Linguistics. You work for British Intelligence."

He stood motionless, now fully aware of her hostility. She placed the gloves carefully together, ensuring that all the fingers matched.

"Your partner for the past two years has been Janine Parke, and your last foreign assignment was Paris."

He made no effort to acknowledge her account of him.

"You realise, of course, that Paris will soon be in German hands."

He stared at her, suppressing an urge to sneer.

"You must be quite concerned about your parents," she

went on. "It's too bad that your father decided to lecture in Vienna when certain members of the Abwehr were in the vicinity, isn't it? Needless to say, he would have been stopped anyway as soon as the German occupational forces arrived in Paris."

Claude licked his dry lips.

"I'm sure you'll agree that your father's Jewish philosophies on free thinking are dangerous and averse to the German goal of racial purity." She did not wait for him to respond. "He obviously could not continue his professorship at the Sorbonne and his writings will be destroyed, of course. For his own good he had to be stopped, you understand."

"What do you mean?" His voice sounded a million miles away.

"He is safe and somewhere where he can do no more harm. Of course, others like him have not survived. Perhaps if you will cooperate........?" She shrugged.

"I am French and an anglophile," he said, his voice barely above a whisper. "Are you asking me to collaborate with the Abwehr?"

She stared at him, her face expressionless. "I don't think you have much choice."

He turned to face her. "You are despicable! Are you not Dutch as your name would imply? Do you not have any loyalty toward your own country?"

"My own country is Germany and I am obviously very loyal to her needs. The Dutch name is a mere convenience."

Obviously highly professional, he concluded that her carefully chosen words, and their unctuous delivery, indicated that her work in skullduggery, assassination and sabotage was most likely flawless. Already reports of the disgusting principles prompting German action against the Polish Jews had filtered westward and he was sure she had savoured every act of murder and deportation. He looked again at her large hands.

"Well?" she said, slowly pulling on the gloves.

"Where are my parents?" he said, cursing the catch in his throat.

"All I can tell you is that they are alive.   They will remain so if you cooperate."

Minutes later he watched her cross the wharf and disappear round the edge of the last building adding a third trail of footprints in the snow.   He stared at them foolishly noting that they now pointed in the opposite direction to his own.

He spent an hour agonising over the situation and made inconclusive attempts at reasonable solutions.   In the end he felt near to tears as each failed.   Because of his ethnic background the enemy had succeeded in entrapping him and he could see no escape. He walked to the edge of the wharf and looked down into the muddy waters of the Ouse.   The river rippled and eddied in the turning tide and a twig spun in a miniature vortex gradually sinking lower and lower as the river sucked it in.

Across the water he could see *Summer Solstice*, yawing gently against the bank and in order to divert the present chaos in his mind, he thought of Yvonne.   If only he could retract his foolish behavior.   He had been clumsy; said the wrong things; acted like an idiot.   It was always like that with her.   She innocently toyed with his affections--although, how could she possibly know that they even existed?   In defence, he found himself speaking unintended words, ruining any hope of enhancement to their flimsy friendship. In his confusion he allowed her to chip away at his demeanour, luring him with her youth and beauty until he was forced to retreat.   Yet he knew that under these new circumstances, he must now disassociate himself from her entirely.

CHAPTER THREE

London, May, 1940

Janine sighed and folded the newspaper in half. She had traveled to London in the hope that Henry might come home to Bayswater this evening in order to enjoy a rare meal together. He would certainly want to read the paper, especially since David was due to report to his squadron at a time when RAF action rapidly accelerated. There had been bombing raids over the Albert Canal and the Fighter squadrons were frantically trying to build up their strength.

She got up and stood by the big bay window. The street below seemed strangely unfamiliar, yet she had walked its length for many years toward Oxford Street and the shops. Perhaps its terraced length of grand old houses was destined to become billets for enemy invaders. Surely this would never be so. England must defend itself against the unremitting German onslaught now engulfing Europe, or lose its identity altogether.

Her parents continued to ignore the ominous prediction

that France would be next in spite of the mass exodus from Paris toward the south. As the Germans advanced and the tangled mass of French vehicles and pedestrians jammed the roads, her parents tenaciously clung to their decision to remain in Aix en Provence. Premier Paul Reynaud had succeeded a disillusioned Edouard Daladier in March and the German forces invaded Norway and Denmark only last month. Now, as May drew to its close, enemy advancement had been steady throughout the month and Belgium, Holland, and Luxembourg cringed under the German jackboot.

Even as the enemy penetrated the French frontier, Premier Reynaud had been shuffling his cabinet and had placed Marshal Philippe Pétain into the slot of vice-premier. Janine wondered how the Marshal, old, and highly militant, would cope with the threat of invasion. But worse, the British Expeditionary Army, along with the French forces, was entrapped at the Dunkirk coastline with nowhere to go but into the sea.   Now that Prime Minister Neville Chamberlain had resigned and Winston Churchill had taken his place, perhaps the threat of German advancement toward Britain might be taken in its proper context. The enemy could not be trusted to conform to any agreements since they obviously had no intention of doing so even at their inception.

The evening light faded rapidly as the sun slid to earth in the west, and the plane trees lining the city street etched themselves for a moment against the sky before disappearing into the inky blackness of a night devoid of peacetime street lamps.

Although never sure of rumour, suspicion, or pure premonition, Janine had quickly assimilated from chance hearsay while at a secret meeting in Baker Street, that plans for the German invasion of Britain had fallen into British hands. An extraordinary bit of luck, yet somehow inconsequential since there was nothing that could be done about it except to brace even more.

Her work with the European refugees had dwindled, and more and more demands were being made on her by the SIS involving obscure geographical locations in France. It seemed ironic that two thousand foreigners had been imprisoned in Britain after a massive roundup of people, some of whom had been born in the British Isles of alien parents; and yet refugees from the occupied countries were flooding in to replace them. Did it not occur to anyone that there may be impostors among them?

While Britain lacked trained agents, Janine knew that she was too well-known to go overtly back to France. In any case, her peacetime role in social undercover listening would be virtually impossible due to her British marital status. However, her navigational experience was invaluable and she now supplied the government with the locations of small airfields throughout France. But more perplexing to her was Claude's continuing absence. Because of their prewar partnership SIS assumed that she knew of his movements, and the question concerning his whereabouts surfaced frequently. On a fleeting visit to the Lewes Rowing Club, she had asked one of the barge men about him.

"You never know with Ben," the man said. "He comes and goes like a phantom. If you need work done on your boat I'll tell him the next time he shows up."

That had been weeks ago.

For some inexplicable reason the child at Mallory Cottage hovered in the back of her mind. The passing remark at Christmas concerning a woman haunted her. Could Claude have been negotiating transport to France? How careless that he should make such arrangements in broad daylight within the boundaries of Long Bottom. Anyone could have seen him. His cover as Ben Boniface could easily lose credence if he began to change his habits.

* * *

June, 1940

The early June days steadily warmed and lengthened into summer. Yvonne looked through the back window of the taxi at the Long Man on the hillside and nodded her usual greeting through the fading light. She felt that he would resent being ignored and might even have some uncanny influence over her own fate. A silly whim, of course; yet she could not bring herself to snub him. As the taxi drove away, she groped into the depths of her handbag in search of keys to Flint House and turned quickly at the sound of someone running along the driveway. Even through the dusk of late evening there was no mistaking Ben's oversized jumper or the ease with which he sprinted toward her. She waited, not without irritation, since she had a hot bath planned and needed time alone to think.

With the promise of an invitational call from Air Transport Auxiliary foremost in her mind, the anticipation of flying again after nine long months of waiting excited her. Still indignant that the two family aircraft were "up on sticks" because of the war, she had ardently pursued every aspect of hope that might get her back in a cockpit--any cockpit. Stringent barriers angered her and made her all the more determined, and a tiny scrap of conversation at a casual luncheon with some members of her flying club sent her in hot pursuit of further information. Apparently Air Transport Auxiliary, initially an offshoot of British Overseas Airways and fully staffed by male pilots not eligible for operational duty, might consider women to deliver single engine trainer planes to storage and other destinations. The RAF was beginning to feel the brunt of pilot attrition from enemy activity, and a heavier load of ferrying had been transferred to ATA.

One influential and tenacious woman had pursued the aspect of female ferry pilots and, at last, her patience was being rewarded.   Because of it, nine women possessing excellent credentials were flying Tiger Moths from Hatfield to Lossiemouth and other northern and western aerodromes, albeit keeping well clear of armed defence areas and potential trouble spots by flying tortuous zigzag routes.   Bureaucratic complications stemming from the question of which authoritative umbrella ATA should come under had caused a new flurry of correspondence and subsequent delays in taking on more qualified women.   But, they assured Yvonne, she would be contacted as soon as permission was received to expand the numbers of female pilots.

"It's rather rough," a woman had said at lunch.   "Open cockpits in freezing weather and no radio, plus no overnight facilities, and a certain amount of hostility from the men, not to mention the media, don't contribute much to a comfortable way of life."

Yvonne already knew of these drawbacks, having had them prodded home by George Ravensbrook last Christmas; but she also knew that they had not curtailed the enthusiasm and endurance of the women.   Neither would they her.   In fact, their accident-free record to date had already begun to prove their point.   The media had been particularly unkind and accused the women of seeking public attention and were, they said, depriving men of jobs.   More strains of George Ravensbrook's biased opinions.   But the media had not bothered to verify their accusations.   Hadn't they noticed that there was a shortage of male pilots?

Avoiding Ben would be impossible and, in any case, there might be something wrong with the boat. She had seen nothing of him since last September yet clearly remembered the manner in which he tried to detain her. His odd habits and uncanny spasmodic appearances gave her the creeps, but something about him interested her. Although certainly charismatic in an obscure way his insinuations nonetheless made her feel uncomfortable. She turned toward the house, hoping to discourage him from coming any further, but he seemed determined to speak to her.

"Is anything wrong?" she said.

"I think that might be an extraneous question since Guderian's Panzers have smashed through the Ardennes and reached the mouth of the Somme at Abbeville." he said. "I would say that yes, something is very wrong."

She squirmed a little under his steady gaze, furious that he was able to embarrass her in this manner.

"I'm aware of that, of course," she snapped. "Mother is very concerned about my grandparents. She's also very concerned because fighter squadrons based in England are losing pilots near Dunkirk. Some idiot told her that the Spitfires were firing on Hurricanes in the confusion. You realise, of course, that David is due to report to his squadron any minute?"

His nod was barely perceptible.

"Then you also know that the BEF forces have been beaten back to the beaches of Dunkirk and are trapped there," he said. "Our fighter and reconnaissance squadrons have flown home from France and so they are virtually unprotected until home based fighters can get there. The large ships can't get in close enough to rescue them."

Yvonne wondered what on earth he was driving at.

"If the large ships can't get in," Ben said, staring at her face. "Then small vessels must do it."

She looked at him incredulously. Surely he could not be thinking of *Summer Solstice*!

"I did some work on your boat while you were away," he said.

"But she can't possibly be seaworthy! She's a river boat!"

"She's sturdy and I'm sure you can vouch for the engine."

"Even if she's acceptable," Yvonne said, stuffing her shaking hands into her pockets. "Who will take the helm?"

"I will. Toby Mallory has agreed to go, too."

She narrowed her eyes. "How dare you assume......."

"......We're required to take her only as far as Newhaven where naval personnel will take over," he went on, ignoring her indignation. "Since you know the engine, it would be advantageous if you would go with us down the river."

His tone was authoritative and his words, demanding. Yet she still opened her mouth to protest.

"I'll meet you at the Rowing Club in half an hour," he said.

Without further word, he turned on his heel and walked quickly away.

If only to prevent this mad idea to take *Summer Solstice* to sea, she knew she had to meet him. His terse determination unsettled her, yet also challenged her to argue her point. She wondered if Toby had been bullied into participating, or if he too felt that the boat was seaworthy and should be offered for service. If this were the case, she would most likely lose the argument. But it still did not make sense to her that the old river boat would be of any use in a military rescue mission across open sea.

There had been many happy days on the river when the family held picnics on the long expanse of the sun deck in the aft section before the war. The saloon, comfortable, high-ceilinged and airy, had been an ample retreat during a sudden summer shower, and the lower cabins could sleep several comfortably. She remembered the rich tones of the teak trim, the shining brass fixtures, and the gay awnings that protected them from the sun. But as her father became more successful, his working hours grew longer and frequently erratic, often keeping him in London. Then she and David went away to school, and her mother's absences abroad became more frequent and prolonged. The boat spent several lonely years moored near the Lewes Rowing Club and began to fall into a state of disrepair. She wondered just how much work Ben had done on *Summer Solstice* while she was away.

Half an hour, he had said. Well, if I do end up going to Newhaven, at least I should be dressed for the occasion, she thought.

With this in mind she hurried to her brother's wardrobe in search of a pair of trousers and a duffel coat, since clothing of this kind did not exist in her own. Minutes later, she clattered down the driveway on her bicycle with all thoughts of the hot bath completely forgotten. In rapidly darkening conditions, she found her way by hugging the curb, often bumping into it and jarring her already tense nerves. She was surprised and annoyed to find only Toby Mallory aboard *Summer Solstice* when she arrived.

*   *   *

I have just enough time, Ben thought, to get a wireless message off before going to the boat. He peddled quickly along the Lewes Road, keeping his eye glued to the curb. The light rapidly faded and, although familiar with the route, he could not afford to take chances. He planned to garble his message to Dierick as much as possible concerning the RDF (AMES) towers along the coast. He had not had much luck in getting close anyway, and his photographs were deliberately unclear. He doubted that the microfilm would give the enemy any more information than they already had.

It puzzled him that his British assignments had continued uninterrupted, although now he operated alone. Janine, they told him, was temporarily assigned to vital cartography work While he could not inform SIS of Dierick's presence in England without jeopardising the safety of his parents, he assumed they had a list of known enemy agents on hand. Yet could it be possible that they were not aware of her?

He had deliberately kept away from Long Bottom, even though he knew his prolonged absence must cause Janine some anxiety. Although his work for Dierick was largely unproductive, he nonetheless felt the need to atone, and the urgent call for small boats to participate in the rescue mission to Dunkirk came at a perfect time. In any case, there were also French troops waiting on those beaches.

The last thing he wanted to do was involve Yvonne, but he had learned only marine carpentry to use as his cover and knew nothing about marine engines. *Summer Solstice* was old and probably unreliable. But he had heard the engine running smoothly as Yvonne tested it all those weeks ago and he knew he had no choice but to contact her.

Having slipped his bicycle through the main door of the warehouse and propped it against the wall, he took the stairs two at a time and quickly lifted the transmitter from its hiding place behind a fuse box on the top floor. Within minutes his distorted message had gone. In spite of the seriousness of his situation, he suddenly felt lighthearted. Even though the trip down river would be short, he happily anticipated the precious stolen time he would spend with Yvonne. As he hurried along the wharf, he noticed a lone figure standing at the end of the Cliffe bridge and the elation quickly slipped away. He immediately recognised his SIS contact who was obviously there to give him an assignment. His atonement would have to wait.

*   *   *

Toby Mallory had been visible in Yvonne's life from the day she was born. A fixture in the village, he knew everyone within a three mile radius and had never been heard to say anything detrimental about anyone. He was, in fact, Ben's only true friend and always stood by him at the Snowdrop Inn, although Ben himself did not seem to acknowledge or appreciate this friendly support. Toby was a retired railway man, yet enjoyed good rapport with the bargees, their common bond being their belief in an honest hard days work. They spoke the same language and understood their mutual needs. He disliked retirement, but his generous heart had faltered two years ago and he was considered a risk on the railway. Making financial ends meet might have been difficult had not Ben arrived and offered to rent a room in the cottage.

The rising moon glowed eerily through the windows of the wooden dodger and highlighted the anxiety on Toby's usually jovial face when she arrived. To avoid being influenced by it, Yvonne directed her attention to the old-fashioned stepped-up trawler saloon brooding on the forward deck in moonlit skeletal symmetry; and then beyond where three other craft moved into a lineup position in the half-light. They would not be alone on the Ouse River tonight. Although in deep shadow, she could just see newly repaired sections in the decking and an entirely new engine hatch cover.

"Where's Ben?" she asked.

"I thought he'd be here by now," Toby said. "We'll be leaving soon. I wish he'd hurry up. I wonder what's keeping him?"

She leaned out from the dodger and listened for any words of instruction from the lead boat. People whispered to

43

one another but no word came back to her.   She looked upwards and saw high gray stratus corrugating the dark sky. A blend of palest pink still lingered at the western horizon.   No breeze disturbed the surface of the river as it flowed like dark syrup on an ebbing course toward its mouth at Newhaven, seven miles to the south.

"Perhaps we should think seriously about this," Yvonne said, hoping Toby would rise to the bait. "The boat has never been to sea, you know."

"It doesn't look any less seaworthy than those in front," Toby said. "Let them decide at Newhaven. As for us, we'll be home in a couple of hours."

She could not argue with that.

"They're calling this rescue mission Operation Dynamo, you know," Toby said. "It's been in progress for several days. I do wonder why the enemy hasn't tried to stop the small rescue boats leaving the English coast, but I suppose they're concentrating on larger ships and the trapped soldiers on the other side.   His eyes widened as he looked forward.

"We're off!" he said, licking his lips.

Yvonne scanned the darkness, hoping for glimpse of Ben.   Nothing stirred on the bank.

"We'll have to go without him," she said.   "All we have to do is follow the other boats."

Toby looked apprehensively toward shore, biting down on his thumb nail.

"Well--I don't know--he said he'd be here," he said.

But Yvonne was already pulling in the lines.   It seemed to her now that perhaps lending the boat might make a tiny contribution to the rescue mission.   The least she could do was take it as far as Newhaven.

The engine turned over immediately and ran smoothly. Easing the bow toward midstream, she followed the boat in front carefully keeping an estimated fifty feet away from the vague outline of its stern.   The four river craft moved without running lights to acknowledge the blackout, or radio contact to avoid detection from any enemy short-wave radio that might succeed in interception.   The boat was veritably blind until Yvonne's eyes accustomed themselves to the darkness.   Only then did the restriction in her throat lessen.

"Ben will be at Newhaven, I'm sure," she said to Toby who stood silently beside her.   "His delay must have been caused by something important."

"Yes," Toby said.   "I'm sure you're right."

But Ben did not meet the boat at Newhaven.   Yvonne jumped ashore the minute they were moored and searched the Newhaven-Dieppe ferry wharf for any sign of him.

"I'll see if I can find someone in authority who can tell us who'll take over the boat," Toby said.   "At the same time, I'll see about an allocation of water and fuel for them."

During the down river run Toby's confidence had noticeably grown and Yvonne was thankful that she could now rely on his help.   He had been alert for the swing bridge at Southease and had pointed out the village of Piddinghoe, hoping that Ben may be waiting there to jump aboard.

"He's not here," she panted, having completed her search along the wharf.   "Any luck with a substitute crew?"

Toby shook his head.   "All naval and Coast Guard personnel are in Folkstone.   All available civilians are already aboard other boats.   They've suggested we wait with our boats for further instructions."

"Does that mean we have come all this way for nothing?"

She could hear Toby breathing in the darkness.

"Ben thinks the boat is seaworthy," he said, at last.

"I've never had the opportunity to test her," Yvonne said, watching the silent preparations going on around her.   "I suppose there's only one way to find out."

"Right.   Well, that's what we'll do then if they can't find anyone else."

"Right. After all, Folkstone isn't that far. Is it?"

"Look, Yvonne.   We'll be with the other boats.   If anything happens, they'll be there to help."

"Yes, Toby.   But did it occur to you that the three boats we came down river with are also only river boats."

"Then.......we're all in the same boat!"

"Literally!"

Toby looked at her bright hair.   "I'm not sure what the reaction will be come daylight when they see that you're.....a woman."

She had not thought of that.   Diving her hands deeply into the pockets of the duffel coat she found a wool hat.   "This should do the trick," she said.

Toby did not look too sure about that, but once every obstinate curl had disappeared from view he said they might get away with it.

"I don't see the ferry, Toby.   But look! There are other boats coming in on the west side of the river mouth.   I think there's going to be quite a fleet of us."

"Indeed there is.   I heard that the ferry went over to Dunkirk from Dover on May 27th.   One of the first to operate under Stuka attack........."

"Where did you hear that?" She had not meant to snap.

"Ben. He said the rescue operations are taking place at night now to avoid these aerial attacks."

He gripped the top of the gunwale and scanned the dock yet again.

"Where the devil is the man," he muttered. "He's had plenty of time to get here, especially now that we've had to wait around like this. It's getting late."

He looked up as a large fishing boat chugged past them.

"That's the *Miss Julie*.   I was told this would be our lead boat.   It looks like we're getting ready to leave." He glanced at his watch. "It's well after midnight."

They both knew that Ben would not come now.

As Yvonne released the mooring lines, she thought about her first solo out of Croydon. While there had been no doubt in her mind she could pull it off successfully, her stomach had felt like a cannon ball. She suffered the same symptoms now as she envisioned the coastline between Newhaven and Folkstone. They would have to stay fairly far out to avoid seaweed beds and shoals, but close enough in to avoid defensive mines.

She smiled at Toby as they pulled out and joined the other boats that were already following the *Miss Julie* toward the river mouth, and drew confidence from his reassuring grin.

After skirting the boundary of the East Pier they heard the slap of waves against the long breakwater to the west as they left the river.

"This is where we find out what kind of stuff *Summer Solstice* is made of," Yvonne said. "We're about to go to sea!"

It occurred to her then that her helmsmanship and seamanship were also about to be put to the test.

As the pale light of dawn hovered at the eastern horizon, she and Toby took stock of the boats around them dimly outlined in a morning mist. At first count they estimated an approximate thirty craft of all shapes, sizes and categories. Their crews matched the general motley array, comprising white-haired men, school aged youths, ruddy-faced commercial fishermen, and a sprinkling of young boat owners who had not yet been called to service. Yvonne saw no other women. On the starboard side of the fleet she saw the black outline of a tug fussing along and, silhouetted ominously both forward and aft, the unmistakable shapes of mounted machine guns.

"Is that our only defence?" she asked Toby.

He nodded, ruefully.

The swell of the Channel brought the boat to life. *Miss Julie* struck out toward Seaford followed by her brood of mismatched Samaritans. This courageous leader would be the first to perish if the fleet encountered a mine.

A sleek thirty-foot, twin-screwed launch crept confidently ahead although its skipper appeared to be improperly dressed for the occasion since he wore riding breeches. He held a gaudy mug and was obviously thoroughly enjoying the liquid contents.

"Tally ho!" he shouted as he passed.

Toby chuckled. "With that kind of fortification, he'll no doubt remain stalwart, cheerful, and decidedly drunk!"

To port, *Summer Solstice* overtook a derelict ancient black tub with the unlikely title of *The Countess Hannah.* The bewhiskered old fellow at the helm wore a battered bowler on the back of his head and a cork life belt around his chest. He continuously mashed his gums since he obviously had no teeth, while furtively glancing behind him. From the cockpit of the *Countess* water rhythmically sloshed out over the side from a bucket, the wielder of which remained invisible.

"Cor lummy, Bert," a young male voice wailed. "She's leaking faster than I can bail. How long did you say it was since she was at sea?"

"Never was," the old rogue at the helm shouted. "Only on the river, and that were about ten year ago."

"But you said.........."

The old man's disjointed words drifted to them on the wind. "...............I lied."

Another fast launch passed. A well-dressed man stood at the helm fully decked out in Riviera yachting gear. On the aft rail streamed a bright Union Jack.

"God save the King," the man said, keeping his upper lip incredibly stiff.

"'Have you got him on board," Bert yelled in the distance.

"No, but a queen is!"

Toby and Yvonne looked at each other incredulously. Were people really treating this whole thing as a lark, or was it simply a facade to disguise an underlying dread of what might be ahead?

"I say," someone shouted through a megaphone.   "Is this the way to the Dunkirk regatta, old bean?"

"Keep left and cross over at Dover," came the reply.

Churning along at an average speed of six knots, the wake from Miss Julie created enough turbulence to make the smaller craft wallow.   Yvonne clung to the helm, feeling the strain in her arms and shoulders.   She glanced at Toby and noticed his thinning gray hair waving like cobwebs in the wind and a pinched pallor about his mouth.

"Are you all right, Toby?"

"Right as rain, m'dear.   Here, let me take over for awhile."

As they passed Seaford Head and the breakwaters, the mist began to disperse.   Beyond, at the east end of the beach stood the old Martello Tower used in peacetime as an excellent landmark for boaters.

Toby inclined his head toward it.   "Probably has a gun emplacement there," he said.   "I imagine a U-boat or two has popped up a periscope to get visual bearings from it, too."

A fiery splinter split the horizon and blossomed into an orange blaze as the sun rose.   Above, strings of cloud changed from black to red reflecting a crimson blush on the boats and crews below.   The frothy bow waves caught the brilliance and shattered it into a thousand rubies.   As Yvonne looked back she could see the scattered sun gems dancing in the merging wakes and thought she had never seen anything so beautiful.

Ahead, the long palisades of white cliffs, shining pink and sugary, curved inland and then swung gracefully forward into the sea to the point of the Beachy Head promontory.   The sun, now only half immersed in the sea, flung a broad golden carpet toward them, too brilliant to look at.   Yvonne wondered what might have happened to Bert and his hapless one-man crew.   Almost indistinguishable among billows of black smoke belching from her cockpit, she could see Bert sitting astride the bowsprit of the *Countess*, legs dangling and bowler-hatted head drooped in his hands while the once-imperceptible first mate, now very much in evidence, attempted to comfort him.   A benevolent fishing boat moved toward them, bent on rescue.

They crossed the soft curve of Pevensey Bay and bustled toward Bexhill along the coast.   Yvonne leaned over the gunwale and saw their bow cleaving through the wake of the *Miss Julie* acknowledging her lead yet forging along abreast of five boats of similar class behind her. *Summer Solstice* was doing well. The sun, now a good six feet up from the sea from her perspective, ogled them from behind a soft cloud sending misty rays downward toward Hastings and the Dungeness land mass that projected out across the horizon in front of them.

Yvonne turned her head sharply, listening.

"Odd," she said.   "The sky's clear, yet I thought I heard thunder."

Toby pointed ahead.   "Cloud banks there," he said, squinting his eyes.

They gasped as a flash of orange light flickered through the dark mass.

"Christ!" Toby said. "That's smoke and gun fire, not storm clouds."

The dull crump became more defined as they rounded the Dungeness point. With Toby still at the helm, they crossed the bight and, passing New Romney, saw the vast cliffs curve toward Hythe on top of which the broad expanse of Romney Marsh stretched back toward Rye for seventeen miles. Hythe, normally sleepy and peaceful, seemed to be listening and waiting as the gunfire grew louder.

Someone stood aft on the lead boat with a megaphone and warned the small fleet that there would be seaweed beds as they turned toward Folkstone. Word relayed back to those out of earshot, but before they could complete the turn, a navy launch streaked out toward them.   Instinctively, all craft slowed to watch the launch pull alongside the *Miss Julie.* A young naval officer stood in the cockpit shouting instructions and pointing ahead, then immediately turned the boat around and roared back at full throttle toward Folkstone.

"Almost there," Toby said.   "I could really do with a cup of tea."

Again megaphone communication was relayed back. They were to go on to Dover.   All available naval personnel were either at the big Cinque Port or en route back from Dunkirk with rescued troops.

Toby looked deflated but followed Yvonne's glance across the water toward the smoke.

"We can do that, can't we?" he said. "We *can* go on."

Yvonne squared her shoulders. Of course they could.

With Dover in sight, they saw a massive black pall of smoke over the French coast that rose and swirled until it veiled the sun, plunging it into mourning.

"The entire French coast must be on fire," Yvonne gasped. "It's nothing short of an inferno."

"It must be the oil tanks," Toby said.

"Are there aircraft there?   I'm sure I heard aircraft engines."

"You're probably hearing the other boats," Toby said. "I wouldn't want to be in an aeroplane in that mess."

A breach in the white cliffs to port indicated the mouth of the river Dour and the narrow valley surrounding it.   They were almost there. On the eastern height of the cliffs the castle ruins of the garrison town balanced near the edge some three hundred and seventy-five feet above sea level.   Below, the lovely old houses and cottages of Dover clustered around the churches and waited patiently for the ships to come home from the sea.   Today, they waited for their rescued men to return from the battle-torn beaches of Dunkirk.

The fleet of small boats passed Shakespeare Cliff and approached the Eastern Entrance of the outer Dover harbour. Yvonne stared at the incredible bustle of activity going on around her, only now realising how enormous the rescue effort was.   Every conceivable type of craft lay alongside the 2,800 foot eastern arm, and others were moving about within the tidal basin.

"There's plenty of depth," Toby said.   "Not that we have to worry about that."   He pointed to a depth gauge on the side of the wharf.   "Twenty-seven feet," he read.

"We probably draw about three," Yvonne said.   "We're like cockleshells!"   She looked around her as their group chugged in, and then at the big trawlers and ferry boats standing by.   "A cockle shell armada!"

Within the southern breakwater that formed about four thousand feet of protective mole, more boats waited while others lined up along the Prince of Wales pier.   Wellington and Granville docks filled quickly and the newcomers were forced to throw lines to boats already tied up and moor alongside, raft fashion.   Two of the Dover-Dunkirk ferries lay behind one another like circus elephants, and upon closer inspection, Yvonne saw chunks missing from their superstructures and deck rails.   Two Isle of Man steam packets rocked gently in the water and Toby pointed to conversions that had transformed them into armed boarding vessels.

He stepped carefully across two boats and joined a group of men on the pier.   Yvonne pulled her hat down further over her ears and followed him, but stood apart from the general conversation stamping her feet and stretching her arms to get the blood circulating.

"....got back after dawn," a man was saying.   "Loaded with troops.   The crews are sleeping and will probably spearhead the next lot over this evening."

She took stock of the scene along the pier, scanning it rapidly for any sign of Ben.   Now that the boat was safely here, she supposed they had better look into arranging transportation home.   It struck her that she and Toby had done rather well to bring it this far and realised that they had not needed Ben's help after all.   But it was still a matter of principle since he had volunteered *Summer Solstice* in the first place.

While waiting for further instructions, she looked around her at the mass of preparations.   Salt-stained east coast trawlers yawed in the churned-up water.   Dover life boats were being secured to a tug, ready for towing.   Dinghies with tiny outboard motors darted about like moor hens.   The Isle of Wight car ferry clung to the Prince of Wales pier, her crew readying her for the task ahead.   Another fleet of fishing boats, nets still slung across their rigs, seemed itchy to get on with it.

The man in riding breeches ghosted past representing the last of the group from Newhaven.   He still held his cup of sustenance and appeared to be a mite unsteady on his feet. Beyond his boat a pair of Dutch barges--Shuits--, geranium pots gaily swinging with the motion, bobbed past a trio of motor boats.

"There aren't enough people to man all the boats," Toby said as he joined her.   "They want us to go."

"What?"

"We could tell them.........who.....what...... you are."

She looked across at the inky pillar of smoke and shook her head.   "That won't let you off the hook, will it?   No.   We'll both go."

Toby held out some papers for her to see.   "T124 forms to claim temporary Navy pay," he said, with a lopsided grin.

Perhaps he needs the money, she thought.   In which case I will see that he gets mine, too.

"This is a makeshift chart," Toby said.   "Obviously we won't have any trouble since we'll simply go along with everyone else.   But it does indicate the mines along the Ruytingen Bank and the general areas we are to aim for, and those to avoid.   We're supposed to try for the inshore channel midway between Dunkirk and Gravelines."

"Then what?"

"We pile on as many men as we can and deliver them to

The Long Man   **Pauline Furey**

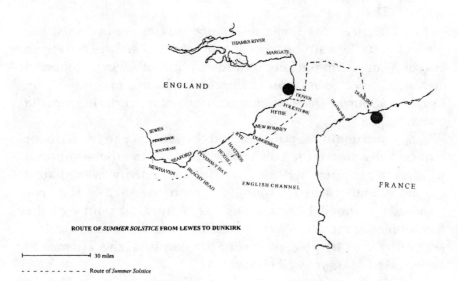

ROUTE OF *SUMMER SOLSTICE* FROM LEWES TO DUNKIRK

|—————————————| 30 miles

– – – – – – – – – – Route of *Summer Solstice*

The Route to Dunkirk

the destroyer which is waiting offshore.   Then go back and get some more and do the same thing again."   Toby looked concerned.   "Look, Yvonne.   This sort of thing will probably go on all night if we don't get hit by gunfire........I'll understand completely if you decide against it."   He hesitated.   "Of course, I shall go in any case."

"Then so shall I."

The need for Ben's assistance was again in focus, but the day went by with no sign of him.   At sunset the converted Isle of Man steam packets moved out and other craft followed suit.   *Summer Solstice* rocked in the backwash of the pleasure boat *Eastbourne Belle* as she got underway, churning up the water.

Once again they approached the entrance to the harbour and as Toby turned the bow toward the east, the incessant thud of distant guns reached them.   But the activity immediately around them affected Yvonne far more deeply.   She saw hundreds of small boats joining them from all points of the foreland.   Some were much smaller than theirs and far less seaworthy.   Toby pointed toward the mouth of the Thames as they passed Margate well to port.

"Look!   Many river boats, Hopper barges, dredge holders, and, would you believe, a Yangtse gun boat?"

This was no small rescue mission.   Hundreds of boats in a great armada converged into a wide gauntlet with every face at every helm looking grimly toward Dunkirk.   What an incredible concentration of concern for the men trapped on the beaches, Yvonne thought.   This must be history in the making and damned if I'm not a part of it.

It seemed in no time at all the dusk closed in and the gun flashes illuminated sudden erratic outlines of boats, faces, clouds, wakes and bow waves in jerky cinematographic movements.   Toby suddenly grabbed her arm.

"Quick!   Get down!" he hissed.   "E Boat!"

She crouched beside him and helped to hold onto the

wheel.   A zip of mini explosions streaked across the top of the dodger accompanied by a burst of staccato shots.   A bright searchlight swept the forest of boats, and another burst of bullets sprayed in a semicircular radius.

"Can you reach the throttle," Toby shouted.   "Open her up! Full out!"

Yvonne stretched her arm up and fumbled about, sobbing with frustration when she could not reach.

Toby raised his head high enough to see what was going on.   "It's veered toward the west.   Those behind us will catch it now.   Bastard!   Nobody can outrun him.   He can pull an easy forty knots."

Yvonne cautiously rose, testing her legs for stability. She stood up, stiffening her knees to keep them from shaking.

"How do you know about E boats?" she said at last.

Toby forced a smile.   "I was in the last war.   Navy. Aboard small craft, actually."

"Toby! You could have told me!"

"I'm a much older man now.   I wasn't sure.........."

With heavy gunfire growing steadily louder toward the east they continued without further incident.   The beaches came into view and in the intermittent flashes they could see patterns of strange black lines looking like dark, irregular snail trails.   Before Yvonne could comment on them, something exploded on their starboard side, rocking the boat alarmingly. The engine faltered as the boat wallowed dangerously and debris rained down upon them.

"Someone struck a mine," Toby shouted as they scrambled to their feet.

"How can we avoid doing the same thing?" Yvonne croaked.

"We can't.   Just keep heading for the beach, Yvonne.....and pray.   I'll keep an eye out for floating obstacles."

As she took the helm, something distracted her out on

the water.

"Toby. There's someone alive out there!"

"Can't stop! Too risky!"

"But we must!   Don't you think what we're doing is already too risky?"   Something moved feebly in the water about ten feet off the port bow and Yvonne yelled frantically. "Please, Toby. We must." She slowed the engine abruptly.

"All right.   But we'll have to be quick." Toby leaned over the side seeking the casualty with a boat hook.

"Can't bring him in alone," he gasped. "You'll have to help."

She scrambled down beside him and together they pulled the floundering man on board. Toby immediately rushed to the helm and brought the engine back up to full throttle. Other boats were rushing past them oblivious to the damaging debris threshing about in the foam.

Yvonne looked down at the prone figure on the deck and knelt to turn him over. She felt the warm stickiness of blood on her hands and saw the dark, saturating stain on the front of his clothes.   He opened his eyes and tried to smile, emitting a strong odour of alcohol. It was the "Tally-ho" man.

"Damn silly, i'n't it?" he whispered thickly, his voice barely audible through the bedlam.   "Came all this way for nothing."

She undid his shirt to see if there was anything she could do about his wound and saw a shining mass.   The vicious injury had laid his intestines bare and blood welled rhythmically amongst them, obviously from a severed main artery.   She reeled back, jerking her head away from the dreadful sight.

"Tally-ho!" the voice whispered.

She forced herself to look at his face as he lifted his chin and tried to wink.   The eyelid stayed half-closed and the eye behind it stared blindly up at the night sky.

"Oh, Toby. We don't even know who he is," she said

through dry lips.

"Take the helm for a moment," Toby shouted.

She obeyed and when she glanced behind her a moment later, the man was gone.

"We'll need space for survivors," Toby said, trolling a canvas bucket for water.

She could hear him washing down the deck in the same manner the commercial fishermen did after a catch and prayed that she might soon wake up from this horrific nightmare.

Ahead the dark hulk of a large ship loomed up, illuminated by gun flashes.   Small craft hovered about the fantail like ducklings around a mallard, awaiting their turn to unload the human cargoes.   Even from a distance, Yvonne could see the wide eyes and white faces of the soldiers as they jumped onto the Jacob's ladders and cargo nets strung from the fantail and gangway and down the sides.

"I think they said that *HMS Malcolm* would be standing by," Toby said.   "She's a destroyer with the capability of moving out at a good clip.   We'll be delivering the men there."

Coming out from the beach a Folkstone pleasure boat, loaded with men and sitting perilously low in the water, churned along toward the English shoreline.

Something hit the water about fifty yards ahead a sent up a plume of spray.

"We're within range of shore artillery," Toby shouted. "Keep down.   There'll be shrapnel."

He changed his course slightly to overtake a small motor boat.   Yvonne marveled at his transformation.   He exuded confidence and capability.   The earlier qualms had disappeared and Toby Mallory was behaving like the hero he was.   She ducked down, raising her head just enough to peep over the side.   Another explosion to starboard.   Closer this time, again rolling the boat and disrupting the engine.   A third shell fell behind them, instantly blowing the little motor boat they had just passed to bits.   Splintered segments of polished wood rained down on the cabin and cockpit of *Summer Solstice*. There would be no point in searching for survivors this time.

The strange black lines on shore were now closer and distinguishable. Hundreds of men stood in controlled queues waiting their turn to be rescued. Yvonne saw that many waded out to the approaching boats until they stood chest deep in water. Others tried to swim to the waiting destroyers, their tin hats bobbing in the water like corks on a fishing net. Around the men on the beaches, columns of sand rose like mud geysers as shells exploded and the water boiled around the swimmers and waders as if it were pitted with gargantuan raindrops.

"Hurry! For heaven's sake, hurry!" she heard herself shouting.

Soon they were in range of the swimming soldiers and Toby threw lines over the sides of *Summer Solstice* and began to help them aboard. Yvonne looked at their ashen, unshaven faces and wondered how they had managed to retain their sanity.

"There's a small bottle of brandy below in the first-aid kit," she shouted to Toby. "It won't go far, but it will help a bit."

"Cor, thanks, son," a corporal said. "I've been waiting two days and nights for you to show up. Thank God you're here." He took a swig from the bottle and passed it on to the man next to him. "Almost made it onto a boat yesterday," he went on. "But it was strafed by a Stuka as it pulled away and kept going round in circles until it sank." His face was expressionless. "Don't believe anyone survived that one because I think the crew was either dead or dying when she went down. I consider myself quite lucky, actually."

This courageous man actually thought he was lucky?

Now they were in close enough for the waders and Yvonne noticed they had unbuttoned their battle dress jackets.

"Thanks," a young private gasped as he came aboard.

"I thought I was a gonner.   Got swept off me feet with the water ballooning up me jumper.   Never did learn to swim."

He collapsed onto the foredeck and then slithered away to make room for the next man to come aboard.

"Look at them poor bloody mongrels up on the beach," he said.   "Never realised we'd collected so many dogs over the past months."

Yvonne, following in the direction his grimy finger pointed, saw an assortment of domestic dogs, some frantically trying to find a familiar hand to lick; others sitting forlornly high up on the beach away from the falling shells; while some lay still, stiffened and bloated.

The young soldier had spoken erratically as he continuously jerked his head as if following the course of a mosquito.   Obviously near breaking point, Yvonne doubted that he would have lasted another day.

"We're full!" Toby shouted.   "We'll deliver this load to the destroyer and come right back."

He looked down at a young soldier in the water.   "Back in a jiffy!"

"Right, Guv," the soldier replied and began to sing "Oh, I do like to be beside the seaside," at the top of his voice. He staggered back to the beach and sat down, wiping away tears from his face with the back of his hand.

"They know we'll sink if we're overloaded," the corporal said.   "But with all this artillery flying about, they also know they may not be there when you get back.....in a jiffy."

An older man on the shore wobbled under the weight of his wet clothes and then collapsed, face down in the water.

"Asleep on his feet," the private said.   "Some blokes drowned like that yesterday.   That was after some of the rescued blokes fell between two destroyers and were crushed to death."   He stared at the water.   "It really ain't been much fun, you know."

Toby turned the boat seaward and suddenly grabbed

Yvonne's arm as the bow bumped against objects floating in the water.

"Don't look! They've been there for quite some time," he said.

He pulled a battered packet of Senior Service cigarettes from his pocket as they wended their way toward the destroyer and handed them around for as long as they lasted. A young officer took a long, grateful draw and narrowed his eyes at Yvonne through the smoke.

"I'm surprised they let a young boy like you come on such a dangerous mission," he said.

She pointed to one of the fishing boats where several young men were hard at work pulling men aboard. "Are you?" she said, and quickly turned her back on him to discourage closer scrutiny.

"It seems to be taking a very long time to get to the destroyer," she said to Toby.

The officer edged under the dodger.   "That's the trouble," he said.   "The men on the beach thought the big ships were much closer than they are and tried to swim for it."

At last they came alongside the destroyer and the exhausted soldiers aboard Summer Solstice rallied their strength to climb the ladders. As the young officer waited his turn he leaned toward Yvonne. "You're very brave," he said, close to her ear. "No one will ever know how brave."

With the last man safely aboard the destroyer, Toby turned the helm toward shore again.

"The tide's turning," he said. "We'll get back to the beach more slowly, but it'll be quicker on the outward runs now." He sniffed the air. "The cordite's getting thick, isn't it?"

Losing all semblance of time, Yvonne worked beside Toby throughout the night ferrying one boat load after another to the waiting destroyer.

"This will have to be our last run," Toby said, looking

toward the east. "Look."

The pale glimmer above the gun emplacements on the beach puzzled Yvonne. It could not possibly be the dawn, could it?

"We'll be visible from the air in a few minutes," Toby said. "Don't fancy providing target practice for the Stukas."

"But there are men still on the beach!"

"We'll take as many as we can back to England," Toby said. "Other than that, what else can we do?"

His face was lined with exhaustion and completely void of colour, yet there was an air of pride about him.

"You've done the work of five men," he said, putting his arm about her shoulders.

Yvonne had not thought about the extreme physical effort she had expended until this moment. Now she felt unbelievably tired. Her limbs were like sand-filled sacks-- heavy and inanimate--and her eyes stung from smoke and fatigue. She looked toward the shore. A larger number now waded out to meet the small boats. They too had seen the dawn. As they approached, a scuffle disturbed the orderliness of the line and she could see men struggling together. Surely the patient control they had exhibited had not broken at last. She wondered how she would cope with their desperation. Then she saw one man being restrained by the others.

"He's gone barmy," a sergeant shouted from the shore. "He's been here three days--he'll die if he doesn't make it this time."

A shell exploded nearby and the restrained man screamed like a wounded animal.

"It's shell shock," Toby said. "We can't take him aboard like that."

"You'll take him," the sergeant shouted as he turned toward the men. "Hold him up!" Yvonne winced as the sergeant delivered a resounding punch to the man's jaw and looked away as he sagged, head lolling forward. Toby hauled him over the side and dragged him into the cabin where he dumped him like a sack of potatoes on a seat.

"Can't be out of his early twenties," he panted, taking off the soldier's tin hat to reveal a shock of snow-white hair.

On shore, the orderly lines were breaking up. Yvonne heard shouting from the beach in French and realised they were also bringing out General de Gaulle's troops. In a supreme surge of strength, men were heaving themselves over the gunwales in wet, stinking clothes, well aware that this would be their last chance of rescue until night fell again.

"We'll have to back off," Toby said. "You can't blame them. But we've got to get back to Dover with this lot and we can't overload."

As he took the boat out several yards beyond the surf, Yvonne saw thin hands desperately clinging to the side of the rear deck and quickly leaned over the side to grab the man's arms. The sergeant came to help and together they hauled him aboard. She would never forget the sheer terror in his eyes as he hung between life and death on the side of the boat.

The shelling had diminished, giving a false sense of respite. With the boat filled to bulging capacity, Toby turned her westward and Yvonne looked down into the water to ensure no one else clung to the sides. Then she saw what he had tried to shield from her. Bloated, uniformed bodies were washing back to shore with the tide and had begun to bump crazily against the legs of those who waited there. As one passed close to the boat it rolled, revealing a distorted face with staring, sightless eyes. She recoiled in horror as the mouth seemed to leer in the movement of the water.

Now battling exhaustion, she clenched her fists as a collective groan emanated from the soldiers left on the beach. She spun around, seeking another vessel that might take their load so that they could go back for just one more. But everything was filled to capacity and the destroyers were rapidly weighing anchor. Out of all context with the battle-torn scene, the beautiful launch that displayed the gallant Union Jack lay at anchor, wallowing abeam in the surf, crammed with men. Its auxiliary dinghy approached from the shore propelled by the now disheveled, wet, and blood-spattered skipper.

"My God!" Toby gasped.   "The idiot's rowing his dinghy stern first."

In spite of the gravity of the situation, Yvonne laughed. "He must have been doing that all night," she said.

"We've delayed too long," Toby shouted.   "Look!"

She instinctively ducked as an olive-green aeroplane rapidly approached, screaming its war cry like a great bird of prey.   The wide-set, spatted wheels seemed to be groping for its victims like giant talons, while the radiator grill under the air screw stretched in a broad, ghastly grin.   It flew along the beach spitting bullets and then zoomed upward, turning to begin a steep dive toward them. As it reached the lowest point, two bombs fell away like excreta and exploded close to the men along the beach. Figures along the shoreline toppled like rag dolls and vehicles, already wrecked by previous attacks, collapsed into piles of smoking metal.

As the demon swooped skyward again, the shiny motor launch suddenly disappeared in a ball of fire spewing out debris and bodies into the water.   Yvonne covered her face with her hands, unable to bear witness to any more atrocities.   She felt a hand gripping her shoulder.

"Hang on, lad. We're on our way home."

The sergeant turned her away from the dreadful scene, but the image of the dead and dying floating around the burning vessel imprinted itself on her mind. As she watched their life's blood colour the boiling sea, her aching body surged with hot anger.

Whether the Stuka pilot miscalculated his dive, or whether one of the futile rifle shots from the beach found a vital mark, no one would ever know.   But as it circled back, the engine abruptly cut and then, coughing and faltering, the aircraft veered and plummeted to the beach, belly-flopping along to a standstill as it slewed against a gutted gun carrier. It seemed to Yvonne that the whole world stopped for an infinitesimal moment while its attention focused on the plane. Slowly the canopy drew back and the pilot emerged, slipping and sliding down the wing to escape the cockpit where flames licked around its rim. He seemed unhurt and obviously had self-preservation in mind. But within seconds, the rifles that had been so ineffectual while he was still aloft, now turned toward him. He died, sprawled across the wing of his machine like a scarecrow.

Toby's voice jolted her into action. "Look for debris," he shouted. "We must get underway. There'll be another of those green devils before we know it"

At last they were beyond the surf, but Toby looked furtively around him.

"We shouldn't be alone," he said. "Jerry can single us out. But there's a fog coming in and I can't see anyone else. Can you?"

Yvonne peered through the rapidly thickening mass and saw nothing. At that moment, the destroyer's antiaircraft guns began to fire.

"The Stukas are back," Toby said. "We'd must get out of here!"

She glanced at his sagging shoulders and drawn, pale face.

"Here, I'll take over for awhile," she said, nudging him aside. "You see if you find somewhere to sit down. Then you'll be rested enough to take us in to Dover Harbour."

She expected him to protest and prepared herself for an argument but he moved away from the wheel, looking behind him for a place to lean. The men were packed in so closely it seemed unlikely that he would find one.

"I don't feel very good about this," the sergeant said with a catch in his voice. "Some of my men are still on that beach.   The same men who shoved me on from behind in that last-minute panic."

"The same way you shoved others on ahead of you for the past three days," a young private said.

The sergeant sniffed and wiped the back of his hand across his face.

"No insubordination now, private," he growled. "Don't forget you're still in the army."

"Yes, Sarge."

Summer Solstice moved along at minimum speed, slowed by her overload of passengers, but since the beach grew smaller and dimmer as the fog closed in, Yvonne felt that they were making at least some progress.

She looked quickly behind her in search of Toby and saw him perched on the edge of the cockpit seat, trying to take up as little room as possible. She caught his eye and winked at him and he quickly responded.   The private observed the exchange.

"I wouldn't be too confident yet," he said.   "We saw *HMS Wakeful* go down with a full load yesterday."

Yvonne gripped the wheel until her fingers hurt.   "Why did it sink?" she asked, clenching her teeth to stop them from chattering.

"Torpedo."

"That's enough!" the Sergeant snapped.

He laid his hand on Yvonne's sleeve.   "Don't worry, we've got a good chance of making it, lad."

Yvonne looked again toward the beach to gauge their speed and saw that the Stuka now burned as a pyre for its German pilot. What could the men still waiting on the beach be thinking as they watched all the shipping pull away?   Did they believe they would perish there? She vowed that she and Toby would bring *Summer Solstice* back for them.

The sodden, silent men around her in the boat were crammed in so closely they could barely breathe and the stench from their uniforms was almost unbearable.   One youth leaned over the side, vomiting.   Who could know if he lost what little he had in his stomach because of seasickness or fear?   One sat quietly in the cockpit, his eyes bandaged and his hands clasped loosely in his lap.   Young, capable hands.   Another stood with his face pressed into the crook of his arm, weeping softly.

Across the water Yvonne could see the ghostly forms of the pleasure boats and the car ferries in the mist.   Other small boats, laden like themselves, were floundering along toward England.   She turned her head and caught a glimpse of the familiar lines of the *Miss Julie*, listing badly, but progressing slowly.

A sudden shot rang out across the water, and everyone ducked.

"It's all right," the Sergeant shouted.   "That came from over there.   I think they're trying to keep themselves awake.   I can't think of any other reason."

He cupped his hands around his mouth and yelled thunderously toward the *Miss Julie*.

"Can you make it? Are you shipping water?"

"We're plugging bullet holes," came the reply.   "We'll make it!"

"We'll send help," the Sergeant shouted.

He turned to Yvonne and shrugged.   "It's all we can do."

Soon they were alone.   They could no longer hear the muffled sputter of the other boat engines, neither could they see them.   Yvonne looked at the compass and saw the needle swinging wildly.

"I think a bullet found its mark," she muttered to herself.

The sergeant looked over her shoulder.   "I think you're right.   Here, use mine.   I've trained it to follow those bluebirds that are supposed to be waiting over the Dover cliffs, you know."

There was a soft pull at her sleeve and she looked down at the seated boy with the bandaged eyes.

"I think your skipper might have fallen asleep," he said. "I can understand that, but I'm afraid I can't hold his weight much longer."

Toby had slumped down against the boy's slight frame and was leaning heavily against him.

"I'll keep us on course," the Sergeant said. "You'd better go and have a look at him, lad. I think he might be ill. Go on! I know how to drive."

The silent men squeezed back as she knelt beside Toby.

"Almost home," she whispered to him. "Do you think you could sit up a bit?"

When he did not respond, the men helped to pull him away from the young blinded soldier and as she took his hand she felt the cold seep into her skin. She held it to her cheek and looked into the glazed blue of his eyes.

"Please Toby. Please wake up."

"He's dead, boy. Can't you see that?" someone said.

She stared in disbelief at Toby's pale face. Why would he be dead?

"Please," she pleaded. "Can we possibly lie him down?"

The seated men stood up, making enough room to lie Toby down along the cockpit seat. Yvonne looked around for something on which to cushion his head. He looked stiff and uncomfortable stretched out like that. Without further thought, she pulled the wool hat from her head and pillowed Toby's head in it.

"He was my friend," she said. "A good man with a bad heart."

She looked up at the faces above her, aware now that they stared.

"You're a girl!" one gasped.

It did not matter any more. She had been to Dunkirk

and there was not a thing anyone could do about that now.

A strange sound came from inside the cabin and she looked into the half-crazed eyes of the shell-shocked soldier. There was a childlike calmness about him now.

"You're a golden girl," he said, reaching to touch her hair. "She's a golden girl."

As she covered Toby with a blanket she looked at the still face and wondered how she would tell Doris Mallory. The couple were inseparable and had relied on each other constantly over the years. Something inside her wanted to snap and shatter the stoic façade she now desperately clung to. If only she could scream, or weep, or yell obscenities at the top of her voice. Instead she straightened up and turned to the sergeant who still held the helm.

"I'll take over now," she said. "Thank you very much for your help."

At last the now familiar cleft in the white cliffs loomed up out of the mist. Some of the men cheered, while others simply stood and stared. Yvonne looked at her watch and estimated that she had been aboard for over thirty-six hours without sleep. Her ears rang so loudly she wondered if perhaps she might have been deafened by the gun fire. Almost overwhelmed with fatigue, shock, and grief she gripped the end of the dodger, willing herself to stay in control.

"Thank God! Thank God!" one man said over and over.

Another coughed loudly and blew his nose on a grimy khaki handkerchief. Perhaps, she thought, the presence of a woman is forcing them to keep their emotions under control, too.

"I hope my missus has the kettle on for a cuppa," the sergeant said. "If she hasn't, I hope she's left the key under the mat," He grinned crookedly at Yvonne. "I'm not sure I'm expected, you see."

The men appeared to ignore the still figure under the blanket and at first this angered her. Then she remembered the bodies rolling in the surf and the desperate men who were still waiting on the beaches.   They had all seen plenty of death. Perhaps they would never be disturbed by it again.

As she slowed *Summer Solstice* for the turn into the harbour the Sergeant touched her arm.   "Well done, Miss," he said.   His mouth twitched downwards at the corners and he turned quickly away.

After the din of Dunkirk, she did not think anything could surpass it, but the cacophony of different sounds in the harbour came very close.   Men yelled into megaphones, ships signaled their intended movements with whoops and sirens, tea cups clattered, ambulances bustled in, medics called for emergency care, people ran hither and yon bent on their many vital errands while the soldiers themselves stood in half bewilderment scarcely believing that they were safely home. As the lines of bedraggled arrivals began to move toward waiting transportation, Yvonne saw a unit of men marching along the wharf, their heads held high and their commander out in front actually strutting.   A man's pride is imperative, she thought. It seems that the rescue mission has been largely successful, but our country lost in battle.   Time now to recuperate, reassemble, rearm and return, to show the enemy the real heart of our military force.

A woman from the Red Cross mobile canteen on the dock offered the men sandwiches, cups of steaming tea, apples, chocolate, and cigarettes--whether they smoked, or not.   Other women, who looked like ordinary housewives, were doing the same thing.   Yvonne accepted a cup from one and looked into eyes as exhausted as her own.   They too had been working through the night.

"You're not going to tell me you were over there," the woman said, inclining her head toward Dunkirk.   Yvonne turned away to watch the young man with bandaged eyes being led away.   He seemed to sense she was there.

"Thank you, Miss," he said, facing where he thought

she stood. "I won't ever forget you even though I don't know what you look like. Not ever."

The woman looked at her with disbelief. "You *were* there. Good God!"

Yvonne wished she would be quiet. She looked down at her hands and saw they were bruised and cut from heaving the men on board. Her duffel coat had blood smeared across the front and she remembered again the Tallyho man. A tremor convulsed through her and the woman's face swam out of focus.

"You look all in. It's all over and you're back now. What you need is a nice long rest."

Yvonne could not agree more as she sat down on an upturned crate and took a sip of tea. The sergeant, satisfied now that the last man was ashore, came toward her. She leapt to her feet. "The *Miss Julie*," she shouted, suddenly remembering the floundering vessel. "We forgot about the *Miss Julie!*"

"No we didn't, Miss. I've already told them and there's help on the way."

She sank back onto her seat. "You deserve a medal, Sergeant."

He patted her shoulder. "We all do, Miss."

He looked up as the young private came running back along the wharf side. "Your missus is here, Sarge," he shouted. "She didn't wait for you to get home. She's brought your cuppa right here to the dock."

The Red Cross tea lady looked to where the soldier pointed. "That woman has been here since Operation Dynamo began," she said. "She's been absolutely tireless and has kept everyone's spirits up." She looked at the Sergeant. "Are you Bert?"

He nodded, dumbly.

"She knew you'd be back. She said you were too evil to get killed. But since she didn't know when or on which boat, she decided to meet them all."

The man had not moved since sighting his wife, nor uttered a word. She came toward him holding out a steaming mug.

"Better late than never," she said.

His face crumpled as he took the mug, and Yvonne looked away.

Now she must turn her attention to the still, silent form under the blanket. As she sighed and rose stiffly to her feet, she sensed that someone watched her. All the men from her boat were gone now and the Red Cross ladies were preparing for the next wave of vessels to come in bearing their precious loads.

"I've just heard about Toby," a familiar voice said. "I'm so very sorry."

She turned quickly, her temples throbbing.

"How dare you, Ben! How dare you!" she shouted, staggering from the effort. Overwhelmed by fatigue, she spun away from him and ran frantically along the wharf choking back hot, angry tears.

"You must understand," he said, easily keeping abreast of her. "No one could have foreseen the reason for my detainment. I had every intention of meeting you at the boat. Have you any idea the mental agony I suffered when I heard you and Toby had gone to Dunkirk?" He moved in front of her and grabbed her shoulders. "Have you?" he shouted, shaking her. Your--our--responsibilities were supposed to end at Newhaven. We have all been victims of circumstances, Yvonne. I was unavoidably detained. Do you understand? There was nothing I could do about it."

Stunned by his unaccustomed outpouring she stared in bewilderment. His face was contorted with remorse and she suddenly felt ashamed.

"We...we had better get Toby off the boat," she said at last.

She watched him board *Summer Solstice.*

"Come on, old fellow," he whispered, lifting the lifeless body with ease. "It's time to go home."

Yvonne could not see his face as she followed him along the length of the wharf, but wondered if he might be weeping for his friend.

Whether it was simply premonition, or *Summer Solstice* found a voice and whispered to her, she never knew; but something made her turn and look back. The old river boat nestled lower and lower beside the dock until the water spilled over the gunwales. With silent dignity she at last succumbed to the bullet holes and shrapnel in her hull and sank out of sight into twenty-seven feet of dark water.

CHAPTER FOUR

June, 1940

Janine turned at the end of her sitting room at Flint House and paced back toward the window, her usual clear-thinking clouded and cluttered. She glanced up at the motionless giant spanning his green hill above Hunter's Burgh at Long Barrow Hill. If only he could influence her reasoning. Perhaps her involvement with British Intelligence all these years had been a mistake. Although her partnership with Claude was a perfect blending of their combined talents, Janine always maintained a complete separation of her secret activities and her personal affairs. But his inappropriate association with Yvonne, albeit under the guise of Ben Boniface, which had resulted in her unintended participation in Operation Dynamo, was a cause for deep concern. Although not entirely his fault, he had nonetheless put her in harm's way. It was most unfortunate that a nest of adverse intrigue had erupted in the south of France that required a more concentrated pocket of British agents in that area, and Claude's subsequent short-notice assignment to Marseilles had been most untimely. But Janine felt he was still to blame for Yvonne's present physical and mental condition, and for Toby Mallory's death.

Two days had passed since Yvonne's return and while still recovering from exhaustion and shock, she was plagued by nightmares, often waking in a state of disorientation and hysteria. Obviously, she'll not be recovered enough to attend Toby's funeral tomorrow, Janine thought as she prepared to leave for Mallory Cottage. Doris Mallory could not be expected to cope with the children under these circumstances and Janine intended to offer her help wherever she could. Leaving Yvonne in the capable hands of Mrs. Dougherty, she clipped Charlie to his lead and left Flint House.

As she passed the stationery shop, Arthur Banberry looked up from behind his post office cage at the back. She knew he was greatly saddened by the loss of his old friend and that it would be some time before he could resume his usual cheerful greeting to passersby.

As she pushed open the gate at Mallory cottage, the little girl from London rushed toward her down the garden path.

"It's Mr. Mallory," Kate Hawkins gasped. Her mouth twitched downward at the corners and her eyes were wide with concern. "I think he's been killed. Killed!" She ran blindly into Janine, obviously in a state of panic. "He's in a box in the parlour. In a box!"

Janine held the child against her, smoothing her hair. "It's all right, Kate. He wasn't killed. His poor old heart gave out, that's all."

Kate drew quickly away, her flushed face filled with dismay. "Oh, I am sorry, Mrs. Parke. I didn't mean to make a scene."

"My dear child," Janine said. "It's been an ordeal for everyone. Where is Mrs. Mallory?"

"Upstairs. She keeps on crying and I don't know what to say to her."

74

"I don't think you've met Charlie, have you?" Janine said, handing the child the dog's lead. "Why don't you take him for a walk around the village while I go and see what I can do for Mrs. Mallory?"

*   *   *

Kate desperately wanted to go home. Mr. Baxter, who lived next door to her home in London, had said the war would last only two weeks and on that assumption she thought a short stay in the country had sounded quite nice. But that was nine months ago! Oddly, he refused to let his daughter Ruby leave, expounding at length that he had no intention of having her labeled and herded off like a sheep. Ginger-haired Ruby Baxter had come to the bus to see Kate off and after saying "Ba-a-a-a" through the window had trotted off on her fat little legs. Their friendship was often argumentative due to stubborn and often opposite opinions about things, but in spite of this Kate missed her friend very much.

Charlie seemed to be listening as she told him how lonely she was and his bushy eyebrows twitched with sympathy. When they returned to Mallory Cottage after a walk around the village, she leaned against the old stone garden wall and laid her cheek against its coolness while Charlie sat quietly beside her.

"There's no point in crying, you know," Kate said. "What good would that do?"

She remembered the day of her departure and her mother's words as she tied the label through her lapel. Keep out of people's way, Kate, and try to be as quiet as you can.

But the wistful bubble growing in her throat suddenly

burst, releasing great choking sobs just as Mrs. Parke came through the gate.

"Oh, Kate! Please don't cry.   Mrs. Mallory is feeling much better now. In fact she's just settling down for a nap."

"It isn't just that," Kate stammered.   "It's everything." She bent down to pat Charlie's head in order to hide her tear-streaked face.   "I'm always in trouble at school because I can't put my gas mask on during the drills. It makes me choke."

"I dislike putting mine on, too," Janine said.   "But we should be prepared......."

"I made a sketch during the gas mask drill at school and everyone looked the same! Like a herd of animals."

It occurred to Janine that everyone felt the same, sharing in the awful apprehension of war and the unknown. "I'm glad you're using the drawing materials I gave you at Christmas," she said. "When can you come to Flint House and show me what you've done? Perhaps you might come by from time to time to take Charlie for a walk. I have to spend quite a bit of time in London these days and I know he would be very glad of the company."

The melancholy tears were fast disappearing.   "May I come soon?" Kate said.   "Since I've drawn just about everyone I know in the village and at school, I really should do a sketch of Charlie, too."   She glanced at the stationery shop as Arthur Banberry appeared carrying a shovel.   He locked the door and came toward them.

"I'm off to do my bit for the war," he said.   "We're joining up with the boy scouts to plant poles in the fields in order to repel any invasion by gliders. We've already taken down or turned around the sign posts, and there isn't a street name to be found anywhere. That should baffle the blighters, shouldn't it?"   His cheerful veneer only thinly disguised the underlying sorrow and Kate sensed that this effort was to shield her from the impact of Toby's death.

"Has the Home Guard been provided with weapons yet,

Arthur?" Janine asked.

"Yes.   No more pitchforks and broom handles! They've sent us guns. Now all we need are the bullets!" He winked at Kate. "We're all very willing, you know. Some of us are even able."

He shouldered the shovel and strutted off down the road "pomp-pomp-pomp" -ing with puffed-out cheeks.

Janine looked after him, shaking her head. "They don't come any better than that," she said, taking Charlie's lead. "Well, I must get back to Yvonne. Mrs. Mallory should wake up soon. Why don't you take another walk until she does?"

Since her arrival in Long Bottom, Kate had been fascinated with the Long Man up on the hillside. Although she had never been to Wilmington, she instinctively knew how to get there. Why, she could see the church spire from where she stood and it did not look very far away at all. No one would possibly know that she had ventured out of the village, since Mr. Banberry was off on his glider-repelling mission and Hugh always played cricket after school in the afternoons. Mrs. Mallory had settled down for a nap. This might be the perfect opportunity to see the Long Man up close.

"The Long Man," she murmured.   "Sometimes the Short Man, depending on where you're standing, I suppose."

It was easy enough to continue through the village and turn onto the Lewes road at the bottom. After a quick walk along a grassy shoulder, she came to the turn that lead her to the village of Wilmington and climbed up the steep road toward the Church of St. Mary and St. Peter at the top. Beyond the churchyard gate within the ancient flint wall the gravestones stood sentry over their dead, their gray shapes softened by moss and erosion that cloaked the names and dates engraved upon them. Kate fancied that soft voices whispered to her in the wind. The meadows beyond the churchyard stretched in a patchwork of varying greens, dotted by grazing cattle and trimmed at the outer edges with brambled frills.   The Long

Man, foreshortened even more now that she was so close to him, stretched upwards in front of her. How many wars has he seen, she wondered? If only he could speak.

Footsteps suddenly pounded across the turf behind her and, startled, she turned quickly.

"Not a step further!" Hugh panted, catching up. "You're too far from home as it is. Besides, Mrs. Mallory sent me up to fetch you because it's tea time. Thank goodness Mr. Banberry saw which way you were going. He's putting up poles in the home field at Farnsworth's farm."

"I don't want to go back," Kate said. "I don't like Mr. Mallory being in that box in the front room."

"They took it away just a few minutes ago. Anyway, you couldn't actually see him."

"He was dead, all the same."

Hugh sighed. "People die all the time, especially when there's a war on, you know. I heard they shot a spy somewhere near Folkstone a few days ago. He's dead, too."

"Spy? There are spies near here?" Kate looked furtively about her.

"There are always spies in wartime--on both sides. Anyone could be one. Mr. Banberry the postmaster, Mrs. Mallory.....even our own mother could be one. Come on Kate, it's tea time."

An old man approached from the lower village as they began to descend the main Wilmington road.

"Him, too?" she whispered.

Hugh nodded. "They know how to use disguises. I'll bet he's one of those Gestapo chaps."

They stood aside to let the man pass and Kate curled her lip into a snarl. The old man muttered to himself as he passed and glanced briefly at her.

"You've got Ribbentrop, Goring, Hess, and Himmler to worry about, you know," Hugh whispered, looking after the man. "as well as all the spies; and don't forget, they all hate little English girls."

As he spoke, the old man suddenly halted and turned around, retracing his steps toward them.

Kate thought her heart would stop.   "That's torn it," she gasped.   "He's coming back to kill us."

Hugh smiled.   "Correction.   He's coming back to kill you.   Remember?   The Gestapo doesn't like little English girls!"

She pressed back against the churchyard wall with her eyes tightly shut, waiting to be killed and opened one tremulous lid as the old man passed.

"Bloody kids," he muttered, as he went into the churchyard.   "Made me fergit where I was going."

Kate opened her eyes and glared at Hugh.

Hugh grinned sheepishly.   "Come on.   The tea's getting cold. I'll race you home."

*   *   *

Janine watched her daughter across the breakfast table and wondered if the change in her temperament might be a permanent thing. A certain empathy heretofore foreign to her nature had penetrated her usual supercilious facade and, while Yvonne would not speak of her own experiences there, she did comment often upon the bravery of the men involved in the Dunkirk rescue, and even wept as news of the aftermath flooded the media. The photographs of heavily damaged ships and dismembered military equipment along the Dunkirk coast needed no captions or explanations and Yvonne obviously grieved for the men who shared the tragic burial ground. Not visible but equally mourned were the three gallant destroyers sunk by enemy action--*HMS Wakeful, HMS Grafton,* and *HMS Grenade*--all fully loaded with men and crew. Although over three hundred thousand men had been rescued, there were still those left behind who would either be taken prisoner or make an attempt to return to England independently. Yvonne Parke, in all her illiberal wisdom, had learned the meaning of compassion.

"Have you seen the paper?" she asked.   "Italy has declared its alliance with Germany.   I should think that means at least another year of upheaval."

She looked steadily at her mother across the table.   "I know you're concerned about conditions in Provence.   Why can't we convince the grandparents to leave?"

"There is talk of an armistice," Janine explained.   "If France is divided, we can hope that the southern sector will remain ostensibly under French jurisdiction. The family estate there is valuable and should be protected.   But you're right. They're getting old and this may prove to be too much for them."

"We'll be next, no doubt.   Everyone's talking about invasion."

"We can only pray for a miracle, Yvonne.   There's no doubt that Britain will be fighting for her life in the next few months."

"Then I'm ready to help in any way that I can."

"Haven't you already done enough?"

"I'll only be able to say that when this war has come to an end. Look at David. He's just about to begin."

*   *   *

"It would be a good idea," Ravensbrook said, "if you drove the MG on the road, David. I don't want my first prang to be the car. You missed that signpost back there by an inch."

"Well at least I missed it, didn't I? Anyway, it was supposed to point toward Chichester--which is the general direction we're supposed to be going in--and it wasn't."

"The signposts have been turned around to confuse Jerry."

"Right. But what about me? I'm confused."

George pointed through the windscreen. "There's the sun and it's moving due west and I suggest you follow it."

Much later than expected they moved with uncertainty through the village of Shopwyke and halted at the barrier gate of Tangmere aerodrome. George handed their orders to the sentry with a flourish.

"Your maintenance flight has been up in Grangemouth since April," the young guard said. "And Regatta Squadron itself......well, sir......it isn't here."

"Not here?" George spluttered. "Not here!"

The guard backed away. "No, sir. On their way, sir. The adjutant came in about an hour ago. Arrived by train, sir." He backed further away and waved them through.

David grinned when they were well out of earshot. "You really had him going, didn't you? What did you expect? A fanfare?"

"Not exactly, but I did expect to see a bit of life around the place."

Camouflaged netting flapped gently in the neighbouring field drawing their attention to the unmistakable shape of Bofors antiaircraft guns and a couple of Hotchkiss and Lewis machine guns lurking beneath. Blast walls along the perimeter of the airfield lay adjacent to dispersal huts and beyond those, in snug U-pens, crouched several Hurricane fighter planes.

"Ah," David breathed. "There they are."

"Ah," George echoed, looking in the direction of the Operations building. "There *they* are! WAAFS, no doubt."

David raised his eyebrows appreciatively. "Yes, but what about your burning love for Yvonne?"

"Oh, it's still flickering. But you have to admit, old boy, it's hardly reciprocal. Anyway, there's a war on and we have to live while we can."

The airfield was uncannily quiet. A hovering skylark twittered above the runway and somewhere in Shopwyke village a dog barked. The two fledgling Pilot Officers looked at one another questioningly.

"Where's all the activity?" David said.

"As far as I'm concerned it's most likely over there with the WAAFS in the Operations building!" George rolled his eyes.

They parked the MG in front of the Officer's Mess and walked around to the back where they found a Flight Lieutenant dozing in a deck chair.

"Well, there is life, after all!" David said.

"He doesn't look very alive to me." George eyed the sleeping man doubtfully and then moved his attention to an ungainly bulldog lying beside him.

"I say, have you ever seen anything as ugly as that?"

The Flight Lieutenant opened one eye. "My mother thinks I'm quite handsome, actually."

"Oh, er, I meant your canine companion, sir."

The man reached down and gave the ugly dog a pat on the head. "He's a bulldog you know. Quite sensitive about rude observations, aren't you, Rosebud?"

George mouthed the word Rosebud?

"Oh, I know he's got plumbing, but there is some logic to the name. I'd stay clear after he's had his dinner, if I were you."

The Flight Lieutenant opened both eyes and looked across the field toward the U-pens.

"Any Hurryback experience?"

"We've just come from Cranwell, sir," David said.

"Then there isn't any point in asking you if you're battle tested, is there?"

"Well, we did have some live gunnery practise at Fraugh and Warmwell," George ventured.

"Yes, well......the CO won't be too happy.   But you'd better not go far because he's due in any minute."

They took their bags into the mess and tried to acclimate themselves.

"By the way," the Flight Lieutenant said from the doorway.   "Which one of you is Parke?"

David cleared his throat.   "I am, sir."

"Well, somebody left off a chariot for you at the gate yesterday.   Some of the chaps from Six-O-One had a bit of fun with it, but it's over by Ops now.   Anyway, you'd better move it because it's in the way."

"Wheels?" George said.   "Well, in that case you won't need to grind my gears any more, will you?"

David recognised his father's dark green Daimler with a sinking heart which sank even further when he saw the expression on Ravensbrook's face.

"Chauffeur's seat," George said, counting on his fingers.   "Communication horn, a sliding partition for privacy-- it even has a blind to pull down--, quite a playground on that back seat, and what have we here..........a strap to hold on to? Since it's supposed to be chauffeur-driven, we won't even have to worry about driving the thing and can enjoy our female company at leisure on the back seat."

He grinned, lecherously. "However, the only thing that seems to be missing is the chauffeur."

"It seems," David said, miserably. "It's me."

The squadron arrived with a roar and flourish within the hour.   Thirteen brown camouflaged aircraft lit down on the field like a flock of Canadian geese and soon the pilots strolled across the field all talking at once.

"They're here!" the Flight Lieutenant needlessly observed. He sniffed the air. "Ah, tea's up! By the way, I'm the squadron adjutant. The name's Kenneth Dillard."

Rosebud arbitrarily raised his leg against the Daimler's rear wheel and waddled off after Dillard.

"By the by," the adjutant said, over his shoulder. "You'd better be prepared for a crash course. We're actually rather short of pilots. Dunkirk and all that sort of thing, you know."

George raised his eyebrows. "Crash course? But I already know how to do that."

"Are we supposed to follow him?" David said.

"You can if you like," Kenneth Dillard said, disappearing into the building. "But it so happens I'm going to the bog."

George eyed the rear wheel of the Daimler. "Well, since Rosebud has ably anointed your luxurious heap here, we'd better give it a name." He closed his eyes and laid a hand on the gleaming dark green bonnet. "I hereby christen you David's Den of Iniquity--DDI, or Dee Dee for short."

* * *

"Do you know that you nearly clipped my wing," a dark-haired pilot was saying as the newcomers entered the Mess. A lock of hair fell across his eyebrow as he slumped into an armchair. "Don't you know how to fly in formation?" He licked the end of a pencil and began writing in his flight log.

A tall, blond Adonis leaned against the door post. "Rubbish!" he said. "In fact, I think you were dozing off..........at least, your head was nodding. I obviously should have clipped something."

"I was memorising lines.   Polly What's-her-name says she's going to follow the squadron here from Wick, heaven forbid. I've got to dream something up to put her off."

"Surely you haven't decided abandon the idea of a woman in your life, Rupert?"

"Well....only the ones who think they can hear wedding bells. Actually, there's a good pub in Chichester, I've heard.....and the feminine natives are friendly.   But we need adequate wheels. I'm not about to walk two miles or so to get there and stagger probably six miles or so back here."

George nudged David.   "Now there's a man after my own heart," he muttered.

Rupert's brown eyes brightened with interest as they focused on David and George.

"Ah! What have we here? Replacements?"   He rose and held out his hand. "Rupert Barlow. That Nordic giant is Adam Tate.....Treacle, if you like.   You know, the Tate and Lyle stuff.   Good chap really, but a bloody awful pilot, God love him."

Treacle raised a hand in recognition as a Flight Lieutenant wandered in and tossed his leather Irvine jacket onto a chair.

"Hello! Where did you two come from?"

"Er, Cranwell," David said.

"Yes......well.....we all have to start somewhere I suppose."

Rupert got up and stretched.   "Me too, last year. Hawker Hinds, Avro Tutors, Harts.....and not a single clue about Hurricanes and Spitfires until I joined a squadron."

David felt deflated.

"Don't worry about it," Rupert said.   "You'll soon learn.   By the way, that's Patrick Kennedy." He nodded toward the Flight Lieutenant.

"Welcome to the mad house," Patrick grinned.

"That's an understatement," an older man said from the doorway.   He edged into the room.   "Anything to report?"

A general negative murmur rumbled through the room.

"Harry Cartwright," Treacle volunteered.   "Intelligence officer.   Have you met the adjutant?"

"Yes, thank you," George said.   "And his disgusting hound.   Would you believe he--the hound--christened David's charabanc with lift of the leg, so to speak?"

Rupert looked interested.   "I say, do you have a heap? Tell you what, I'll show you the Hurricane's preliminaries, if you'll drive us to Chichester one evening or six."

"I'll do better than that," George said.   "I'll even throw in a chauffeur!"

"You might consider this a rather inane question," the adjutant murmured.   "But where's the Squadron Leader?"

"Fuel trouble," Patrick said.   "He had to land at Grangemouth.   He'll be along directly." He looked toward the window as a Miles Magister two-seater touched down.   "As a matter of fact, I think that's probably him now."

As the CO strode in, pulling off his gloves, David and George straightened their backs, noting his tallness and the craggy outline of his face.   He appeared to observe everyone in the room to a man with one sweeping glance.   He exuded leadership and experience and David immediately felt a sense of respect for him.

"Well at least the trains are running on time, aren't they?" he said, addressing Kenneth but obviously not expecting an answer.   "I trust you and Harry were here before the rest of the squadron came in?   Have the replacements come in yet?"

David and George eased forward hoping to draw approval from the shrewd blue eyes.

"Two kites in the hangar and three more due," Harry said.   "Oh, and by the way, we have two new.....officers.....just down from Cranwell."

86

The Squadron Leader eyed the two pilots who stood eagerly at attention, and returned their smart salutes with a flick of his forefinger. He walked into a small office, indicating that they should follow.

"My name is Donald Moore," he said. "I ought to send you two to a conversion course since you've obviously had no experience with fighters, but we're short. We're already on alert due to the wrap-up of Operation Dynamo. You won't be ready in time to do anything about that, but at least we can get you started.......first thing in the morning!"

"The infamous crash course," David said as they gathered up their luggage.

"Off the cuff, you understand," Treacle said, catching up with them. "Rupert can't blackmail you into a ride to Chichester after all. He's been ordered to familiarise you with the Hurryback at first light tomorrow." He grinned, impishly. "He's actually a good pilot, but you don't have to let him know that. The CO wasn't joking, though. The squadron is operational."

"But you've only just arrived!" George said.

"In case you hadn't noticed, there's a war on. You'll see a lot of new stuff coming in because Tangmere is the centre for funneling replacement aircraft. You'll also notice there'll be a lot of those replacements. As I said, there's a war on."

George picked up his bag. "No hope of joining a rugby game, then?" he asked ruefully.

"I'm for cricket myself, but we haven't even time for a game of ping-pong at this stage. See you in the Mess."

The thought of a drink and some shop talk was enticing, but David felt a quick look at the Hurricane would be to their advantage. He and George were pleased and grateful to the ground crews who were most obliging, and Rupert found them two hours later studying the instrument panel so intensely they did not hear his approach.

"Ah, so that's how it works, is it?" he said, hopping up

onto the wing and peering into the cockpit.

"I can't wait to take her up," David murmured, standing on the port wing.

"Well, just remember that she's bloody quick compared to what you've been flying. After you get the hang of it, it's a piece of cake. But right now, the bar's about to close because everyone has early appointments in the morning--B section with Jerry, and me with you two."

George reluctantly climbed out of the cockpit while David questioned Rupert about combat tactics. Rupert quickly outlined his point of view as they returned to the Mess.

"Every sortie is different, of course. You can never really predict what Jerry has in mind. The Me109s usually fly protectively above the Stuka schwarms and theoretically the Spitfire squadrons are supposed to take them on. The Hurrys go for the bombers. Just remember that a Stuka is most vulnerable when it has climbed to its assigned height in preparation to dive--little power and speed then, you know." He put his arms across the shoulders of the two new arrivals. "Of course, it's all theory. When you've got the Hun on your tail you do what's necessary--it's either him or you whether he's a bomber or a fighter. Just try to keep up sun, that's all."

David stood outside the Mess at dawn and watched B Flight take off. Treacle had waved as he clambered aboard the lorry. "Rupert's a pretty good tutor when he's not thinking about women," he shouted. "You're in for a treat."

Rupert wandered out, yawning noisily. "There go the Spits," he said nodding toward a group of aircraft taxiing to the runway from another part of the field. He peered up at the sky, spilling tea from the mug he held. "A bit murky up there. Hope the weather holds."

"I hope they've left a couple of aeroplanes for us to play with," David said. "I understand we're to take a lesson with you this morning. CO's orders!" He grinned, knowingly.

"The ground crews will be all ready for us, mark my

words. Yes, it was the CO's orders. But can I still have a ride
to Chichester?"

David feigned indecision. "I suppose a lot depends on
whether we're considered good enough to fly Hurricanes."

"Point taken. By the way, have you ever had to bale
out?"

"No, but I've done a few fancy landings that weren't too
popular!"

"Well, if you do, point your aeroplane away from town
and find a nice soft spot to float down to on the end of your
parachute. I always do. As a matter of interest, where's your
eager friend?"

"Always?"

"Well, at least once."

"To answer your question, my eager friend wasn't very
willing to get up, but he's on his way."

Rupert eyed DDI and the MG as they passed by them.
"I say, what a duo! The sporty one is superb for attracting the
fairer sex, and the other one's a veritable bedroom, isn't it?"

"My thought exactly," George said, joining them.
"We'll use the green one for Chichester though, don't you
think?"

"Absolutely, old boy. Now, are you ready to go up and
kill yourselves?"

As they walked toward the hangar, Rupert's flippant
mood quickly changed.

"Now you know," he said, "that the Spit and
Messerschmitt are faster than the Hurricane by a good thirty
miles per hour. But don't let that discourage you. The
Hurricane is a gem when it comes to maneuverability and
survivability. She can out-turn a Me109, so bear that in mind if
you find yourself in a bind. The visibility is better on the
ground than that of the Spit and I think the Browning machine
gun configuration is superior. She's easier to land than a
Spitfire, too. You'll find her responsive and willing."

"Ah, yes," George said, looking wistfully toward the Operations building. "Responsive and willing."

Having been forewarned that the engine coolant heated rapidly, David anxiously watched the gauge as they taxied the aircraft to the end of the runway. At last, with the glycol almost at boiling point, the trio of Hurricanes took to the air and the gauge began to subside.

"Don't forget the legs have to go up," Rupert said, over the radio telephone, commonly known as the R/T. "You didn't have that to think about that at Cranwell, did you?"

David looked quickly at the instrument panel and saw the "landing gear down" light.

"You'll have to pump with one hand and fly with the other," Rupert said. "Sort of like rubbing your stomach and patting your head at the same time. You'll soon get the hang of it."

With sweat trickling uncomfortably down his neck, David drew a sigh of relief as the light went off. He looked ahead and saw tree tops coming rapidly toward him.

"Where the devil are you two?" Rupert shouted.

"Just coming, Mother," George called. "Glad I got the wheels up or I might have had quite a collection of top branches in them."

David concurred as he again checked his altitude, amazed at the speed of this nifty aeroplane. He concentrated on Rupert's plane, knowing that any minute they would begin maneuvers. The intense studying of the previous evening was paying off since he knew the instrument panel and other positions in the cockpit by heart. The Hurricane was indeed a pleasure to fly and she was as responsive and willing as Rupert had so eloquently described.

"Now we'll do some tricks," Rupert said. "Follow me and stick like glue."

The series of routine dives, banks, climbs, turns, rolls, side slips, stalls and slides became progressively more exciting and David's exhilaration peaked.

"You'll do," Rupert said. "Let's go home."

"Just a few more minutes?" George pleaded.

"Look at your fuel, old man. Vital when in combat, you know."

The gauge registered low and David glanced across at George in astonishment.   Had they really been flying long enough to use up that much?

"That Merlin engine guzzles fuel quickly and it's imperative that the pilot keep an eye on time aloft, especially in combat," Rupert said. "Don't forget to put the wheels down, chaps. It makes landing much nicer."

And so it was. David shut down the engine, aware that a straggle of pilots lingered outside the Mess, and knew that the performance had been closely watched.   He wondered how they had fared.

"Not bad for beginners," one said as they approached. "I wouldn't try too hard if I were you.   You'll find yourself facing old Jerry in a day or so if you're not careful."

It was a backhanded compliment which David nonetheless appreciated.

The speaker looked up, shading his eyes.   "B Flight," he said.

The anticipation of hearing battle experiences quickly faded as all but one of the aeroplanes came in. When they landed--some in difficulty, others with barely enough fuel to keep them going-- young pilots staggered from the cockpits, their zip and panache now deteriorated into shock and exhaustion. All of the aircraft were badly shot up and several of the pilots were bespattered with blood.   Two were taken away by ambulance.   Rupert stood quietly watching, hands clasped behind his back and mouth drawn into a thin line.   Donald Moore dropped his gear to the ground and stood with him while David and George kept their distance, knowing that to speak would be indiscreet.   They waited for nearly an hour, but

The Long Man   Pauline Furey

the last Hurricane did not return.

CHAPTER FIVE

June, 1940

David wondered how long Rupert would be able to retain his composure. Losing someone who had been his close friend must be pure agony for him and although he brooded, he made no mention of it. Squadron Leader Moore reported that he thought he saw Treacle bale out somewhere over the Channel, but could not be sure since there had been no communication over the R/T. Clouds, and the general mayhem of dog fighting made positive identification almost impossible. Two days had passed without a word.

George and David qualified for operational flying just after the Dunkirk rescue was officially terminated. One significant event after another made news headlines each day, but understandably nobody in the Squadron indulged much in political and international discussion since the entire focus centered on victory and survival in air combat.

But the continued enemy infiltration into France festered in the back of David's mind. He remembered the happy hours spent on his grandparent's estate near Aix-en-

Provence and the lush scenery surrounding the Sainte-Victoire mountain and the ancient buildings steeped in history. He thought of the friendly people in the village of Luynes when, accompanied by his grandfather, he bought warm croissants and fresh fruit to carry home for breakfast before the rest of the household even thought of stirring. Now the Germans were in Paris. Premier Reynaud had resigned and David had heard that masses of carts, trucks and pedestrians were leaving Paris in frantic flight from the Germans. He wondered how Pétain, who was Reynaud's replacement, would cope with the enemy. General Charles de Gaulle had left France and was setting up a Free French organisation in London. The words "Ici Londre" had become familiar with the BBC listening public when broadcasts were made to France. Would there be an armistice? Would France be totally occupied by the enemy?   Would David's grandparents be directly affected? He thought of his mother and knew she must be deeply concerned at this unsettled time.

George stared dolefully out over the airfield.

"I feel a bit redundant," he said.   "The excitement's over.   I'd hoped that we would have been in time to find out what it's like to be on the offensive up there."

"You're offensive enough on the ground," David said. "Anyway, things are already hotting up again.   Don't worry, our turn's coming."

Rupert drummed his fingers on the window sill.   "Can you imagine," he said to no one in particular.   "We were supposed to rendezvous with a French squadron over Hawkinge yesterday, and the bloody cowards didn't show up."

His bitter mood smoldered and anyone could see he was about to explode.   He turned away from the window and wandered off, pontificating about the unreliable French and how anyone barbaric enough to eat snails and frogs could possibly understand the tactics and strategy of modern warfare. Patrick Kennedy looked after him, shaking his head.

"It was a bit sporty over there," he said. "I don't know what Treacle's chances are. If he went into the water, he would have to rely on whatever shipping happened to be out there to pick him up. If no one saw him come down......well......Rupert's putting on a good show, but....." He shrugged.

"What about the seagoing defences in the Dunkirk area?" George asked. "I mean, surely the RAF wasn't the only protective force out and about that day."

"Oh, yes. Plenty of shipping there, but we heard that three destroyers and two transports were sunk, all loaded with rescued men. Poor devils. As it was, the concentration of shipping was in the Dunkirk area and only by remote chance would there have been anything in the area where we were dog fighting and where Treacle went down." Patrick shook his head again and glanced at David. "Can you imagine all those little boats going over? Is it true that your sister took part in all that?"

"I don't really know the details," David said. "I do know from news relayed by my mother that she helped take our river boat over. At the moment she's seen more action than I have. According to my mother, Yvonne claims that the RAF was not in evidence, but of course, we know differently......."

"Running air battles don't stay in one place for long," Patrick said. "We were chasing the bastards off further along the coast. But your sister's opinion seems prevalent amongst the Army blokes. One made a rude gesture and swore at me in Shopwyke yesterday."

"They should have seen you come in flying your shot-up aeroplanes," David said. "And in Treacle's case, not come in."

"Squadrons Two-forty-five and Seventeen took a pretty savage licking, too. It's a bloody rotten war."

Patrick turned on his heel and left, continuing to let off steam simply by talking to himself.

"Think you're ready for tomorrow?" David asked George.   They were slated to fly a patrol with Donald Moore the next morning.   "I mean, do you know the meanings of all the usual acronyms we'll be using?"

"Of course!"

"All right.   What does IFF mean?"

George laid the back of his hand across his forehead.   "I Feel Faint?"

"You will if you don't know.   Identification, Friend or Foe.   Remember?"

"Ah yes, of course.   One of us switches over to a device called Pip-squeak which sends out location signals that Direction Finding picks up."

"What else?"

"Cross bearings from these fix our position and we can be continuously plotted on the ground."

David sighed, well aware that George had faked his ignorance.   "So we are then fed information concerning the location of incoming enemy."

"Marvelous, isn't it?" George said.   "All those little dots on a cathode ray tube actually mean something.   I wonder how much longer we'll have to wait to become a dot?"

"Only until tomorrow morning--and the word is 'blip'. By the way, I don't think we're considered the New Boys any longer.   New replacements are due tomorrow."

Rupert wandered back, still muttering to himself.   "It was bloody awful up at Wick," he grumbled.   "The only consolation was Polly What's-her-name until she started getting serious and ruined everything.   But it was the mud that was really awful.   Tons of it. I swear Wick has more rain than the rest of the country put together. And that, my friends, produces mud."   He threw back his head and began to sing: "Mud! Mud! Glorious Mud! Nothing quite like it for cooling the blud!"

"I say," a faint voice from the doorway complained.

"Do you mind singing in tune. You're hurting my ears."

Rupert stared in disbelief and scrambled to his feet. "My God! He's come back to haunt me!" He rushed to the door, stumbling over George's feet on the way. "You're late!" he yelled, thumping Treacle on the back so enthusiastically he nearly knocked him over.

"Hang on," Treacle protested, attempting to hold on to a large bundle of grubby white silk which he held against his chest. "I'm only two days late. I would have been back sooner, but I had to walk because they wouldn't let me on the bus." He grabbed at the unfolding cloth as it began to slide from his arms.

"Why?"

"Because I smelt fishy."

"Yes......well.....I see what you mean," Rupert took a step backwards, holding his nose.

Treacle reeled and put out his hand, groping for some kind of support. The mass of silk fell to the floor and billowed up in undulating waves around him.

"I say, is that your parachute?" Rupert said, peering closer.

Treacle yawned and rubbed his eyes with grimy knuckles. "Well, yes, actually. I suppose it is. You see, I didn't want to lose it because I know this one works." He swayed sideways and David grabbed his arm.

"He's asleep on his feet!"

"Sleep?" Treacle said, looking closely into David's eyes. "Yes, please."

"Better report in first and tell them who you are," George said. "I doubt that anyone would believe it's really you, otherwise."

George gently led the half-conscious pilot from the Mess while David insisted that Rupert sit down.

"I always said he was a rotten pilot," Rupert said, brokenly. "But at least he knew how to bale out." He tried to smile without success.   Instead, his handsome face crumpled and he got up, knocking the chair over, and quickly walked away.

*   *   *

Although air activity was accelerating along the French coast David's first flight over the Channel proved to be a disappointment.   British squadrons were constantly on patrol during daylight hours out looking for trouble and both he and George had scarcely slept the previous night anticipating all the excitement that must inevitably come the next day.   He had taken special stock of the ground crews as they readied his aeroplane and saw that they were superbly efficient.   There seemed to be an almost parental attitude about them as they carefully checked each facet of the aircraft's mechanics.   A short, serious-faced cockney named Fred Beggs stood in charge over his crew with quiet authority and there seemed to be some kind of mental telepathy between him and his trusty second, Jim Patch.

The patrol was scarcely over the coastline, when the R/T crackled and Donald Moore--Red Leader--announced that they were turning back.

"Look ahead, chaps.   A pea souper if I ever saw one."

David immediately banked his aircraft and followed the rapidly dimming outline of Red Leader.   One swift distracting glance at the instrument panel cost him his cohesion in the formation and he knew immediately that he was flying blind. As the swirling mist whispered against his windshield, he fought down panic prodded by persistent thoughts of midair collisions.   Garbled voices jammed the R/T and gradually petered out.   He was suddenly alone in dense fog, utterly lost and very frightened.

"Northwest," he muttered.   "I may end up hopelessly off course, but at least I should be somewhere over the British Isles--I hope."

He knew a too low altitude would bring him in collision with the chalk cliffs along the southeast coast.   Yet, climbing too high might deprive him of the glimpse of land he now prayed for.   As he peered down into the dense mass, it suddenly thinned and he saw a flash of green.   Then, even more surprising, a flash of white.

My God, he thought.   I'm flying directly over Flint House.   That was the Long Man! If I continue north, I might be able to land at Biggin Hill in Kent, or Croydon.

It might have been a miracle, but more likely an attribution to the lie of the land since he was well away from the sea now which was the source of the fog. Whatever the cause, the visibility suddenly improved and he flew in brilliant sunshine on a direct course for Tangmere.

Still in a state of complete astonishment, he landed without incident and came to a halt in front of the U-pen.   He threw back the canopy, hesitant to leave the cockpit and face the reprimand he knew was due from the CO.   Climbing shakily from the cockpit he became acutely aware of how terrified he had been.   Patch helped him from the wing.

"Well done, Sir.   You're the third to make it in so far."

"W-what?"

"Only two others, Sir."

David pulled off his helmet and felt the cool air grip at his scalp.

"Pilot Officer Ravensbrook is in, and Squadron Leader Moore."

David's relief quickly changed to consternation.   Where were the others?

Patch smiled crookedly.   "Pilot Officer Ravensbrook

is....er....injured, Sir."

"What!"

"Very slight, Sir......although I don't think *he* thinks so."
The smile broadened.

David began to run. George had always taken his rugby
injuries in his stride. Patch must be underestimating this one.
Had George crashed? Was he out of commission?

He found the patient slumped in a Mess armchair
holding up a swollen thumb toward the light. David sagged
with relief.

"Bumpy landing?"

"You could say that. I took the top off one haystack
and landed in another." George turned the digit round and
scrutinised it from a different angle.

"Well, a jammed thumb isn't so bad," David said.

"And a chipped tooth. Listen, I can whistle through the
hole."

"What about your aeroplane?"

"Oh, that. Well, it's full of hay but otherwise sustained
less damage than I did."

David went to make his report to Harry Cartwright and
learned that three of Red Section had landed at Croydon and
one at Biggin Hill, all pretty much out of juice because they
had floundered about for a while and then followed the
coastline whenever it became visible. Two found the mouth of
the Thames and followed the river westward and thence out of
the fog.

"Two of the young replacements went into the cliffs,"
Harry said, quietly. "Damn shame!"

"What about Barlow, Sir? And Kennedy?"

"Barlow pranged....slightly..... in a field near Arundel
out of fuel, but he's fine. Tate went out in the Tangmere lorry
to bring him in. I gather his aircraft is repairable."

"Obviously Treacle--er Tate--is none the worse for wear
after walking all that way with his parachute," David said.

Harry shook his head. "I cease to be surprised at the antics of this squadron," he said. "But he's damned lucky. The Germans have a pretty effective search and rescue programme for their downed pilots, but we have to rely on civilian seagoing craft or whomever happens to be in the area. Some of our chaps have drowned waiting to be rescued, I'm afraid. A French fishing boat saw him and pulled him in and, as luck would have it, met a British herring boat out from The Wash. He has the French to thank in spite of Barlow's adverse opinion of them."

David turned to leave the office. "Oh, and what about Kennedy, Sir?" He had liked Patrick from the start. A steady pilot with a great love of aviation, David discovered that he was also something of a writer. Genuinely modest concerning this talent, David insisted that he read aloud one of his poems when they were alone in the Mess one afternoon and was touched by both the significance of the words and the beauty of the voice that recited them.

"He landed at Friston almost out of fuel. He's on his way."

* * *

An uncanny air of desertion hung over the coast of France. Continuing patrols were uneventful and while the time aloft offered those unfamiliar with their aircraft time to accustom themselves to it, the lack of enemy action suggested an ominous threat rather than relief.

"I think it'th time," Rupert lisped having badly bitten his tongue when he crashed, "that we theek out the flethpots of Chichethter."

Although George continued to make the most of his injured thumb, the rest of the squadron had adopted his chipped tooth-inspired whistle along with Rupert's lisp. During routine patrols Donald Moore had to put a stop to it since neither he nor Ground Control could understand a word they were saying.

"It's bad enough," he said, "that we can't convince the Poles and Czechs to stop jabbering over the R/T without you chaps complicating things further."

"How many," Rupert continued, "can DDI hold?"

"Three on the back seat, two on the jump seats, and one in front with the driver," David said.

"I'll drive," George volunteered as he watched a mass of bodies rushing for the door.

After a great deal of wedging, stuffing and pushing, DDI rumbled through the gates of Tangmere with her sides bulging. Somehow, David had managed to commandeer one of the jump seats and winced as George ground the gears alarmingly.

"Don't worry, old boy," Rupert's muffled voice said from underneath a pile of arms and legs. "He'll get the hang of it."

"He'd better," David groaned.

Used to the speed and maneuverability of his MG George urged the Daimler on like a race horse until it arrived outside The Unicorn pub literally gasping.

Cigarette smoke, noise, and laughter greeted them as they entered. George and Rupert immediately cleared a path to the bar and soon had their arms around two local girls who somehow knew the words to the bawdiest rugby songs. David and Treacle willingly took back seats and watched the fun, feeling the warmth of the welcome that Chichester gave to the pilots of Westhampnett and Tangmere.

The evening might have been a complete success but for the boisterous arrival of several young Army corporals. Obviously not the first pub they had visited during the evening, their beer-filled bellies predominated over good sense and, upon seeing the RAF contingency, their mood changed from high-spirited conviviality to accusative sarcasm.

"Well, if it isn't the Brylcreem Boys," one said, sidling up to George and Rupert, apparently looking for trouble. "Where were you when we were dying at Dunkirk?"

George carefully put down his beer mug and faced his tormentor. "The Raff *was* there," he said, shortly.

"Hear that?" the soldier said. "He says they were there. Don't see any walking wounded amongst you like young Norman here." He shoved a young man forward whose eyes were heavily bandaged. "Norman didn't see you there, either. Did you Norman? Poor bugger can't see much of anything now. Come on, Brylcreem Boy, show us your walking wounded." The soldier strutted forward with his fists up, weaving menacingly in front of Rupert.

David knew that one punch from George would put the drunken man flat on his back. Treacle stood up and the soldier immediately turned to face him, taking note of his height.

"Now it's my turn to hit you below the belt," he bellowed, prancing about in front of Treacle. He was a good six inches shorter and would quite likely deliver his first blow exactly where he predicted.

The publican came out from behind the bar and the soldier turned on him. "You're all in on it," he shouted. "Nobody knows what it was like over there and nobody cares."

"Look, old fellow," the publican said. "You've got your facts mixed up. It's Jerry who's the enemy. We're all in this war together you know."

"Quiet, everyone!" someone shouted. "The news is on the wireless. Quick, turn up the volume so we can all hear. It's Winnie making a speech in Parliament. Pipe down for Christ's sake and listen!"

The soldier looked bewildered and seemed undecided

whether he should conform to the publican's plea or lash out at him.   But as the distinctive voice of the Prime Minister filled the smoky room, his hands dropped to his sides and he stood quietly listening.   The message was emphatically clear.   While the successful evacuation at Dunkirk must be considered a military defeat, the war in the air was no less than a victory. While commendations went to the Navy and the civilians in their little boats, there was "a victory inside this deliverance-- gained by the Air Force."   The Prime Minister continued his speech emphasising that Britain would never surrender and that she would remain strong in unity.

The soldier unclenched his fists and extended his hand toward George who shook it warmly.

"He's right you know," Treacle said.   "We are all in this together."

The soldier lifted his mug of beer and hiccuped.   "I'll drink to that," he said.

*   *   *

London

"It's a despicable situation," the man said.

Janine listened to the report and tried to make sense out of it. Even to this day she did not know how to address the speaker since his suggestion that she use his code name 'Charles' simply stuck in her throat.   That was the name of David's dog, for heaven's sake!

"But I've worked with Claude for years," she said. "Surely there must be some mistake.   What will happen to him?"

"He isn't aware that we know of his compromised situation. We feed him erroneous information to take to the enemy. He is, in fact, a double agent. He can be quite valuable to us in that way because they, in turn, will do the same, believing that we will accept it as fact. They know nothing of our discovery, either."

"He's a Jew, you know."

"Yes. We've known that all along. We've also known about his father being well-published and widely read in France--especially amongst the students. It's been a source of concern since the beginning and we rather predicted that he might be placed in the confounded situation he now finds himself. The sad thing is that it's doubtful that his father is actually still alive. We don't know that for sure, of course."

"How did you find out that he had been approached by the enemy?"

"He operates a transmitter from a warehouse in Lewes. His code was picked up by mobile detection and decrypted at Bletchley. He was sending them insignificant drivel. Needless to say, we don't know what they might do to ensure his usefulness. If he feels he would be responsible for any harm that came to his parents, he may change his tactics. We know something about the enemy agent who contacted him, but have not been successful in tracking her down. She assumes a number of different characters--an art she learned as an actress in Germany--and manages to elude detection each time. One thing we are sure of is that she has been watching Claude and his associates for some time and there's little doubt that she knows who you are. Obviously, you must avoid contact with him completely."

Janine looked at him questioningly. "That will be difficult. As you know we live in the same village in Sussex, and he uses an assumed name."

'Charles' offered Janine more tea which she refused. "But you have a house here in London."

"He's aware of that, too."

"Are you in touch with your parents in Aix-en-Provence?"

"Yes. But I don't know how long that will be possible."

"Had you thought about bringing them to England?"

"Yes."

"We could kill two birds with one stone, Janine.   If you would be willing to spend a few weeks in southern France we would be able to help you bring them out in exchange for a small service."

Janine did not like the tone of the conversation at all. Eavesdropping and discreet observation in pre-war conditions were one thing, but 'Charles' obviously had something else in mind.

"If this German agent knows about me, then surely it would be risky......," she said.

"It's always been chancy. But look how well you've always carried it off. Needless to say, you would have to arrive, operate, and depart secretly this time."

Perhaps it would be safer to carry out her plan to bring her parents out with some professional assistance. Somehow she would have to explain away several weeks of absence to her family. Yet perhaps even that might not be necessary. Henry's work at the hospital occupied much of his time and David would scarcely know she was gone if she arranged to have letters posted at intervals to him. He was exceptionally busy, and trying to ring him on the telephone had become impossible. Apart from anything else, such personal calls were entirely discouraged by the government in order to leave the lines free for more urgent business.   It appeared that ATA would very likely take Yvonne as a ferry pilot since that programme was expanding rapidly. If it were to be only for a couple of weeks then, why not?

"What is it you want me to do?" The brittleness of her tone surprised her.

"With your experience as a pilot and your familiarity with the French terrain, and of course, fluency in the French language, you're our obvious choice to seek out suitable landing spots for our agents to parachute in. Also, the relatively safe areas where people could be delivered and others picked up by aircraft. The fields would have to accommodate adequate landing and rapid take-off space, of course. We believe you would be perfect for the job."

"Hasn't that been in operation already in the vicinity of Paris?"

"Yes. But Alsace and Lorraine have been annexed to Germany in the armistice agreement with Pétain and they have claimed rights north and west of a line drawn across France from the Swiss Frontier, somewhere near Geneva, through Bourges to a point east of Tours, and then south to the Spanish Frontier at St. Jean-Pied-de-Port. You know, of course that Petain has established his government in Vichy in the southern sector, but what you may not know is that they have just broken relations with Britain and are obviously leaning toward full cooperation with Germany and Italy. We can no longer assume that overt operations by us will be tolerated in the southern sector."

Janine suddenly thought of Claude and the untimely assignment to Marseilles.

"Then is Claude still involved?"

"No." 'Charles' hesitated for a moment. "Knowing how well you manage to acquire and conceal information," he said, obviously unwilling to pursue the subject of Claude, "there's little doubt that you know about the Baker Street Club."

Janine nodded. "Yes. I understand that there is far more to our relationship with the United States than is generally known, even though they have chosen to remain neutral. Do they not have duplicates of vital plans and high level documents of ours in safekeeping? Are they not working in conjunction with Canada?"

'Charles' said nothing.

"At least duplicates of our secrets are relatively safe if they are in New York," Janine went on, hoping he would acknowledge the rumour she had picked up. "Should this country be invaded and we are forced to destroy such papers here, at least we could have representatives working in America and Canada using these duplicates."

"That's partly true," 'Charles' said. "Duplications of plans are there as you say, but we still have a quantity of information here which would be invaluable to the enemy. We must continue to think positively and trust that this country will never succumb to Nazi domination."

Janine looked down at her hands. This man knew far more than she could ever even imagine. Perhaps then, England might be relatively safe if America was now fully aware of Nazi treachery. Undoubtedly, they still had their business interests in Germany to think about, which must create a difficult situation among commercial, political and military arenas. However, surely they must be aware of the obvious German desire for European, or indeed world domination. Yet southern France seemed to be ignoring this. The Germans may be acknowledging the terms of armistice now, but she doubted that it would continue. They knew better than to give anyone even the merest semblance of independence. Her impressions during that last diplomatic party in Paris continued to disturb her. Representatives from large American corporations had been there and, in the interest of protecting their business interests in Europe, made it clear that they would be reluctant to assist Britain in any retaliatory actions against the Germans.

The personal American commercial interests combined with those French who chose to collaborate with the Germans would make the business of intelligence-gathering far more difficult than it had been before the declaration of war. Janine knew that her work in France--if she agreed to go--would be dangerous.

After the meeting, she decided to return to the house in Bayswater. In her mind the myriad of questions and options plagued her, pushing first one and then another into a place of indecisive priority. She had orders to avoid Claude at all costs which meant she must also avoid Ben Boniface. The plan to close up Flint House filtered to the top of her mental list and stayed there. She must talk to Henry about that as soon as possible. Under normal circumstances she would wait until evening to do this, but he had lately been touring the military hospitals with a prominent plastic surgeon named Archibald McIndoe who was from New Zealand and who selected the worst burn cases for his personal supervision. It was impossible to even guess when or if Henry might be home.

After over an hour of trying to get through to the hospital by telephone, Janine left the Bayswater house in exasperation and hailed a taxi. She would just have to wait at the hospital until Henry was available.

*   *   *

As the London-bound train steamed into the terminal, the shroud of desperation continued to cloud Claude's usual sharp-thinking. Hopelessly entrapped like a fly in a spider's web, he had almost ceased to struggle. Yet, somewhere in the back of his mind, he knew there had to be a way out. Did a fly ever escape from a web? Perhaps there might be some way to disentangle himself. He looked at his watch. First he would keep an appointment with his solicitors. Then he would make a decision that could possibly change his life for ever.

CHAPTER SIX

July, 1940

A gaggle of six Air Transport Auxiliary deliveries, all flown by women, started out from Hatfield early one golden July morning. The bi-wing Tiger Moths were destined for various airfields in the north and northwest of Britain. Two banked away toward the west, leaving the depleted flock to continue northward. Yvonne's destination was RAF Lossiemouth in Scotland and she would finish her journey alone.

This was her twenty-sixth delivery since her call to join ATA in mid-June and, because the daily delivery demands were heavy, she had seen nothing of her family--not that they were readily available anyway. Telephone messages were impossible since circuits were primarily reserved for vital needs and private calls were therefore discouraged.

News of the armistice in France, and continued talk of the invasion of England frightened her. People said that the Germans would land on the southeast coast and that

Eastbourne would probably be one of the first to be seized. This rumour made sense since a strict British military curfew had already been enforced along the sea front. Orders were circulating to pollute petrol in car tanks with sugar and to put up road barricades when invasion alerts were sounded. At the end of the first week in July a Dornier Seventeen had unleashed a stick of high explosive bombs on the town which marked the point of first blood since over twenty people were injured and two were killed. Yvonne thought of Arthur Banberry and his anti-glider poles and realised that his enthusiasm was not so comical after all. All this preventative activity was occurring so very close to the quiet little village of Long Bottom.

In order to subdue her concern, and to clarify the often conflicting rumours, she thought she might seek out her mother who always kept up to date with news, and often with occurrences that had not yet made the media, although Yvonne often wondered how she did that.

She glanced at the map on her knee and looked down at the road below her. Familiar with the topography from her flying club days, she was nonetheless not used to radio silence. Due to security and the necessity to keep the airwaves open for operational aircraft, none of the trainers was equipped with a radio. The pilot alongside pointed below and then gestured with her thumb toward the west. They must be near defensive antiaircraft emplacements and it was time to deviate from the set course to avoid them. Understandably, gun battery personnel were edgy and quick to fire even though the aircraft flew at such low altitudes and were clearly identifiable. However, the enemy was using captured British aircraft for reconnaissance and this in itself had presented a hazardous problem to the ferry pilots. For obvious reasons, none of the military installations was marked on any map and knowledge of their presence by the ATA pilots had been learned purely from familiarity and word of mouth.

After a restless night in a cold boarding house near the

airfield at Lossiemouth, Yvonne was relieved to see an ATA Anson taxi aircraft on the tarmac when she arrived at the airfield the next morning.   Other ferry pilots were already boarding which meant there were no aircraft to deliver to the south. She hurried to join them, dismissing the gloomy prospect of a long, cold train journey back to London.   Apart from the camaraderie of her friends aboard, the earlier arrival at Hatfield would lengthen her allotted time off from duty and she decided that she would go directly to Bayswater and try to locate at least one of her parents.

*   *   *

London

Claude knew that Janine would be able to understand his predicament, yet he continued to wrestle with the decision to seek her advice. It occurred to him that she may already know that he had been forced into counter intelligence, but to openly confess to someone that mattered must be better than the lonely hell he found himself in now. He was prepared to risk the consequences.

In order to keep his mind fresh, he chose to walk from his solicitors' office in St. Martins-in-the-Fields to Bayswater, rather than take a taxi. He had never actually visited the Parke's London house, but knew exactly where it was. He also knew that while maintaining the middle section of the house for themselves, the Parkes had let out the top floor, the ground floor, and the basement to military officers who were currently assigned to the War Office. He would have to ensure that only Janine was home.

Since his dark business suit blended well into the city scene, he felt reasonably inconspicuous as he watched the house from across the street. It seemed strange that the front door had been left slightly open and he wondered if Janine were there, or perhaps one of the officers had inadvertently forgotten to close it after him. After fifteen minutes Claude walked quickly across the road and rang the doorbell. No one came. He knew the military officers worked long hours at the War Office and their likelihood of being in the house was remote; yet he also knew they worked staggered hours since the War Office operated on a twenty-four hour basis. Perhaps a tired soldier had inadvertently left the door open in his haste to get to bed. In which case, he would most likely be sound asleep. Claude decided to risk entering and wait for Janine. Under gentle pressure, the door swung open easily to reveal the broad sweep of stairs toward the rear of the foyer. He listened for any sound and heard nothing. The carpet caressed his shoes as he ascended silently and he noted with pleasure the carefully chosen French furnishings. Although he had not exactly broken into the house, he felt uncomfortable. How would he explain his presence if a tenant were in fact home? He hesitated, deciding whether he should continue. Now that he had made his decision to confide in Janine, a change in plans would undoubtedly deflate his confidence. With this thought goading him on, he approached the nearest door at the top and was about to knock when he heard someone enter the foyer below. He quickly turned the handle and entered a vestibule from which several closed doors lead, he supposed, to bedrooms. Fearing discovery and perhaps an accusation of intended burglary, he entered one of the bedrooms and waited behind the door, cursing himself for his stupidity.

Hearing no further sound he opened the door a tiny crack just in time to see Yvonne push the vestibule door with her hip and hold it open in order to bring in her overnight bag. Claude looked quickly behind him and surmised that the room he was in must be shared by Janine and her husband. Large, and beautifully furnished with an oversized bed, plus both masculine and feminine appointments, it was obviously a master suite. Perhaps Yvonne would use a smaller room. He smiled as she kicked off her shoes and left them in the middle of the vestibule.

"Bath! Lovely bath!" she muttered as she took off her uniform jacket and, as he had hoped, went into another bedroom.

He relaxed a little, knowing that it would be easy to slip out while she enjoyed her soak in the tub. He watched for her to reappear and within a short while she emerged, stark naked, and tripped across the vestibule to another door.

"Bath robe," she muttered.   "Must be in the bathroom."

Claude stifled a gasp of pleasure as the beautiful body disappeared from view.   Stunned, he waited to gather his composure, wondering if she would make a return trip to the bedroom.   Soon he could hear the water running followed by her groan of pleasure as she slid into the bath. He sped noiselessly down the stairs and out into the cool air.

Impatiently nudging people aside, he hurried down the Notting Hill Gate Underground escalator failing in every attempt to dismiss Yvonne's naked image from his mind. Now aware that to confess all to Janine would not only have been insane, but in making contact he might have also jeopardised her cover . Upon leaving the house he had scanned the street, seeking any lingering figure that might have ulterior motives. While the street was clear, the possibility of observation from one of the houses still existed. He indulged himself in a tirade of silent self-reprimand. Why, he wondered, was he destined to place the two people he cared for most in potential danger? Although it was doubtful that Yvonne would be subject to enemy suspicion since their association rose from a purely casual interest in the boat at Lewes, he nonetheless seemed destined to inadvertently involve her.

As he clung to the overhead strap on the crowded tube train, the elusive answer to his dilemma suddenly came to him. He knew he could not endure the hold the Germans held on him without attempting to escape from it in some way. The entrapment stemmed from the incarceration of his parents and in order to free himself from it, the solution was clear. Since his meeting with Dierick in the warehouse, he had neither seen nor heard from her again and he did not know if she was even in England. He had only assumed that he was being watched.

He began to sieve through the names of people he knew in Paris who may have stayed on and who could be trusted. Perhaps a Christian friend of his father's who was a professor of medical science might still be there. Doctor Noe Marceau would surely want to assist in the rescue of Claude's parents, who were his old friends. It was a bold scheme and it had to work, or Claude vowed he would die in the attempt. The recent visit to his solicitors had put his personal affairs in England in order, and should he not return, there would be no legal complications. He slid into a newly vacated seat and stared at the Underground station diagram above the opposite window. But Claude Simone had no need of a map. He knew exactly where he was going. The only question now was how was he going to get there?

*   *   *

Long Bottom

Mrs. Mallory still looked the same, but Kate was sure that the poor lady's heart had broken. The cottage felt incomplete without Toby's cheerful presence and even Mr. Banberry hadn't recovered yet from the loss.

The school summer holidays began and Kate wondered how she would fill her time.   Hugh went off on the Lewes bus to play cricket almost every day and Mrs. Parke spent most of her time in London and was not available to look at all the sketches Kate had made.   Mrs. Dougherty mentioned that she was looking for another position as a cook since all indications pointed to the fact that Flint House would either be closed up or put to use by one of the military branches. If this happened, Charlie would have to go to London, too.

The village seemed smaller than ever and even Charlie was bored with the monotonous walk up one side of the street and down the other.   There were no other children from her school nearby and the four that lived in the village besides Hugh and herself were much older. It appeared to her that nobody would know, or even care, if she went back to Wilmington to visit the Long Man again. She could let Charlie off his lead for a good run and they could go together right up to the head.

She found Mrs. Dougherty grumbling to herself in the kitchen at Flint House.

"That girl couldn't even walk up the stairs without tripping over.   Heaven only knows what she'll be like working on the farm for John Farnsworth.   Land Girl, indeed!"

"Has Jenny gone, then?" Kate asked, carefully wiping her feet before entering the kitchen.

The old cook snorted. "She gave up waiting for David to come home on leave--not that he ever took much notice of her--and decided it was high time she did her bit for the war. Her assignment to the Farnsworth's farm as a Land Girl came as a complete surprise even to her."

She watched Kate take the dog lead from its hook.

Kate smiled as she clipped the lead to Charlie's collar attempting, without success, to envision Jenny and David

116

together in an amorous clinch. At least the baggy corduroy breeches the Land Girls wore would prevent Jenny from showing off her legs so much.

"You won't go too far now, will you Kate. The air alerts are getting more frequent and you don't want to be caught somewhere where there's no cover."

"I'll be careful Mrs. Dougherty."

It was true. The air raid siren wailed almost every day now, although there had been no hostile activity directly in the Long Bottom area. Eastbourne was the focal point since it was surmised that this would be where the enemy would land in the event of invasion. British fighter planes flew over quite often heading toward the Channel and Kate had mentioned to Mr. Banberry that their formations of the V-three had changed to Fingers-four, like the varying lengths of four fingers.

She and Charlie had scarcely reached the Lewes road when Hugh again caught up with her, out of breath and obviously angry. She sighed with exasperation.

"Where do you think you're going?" he panted. "It's a good thing they canceled the cricket game because of a soggy field. You know Mrs. Mallory doesn't want you to leave the village."

"Mrs. Mallory doesn't even know I'm alive any more, Hugh. Anyway, I still haven't been all the way to the top of the Long Man and this time, I'm going.   I'm tired of walking round the village."

"Well, I suppose I've come this far," Hugh said.   "I'll go with you the rest of the way.   Mrs. Mallory didn't seem to know where you were and the only other place I could think of was Flint House.   Mrs. Dougherty said that she had told you not to go too far."

"Everyone's telling me what not to do," Kate complained.

"Well this may be your last chance to see the Long Man," Hugh said. "I've heard that we'll be going home to

London very soon."

"Home?"

"Things are getting too hot in this area. You heard the bombs dropping on Eastbourne, didn't you?   There's a lot going on elsewhere, too.   Malta was bombed, our convoys are being bombed, the Channel Islands......."

"Bombed?"

"......yes, and occupied. The Germans are almost here." He stuck his hands in his pockets and looked glum. "Even the Eastbourne children are being evacuated now. They're being sent to the West country....Wales, I think. That last German aeroplane--a lone wolf they called it--dropped bombs near a school. I do wonder why they sent us here in the first place but if we don't get out of here, we're going to be bombed. Anyway, it's pretty obvious that Mrs. Mallory can't cope with us any more."

As they walked through Wilmington a couple of Hurricanes streaked overhead and disappeared behind the hill.

"David Parke flies one of those," Kate said, glad that she could offer Hugh some information for a change.   "I suppose they're in more danger than any of us."

She stopped and looked at the church gate where they had met Hugh's "spy".

"If the Germans invade, will they kill off all the little English girls first?" she asked.

Hugh took her hand in an unaccustomed gesture of fondness--or perhaps remorse.

"I was only teasing," he said. "The enemy doesn't like any of us."

"Did you know that Mr. Banberry's not only doing something with the Home Guard, but he sits up in the belfry here with a pair of binoculars--something to do with "observing". I suppose he's looking for the enemy up there."

Hugh grinned. "He said there were bats up there."

"Yes, and he called them little buggers because they

kept flapping about his head.   But, you know, those little
buggers were there first, weren't they?"

Hugh's grin broadened.   "I heard he shooed one into
the bell and it got entangled with the clapper.   Everyone in
Wilmington thought they were really being invaded then."

They released Charlie beyond the church and he tore in
and out of the hedgerow like a wild thing, emerging with
sprinklings of seed and burrs sticking to his eyebrows.   Kate
sniffed the heady perfume of the wildflowers and watched a
whiffling breeze jostle the foxgloves and daisies in the banks
making their flowered heads nod indecisively in different
directions like blind children in sun bonnets. At the base of the
hill, the Long Man was too near to determine his shape and his
outline transformed into a maze of meaningless white paths. A
stile through the hedgerow offered the only access to the field
beyond and Kate hesitated as a large cow stopped chewing to
offer them a walleyed stare.

"She doesn't look friendly," Kate said.   "She isn't going
to let us over the stile, you know."

"Animals know when you're scared of them," Hugh
said.   "We'll just pretend we don't care.   I'll bet she'll move
when we challenge her?"

"What if she chases us?"

Hugh shrugged.   "I doubt that she could.   Look at
those udders!"

Kate looked to where Hugh pointed and saw the huge,
veined bag hanging from the cow's belly.

"That's disgusting!"

"Well, fresh milk isn't disgusting, is it? Come on. She
won't do anything.   Have you ever heard of anyone being
killed by a cow?"

Hugh stood on the opposite side of the stile, poised to
leap back over it if the cow moved.   Kate followed just as the
animal deposited an odoriferous, steaming pancake behind her.

"She's revolting," Kate said, holding her nose.

The cow bellowed a bovine response and added a bit more to the pancake into which Charlie stepped with all four paws.

A fresh breeze from the sea tousled their hair as they climbed the hill and the springy turf lightened their steps. At the top they stood together surveying the rural panorama below them. A patchwork of contrasting greens and browns picked out the Farnsworth farm where a tractor, barely larger than a toy in the distance, droned back and forth like a bumble bee.

"That's probably Jenny," Kate said. "She's a Land Girl now, you know."

"She'll be good at that since she's also a Haystack Girl," Hugh smirked. "Also a Barn Loft girl."

Kate knew all about Jenny's legs, but was not quite sure about haystacks and barn lofts.

The village hid quietly behind its screen of poplars, while Wilmington lay directly below, dozing in the afternoon sun. A single movement at the church gate caught Kate's attention and she saw the unmistakable feather bouncing in Mrs. Mallory's hat as she went into the churchyard.

"Mrs. Mallory! Mrs. Mallory! Here we are," Kate yelled.

Hugh sat down on the turf and clasped his knees. "She can't hear you. We're too far away. She's gone in to visit Mr. Mallory's grave, of course." He looked eastward toward the horizon and suddenly stood up. "There's a very large aeroplane coming this way," he said. "I think we had better go." He took her hand and they began to careen down the hill.

"Stop, Hugh! I can't run this fast, I'll fall over."

"It's a Jerry," Hugh yelled, ignoring her plea. "It's a Dornier Seventeen."

Unable to keep up the pace any longer, Kate fell headlong and sprawled painfully on the rough turf. She could hear the engines coming nearer and tried desperately to get up. Hugh hauled her to her feet and again pulled her down the hill.

All at once, the familiar sound of fighter engines reached them as four Spitfires zoomed up over the hill.

"Charlie!" Kate screamed as Hugh pushed her under a blackberry bramble into the hedgerow. "Charlie!"

The jubilant dog arrived, stinking to high heaven from the cow pancake, and snuffled under Kate's legs anxious to join in the fun.

Kate struggled to see through to the other side of the hedgerow.

"The Spits are after him!" Hugh yelled. "Look at that! They've made a hit!"

Black smoke trailed from one engine and the big aeroplane began to lose altitude. On top of the fuselage, she could see the glint of Perspex from which a sudden streak of red tracer bullets burst forth. By now, the victim was nearly over the Lewes Road and Kate saw for the first time the black and grey crosses on the wings and the unmistakable Swastika on each of the twin tail fins. A Spitfire came in for another attack and this time hit a fuel tank causing it to explode. Kate ducked as the great plane wheeled, obviously in an attempt to avoid hitting the hillside, and turned northward, spewing fire and black acrid smoke. Coughing and spluttering, Kate looked up again fervently hoping that the worst was over, and saw the gun turret swivel and aim its guns toward the exposed underbelly of the Spitfire as it banked away. At the same time the Dornier's port propeller feathered and the plane dipped slightly in that direction, sending the stream of misfired bullets into the hedgerow spitting bits of twigs and leaves high into the air a good fifty yards down from where the children hid.

"Look out!" Hugh yelled, as the Dornier continued to bank in a wide semicircle, billowing black smoke and fire like a wounded dragon.

The remaining engine screamed in an eerie monotone as the great shadow passed over them and Kate clapped her hands over her ears to block out the sound. She felt the ground shudder as the dreadful death cry ended and they were engulfed with the sickening smell of burning oil. A massive explosion pushed her forward and forced her face down amongst the flowers. Afraid to move, she lay listening to the roar of flames while oily black smoke drifted over them. She heard Hugh struggling with the briars behind her, groaning with pain as the thorns tore at his skin. He broke free at last and stood up with blood running down his bare legs and arms. Feeling nauseous and numb from the icy grip of shock, she began disentangling herself from the clawing thorns and was able at last to take Hugh's outstretched hand and stagger to her feet.

"Stay here, Kate," he said. "Don't follow me! Stay right here."

He dropped her hand and stumbled along the hedgerow with Charlie limping along behind him. He broke into a painful trot and stopped briefly to look at an object fluttering in the hedge. As strength returned to her wobbly legs another deafening explosion knocked her to the ground again. In sheer panic she ignored Hugh's warning and scrambling to her feet, tottered after him. Acrid smoke swirled about, choking her and filling her eyes with tears.

"Hugh! Where are you!" she screamed.

The object in the hedge was Mrs. Mallory's porkpie hat. The dented crown looked odd without its owners head to fill it, and a jagged pattern of scallops altered the once symmetrical brim. But the indomitable feather still fluttered unscathed in the heat of the burning plane.

"Get back!" Hugh bellowed. "Don't come any nearer!" His voice faltered. "Oh, God!" she heard him say brokenly. "She must have come to find us."

But Kate continued on, blinded by smoke and deafened by terror until she saw Mrs. Mallory lying on the ground. The summer skirt billowed in the heat and revealed a pair of white legs. Kate stared stupidly, realising that she had never really seen Mrs. Mallory's legs before since they were always covered by an ample skirt.   There were dimples of fat pocking the bulky thighs and a fine network of purple veins that extended delicately down toward the inner calves. Charlie sat quietly beside Mrs. Mallory, licking a lacerated paw.   Hugh grabbed Kate's arm to pull her away, but not before she saw the dreadful, unrecognisable, shattered mess that had once been Mrs. Mallory's face.

Kate reeled, unable to tear her eyes away from the awful sight and leaned weakly against Hugh, swallowing the bitter bile that burned her throat.   At last, she turned away and looked up toward the Long Man.   Blinking, she wondered if she might have gone a little mad.   Through the shimmering haze of smoke the indistinct figure leaned toward her and the outline of the featureless face appeared to move as if it were speaking.   At the base of one of his supportive poles she saw a dark, steaming mound and took a few faltering steps toward it. Like Mrs. Mallory, the ill-mannered cow lay dead, its carcass reduced to a bloody mass, and the summer flies were already swarming in for the feast.

* * *

The small flat over Mr. Banberry's shop smelt of cooked Brussels' sprouts which was not surprising because there was really not much else to cook.

"If I have to eat another Brussels sprout," Hugh complained, "I shall go green around the gills."

"You haven't got gills," Kate said. "Besides, we're going home. I suppose Mr. Banberry did his best."

Food did not appeal to her anymore anyway.   Each time she thought of Mrs. Mallory and the dead cow her stomach heaved.   Mr. Banberry tried to keep her mind off it and Hugh pretended he did not remember the incident at all.   She decided to get away from the smell of food and pick up Charlie from Flint House for a last walk around the village.   She knew the Long Man was still there, but could not bring herself to look up at him. Neither could she look at Mallory Cottage.

Charlie seemed to sense that changes were imminent. He lay with his head on his paws when she arrived and showed little interest in the idea of a walk.

"He'll be going up to London tomorrow," Mrs. Dougherty said.   "He won't like that very much."

"We all have to do things we don't like sometimes," Kate said.   "Have you found another position, Mrs. Dougherty?"

The old cook sat down with her hands clasped loosely in her lap.   "You know young Kate, I really don't know if I want one. I'm getting too old for change.   For the next few days I'll be busy helping Mrs. Parke close up the house and then after that, I really don't know............"

Even Mrs. Dougherty, usually decisive and confident, seemed at a loss. If only some miracle could stop the war and allow everyone to smile again. As Kate led Charlie through the gate, a large green car coasted slowly through the village and stopped near her.

"It's Kate, isn't it?" the driver said through the open window.

She recognised the Air Force uniform immediately and the face peering through the window.

"Have you come to take Charlie to London, David?" she asked, pulling Charlie closer to her.

"No. I'll be home for only a few hours. I need to get a few personal things.   Anyway, we already have a ....dog.....sort of.......at the squadron."

"Where's your friend, George?   The one with the black eye?"

"He's rather busy.   I will be too as soon as I get back to Tangmere."

"I'm going home to London, you know.   But I'll think of you when I see a Hurricane fly over."

"Well, thank you, Kate; but I hope you won't be seeing me over London.   Most of the defence action is along the coast at the moment and I hope it stays that way."

"Hugh will let me know if the war is on its way to London," Kate said.   "He knows so much about it, you know. By the way, did you ever think that we might be spies?"

"Well......actually......yes, I did.   Exactly whose side are you on?"

"I didn't say I was a spy.   Anyway, if I were I would be on our side of course.   I don't really like the Germans, David." She glanced down at Charlie sitting quietly at her feet.   "He's not going to like it in the big city, you know.   Who's going to look after him there?"

"I didn't know he was going to London.   I'm sure Mrs. Mallory would be glad to take care of him after Flint House has been closed up."

Kate stared at him.   "You don't know, do you?   You don't even know that she's dead."

David frowned.   "Don't you mean *Mr.* Mallory?"

"Mrs. Mallory was machine-gunned.....right in the face. Up there by the Long Man."   She pointed toward the downs without looking toward them.   "We were up there, too.   We saw the Spitfires shoot down the Dornier that did it.   It almost crashed on top of us.   Didn't you know that?   Didn't you? Didn't Mrs. Dougherty tell you?"

She realised that she was shouting and took a step backwards.   The shocked expression on David's face made everything even worse.   She hadn't meant to make him unhappy yet she simply couldn't stop talking about it.   "Mrs. Mallory didn't have a face.   Oh, David!   She didn't have a face!"

She covered her face with her hands, trying to block out the awful memory and even when the car door slammed, she could not look up.   As young, strong arms encircled her, she choked back the huge, hot lump that lay stubbornly at the base of her throat.

"It's all right.   You mustn't think about it."   His voice was barely a whisper.   "Do you think you might help me and Mrs. Dougherty make a cup of tea?   You see, I'm really not very good at it."

*   *   *

Later in the day David stood in the doorway of the dispersal hut and watched the vigilant ground crews preparing the aeroplanes for Alert readiness.   He looked up at the fuselage of his Hurricane and noted with satisfaction that Patch had painted the word Hawkins just under the cockpit window. There was something about that London evacuee that affected him deeply. A quiet courage perhaps? An intrinsic logic with observations that were quite astonishing for her age--she was ten when they first met, so she must be about eleven.   Now, with her name endorsing his Hurricane, he felt invincible. He smiled, remembering her astonished expression when he told her about the Hurricane he had named Hawkins.

"Come on David," George said, barging past him. "The CO has called a briefing."

They learned that orders had just been received from Eleventh Group Headquarters at Uxbridge directing them to intercept enemy attackers on British shipping in the Channel.

Now, David thought, we should see some action. He slumped back in a deck chair watching the summer heat shimmer above the grass across the field.   Rupert, his lisp gone, moodily flicked a deck of playing cards one by one into a rose-sprigged chamber pot.   Treacle shaded his eyes with his arms as he lay on his back on the grass with Rosebud beside him grunting out each breath. Patrick thumbed through an old copy of Hotspur while George watched several wasps struggling and dying in an empty but unwashed jam jar.

The telephone bell, piercing through the silence of the afternoon, brought everyone immediately to their feet. After a short silence they heard the telephone being replaced.

"Scramble!" someone yelled through the dispersal hut window.

David ran awkwardly across the field toward his aeroplane, encumbered by his Mae West life vest and heavy flying boots. He climbed into the cockpit and quickly settled himself on top of his parachute pack. Working fast, Beggs had him strapped and plugged in within seconds.

"Good luck, sir," Beggs shouted, and gave the side of the Hurricane a thump.

George raised his thumb as he taxied alongside and David returned the signal. This was it!

Red section taxied out onto the field and were soon soaring into clear blue sky.   They spearheaded a triple formation as two other sections from the Tangmere Wing joined them.   Concentrating on formation, David had little time to think about their mission and they were over the English Channel in a flash. He could hear Ground Control giving enemy positions over the R/T:

"Vector 132. Angels 15.   10 or more bandits attacking shipping."

But he could see for himself.   Ahead, a circuitous formation of Stukas, too far for detail, but close enough for silhouette identification, wheeled like vultures over the convoy. Their venomous intent appeared leisurely--almost like a romp in the sunshine--as they took turns in swooping down on the vulnerable ships.

Red Leader began to climb, moving into position between the sun and the dive bombers.   David's heart thumped against his ribs as he quickly scanned the sky expecting a surprise attack from above. He was right!

"Bandits at nine o'clock!" Treacle's voice sounded young and shrill.

A group of Me109s advanced rapidly from the east.

"Line abreast! Red Leader ordered. "Attack head on! Going in.........NOW!"

Sweat flowed freely inside David's helmet and he thought his oxygen mask would stifle him. He reached for the firing button, poised his thumb above it, and waited for the right moment to press it.   But before he had a chance to aim, the Me109s scattered and left nothing but clear blue sky in front of the windscreen.

"Behind you, David!" George's voice.

A mottled gray Messerschmitt loomed in the rearview mirror, advancing rapidly.   With that kind of speed David's only alternative was immediate evasion and, jinking sideways, he turned his aeroplane onto its back and rolled into a dive. The Messerschmitt followed like an object in tow.   The Hurricane involuntarily shuddered as the spang-crack of machine gun bullets hit somewhere in the rear. Hawkins had received her first injury.   David remembered the Hurricane's unique ability to make tight turns, and thus outmaneuver the Messerschmitt. He quickly took action. Banking, he turned in the tightest circle he could manipulate and found himself beneath and behind his pursuer.   Now the expertise of the German pilot prevailed.   The Me109 slid rapidly to port and began to barrel roll downwards. David followed, ready to fire as soon as the enemy plane leveled out. His bullets, fired at an approximate range of four hundred yards, sprayed harmlessly into thin air. The text book estimate in class must have been wrong, he thought feeling beads of perspiration forming along his upper lip. The German plane had leveled out again, and David moved in closer again taking aim. This time he fired at an approximate two hundred yard range and black smoke spumed from the enemy's wing. Turning to return for the kill, he saw George's plane follow the crippled plane giving it a series of spurts until it burst into flames.

"Look out, Red Two. Behind you!"

As David took evasive action he saw another enemy plane in his rearview mirror explode in a fiery mass.

"That's two!"

George was having a field day.

But obviously the German fighters had had enough of him and converged on his Hurricane, singling him out for a kill. David watched in horror as they hammered George's aircraft with numerous hits. Within a split second, a white trail spurted from the fuselage and rapidly extended as his plane began to lose altitude. David charged at the pursuing Me109s, with Browning machine guns blazing. Perhaps the enemy was satisfied that they had disabled George sufficiently, or perhaps they were low on fuel and ammunition. Whatever the cause, they did not follow the crippled aircraft, but allowed it to wheel like a seagull, oozing glycol and now trailing a thin line of orange fire in a long graceful decent toward the sea.

David looked desperately for a parachute. He saw none and his face turned ice-cold while the warm sweat inside his helmet felt like melted ice cream. He turned to follow the doomed Hurricane in order to gauge the general area of impact, but it had completely disappeared.

"Where are you, George?" he shouted. "For God's sake answer me."

There was no response. Fierce anger burned inside him as he scanned the sky. With throttle fully open he soared in pursuit of the executioners and, flying like a maniac, he attacked and damaged one enemy aircraft after another. Ignoring the acrid smell of cordite as bullets bit into his own fuselage, the scarlet haze of his fury lent him sadistic courage. He wanted to ignore Donald Moore's command that they reform and return home to refuel and rearm. He pressed his thumb once more on the firing button and only then did he realise that he was completely out of ammunition.

Surprised, David could see the English coastline below him. He looked around as the rest of the squadron moved into position and saw that their numbers were badly depleted. There was little to say over the R/T. The gaps in formation spoke for themselves. At last, he felt the stutter of his wheels on the grass and suddenly felt terribly tired. He sat in the cockpit of his stationary aeroplane and tried to gather his wits. His body felt as if it had been through a mangle and he wondered if he would ever be able to move his limbs again. In his peripheral vision his weary mind registered Rupert climbing down and relieving himself on the grass. Weakly David heaved himself from the cockpit and joined his friend.

"Bad day at the races," Rupert said, shaking his head. "But we didn't exactly lose."

His expression remained unchanged as Treacle approached, counting on his fingers. "One definite, one probable, one shared with Ravensbrook......." He looked at David. "Sorry, old chap."

Donald Moore joined them. "We have seven pilots and seven badly shot-up Hurricanes all receiving sticking-plaster repairs......and we're going back up, sticking plaster and all. Jerry's not done yet for the day."

He ignored the barely audible collective sigh as he looked round the semicircle of young faces.

"Two minutes and the ground crews will have us ready. Good luck, chaps."

David eyed the tattered side of his aeroplane as he climbed back into the cockpit. Hawkins had taken her beating bravely. Everything he did seemed to be purely by rote as he followed Red Leader back up into the sky. The enemy was apparently attempting to lure them closer to the French coast and soon, black puffs of flak appeared and flashed by. They had been joined by segments of three other Hurricane squadrons and since all were on different radio frequencies, communication cohesion was impossible. But there seemed to be little point in conversation. He calculated that the mass of enemy aircraft ahead amounted to a ratio of four Germans to one British and that this impending encounter would take all of his courage.

The next ten minutes engraved themselves on his mind like words on a tombstone. He saw blood-streaked windscreens and slumped bodies in aeroplanes that flew straight and level by themselves--one completely upside down. There were shattered rear gun turrets on the Me110s and limp figures drifting into oblivion under silky canopies--some floundering or streaming. Fireballs that were once aeroplanes plummeted and disintegrated as they fell to earth. He heard screaming voices over the R/T sometimes celebrating a victory, but more often than not sobbing their last terrified words.

His neck ached from continuously scanning the sky, yet he knew if he stopped, it would be his last flight. At last, the German aircraft reformed and flew toward the French coastline leaving the British thankfully watching their retreat from mid-Channel. David wondered if he would have enough fuel to see him home and saw that the reserve tank registered dangerously low. There were no familiar squadron spinners in sight and he crossed the English coast alone. Flying at low altitude he looked down at the chequered fields spreading in a thin haze below him and brought the aircraft down even lower. As he pulled off his oxygen mask and pushed back the cockpit canopy, the sudden rush of wind took his breath away. He could see the southern coastline with its froth of surf and the roofs of Worthing soon passed beneath him. The broad expanse of Tangmere field stretched before him and a green flare shot into the air. Almost empty of fuel, he touched down and saw the fire crews rushing toward him and wondered why. Then the aircraft pulled sharply to the left and he hung on for dear life trying to straighten it out.   Skidding and slithering he finally came to a halt facing entirely in the opposite direction and smelt the pungent odour of burning rubber.   Immediately, the ground crew appeared as if from nowhere and the fire tender quickly dealt with the smoldering tyre.

"Brilliant, sir!" Patch said, appearing beside him on the wing.   "The other tyre was about flat."   He looked back along the fuselage.   "I'd say you have taken quite a caning today."

The voice sounded far away as David stepped out onto the wing and he thought for a moment that he might faint. Beggs held his arm to steady him.

"It's all right, sir."

David looked up at his aeroplane and saw that it was riddled with bullet holes.   Suddenly exhaustion hit like a blow to the head as he tottered away. Halfway across the apron, he vomited.

Donald Moore met him at the door looking twenty years older. His shoulders drooped, and fatigue masked his face.

David pulled off his helmet and ran his fingers through sticky, wet hair.   He wanted to tear off all his clothes and plunge his incredibly tired, naked body into the cool cleansing waters of a deep lake.

"I've briefed Harry," Squadron Leader Moore said. "You'd better go and tell him your record for the day."   He looked toward the horizon.   "I think I'll just stay here for a little while longer."

David stepped over Rosebud who lay disconsolately across the threshold of the doorway.

"Believe it or not," Harry said, "we've received orders for tomorrow's operations from HQ."

"Two fagged out pilots flying a couple of sieves? What good would that do?" David spoke with difficulty.   His tongue stuck to the roof of his mouth and his teeth felt enormous.

"I told them that.   So the squadron's now in some kind of training capacity for the time being."

Donald's shadow stretched long across Harry's desk and the light behind him threw his face into darkness.   His damp, flattened hair stuck to the back of his neck like strands of kelp and as he turned, the pallor of his face gleamed in the light. David wondered how old this man might be.   Surely no more that twenty-eight.   Perhaps less.   Yet the weight of responsibility lay heavily on his shoulders.

"What do we train for?" he said.

"They didn't say, sir."

Donald put his hand on David's shoulder.   "Come on, old fellow.   Let's go and have a well-deserved drink."

David tried to smile and failed.   "Thank you, sir. Let's go and have several," he said.

CHAPTER SEVEN

Eastbourne, August, 1940

Kate looked up at Ben's wooden expression and then down at his hand gently holding hers, wondering what he might be thinking. They stood in drizzling rain on the railway station platform in Eastbourne waiting for the London train. The weather matched her mood as she miserably watched Hugh who hovered near the edge of the platform anxiously peering down the line. He seemed impatient to be away, which was understandable since the station had been heavily damaged in the last bombing raid and that was enough to scare anyone.

It seemed odd that Ben would be the one to see them on their way. Although she had known loneliness in Long Bottom, somehow the people there were now a part of her life and she did not like to think that she would never see them again. At least David Parke had given her his squadron address and she had every intention of writing to him whether he answered or not.

Yvonne Parke was busy ferrying aeroplanes and usually went to Bayswater on her days off, according to Mrs. Dougherty. Even Mrs. Parke was always in a hurry and rarely at Flint House. Just by chance she had been on a flying visit to collect more items for the Bayswater flat yesterday and had kissed Kate's cheek and held both her hands very tightly.

"Charlie will miss you so much," she said. "He'll have to make do with the London parks for walks now. I hope you'll come back and see me after the war is over."

Mrs. Dougherty, arms deep in a crate of china, quickly withdrew one hand to search for her handkerchief. Mr. Banberry had to see to the first postal deliveries of the day and could not leave the stationery shop. He did, however, invite them to stay with him any time. Hugh had simply raised his eyebrows at that and mouthed the words Brussels sprouts.

It might have been left in the hands of the local taxi driver to see them safely onto the platform if Ben had not come forward. Although he continued to keep his room at Mallory Cottage he rarely stayed in it, but just happened to be home when they were due to leave for the station. His lack of conversation did not affect her one way or the other since she had grown used to it. Today she had no inclination to say anything herself anyway since it seemed to her that all the words in the world would be pointless at this moment. In spite of his silence Kate knew that Ben was her friend.

"Here she comes!" Hugh shouted.

A gleaming wet engine clattered in with brakes screeching as the pistons churned to a halt. Clouds of hissing steam spurted from beneath as the entourage of carriages followed and came to a jostling stop along the platform. Ben picked up their bags and selected a carriage door.

"Your father will meet you at the London terminal," he said. "It's all arranged."

He helped them aboard and as the train began to move

Kate saw his expression soften.

"Are you going to stay at Mallory Cottage?" she shouted, thinking now of a million things she wanted to say.

Ben grew rapidly smaller on the platform as the train moved away and Kate was sure that he pretended not to hear. The lone figure looked ghostly, shrouded as it was in misty rain. Ben barely raised his hand in response to her wave although he made no move to leave the platform.

"We'd better close the window," Hugh said.   "The rain's coming in."

She watched drops of rain run a disoriented race down the grubby window.

"He'll be lonelier than ever now. I didn't know him very well, but I think he's very lonely."

*   *   *

London

Old Bertie, a stuffed clown Kate had owned since an infant, lay on her bed exactly where she had left him nine months ago. It seemed to her that he had been patiently waiting for her to return and was the only one in the household to offer a true welcome. A new baby and an obviously unwell mother gave the house a strange aura which detracted from the customary familiar warmth of home.

Perhaps the garden might offer solace, she thought, picking up the doll and tucking him under her arm. Ruby Baxter greeted her briefly upon their arrival and Kate noticed that she still looked fat and robust, in spite of food rationing. She looked hopefully over the fence to see if Ruby might reappear, but only Mr. Baxter leaned against his back door post and rolled a cigarette on that peculiar machine of his. The cigarettes he made always looked ragged and limp and invariably left a deposit of tobacco on his lip which he unceremoniously spat out. He surveyed the extent of his colourful back garden while making opinionated comments about things in general to his wife inside the house. Kate turned her attention to the Hawkins' garden which looked vastly different with its rows of vegetables and berry bushes.

"It's a Victory garden," her father explained as he joined her. "Those vegetables will come in handy if Hitler decides to put us under siege."

He pointed to a large mound protruding like a carbuncle where the lawn used to be.

".....and that's an Anderson shelter. The marrow vines serve as camouflage, you see."

"What's it for?"

"We go into it to shelter from air raids."

"Air raids!" Kate said to Bertie after her father had left. "What do they know about air raids!"

"Probably a lot more than that stuffed clown does!" Ruby Baxter's freckled faced appeared above the fence.

"He's no more stuffed than your head," Kate retorted.

"Would you like to come over to my garden--where we still have a lawn--and play dress-ups?"

"Aren't we a bit old for that game now?"

"Well, if you feel that way about it, never mind. Anyway, if you're too old for dress-ups you're too old for stuffed clowns, too."

Kate took Bertie back indoors. If she were to keep Ruby as a friend she had better conform to her whims of make-believe. Later they sat in deck chairs dressed in a bizarre assortment of adult cast-off clothes.

"We should be in New York in a few days," Ruby said, flicking an imaginary cigarette ash from the end of her drinking straw.   "The Queen Mary's jolly fast you know--although the sea's a bit rough today, don't you think?"

"Well, you'd better hold on to your gin and tonic, because you're spilling it down your front," Kate said.

Ruby looked at her glass of reconstituted lemonade with disgust. Her oversized hat flopped forward over her nose and caused her to spill even more down her front.

"D'you think you could find a steward, m'dear?" she said, pushing the hat back and exposing a red tuft of hair in the front.

"I don't know about a steward," Kate said.   "But Hugh said we'd better watch out for U-boats."

"You boats?" Ruby said, pointing at Kate.

Kate clucked with exasperation.   "They're German submarines. The "U" stands for "underwater"."

Ruby dabbed at the stain with her sleeve.   "Where's that stupid steward?" she muttered.

"You can't expect the steward to mop you up all the time," Kate said.   "Anyway, it's the U-boats that are blowing up the merchant ships that bring food to us.   That's why our rations are so small and why my father has planted a Victory garden."

Ruby got up and gathered up her oversized skirt.   "If you're going to talk about the war all the time, I'm getting off this cruise. The war is silly. My dad says it's a lot of propaganda--although I'm not sure what well-mannered ganders have to do with anything."

"Well Hitler's got a gang called the Gestapo who walk like geese. Hugh says they hate little English girls and they wear badges--sort of like our Ovaltini badges--only theirs are stuck on."

"Stuck on?"

"Yes.   They're called Swass-stickers.   They wear borrowed boots, too."

"Borrowed?"

Kate nodded. "They borrow them from someone called Jack. Hugh told me that, too."

Ruby minced away, holding up her skirts. "My dad says the invasion will never happen," she said as she disappeared through her back door. "And by the way, it's a good thing you didn't bring Bertie the clown on this trip because he would have been seasick and thrown up all his stuffing."

Kate leaned back in her deck chair and looked up at the sky. It was not unusual for Ruby to leave in a huff; she would soon be back. Kate squinted her eyes and watched a maze of fluffy vapor trails drifting from the south. Even as she watched, they slowly melted away until there was nothing left but a canopy of clear blue. She closed her eyes and the negative images floated against her eyelids. *....thank you, Kate,* David Parke had said, *but I hope you won't be seeing me over London..................action is at the coast and I hope it stays that way......................"*

*   *   *

Tangmere

Although emotionally drained from waiting for news of Regatta Squadron, David's dreams robbed him of beneficial sleep. They were vivid and frighteningly surrealistic; bizarre and yet uncannily symbolic. He awoke each morning unrested and irritable.

Last night children had hovered above his head like Christmas cherubs. Their wings were made of labels bearing names and addresses and their gifts, held in chubby hands, were gas mask boxes. He strained to hear their voices but instead of ethereal praises they wailed in anguish, crying for their mothers. As their cries faded, a barrage balloon began to deflate above him. He watched in wonderment as its gargantuan size writhed into wallowing folds, twisting in tortuous distorted shapes as it drifted down upon him. As it silently enveloped him he saw the bullet holes that had pierced its side. He awoke, gasping for air.

Later in the day, a cirrus cloud formation lay motionless and unchanging across the washed blue above Tangmere air field. He lay back in the arm chair he had dragged from the Mess and shut his eyes, simply listening to the silence. If Hitler does follow through with his intentions to smash the southern air fields, he thought, he had better not do it today because the weather's just too perfect. He had spent two agonising days in London, trying not to think about the others yet hoping desperately for good news. Unable to bear the stress of waiting and wondering, he returned to Tangmere and found a still-empty Mess.

A day later the first letter arrived from Kate Hawkins and took him completely by surprise. In the midst of her distress concerning the death of Mrs. Mallory, and while Mrs. Dougherty had insisted on her drinking hot, strong tea at Flint House, he had given her the address of the squadron and then completely forgotten about it. When that first letter came, he had opened the envelope with amusement, but her words immediately caught and held his interest, while the accompanying sketches--of extraordinary quality for her age and with a suggestion of subtle humour--quickly lifted his dampened spirits. He decided to reply at once and then found himself pleasurably anticipating her next letter. In following notes, her concern for his safety astonished him. She made him see his war from her aspect and realised with sudden pride that civilians watched from the ground and cheered for his victories as he fought in desperate air battles. He learned from her that the pilots of Fighter Command were considered heroes of the hour and that people included them in their daily prayers as they watched the vapour trails left by their aeroplanes drift toward the east and into history. She told him that they mourned the bleeding earth beneath, potmarked with jettisoned German bombs and the wreckage of destroyed aircraft. She drew pictures of sunken ships and broken planes as she imagined them cradled at the bottom of the sea, entombing their dead crews. In an odd, sometimes misconstrued way she seemed to know the intricacies of war. How could this child be so perceptive? Had war succeeded in stealing away so perfectly the fantasies and innocence of childhood?

He pressed his fingers to his temples in an attempt to ease the ache. Where were all the others? Where were Ravensbrook, Barlow, Tate, and Kennedy? Donald Moore had been glued to the telephone all day demanding replacement men and aircraft. This seemed so final. Could he not wait just a few more hours for the others to come back?

David felt the comforting softness of silk about his neck. His starched uniform collar had left welts from his constant lookout for the enemy aloft which stung from the salt of his perspiration. A small parcel had arrived from his father containing several silk scarves accompanied by a short note directing him to take good care of himself. Was this a mere coincidence or had his father been informed of the discomfort during the air battles by injured pilots in his care?

Rosebud lumbered to a grunting halt and lowered his cumbrous body into the nearest resemblance of recline as it would allow.

"Go away, you smelly ogre" David snarled.

"I could go away," the adjutant said, sulkily. "But you wouldn't hear the news then, would you?"

The armchair fell backward as David leapt to his feet.

Kenneth sighed, righted the chair and sat in it and began to doze.

"Sir!"

"Oh, yes, Parke.   Well, I forgot to mention that Tate came back while you were in London. He arrived in the worst looking Hurricane I've ever seen. He says he borrowed it but I can't imagine from where.   It had only one fuel tank and he sputtered in here practically flying on fumes and with a fuselage full of bullet holes. Pure madness!"

"I'd call it skill and loyalty."

"Damn good show, actually. He's gone on leave which is where you ought to be."   The adjutant settled himself more comfortably in the chair. "Then Barlow came back in his own kite with an inoperable landing gear, but did a magnificent belly flop and didn't even bite his tongue this time."   Kenneth closed his eyes.

Damn him, David thought. I'm not going to give him the satisfaction of pleading.

"Don't you have a girlfriend, Parke? I mean, you're getting on my nerves hanging around here."

David stood his ground.

"Well, all right! Kennedy crashed at Hawkinge and is in hospital badly burned."

David drew a deep breath. Had Patrick Kennedy come under the indirect care of his father? Had it been Patrick who mentioned the comfort of the silk scarves?

"The three new boys are all in hospital with various injuries but should be fit to return to duty in a week or so......and there's no word concerning Ravensbrook."   The adjutant's supercilious expression briefly softened.   "You saw Tate come back," he said. "So it could happen again, you know."

He shaded his eyes and looked across the field. "Would you believe that the RAF has only nineteen operational Hurricane squadrons?   We needed experienced people like

Patrick and George."

As the days went by, David watched the replacement men and aircraft drift in. Aircraftman Patch had stenciled two-and-one-half swastikas under the name Hawkins, depicting David's two confirmed enemy kills, and one shared with Treacle. Rupert and Treacle arrived with two Sergeant Pilots from Biggin Hill aerodrome and a battle-tested Flight Lieutenant from Tenth Group in the north who was to replace Patrick Kennedy. Two more Pilot Officers came the next day followed by six brand new graduates from Officer Training Units who were full of courage, enthusiasm and panache, but had yet to fly an operational machine or fire their first Browning. Only one of them had something in the region of one hundred and eighty hours. The others, considerably less. As they hauled their gear toward the Mess, the Flight Lieutenant from Tenth Group joined David.

"They haven't a real bloody clue, have they?" he said. "They'll learn soon enough, won't they?"

Yes, David thought. They will. Could it be only a matter of weeks ago when he and George found themselves in exactly the same position?

"It's like running a nursery school," Donald Moore said, shaking his head. "I swear half of them haven't even had to shave yet." He glanced at David. "Now you can make yourself useful and teach them how to fly a fighter plane," he said. "By the way, we've received our first allocation of one hundred octane fuel from America. You're going to notice a remarkable difference in performance now. The replacement planes have all been fitted with a metal disc insertion in the fuel system. No more turning over on your back to dive. Yours is in the hangar now, David, for modification."

More than once, when he had first begun and was still in the process of learning the few idiosyncrasies of the Hurricane, David's aircraft had almost stalled in an attempted dive due to gravity holding the fuel back from the engine. To compensate for this structural flaw, the pilot was forced to turn the plane upside down in order to dive while at the same time, keep the engine running. This latest announcement from the CO was indeed good news.

The grim war news plunged everyone into apprehensive gloom as the Germans launched massive attacks on British ports, convoys and lately, airfields. As other squadrons became operational, pilots from already active squadrons were glad to see their numbers swelling as they were joined in the melee over the Channel. They fought there so frequently they had named the area Hellfire Corner.

"The Luftwaffe is now operating from occupied airfields closer to the coast in France, the Lowlands and Scandinavia," Donald Moore explained. "The aircraft are arriving over the Channel well-fueled and fresh for a fight. Be aware of it!"

David nursed a mug of beer in the Mess one evening feeling pleased with the progress of his young students. Although he had lost one newcomer on his first flight--a boy of eighteen who had shown fear right from the start--the others were already chalking up kills and assisted kills. Donald came and sat beside him.

"I thought you might be interested to know," he said, quietly. "I have word of Ravensbrook from Headquarters."

David closed his eyes, waiting for the worst.

"We believe he's alive in France. We do know that he is not in captivity and are baffled because he doesn't seem to be making an attempt to get back to the squadron. If I hear any more, I'll let you know. I know you and he were--are--good friends."

David wanted to shout with joy. Instead, he rose and walked out into the night. Shining in the moonlight George's MG stood waiting patiently beside the big green Daimler. David patted the crimson hood.

"He'll be back," he whispered.

The next morning they were scrambled to attack enemy

aircraft already inflicting grievous damage to a floundering merchant convoy just northeast of Dover.   Three young replacements flew with the squadron for the first time and David could see his young protégés leaning forward eagerly in their cockpits. Easily detected in the bright sunshine, he could also see a clutch of Me110s busily taking turns to attack the convoy.   As he listened to the CO and positioned himself as instructed, line astern for the attack, he saw a Messerschmitt peel away and dive toward an already crippled and sinking merchantman whose crew was rapidly abandoning ship. Crimson anger surged as he saw the enemy gunner train his sights on the floundering men in the water. Donald's ensuing command steeled him further for action.

"Going in..........NOW!"

The enemy planes drew into a defensive circle as if pulled by centrifugal force and David singled out one, intent on personal vindication.

"Bandits! Three o'clock! Angels fifteen."

A group of nine Me109s swooped toward them from the direction of Beachy Head.

"Obviously bomber escorts coming in for the attack!"

David quickly took stock of the situation and saw they were now caught between the defensive circle of cowardly bullies and an offensive gang of hooligans, the squadron fanned out to battle individually with the enemy.   Within five long minutes the mayhem of battle resulted in the 110s retreating and the 109s returning to protect a massive *schwarm* of approaching enemy bombers now clearly visible toward the west. Suddenly, a lone wolf sprung from behind in hot pursuit of Donald's plane.

"Get on with it then!" Rupert's voice. "I'll follow you in."

Together they formed a line astern attack and shared another kill, but not before the German pilot had disabled Donald's aircraft with a rip of bullets along the length of the fuselage.   David saw the propeller waver and a string of glycol spurt from behind, spreading rapidly into a wide, white ribbon. He heard Rupert urging the Squadron Leader to bale out.

"I'm on course for Eastbourne."   The words were barely audible. "I'm going to try for Friston. Can't risk hitting the town. Stay clear--there might be a big bang!"

The cockpit canopy was clouded with glycol and the pilot, now invisible.

David and Rupert ignored the warning and stuck with their commander, flying slightly above him. As the emergency runway at Friston came into view he saw the crippled aircraft losing altitude far too quickly and there was no sign of the wheels coming down.

"Wheels, sir!" he shouted.

There was no response.

Upon impact, the plane cartwheeled, landing upside down and skidded along on its ruined airscrew to a teetering halt. Miraculously, no fire ensued probably because the fuel tanks were near empty. A flare went up, waving them off. Neither attempted to communicate, each acutely aware that the chances of surviving such a crash were extremely remote.

Treacle waited for them at Tangmere when they returned, barely able to speak.

"He's alive.....brutal injuries.....both legs."

Added to this grievous news, they also learned that four of the untried youngsters were bounced, and all had spun in without firing a shot.

*   *   *

Squadron Leader Ian Lowery was the antithesis of

146

Donald Moore in appearance, yet he exhibited the same consideration and fairness of his predecessor. A man in his early thirties, his record of experience and longevity in the Royal Air Force preceded him and the squadron knew that it was in good hands. Perhaps a little rambunctious, he seemed oblivious to the unpleasant stink of his favourite rose briar pipe as he trailed behind him a reeking genie of Balkan Suprani tobacco. Yet, in spite of this characteristic, everyone liked and respected him as he coped tirelessly with his exhausted pilots and replaced missing ones along with their aircraft as the air battles continued unabated. David missed the special relationship that had developed between him and Donald Moore, yet he saw how well Ian Lowery endeavoured to conceal his own fatigue and watched him strive to keep up spirits and morale. But too often coughing, spluttering aircraft returned, tottering down to land like asthmatic old men. Too often the young pilots who were lucky enough to survive--shocked and fatigued--trembled and often vomited in anticipation of the next sortie. Some would ask who was missing. Others hurried to the lavatory, while others slumped into chairs and stared into space. A few talked excitedly about their engagements with the enemy and demonstrated their prowess with swooping hands. David wondered how long their luck would hold--how long could anyone's luck hold?

Medford-Smythe--a veteran of twenty sorties, the son of a high ranking RAF officer, and a veritable expert of aircraft types--suddenly looked up from his book and tilted his head to one side.

"Bombers!" he said. "German night bombers!"

Someone doused the lights as everyone rushed to the door to look up into the twilight sky. They saw the escalated formations moving relentlessly forward as searchlight beams inconsequentially swept over them.

"The night fighters are trying hard," Rupert said. "But it's like tickling an elephant with a feather!"

147

"Ground defence isn't doing any better," Treacle added. "The Hun hit the RDF towers along the south coast yesterday before they moved on to bomb the hell out of South Wales and the Midlands."

Medford-Smythe nodded.   "The RDF at Ventnor, Isle of Wight took a pasting, I heard.   There's a ten mile gap in communications now."

Squadron Leader Lowery joined them puffing on his odoriferous pipe.   "Better try and get some sleep," he said. "Our turn in the morning.   At least we can see who we're fighting in the daylight."

At half-past twelve hundred hours the next afternoon the entire squadron was scrambled to face a reported very large incoming force of German bombers and their fighter escorts.

"All set, sir," Beggs said, jumping down off the wing. "Good luck, sir."

David noticed that Beggs showed genuine concern for his safety plus respect for his now commendable battle record of six kills and five assists.   He held up a gloved thumb.

"Formation of bombers approaching Selsey Bill.   We have three other squadrons joining us.   We'll go in line abreast and break up the formation."

"Christ Almighty!" Rupert's voice.   "How many of the bastards are there?"

David glanced at his altimeter and saw that it registered at 15,000 feet.   Coming toward them he calculated at least one hundred Stukas, stepped up between 12,000 and 15,000 feet.

"Line abreast! Head on! Going in........NOW!"

"Tally-ho!" Treacle's voice.

The formidable oncoming enemy seemed impenetrable. Could this David against that Goliath make any impression at all? Strangely, the bomber formation began to break up as if in panic and soon several plummeted, streaming black, boiling smoke behind them.   Momentarily astonished by this turn of events, David's confidence soared and he plunged into battle with icy determination. Five minutes passed in a flash and only vaguely could he remember how many enemy aircraft he encountered and helped to destroy; how many he encountered and destroyed alone; or how many times his own aeroplane received punishment.

Twenty minutes passed, and he had already switched to his reserve tank which meant he had little fuel left. He was well along the southwest coast and would be able to make a quick stop at Tangmere for refueling, rearming, and to replenish his oxygen. The rest of the squadron was indistinguishable in the maze of aeroplanes around him, and he decided to go down alone. But as he approached the field he saw the Hurricane squadrons from Westhampnett were up trying desperately to prevent the Stukas from making more dive-bombing runs across Tangmere. Great clouds of smoke rose, and massive, angry fuel-fed flames roared from the roofs of two hangars.

A gummy abstract design of dead bugs on David's windscreen added to the enveloping pockets of soot-filled smoke and obscured his vision as he searched for the ground. At last the wheels bounced over two freshly filled craters and he taxied in the general direction of his dispersal area. Relief flooded through him as Fred Beggs ran alongside, hanging on to his tin hat and urging the rigger to grab and wing and help turn the plane.

"Be ready to duck, sir," Beggs yelled. "Ground gunnery couldn't fire before because there were too many of our chaps taking off, but they're making up for it now. It's a miracle you got down."

Shrapnel clattered against the blast walls as they ran for shelter.

"Two hangars gone," Beggs shouted, gasping for breath. "Seven Hurrybacks gone and six Blenheims.........and God knows what else. There were Airspeed Oxfords in one of the hangars and a Fox Moth, all with full fuel tanks.......watch out, sir!"

149

They cringed against the wall as a Stuka roared over, spitting machine gun fire.

"Bastards got some WAAFs over there," he said, inclining his head toward the Operations building. "My God! Look at that!"

The Crossley fire tender took a direct hit and split asunder in the middle of the apron and at the same time a blazing Spitfire crashed and disintegrated at the end of the runway, raining down debris across the field. David glanced up and saw three parachutes drifting down through the haze and fervently hoped that the pilot of the crashed Spit was amongst them.

"It's hell on earth!" Beggs said, chokingly. A trickle of blood seeped from his temple and ran across his chalk-white cheek.

"Where's Patch?" David yelled. Beggs was obviously about to break and the only person who came to mind who might be able to deal with it was Patch.

Beggs pursed his trembling lips. "Adjutant's bloody dog ran amok after the first bomb. Jim ran out to try and calm him down." Tears joined the trickle of blood. "They're both over there........." He covered his face with his hands.

David followed the direction of Beggs' trembling finger and saw two still bodies lying side by side near the dispersal hut. He had always hated the dog, but would never have wished this kind of death upon him. Always willing to do that little bit extra, Jim Patch was a favourite amongst both the ground and air crews. David looked up at the line of kills on his fuselage and felt a great wad of fury congeal in his chest. He sprang to his feet and ran toward his aeroplane, shouting.

"Hurry up! Hurry up! We haven't got all day. Get on with it then."

The ground crew was already working as fast as it could in spite of the onslaught from above. David slowed down, immediately regretting his churlishness. The mechanics, fitters, riggers, armourers, and all the supporting arm of maintenance were getting as little sleep as the pilots and yet had not failed him once.   What right had he to reprimand them?   Fred Beggs caught up with him, ready to defend his men and David grabbed his arm.

"Sorry, old man.   Truly sorry.   Sorry for everything."

Somehow he managed to take off without sustaining further damage and climbed rapidly to again join in the melee. The R/T was jammed with the excited voices of Czech, Polish, Belgian, and a myriad of other foreign pilots who flew with the RAF and who were obviously elated at this opportunity to get back at the Germans for whom they harboured a deep hatred. Bitter, angry, and vitally anxious to return to their homelands, they fought vindictively and bravely;   although vociferous, they were extremely effective.   David now understood their rage and spurred his aircraft into the middle of the action.

Two German bombers collided below him in the confusion and tandemed down in a fiery spiral waltz.   Toward the rear of the next wave of Stukas, several broke formation and began to skid sideways and upwards to begin their pre-dive climb.   David flew southward, selecting one that had almost reached its appointed apex and, as it arched in readiness for its screaming dive earthward, he knew it was at its most vulnerable.   With his thumb poised over the firing button he waited for the right moment and then let fire.   Forced to jink sideways to avoid the fiery ball resulting from his direct hit into a fuel tank, he thought of Patrick Kennedy and felt he might have avenged him.

Suddenly, Hawkins shuddered as three successive explosions raked through her.   The engine coughed and died as David smelt the tang of cordite.   A fourth explosion deafened him and a great orange wall of fire roared toward him from under the instrument panel.   Unable to see through his goggles, and unable to think rationally in his panic, he tore at anything that restricted his ability to reach for the canopy latch.

The searing heat jabbed unthinkable pain across his eyes and forehead. Instinctively, he flung his oxygen mask from him to avoid further combustion and realised, too late, that he had exposed his entire face to the flames. With inhuman strength he opened the canopy, only to fall back into his seat, pinned in by the Sutton harness.

"God! Oh, God!" he screamed. "Help me! Help Me!"

He looked at his smoldering gloves and resisted the temptation to remove them. Somehow he released the straps and, acting purely by instinct, half rolled the aircraft and fell out into blessed, cool space. How long it had taken him to get out of the inferno, he had no idea. He heard his voice whimpering, but could not remember having made a sound. He saw his smoking gloves floating on the ends of charred sleeves on either side of his body. Perhaps, he thought stupidly, they might still be attached to me. His vision blurred as tears stung his rapidly swelling eyelids, although he was not aware that he wept.

I suppose, he thought, I ought to do something about opening my parachute, but first I'd better bring one of those smoking gloves over this way in order to do so. Aware now that he tumbled over and over in the cool air, he thought he would like this weightlessness to go on for ever.

"If I were you," a small voice said.   *"I'd get a move on."*

"Kate? Is that you?"

"All that time at Cranwell, and you've forgotten how to pull the ripcord? Shame on you!"

The glare of daylight almost blinded him as he painfully forced his eyes open. Somewhere near a bank of cumulus her face floated in and out of the shadow.

"Hit the silk! You're waiting too long!"

With inconceivable effort he forced his arm inward and fumbled for the ring of the ripcord.

"Go on David. Pull it!"

"Can't. Can't do it."

"Of course you can! I'll help." She sighed with exasperation. *"Really! You're being such a baby. Here!"*

She pushed his hand and he felt the shape of the ring against his gloved fingers.

All at once he was not falling any more. He raised his chin barely high enough to see the spurt of white silk shoot skyward above him. A sudden jerk assured him that the parachute had not been burned and functioned now to bring him safely down under its billowing white umbrella.

"I told you you could do it. Now I have to go."

"No! No, Kate. Please stay with me."

Through rapidly closing slits he looked downward. His trousers and boots must have been blown or burned off since his bare legs hung limply. A stream of blood ran down one of them although he felt no pain there. At the end of his bootless foot he saw that his toe protruded through that inevitable hole in his sock.

Mother will be furious, he thought.

He looked beyond his feet to the sparkling water below. Water? Wasn't I over Tangmere? Wait! I headed south. I must be over Selsey Bill somewhere. Turning his head he saw a rapidly widening oil slick on the surface of the water, above which a haze of blue smoke hung in strips like wisps of tattered chiffon.

"Goodbye, old girl," he mumbled through swollen lips. "We did our best, didn't we?"

Above him, the ghosts of disintegrating vapour trails drifted toward the French coast. He hoped the enemy had gone home. It would not do for them to find him here hanging about like a rag doll. Perhaps they might shoot down what was left of him. It seemed now that this particular problem would soon be resolved since the surface of the water came rapidly toward him to receive him in a salty, frigid embrace.

Fascinated, he watched the flurry of bubbles swirl around him brightening the dark canopy of water to a brilliant emerald green. Perhaps he would not bother to go back to the surface. But the sweet, inertial coolness of the water against his burned skin quickly changed to fiery pain as the salinity penetrated the injuries to his face and hands.

"Going up?"

"Must I?"

"Better that you should."

He burst through the surface, gasping and choking up sea water.

"You haven't finished yet, you know.   You've got to release the parachute so that you don't get dragged down. Go on! Push the punch plate."

"I thought you'd deserted me."

"Oh, David! I'd never do that."

He pushed the punch plate with difficulty and released the shrouds. Looking like a giant cuttle fish, the white silk puffed out on the water's surface, dragging the cords along behind it like tendrils. Within seconds it began to sink, section by section, until it disappeared entirely under the waves.

"Life jacket!"

"I think you'll find it's a goner.   Burned to a crisp, actually. But don't despair.   You're a good swimmer, aren't you? Why not do a leisurely dog paddle to the shore. It's really not very far."

"Think I can?"

"Sure of it. That's the ticket. Keep the chin up and the water out of your mouth and you'll be fine."

CHAPTER EIGHT

London, August, 1940

The Prime Minister's speech was brilliant yet Janine's anger and resentment would not abate. Never, indeed "in the field of human conflict was so much owed by so many to so few". There were many mothers like herself who grieved over the ghastly injuries their sons or daughters were enduring and others who mourned the loss of their sons or daughters entirely. The tragic news from Tangmere reported that several young women had made the supreme sacrifice as German Stukas attacked the airfield with bombs and strafing. Now David lay in delirium at the Air Force wing of the Masonic Hospital in London, his face and hands swollen beyond recognition and looking toward a future of probable gross disfigurement. Janine stared down at the London street from her upper window and tearfully vowed that she would somehow avenge her son's brutal injuries.

Expecting an immediate exit from England after her meeting with 'Charles' her role in clandestine activities had actually dwindled to a form of cartography which, for the moment, pinpointed the small aerodromes both public and private that were familiar to her throughout France. Her presence at the London house was rare, but the terrible news of David's savage injuries had temporarily relaxed the tight security that surrounded her. She normally worked and slept in a small flat near Euston Station which she rarely left. When Henry was able to take a short break, arrangements were made for her to meet him in Bayswater, primarily to prevent arousing any suspicion on his part. Later she knew that she would be assigned to intensive training courses in parachute jumping, silent assassination, and self-defence. Even some instruction concerning the handling of carrier pigeons would be included.

An odd incident occurred on the 24th of August. While London itself had been left untouched by the enemy, areas around all cities and coastal installations had taken a dreadful thrashing. It came as a surprise then that several bombs did fall on a residential area of Stepney on the 24th. The attack was haphazard enough to be considered an error, yet a retaliatory raid on Berlin by RAF Bomber Command nevertheless followed. Judging from overheard comments from German officials before the war in Paris, Janine knew of their pride and temperament and that the British justifiable response would not end the incident. A counter attack was sure to come. This, however, was an assumption that no one could accurately predict.

Conversation over dinner with Henry focused on this, the children, and then on the subject of Flint House. Mrs. Dougherty had agreed to keep an eye on the Bayswater property from time to time and had moved into a flat in Victoria where she looked after Charlie. Flint House stood in sad abandonment now that the family was preoccupied elsewhere.

"The wounded need safe places to convalesce," Henry explained. "The location and relative serenity of Long Bottom and the adequate accommodation that Flint House can offer make it an ideal place for the injured to recuperate. We should seriously think about that."

His eyes shone in the candle light and Janine knew that this interest stemmed from his personal involvement with young wounded servicemen. Beneath the momentary sparkle of enthusiasm, she saw that he was desperately tired.

"I agree," she said, glad to witness the pleasure her positive response gave him.

"You are so beautiful, Janine, in many ways. Thank you for your patience and understanding."

"I'll begin to move our personal things out tomorrow," she said. "Mrs. Dougherty and I have already packed up much of the household necessities and brought them here. The rest we'll have to store. Will you arrange for the hospital beds and whatever else they will need?"

He nodded and she saw the brightness of tears along his lashes. "Our own son could quite easily go there later on," he said. "Archibald McIndoe saw him yesterday and is having him transferred to the burn unit at the Queen Victoria Hospital at East Grinstead. I expect to spend a good deal of my time there, too, since reconstructive bone surgery is also involved. I've thought about renting a cottage in the area to avoid the commute from London and to be near at hand should I be needed. Would you mind?"

Janine gathered the dishes together and took them to the kitchen as Henry watched. "Of course not, my dear. I'll come down and stay whenever I can. You do understand, of course, that I must spend most of my time here in London."

"How are you filling your time, Janine? I mean, I know you always manage to keep very busy and half the time I don't know what you're doing, but I wondered if you were still using your language skills with the refugees?"

"Their need of my help is minimal now," she said. "They've begun to set up their own special Executives in this country, and are bound and determined to do what they can for their occupied countries.   I'm pitching in here and there and, yes, I'm very busy."

She returned to the dining room and saw that her husband was fighting sleep.

"There's still a little brandy left, Henry.   Let's have some.   It might help you to forget some of your concerns and allow you to have a good night's sleep."

He made no protest and did not pursue the subject of her activities any further.

Later, as Henry lay gently snoring beside her, Janine tried to create some order out of the chaos in her mind.   The various branches of secret activities and intelligence in London seemed not to be cohesive and the War Office appeared cool toward all of them.   Yet she knew that all military personnel who found themselves separated from their units in Europe were encouraged in lectures given by MI9 prior to embarkation, to evade capture and to endeavour to return to their units in England.   David had mentioned that this pertained also to pilots who were shot down over enemy territory.   There were soldiers--over 2,000 it had been estimated--left over from the Dunkirk rescue who were still there.   A large number had been taken prisoner and Red Cross parcels were already being delivered to the numerous prison camps.   But some would, without doubt, attempt escape and somehow these men have to be helped. She mulled this thought further around in her mind. Many did not speak a language other than English and all, of course, were in uniform who, if captured, would warrant certain imprisonment for the duration of the war.   Even under these circumstances, they were encouraged to escape and find their way back to England. Surely the War Office must see that they need assistance and clothes, food, money, maps, some form of escape route, and bogus papers to get them across frontiers, she thought.

Janine knew that the students in Paris would not keep silent for long; that is if the Germans did not round them all up for service in their own country. If they were left alone they would undoubtedly rebel, albeit in some unobtrusive manner. Perhaps they may be willing to help. She remembered her days at the Sorbonne when she too aired her political inclinations at inconsequential rallies and experienced again her somewhat radical indignation at injustices. The Free French were already assisting, and rumour had it that they sought arms to secrete until the time came to uprise against the Wehrmacht and worse, the dreaded Gestapo and SS. The students were bound to get caught up in all that.

She got up from her bed, careful not to disturb Henry, and wandered out to the kitchen. The Vichy Government in "unoccupied" France would not help now that they had broken relationships with Britain. This in itself disturbed her since she knew that the situation in southern France was precarious at best and she wondered how her parents were coping.

She grabbed the teakettle before it had time to whistle and made herself a small pot of tea.

Locating suitable landing fields for aircraft in France was all very well, but she felt sure there was something far more significant for her to do. She spent the balance of the night on a sofa and although sleep evaded her, by morning she had the outline of a plan formed in her mind. If only she could solve David's devastating problem so easily.

*   *   *

Since no Anson air taxi was available after her last aircraft delivery, Yvonne took a train from the North country. She felt weary and disheveled, but had earlier made the decision to change trains in London and continue on in order

to visit her brother at the burn unit in East Grinstead. As the
northern train approached the London suburbs she watched the
sombre city structures slide by in a sooty parade. The backs of
terraced houses looked forlorn with their taped windows,
blackout curtains, and minuscule vegetable gardens abutting
the railway lines. The train's metallic brakes squealed as it
entered the terminal and she looked glumly at the weeds
growing from pavement cracks at the end of the platform and
felt her melancholy mood deepen. There seemed to be an air of
abandonment about it all. The throng of people in the station
were mostly in uniform and all anxious to get to their
destinations. After an exasperating half hour, Yvonne had
almost abandoned the idea of getting to Kings Cross station
where she would catch the train for East Grinstead. At last, two
WAAFs (Women's Auxiliary Air Force) who were eager to get to
the Air Ministry agreed to share a taxi with her.

    In pleasant contrast, the station at East Grinstead
offered the quietness of the countryside which helped to calm
her apprehension. As luck would have it the local taxi drew up
outside the station just as she came through the ticket barrier
and she was soon on her way to the hospital. She tried to
envision what David must look like. Swollen, her mother had
said. Swollen beyond recognition. Yvonne steeled herself yet
again for the ordeal that faced her and prayed that she would be
able to maintain her self-control.   Conversations between
herself and her brother had usually been pleasantly flippant,
witty, and often argumentative. How would she speak to him
now? How would he reply? She thought of that last Christmas
dinner and Jenny's inept attempts to flirt with him. She
remembered how attractive he and George were in their
uniforms and how badly she had handled the conversation. If
only she might have another opportunity to reveal her better
side. If only she could tell George how much he really meant to
her and to demonstrate the true affection she felt for David.

* * *

"It's the wooden building in the back of the main hospital," the nurse said. "Ward III. Air crew are all in there together."

A display of flowers around a flag pole in the central courtyard reminded Yvonne of Flint House, and she wondered if she should return to town to buy a bouquet for David.

"......infection is always the most prevalent problem," her father had said. Perhaps flowers would not be allowed.

Ward III had obviously been built as an annex to the hospital and left much to be desired with regard to architectural imagination. She wondered if it had been erected specifically as a military wing and therefore was not required to be particularly attractive. As she approached the hut, the main door suddenly opened releasing a clammy, sickening odour. She held on to a pole supporting the covered walkway, and stood aside to allow a stretcher to wheel past, deliberately avoiding the impulse to look at its occupant. The attendants eyed her ATA uniform with interest as they passed. A nurse wearing a gauze mask stepped out from the ward in order to close the door behind them.

"I'm here to see Pilot Officer Parke," Yvonne stammered.

"Relative?"

"His sister."

"First time?"

Yvonne nodded.

"Your parents, of course, have seen him several times. Your mother was remarkably brave, you know. Pilot Officer Parke is in bandages at the moment, so you won't be able to see much of him. It's always a bit of a shock at first, though.   He's in the third bed on the left."

Yvonne peered into the ward, clinging to the door frame, and taking shallow breaths to avoid the stench.

"Look, I'll go with you if you like."   The nurse's eyes smiled above the mask.   "Did you know that your father has been here with the other surgeons most of the day?   He's in the main hospital at the moment but said he would return shortly. Did he know you were coming?"

This indeed was a pleasant surprise and a great source of relief.   Yet as Yvonne clung to the door frame, she knew that she could not wait indefinitely for her father.   Perhaps David had heard her voice and was now expecting her.

Yvonne shook her head.   "It's difficult these days to make such plans," she said.   "But I'm pleased he'll be here."

She took a few faltering steps into the overwhelming odour of burned flesh and antiseptics.

The ward could not have been more basic with its exposed beams and dingy paint.   She counted twelve beds, six to a side, and noted the three large heating stoves at regular intervals down the middle of the room.   Keeping her eyes trained on the far wall, she nonetheless smiled as appreciative whistles followed her.

"Are you Yvonne?"

She turned at the sound of the pleasant voice expecting it to belong to an equally attractive man.   Instead, she faced a monstrous apparition wearing a Flight Lieutenant's uniform jacket draped around the shoulders.   His face was a distorted mask of angry welts and, in the area where his nose should have been, a long roll of flesh protruded like a trunk, the end of which disappeared under the collar of his open-necked shirt. She felt the blood drain from her face.

"I'm Patrick Kennedy," the pleasant voice said. "David and I flew together at Tangmere."

He held his bandaged hands across his stomach,

cradling them like a pair of white kittens. Her initial horror subsided into profound compassion.

"Yes. Yes, Patrick. I've heard him speak very highly of you."

"Well, the feeling's mutual. He's one terrific pilot."

She fumbled for further words and was relieved to see her father enter the ward.

"Ah! I see you've met the star patient," he said, nodding to the nurse who left to pursue her duties.

"I think I scared her to death," Patrick said. "Sorry, Yvonne. One tries to forget the pedicle after a while."

Henry took her arm. "It's a pedicle of skin you see--a flap that's still attached to living tissue at the upper chest to keep it nourished with blood--that's attached to the nose area. It's rolled like that to avoid infection. After the graft takes, the flap will be detached and a new nose will be formed."

Patrick's attempted smile, limited by atrophied scarring, resulted in a grimace.

But her father's professional explanation lessened her dismay and she wanted to know more about the newest grafting techniques. She vaguely remembered hearing her father speak of them during the Christmas holidays, but at that time she had been absorbed in self-centered interests, mostly due to her great desire to get back to flying--and to George Ravensbrook's disturbing presence.

"They have already given him a temporary set of eyelids," her father went on.

"Without eyelashes," Patrick added. "Perhaps the permanent set will have plenty of them to flutter."

"I wonder," a muffled voice said from the third bed, "if my visitor is ever going to get this far."

Yvonne went quickly to him. "Oh, David. How did you know?"

"Well I might not be able to see much, but I'm not deaf, you know."

The all-enveloping bandage about his eyes and head robbed him of identity, and she wondered if she would have recognised him had she not been told which bed was his. His hands, also heavily bandaged, lay like detached puppets on the coverlet, and the outline of his body appeared emaciated and lifeless under the covers

"Not a good way to lose weight," he quipped through swollen lips. "But we get eggs here. Can you imagine. Real eggs!"

"What can I bring you? Just ask, David. What can I do for you--I mean anything--anything at all?"

"Can you turn back the clock? I would give anything if you could do that."

He became noticeably restless as she made inane conversation and when Patrick appeared at the foot of the bed indicating that he wanted to speak to her, she moved away and looked at him questioningly.

"It's the pain, you see," he said. "He needs morphia, but it will end the visit."

She returned to the bed. "David....I have an appointment with a bi-wing. But I'll come again very soon. I promise."

The bandaged head moved slightly, but David made no further comment. Patrick followed her to the door. "Keep that promise, Yvonne," he whispered. "It will mean so much to him."

She gulped in the fresh air as her father joined her.

"Don't fret. He will get better. The bandages cover a paraffin-soaked wool pad and tulle gras dressing to soften the scar tissue. You see, the original treatment called for a coating of tannic acid which is 2 1/2 aqueous, but is so difficult to remove. Also the application of silver nitrate has been abolished due to corneal ulcers. Archie McIndoe is the best, you know, and David is in excellent hands." He took her arm and led her toward the main foyer. "His upper and lower eyelids began to retract, making it almost impossible for him to close his eyes....tarsorrhaphy, meaning to keep the eyes covered during the relaxation of sleep. He has to be built up for further surgery since he's lost a tremendous amount of weight. He's already being saturated with vitamins plus a high protein and carbohydrate diet."

"Eggs!" Yvonne murmured.

"Yes, eggs. He's also lost a great deal of body fluid and we have to watch for seepage into interstitial spaces which form a generalised oedema. He's being given plasma and whole blood, too, to avoid red blood cell loss. So you see, there are a number of prepatory tangents to follow before the final grafting can take place."

"He seems reasonably lucid at the moment....has he been aware of his condition all along?"

"For the first two weeks he was delirious and in shock. He kept speaking to someone named Kate. Do you know who this might be?"

Yvonne shook her head. David had many friends and this must be somebody he knew at Oxford. Yet that name.........wait a minute!

"Did you say Kate? Surely it couldn't be the child who was evacuated from London. The one the Mallorys took in with her brother."

"I don't think it could be a child. He continuously asked her for advice."

"Then I have no idea who it is."

* * *

165

London

Mr. Baxter changed his mind when the Germans dropped bombs on Croydon. He stood on his back step rolling the inevitable limp cigarette and made the announcement across the fence to anyone who happened to be listening.

"They're leaving," he said, referring to his wife and daughter. "They're leaving as soon as possible."

"I don't know where you think you're going," Kate said to Ruby later on. "There really isn't anywhere that's safe. Hugh says the invasion will come from the south, and the Germans are dropping bombs all over the place....except London. The way I see it, we're just as safe here as anywhere."

Ruby looked askance at Kate and snorted. "That's all you know. We're going to Nova Scotia and that's not even in England."

"Scotland isn't safe, either."

Ruby yawned. "It's across the Atlantic--the real Atlantic, and I'm going on a real ship."

Kate's heart sank. "But you can't do that! You're the only friend I have!"

"There's always stuffy old Bertie, isn't there?"

Kate bit her lip. "When are you going?"

"Soon."

"Well, the Gestapo could come before you leave so we had better practice invasion precautions."

"All right. What do you suggest?"

"If we hold arms with you walking forward and me walking backward we should be able to keep a lookout in all directions."

They hooked arms and set off down the road with their heads swiveling from side to side.

"All clear in front!"

"Behind, too, except for Mrs. Parker and snotty-nosed Albert. There's a cat with a bent tail following them."

"That's the Belcher's cat. Sidney Belcher shut its tail in the door."

The air raid siren suddenly cleaved through the quiet afternoon and both girls froze.

"Run! Run!" Ruby screamed. "It's the Gestapo!"

Her plump knees became a blur as she galloped off toward home with Kate in hot pursuit. Speedier than her friend, Kate soon took the lead and tore along the pavement at a brisk clip. As Ruby's footfalls faded behind her she heard her friend scream. Should she stop? Would it be too late to help? As Kate slowed down, she heard the resumption of footfalls, but these were much heavier and faster and she began to speed up again.

"Don't let the Gestapo get me," she sobbed as she tore along. "Please don't let them get me."

Perhaps that was another Dornier Seventeen she could hear. Would it render her dead and faceless like Mrs. Mallory?

Arriving in sheer panic at the entrance to the Anderson shelter, she leapt blindly into the darkness and landed in an oozing mass of yellow mud. She cringed against the corrugated wall, and felt the damp chill creeping through her clothes. Her feet sank lower, displacing she was sure a myriad of slimy things that would undoubtedly slither into her shoes and down her socks. As her eyes became more accustomed to the darkness she could see that she stood in a quagmire of stagnant, rotting clay. But far worse, the heavy footsteps had arrived outside. Had the Gestapo killed Ruby? If so, how did they do it? Would they do the same to her? A dark figure loomed in the doorway and flung its arms wide, ready to leap. She saw the cruel gleam in its eyes as it sprang toward her, rendering her speechless.

"Oh, bugger!" Hugh said, as he landed. "I've jumped into a bloody latrine!"

"Hugh?"

"I'll say one thing for you, Kate," he said pulling one

squelching shoe from the mud.   "You can run."

Ruby appeared in the doorway, panting and rasping, followed by Kate's mother who held the new baby tightly against her.

"I tried to shout to you," Ruby gasped. "I shouted to you that it was Hugh, half scared out of his wits, but you wouldn't listen."

"I wouldn't come in here if I were you," Hugh said, scowling.   "I think I'm going to take my chances with old Jerry at ground level from now on.   As for you Ruby Baxter, I wish you'd hurry up and go to Nova Scotia."   Holding his nose, he scrambled from the shelter.   "I'm never going back in there again.   Never!"

The All Clear sounded.

"What happened to the Dornier Seventeen?" Kate asked, squelching her way to the door.

"Fat lot you know," Hugh scoffed.   "It was probably a reconnaissance type.   They used to call it a phony war, so that must have been a phony air raid.   Drole de Guerre the French called it."   He looked at Ruby and arched his eyebrows.   "I learned that in school, you know."

"But what does it mean?" Ruby asked.

"Phony," Hugh said as he bent to pick up several pieces of paper that fluttered between the rows of cabbages. "Obviously this was not a bombing raid.   These are pamphlets from Hitler telling us to surrender."

Mr. Baxter arrived to investigate all the fuss and quickly read one of the German pamphlets.   Without reservation he made an obscene gesture skyward and since Mr. Banberry had set Kate straight on hand gestures, she knew exactly what Mr. Baxter was thinking.

The day arrived for Ruby's departure and Kate sat in the kitchen dolefully chasing the last cornflake around her breakfast bowl.   Although the summer holidays were almost over, there had been no indication that school would resume.

Too many teachers and children were still away and the unpredicted return of London evacuees plus the lack of facilities, materials, and teachers had created a serious problem.

Kate wandered out into the garden and saw that the marrow vines growing over the shelter were approaching fruition and the hollyhocks along the fence of the Baxter's garden were so tall they leaned on one another for support. She sniffed the sweet scent of the lavender borders that surrounded Mr. Baxter's lawn and stood on tiptoe to see the wayward lupins and nasturtiums struggling to survive amid the potato plants at the end of her own garden. She looked a little closer. Lying comfortably amongst them and sunning himself luxuriantly was none other than the Belcher's cat.

"What are you doing here?" Kate said.

"He's hungry."

Ruby's freckled face appeared suddenly between the hollyhocks. "He came here first and my dad told him to buzz off. I think the Belchers must have gone away and left him to fend for himself."

The big ginger cat blinked his yellow eyes seductively and feigned a yawn.

"What's his name?"

Ruby shrugged. "I've always called him Belcher's Cat. I heard they went away. I suppose he'd be counted as a stray now."

Kate bent to stroke the cat's head. "BC," she said.

"You can call him what you like. I'm leaving for Liverpool as soon as the taxi gets here. The ship doesn't sail for a few more days yet, but my dad thinks things are going to heat up in London."

"Why?"

"Because they dropped bombs on it and we bombed them back, that's why." Ruby looked up at the sky and pointed. "Look up there. What's that?"

As she spoke the air raid alarm sounded.

"Dog fight!" Hugh shouted, running from the house.

High in the blue and barely visible, a scribble of vapour trails blossomed and faded. Chattering machine guns--the sound less than that of a watch being wound--drifted to them and a sudden fiery ball plummeted earthward like a red comet. It was followed by a tiny white canopy that drifted on the prevailing wind.

All at once two much larger aircraft, flying at low altitude, roared over the roof tops. BC immediately disappeared under the marrow vines and Kate instinctively flung herself to the ground. Several loud explosions shook the ground and she felt a warm rush of air pass over her. Had the planes crashed like the Dornier on the downs? She lay face down, pressing her body into the earth. Ruby screamed in terror on the other side of the hollyhocks and Kate raised her head to see huge mushrooms of smoke rising above the trees tops on the common, expanding and billowing until they blocked out the sun.

"Get inside!" Mr. Baxter yelled from his back door. "Do you all want to be killed?"

Hugh had remained on his feet during the onslaught and now stood staring at the satanic sky as if he were in a trance.

The raid had lasted only a matter of seconds, but it caused a delay in the arrival of the Baxter's taxi. Mr. Baxter grumbled a great deal about incompetence and unreliability. But a BBC bulletin finally convinced him that the lateness was justified due to the air raid. According to the announcer, a Heinkel 111 and a Junkers 88 bomber, apparently both badly damaged from their encounters with the RAF, retreated eastward and haphazardly jettisoned their bombs. Several had landed on the common, narrowly missing the gun and barrage balloon emplacements there, and one had made a direct hit on a house in Balham occupied by two old ladies, killing them both.

"It won't make that much difference," the taxi driver said when he arrived at last. "There's debris on the Streatham Hill railway line, and your train will be late anyway. There's a war on, you know."

He winked at Kate as he helped Mrs. Baxter on board.

"I don't want you to go," Kate shouted. "Please don't go."

"I'll be back when it's over," Ruby said through the taxi window. "You'll just have to make do with Bertie and BC 'til then. You *are* going to keep BC, aren't you?"

Ruby waved through the back window, and she kept on waving until the taxi turned the corner.

Now, Kate thought, I'm back where I started in Long Bottom village. But at least I had Charlie there and I liked all the people that I eventually met. She bent down and picked up BC. Although only a short time had elapsed since her departure from Sussex, the faces she had sketched were quickly fading from her memory. If only she had not left all her drawings behind in her bedroom at Mallory Cottage. She had not wanted to go back in to retrieve them after Mrs. Mallory was killed. I'll never get the people right if I try to draw them from memory, she grumbled. Even the familiar faces of Mr. Banberry and Mrs. Parke were beginning to fade. She wondered if, in time, she would forget Ruby, too. But she would never forget how to draw David's face; of that she was sure.

*   *   *

Early September, 1940

171

The soft perfume of the summer evening filtered to Janine as she drove southward from East Grinstead toward Long Bottom.   On the back seat Charlie seemed to know he was going home. As they drew closer to the village he began to whimper excitedly and ran across the seat from window to window.   Soon, as the dusk deepened into night, the searchlights would begin to rake the sky for German aircraft and the Beaufighter night crews would stand ready to combat the incoming enemy bombers and their fighter escorts.   The battle in the sky raged during the daylight hours too, and the results were highly visible as the military wings of hospitals around the country filled with the burned and badly injured. Henry, now barely in evidence at all due to his busy schedule, had mentioned that two hundred and seventy-seven RAF pilots had been lost, out of which one hundred and three pilots were killed and one hundred and twenty-eight seriously wounded during the past few weeks.   In fact, David's squadron had withdrawn to Acklington to rest and regroup since they had suffered so many casualties. Aircraft production was unable to keep abreast of replacement requirements, and factory personnel were working long hours to keep up production demands. If the enemy were not losing hundreds of men and aircraft too, Janine wondered how Britain could possibly continue to fight.   Ironically, the Luftwaffe had turned its attention away from the airfields and was concentrating on devastating towns and cities throughout the country.

She heard the crunch of gravel beneath the tires as she drove through the gates of Flint House. While her pending two-part mission to France was clearly defined, she hoped to pick up an accurate feel for the atmosphere surrounding the Vichy government.   Delivery of letters from her parents had decreased and she needed to know if they were in fact being intimidated in some way.   The new Special Operations Executives' highly efficient, complex network had become a vital link in intelligence-gathering, although no clear form of supportive British intelligence was yet in operation.   However, Janine knew that the resistance movement in France was asking for arms and advice.   Oddly, there seemed to be some animosity between this movement and the leader of the Free French in London, General de Gaulle.   Although entirely top secret, she also knew that the code-breaking operations north of London were enjoying some great successes and only two days ago it came to her attention that Prime Minister Winston Churchill was essentially supportive of further intelligence operations which made the future look much brighter for the military evaders and escapees.

Flint House smelt musty from disuse as she opened the front door.   Although the early September evening was still warm, she nonetheless lit a fire in the drawing room and flung open windows throughout the rest of the house.

Soon Yvonne will be here, she thought, and having just recently visited David for the first time, will no doubt welcome the familiar comfort of home.   It seems an eternity has passed since the young people enjoyed Christmas dinner together here. Now George Ravensbrook is missing, perhaps dead, and David is horribly burned.

Yvonne arrived earlier than expected, looking older than her nineteen years.   At first Janine attributed this to the shorter hair and distinguished uniform. But as they talked it became quite evident that her daughter had matured both in appearance and outlook.

"I feel fortunate that I couldn't see very much because of the bandages," she said.   "He's obviously in considerable pain."

Janine could see that the visit to David had deeply affected her daughter.

"Have you met Patrick?" Yvonne asked.

"Yes. I suppose I should have warned you."

They stood by the drawing room window looking up at

the almost obscured outline of the Long Man.

"I often wonder if the Long Man has some kind of uncanny influence over us," Yvonne said. "It's a silly thought, really, but do you agree? Considering the size of the village and the number who have suffered here, there seems to be an imbalance somehow. We were all so happy and safe before."

Janine sighed. "I know young Kate Hawkins felt she had a special relationship with him."

"How well did David know that little girl?" Yvonne asked. "He apparently mentioned the name "Kate" often during his delirium."

"Hardly at all. Perhaps he knows someone else with the same Christian name. We'll have to ask him when he's more up to it."

Even though George Ravensbrook had been a visitor, perhaps he too had been influenced by this odd adversity in the village. Yvonne found herself thinking often of him, remembering the unaffected nonchalance and ready wit. Sometimes she felt him close to her as she had at Christmas time and remembered how pleasurable it had been. If he were not dead, why then, she wondered, was his name not on the prisoner-of-war lists? If he had been badly injured, was he lying in some French barn loft slowly dying of infection? If he were at large, why had he not attempted to return to his squadron?

Below the hill she could see the hedgerows glowing crimson with berries predicting an early autumn. The broad leaf trees burned brightly with rust and gold, mingling their colours with the trembling pale yellow of the silver birches. The poplars held up their brilliant amber arms waiting for the slightest stir of wind to fashion a festoon of showering multicoloured jewels as the dying leaves drifted earthward. Above, an orange sun pursued it leisurely path westward, its brilliance subdued by the interfusion of evening mist and fragrant firewood smoke. If only David and George were here to see this.

She went upstairs to help fill steamer trunks with clothes for all seasons while Charlie joyfully reinstated his old territories in the grounds, and tunneled through the fallen leaves to let off the steam that had been long suppressed in the confines of the London flat and the surrounding limitation of the parks.

"He was such a forthright boy," Janine said as she folded one of David's pullovers. "Always knew exactly where he was going. I sometimes wonder if he would have ever finished his studies in medicine. Your father did rather force him into that field and it was obvious from the start that David wasn't keen."

"He loves flying," Yvonne said. "Perhaps........."

"He'll never fly again," Janine said. "Isn't it enough that you're still at it?"

Yvonne sat back on her heels having filled the trunk. How she longed to talk to her mother about certain recent occurrences in her life. A strange official-looking--yet unsigned--message had arrived for her at White Waltham ordering her to report to a building in Berkeley Square on a specified date. Since the message warned that under no circumstances should she speak to anyone concerning this request, she destroyed it as instructed. ATA would never communicate with her in this manner and she thought this indirect approach somewhat ominous. At first she considered ignoring it, yet the letter was undoubtedly something official. If only she could discuss her dilemma with her mother.

CHAPTER NINE

London. September, 1940

On the first day of September--a Sunday--Kate found herself in trouble again. As she sat in the chancel of St. Alban's church looking up at the big stained glass window on the west wall, it seemed to her that anything to do with religion had an air of mustiness and dust about it. The window was set between a pair of saintly statues and together with the lofty arch that formed the ceiling they were all too far removed and holy to allow close scrutiny. Yet even there a diaphanous cobweb drifted to and fro and sometimes glittered against the sculptured frieze of the great stone wall. As the sun filtered in through the Byzantine stained glass window on the opposite side, the cobweb was caught in prism of rich reds and blues. She stared hard at the window and tried to block out the exasperated words of the middle-aged matron who reprimanded her.

"You don't question things like that, Kate Hawkins! God loves everyone--even the Nazis." The elderly lady clucked with irritation. "And I suggest you look at me when I speak to you."

"But God doesn't love evil!" Kate argued. "The Nazis and the Gestapo and the SS are evil!" She clenched her fists in her pockets, determined not to be influenced by this grizzled old woman. "I simply can't agree with a God who likes Hitler."

The woman looked deflated. "I think you'd better go home, Kate. And I also think you'd better wait until you're less of a skeptic before you come back. You've got to have faith don't you know. You've just got to accept some things as the truth."

Kate dawdled home, pondering over the concept of evil versus good, and decided that it was quite possible that she might always be a skeptic. Upon reaching the short road that lead to her house, she saw a boy she did not recognise waiting by her gate. It had been some time since Ruby's departure and although Mr. Baxter said she still waited to sail in Liverpool, there had been no word from her. Perhaps, Kate thought, it might be time to make a new friend, even if it has to be a boy.

"I'm Peter Trimble," he said as she approached. "We were bombed out in Croydon, you know, and have just moved into number eleven." He nodded toward a house further along the road.

"I'm Kate Hawkins and I'm a skeptic........bombed out, you said? Did you see dead people?"

The blue eyes widened. "What are you skeptical about?"

"God."

The eyes widened further. "I'm not sure if I saw dead people. There were some bodies lying about, but I'm not really sure if they were dead."

"I saw a dead person once. She didn't have a face."

Peter took a step back.   "Look, your next door neighbour, Mr. Baxter, said you might be interested in meeting some new friends.   But if you're only interested in being a skeptic and talking about dead people........................."

"Oh!   I'll talk about anything you like," Kate said, quickly.   "You can meet Bertie and BC and I'll tell you all about the RAF pilot I write to sometimes, and I'll show you the pictures I draw."

Peter looked relieved.   "I've met a couple of other children in the neighbourhood," he said.   "They're twins and have an empty garage by their house; it's empty because their father has lent his car to the army.   Perhaps we could have a club, or something."

"Could Bertie and BC join?"

"Are they your brothers?"

"Sort of."

*   *   *

The thirteen-year-old twins, Pamela and Mark Hamilton were hard at work sweeping out the garage when Kate arrived with Peter Trimble.   It stood apart from the house and was obviously being used to store discarded household items since the car was out on loan.

"If you want to join the club," Mark said.   "You'll have to help.   You and Peter can pull that old overstuffed armchair out into the sunshine.   It's rather damp."

Kate eyed the dirty chair and grimaced at the big spider sitting exactly in the middle of the lumpy seat.   "There's a spider on it."

"The spider doesn't need airing," Mark said. "Knock it off."

Four o'clock found the four children draped over the big armchair in various strange positions like a pride of young lions, soaking in the sun and congratulating themselves on a good afternoon's work.

"Aaron Cohen and Wendy Shor want to join," Pamela said. "Think we should vote on it?"

"I don't know them," Kate said. "Besides, they didn't do any of the work."

"We didn't know you," Mark said. "But you're in, aren't you and you're younger than the rest of us. Do you have something against Jewish people?"

"I didn't know they were Jewish, either. I just think they should have shared in some of the work, that's all."

Peter stood up and stretched. "We could even up that score," he said. "Why don't you ask those two brothers of yours if they would like to join......now that all the work is done?"

"I told you they were sort of brothers," Kate said, wishing she had never mentioned Bertie and BC. "Actually, one's really the Belchers' cat....although I think he might be ours now because the Belchers when away and left him......and the other one is a harlequin....doll, sort of....named after Bertram Mills' circus."

Pamela smirked and Mark's grin widened, but neither said anything.

Peter squinted into the sun. "Well.......that's all right, isn't it?" he said. "I mean BC can be our mascot, and Bertie will do to make up a quorum when we do any voting."

"Quorum?" Pamela's smirk faded.

"It's what you need to vote with and Bertie can be it."

Kate looked smug. At least Peter understood the importance of being Bertie.

That evening she wrote to David giving him all the details of her new friends and the club along with several sketches, which included the spider. She did not, however, mention her dilemma concerning good versus evil.

"I think our first activity should be an expedition," Mark said from his presidential seat in the armchair, the following weekend.

Kate had made a point to surreptitiously study Aaron and Wendy in order to learn what it meant to be Jewish, and had come to no conclusions. As far as she was concerned, they were no different from anyone else. The spider, duly ousted, now sulked in a dark corner.

Pamela, as self-appointed Secretary, licked the end of her pencil in readiness to take notes.

"Where to?" Peter asked.

"The common. More specifically, the barrage balloon battery."

"What for?" Aaron asked.

"Aren't you interested in the defense of our country?" Mark said. "If Jerry really does try to bomb London, those balloons will do a good job of stopping the bombers from getting through."

"How?"

"Aaron, for a Jewish boy you really don't know very much, do you?"

"Well, I'll know more when you tell me how the balloons will stop Jerry from bombing us."

"My brother says that they stop the dive bombers and low-level attacks," Kate said, propping Bertie Quorum up beside her.

"Would that be brother BC or brother BQ?" Pam said.

"I really do have a brother. His name is Hugh and he knows lots of things about the war. He puts flags on maps in his bedroom to mark all the places the Germans have invaded."

"I hope they don't invade here," Wendy said. "They don't like Jewish people."

"Well, Hugh says the Gestapo doesn't like anyone much."

"What else did your brother say about the balloons?" Aaron asked.

Kate thought hard. "He said that they go up to 5,000 feet and if an aeroplane hits the cables, little knives cut through those cables, which are heavy, and this separates them from the balloon. The cables drag along behind the aeroplane and makes it stall. Then two parachutes open at either end of the cable and that finishes off the aeroplane."

"A likely story!" Pamela scoffed.

"I vote we go and look," Mark said.

Kate lifted BQ's hand and said "Aye", which made the vote unanimously in favour.

While BQ stayed behind to mind the Presidential Chair, BC led the entourage to the common, waving his bent tail like a banner.

Beyond the thorny obstruction of barbed wire, they saw several flatbed lorries standing at various stations with guns mounted on them. Beyond them a huge lensed cylinder winked in the sun. But far more obtrusive and massive even at a distance, a floundering monster wallowed at its moorings. Several uniformed women had tamed the beast and now hurried about looking very efficient and small in contrast.

"Cables. Parachutes. Little knives," Kate said. "See?"

"But...I thought they were smaller than that," Wendy said. "I mean they look like a school of silver fish when they're up there in the sky--all facing in the same direction."

Pamela said nothing as she eyed an approaching policeman.

"Move along now, kiddies," he said, hopping off his bicycle. "This is no place for children."

181

"We're only looking," Kate said.   "Besides, it wouldn't take much for a spy to see what's going on here, would it?" She pointed.   "That's a searchlight, and those are mobile Bofors. You ought to be pleased that we're not spies."

The policeman slid one finger under his helmet and scratched.

Suddenly the great silver fish began to arise from its pad, nodding and weaving toward the sun and casting everyone who watched on the ground into deep shadow.   As if to accompany the ungainly dancer, a chorus of air raid sirens began to play their dismal atonal melody.

Before the policeman could speak, the entire group of youngsters, including the cat, had disappeared over the hill, running hell for leather toward shelter.   Kate tried to look up as she ran, searching the sky for the inevitable dog fight and hoping no more wayward bombers would fly over.   No fighters wove and dodged all over the sky, but she could hear the throb of many much heavier aircraft approaching.   She ran faster, shouting at BC who insisted on running under her feet. Distracted by the cat, she crashed blindly into Mr. Baxter who stood waiting anxiously at the gate.

"Quickly!" he shouted, ushering her toward her house. "We'll have to make do with sheltering under the stairs.   The bombers are very close."

Kate took one last look up and saw a huge formidable swarm of black silhouettes against the blue approaching over the tree line that marked the edge of the common.   The aircraft filled the sky to such an extent no one could possible gauge how many there might have been, or from which general direction they came.   One thing was excruciatingly clear;   the mass of bombers withheld its bombs for good reason. Obviously their intended target must be the City of London. What had Ruby said? They'll be back, because they dropped bombs on London and we bombed them back.....

Her mother crouched under the stairs holding the baby, Annie, close to her as Mr. Baxter hurried Kate in. Since her return from Sussex the initial resentment had faded concerning the new little sister. She was, after all, only a baby and could not possibly be aware that she had stolen Kate's position in the family. She did, however, blame Annie for her mother's continued pallor. But as the baby's frightened wide eyes swam with tears, Kate touched one tiny foot as a gesture of reassurance.   The noise was deafening which made it impossible to speak and Annie pressed her face against her mother's shoulder as the mighty roar of the planes shook the house. Kate covered her ears and looked about her in search of BC. At last, she saw two yellow eyes glinting from under the hall stand and even as she watched, the eyes grew dim as the cat drew back further into his chosen shelter.

"We're in for it now," Mr. Baxter muttered.   "Where's the RAF for God's sake?"

* * *

Janine took one last look around her London bedroom and closed the big canvas bag.

"Dougherty will take care of you until I come back," she said to Charlie, who sat looking hopefully toward his leash.

At the curb outside the house the green Daimler glinted in the sun and she looked down from her window and shook her head in disbelief. Tangmere had been rendered inoperable by enemy raids and it astounded her that the big car had come through barely scratched. When Squadron Leader Ian Lowery telephoned concerning the delivery of the car by a Pilot Officer on leave, he had mentioned that George Ravensbrook's MG

183

had been entirely demolished even though the cars were parked side by side. How strange, she thought, are the selective whims of war. In order to put the car to good use now that David would not be able to drive it for some time, she had offered it to his friend, Rupert Barlow.

"It's very kind of you, Mrs. Parke," he had said on the telephone. "DDI...er....the Daimler has been an invaluable asset to the squadron and I shall take very good care of it. I'll be in London this afternoon to pick it up and will look forward to meeting you."

The train to Lincolnshire was due to leave in twenty minutes and Janine knew she could not wait for him any longer. Her intensive training would begin tomorrow and she had to catch that train. In the event that she would not be at home when Rupert arrived, she had advised him where the car would be. David had spoken of his friend often, and Janine looked forward to meeting him. She glanced again at her watch as her taxi drew up and peered up and down the road hoping to catch sight of a young man in RAF uniform, but none came. As she opened the taxi door, the air raid warning sounded.

"Oh, blast!" she said to the driver. "Look, it'll be just another dog fight. I'll double your fare if you'll get me to the station."

The driver looked doubtful. "Well, missus. It's on your head if we get caught. We're supposed to take shelter."

Janine clung to the hand strap in the back seat as the panicky driver took the corners at high speed and after a hair-raising ride they arrived at the station in record time. As Janine prepared to leave the taxi the driver looked up, cupping an ear with his hand.

"Crikey!" he said. "What the hell is that?"

They both looked expectantly toward the southeast and listened to the ever-increasing volume of sound. As the leaders of the immense aerial armada passed overhead with their fighter escorts weaving back and forth in order to keep abreast of their wards, the driver abandoned his taxi and took off toward the nearest pub. Janine left the fare on the driver's seat and hurried toward the station entrance.

"I wouldn't if I were you, miss," a porter shouted, pointing toward the glass canopied roof. "There's room in here. Come on."

"But my train............"

"It won't run until this lot's gone," the porter said, ushering her into the Left Luggage office. "It's safe enough in here if we lie low. My bet is there's going to be some flying glass."

As if on cue, the bombardment began and although the noise of the raid shook and shattered parts of the station, the concentration of the bombardment seemed to be elsewhere.

"Sounds like the docks to me," the porter said, brushing ceiling plaster from his shoulders. "Where the hell is the RAF?"

Janine ran the back of her hand across her forehead, knowing full well why the air force was not in evidence. Rupert had telephoned from Acklington where the squadron had been sent to recoup. While the crux of the conversation concerned the car, he indicated that RAF Fighter Command had been brought to its knees by severe losses and complete exhaustion. We need a miracle, he had said.

"Well, the guns in the parks are having a go," the porter said. "At least somebody's trying."

Janine had no heart to tell him that this was quite likely the beginning of the end of Britain as they knew it, since invasion and occupation must surely follow. As the All Clear sounded, they hurried outside to join the throng already staring up at the sky.

"It's an omen," a woman cried. "The sky has turned to blood!"

Janine fumbled for her handkerchief as she choked over the bitter fumes and dust-filled air. Charred fragments fluttered down like black snow, while paper, weightless and blackened, soared upwards on drafts of wind like swarms of bats. A bus driver passed with windscreen wipers working to the hilt to clear the dust while the female Clippie clung to the boarding pole on the back platform and shouted that both sides of the Thames were ablaze in the dock areas of East London.

"Houses, too!" she added. "Poor blighters didn't know what hit them."

Janine closed her hand around the train ticket fare she had put in her pocket. She had no desire to desert her home and family, yet under German occupation here she would be useless. If she operated directly in southern France, she could at least function advantageously. Without a further glance at the ominous red sky, she walked quickly toward the ticket office and bought a one-way ticket to Lincolnshire.

* * *

Stunned, Yvonne left a basement in Berkeley Square with the word *Résistance* reverberating through her mind. Sometimes she simply forgot that her mother was French-born although they often spoke the language at home. Obviously, as a pilot, she knew something about the French terrain since she had flown over it enough times with her mother en route to Aix-en-Provence. But surely there were others better qualified to assume the role of an agent in the French Special Operations Executive (FSOE) under General de Gaulle? Didn't the fact that the break in friendly relations by the French Vichy government with Britain indicate that it intended to cooperate with the German liaison between the north and south? How could a member of the FSOE in Vichy expect any assistance or sympathy under those circumstances?   Also, was not the credibility of the entire demarcation line separating midi and southern France from the occupied zone at risk?

This disturbing and unwelcome intrusion into her life was irritating enough, but the fact that the meeting was conducted in a basement air raid shelter added to her agitated mood. The two uniformed Frenchmen seemed unperturbed by the noise of the unpredicted air raid and conducted the inquiry methodically to its end. With instructions to seriously consider the proposals they had outlined to her, she left the building immediately after the All Clear sounded.

Completely preoccupied with her thoughts she pushed her way through the throng of people on the pavement, only vaguely aware that they stood staring with disbelief at the sky.

"They'll be back," she heard someone say.   "Mark my words, this is just the beginning."

She looked up and saw for the first time the scarlet clouds billowing above her, only then realising how serious the air raid had been. If this were the first step toward invasion, she wondered, how much longer could ATA operate, ferrying unarmed aircraft inland under enemy attack?   On a more personal level, what would happen to her?   Forced labour, perhaps? Internment?

The stunned crowd began to disperse and Yvonne looked into faces ashen with shock and apprehension. While sworn to secrecy concerning her covert meeting in the basement, she nonetheless felt in need for conversation--any conversation. Perhaps, by some remote chance one of her parents might be at home in Bayswater.

*   *   *

Claude returned the doorman's greeting with a nod. The elderly man, immaculate in his uniform, hovered inside the sandbag barricade embracing the door of a gentlemen's club in Saint James.   After weeks of anxiety and a sense of hopelessness, Claude's mood had shifted to one of unmitigated relief. He had spent a constructive and beneficial afternoon with his solicitor, and left the office with his affairs in good order.   The entire dossier, filled with positive and conclusive decisions, left him in excellent spirits.

Seated in a deep leather chair in the silence of the smoking room, he savored the rich taste of aged whiskey with satisfaction. One small irritation lingered in the shadows of his mind and he could only trust that time would take care of it. While the child, Kate, had a remarkable artistic talent, he hoped her recollections of past drawings might not be so pronounced. Upon finding the sketch of Beatrix Dierick amongst the others in the bedroom at Mallory Cottage, his blood had run cold. The pale, cold eyes had mocked him from the paper and he derived great pleasure in watching them writhe and shrivel as the flame crept across the paper. If only it could be that easy to obliterate this likeness from the mind of the child who drew it.

The old waiter, in service at the club for as long as Claude could remember, appeared quietly at his side.

"The Air Raid warning has just sounded, sir," he said. "May I take your whiskey down to the basement for you?"

Away from the confines of club rules, Claude would not have bothered.   There had been no bombing on central London and the alert usually sounded simply due to enemy aircraft crossing the coastline. But the unfamiliar throb of bomber engines over the city quickly conveyed a new enemy intent, and other club members were hastening toward the stairs.   Once below, the joints and rafters creaked as the bombardment ran its course, although it was obviously not in the near vicinity.

"Not this side of town," someone said. "I wonder what they're after?"

"The docks, most likely," said another. "That would make sense, wouldn't it?"

When the raid ended, Claude felt the dryness of dust in his nostrils the minute he left the building and instinctively looked up at the sky. Great black billows of smoke belched upward, eerily stained with flickering blood-reds and vivid oranges. The air smelt of death and devastation. Frightened people, bewildered by the awful sight, seemed unsure what to do--where to go.

Aware that transportation would be hampered by the air raid, he decided to walk to the station and deftly wove his way through the stunned crowd toward Marble Arch. A little ahead he thought he saw a familiar figure hurrying along and he quickened his pace to catch up. There was no mistaking the brisk, determined walk, and the bright copper hair curling from under the smart ATA forage cap. As always, the full pilot's brevet on the uniform jacket brought puzzled glances from passersby, but the wearer seemed oblivious to the stares. Although he had made every attempt to dismiss Yvonne from his mind, all caution and discretion immediately vanished at the sight of her, and he broke into a run to catch up.

At first she seemed not to know him. Then she stared in surprise at his well-tailored suit.

"Ben Boniface? I hardly recognised you."

He smiled. "I don't think my oversized jumper would be well accepted in London, do you?"

She looked at him questioningly?

"I don't come to the city very often," he lied. "But perhaps since we're both here, you might consider joining me for an early dinner." He nodded in the direction of Park Lane. "I think one of the hotels might find something for us to eat."

"I'm on my way to Bayswater," she said. "I haven't seen my parents for some time."

"I imagine your father will be very busy this evening after......this." He looked up at the sky.

"Well, perhaps my mother........"

He said nothing; but not wanting to miss an opportunity for a little more time with Yvonne, he thought quickly. "Well, a quick drink then before you go. I can give you some news of the village, if you like."

He took advantage of her momentary hesitation and held her arm to guide her across the road.

Time passed quickly as he talked about the village; of Lewes and the river; and of Eastbourne. The quiet luxury of the hotel lounge served to detract from the earlier disaster at the docks. Yvonne showed interest in news of home and Claude sensed that the prior imbalance of their relationship had begun to level. A certain mutual interest blossomed between them, but he chose to ignore its warning.

A young page hurried through the area announcing that another mass of German bombers had crossed the coast and that everyone should hurry downstairs to the basement shelter. The earlier raid had changed the public's apathetic attitude toward the air raid sirens, and hotel guests quickly obeyed. But aircraft were overhead before Claude and Yvonne had reached the top of the stairs.

"In here!" he urged, quickly taking her arm and pulling her toward a door behind the concierge's podium.

At that moment the hotel lights flickered and died plunging the luggage room into darkness. Acutely aware of her nearness, he stood in silence listening to the distant attack. A sudden closer blast brought a smattering of ceiling plaster down on them and he reached out into the darkness to find her.

"Are you all right?" he asked, taking her hand.

"Probably dusty," she said. "But I can't see, of course."

The room creaked as a second explosion brought more plaster down, and she moved closer to him.

"The docks again--and more," he said.

"Yes."

He felt her tremble against his side and instinctively turned to protect her. He closed his eyes, remembering how often he had dreamt of such circumstances, always aware that she would undoubtedly object. But she made no protest as he whispered her name and brushed his lips against her cheek. As he sought her soft mouth, she put her arms about him, drawing him closer and he rejoiced as their passion mounted.

Suddenly, the door flew open and two small circles of light danced along the wall toward them.

"There's two in here," a lively Cockney voice said, as the light beam settled on two red buckets of sand. "Hurry up before the entire kitchen goes up in smoke. If any more wires short out then things will really get hot."

The men left with their buckets while Claude gaped in astonishment.

"Well," he choked. "I knew things were heating up-- but buckets of sand?!"

*   *   *

Late September, 1940

David tried to close his eyes against the brilliance of the surgical lamp without success.

"It's all right," someone said. "We'll soon have you under."

He might have protested against the sudden intense sting in his arm if the light and pain had not quickly faded away. Yet, uncannily he tasted sea water and felt the weight of his wet clothes pulling him down.

"Keep going!" Kate said. *"Help is on the way."*

"How do you know? We're in the middle of the Channel. How could you possibly know?"

"Listen!"

"I can't hear anything!"

"Listen harder! It's a boat."

Through swollen eyes he could barely see the hazy outline of a small launch.

"Are you British?"

The voice sounded very far away.

"Yes....Brish........"

"If you're a Jerry, you can bloody well drown," the voice shouted.

"No! No! Not a Jerry!" He was sure he had screamed the words.

"Speak up, boy. What are you then?"

"Brish.....British!" he yelled. "Bloody hell.....can't you see? I'm British!"

The effort sapped his little remaining strength and he felt himself sinking.

"Grab him! He's going down!"

Strong hands grasped his arms and jerked him back to the surface.

"Sorry, young fellow. We had to be sure, you know."

He tried not to cry out when one of the men inadvertently caught hold of his burned hand and was ashamed of the awful involuntary scream. Perhaps he might have fainted, but could not be sure. While unable to remember his entry into the boat, he looked up at the sky and realised that he no longer struggled to keep afloat. He tried to move his arms and found they were pinned snugly by a blanket against his body. The bile rose in his stomach and he fought feebly to move.

"H-help me," he pleaded. "I have to be sick."

"It's all right, boy. We understand."

"No. No, please help me to the side."

The men gently lifted him to the gunwale and he wondered why on earth he had needed to retain the last remaining segment of his dignity, since the pain was almost unbearable. He wretched pitifully and each upsurge sent throbs of pain through his face while his blistered hands slid from the rail, no longer able to support him. At last he fell back, exhausted.

"God love him, he's truly fried," he heard one man say. "Can't be much more than twenty."

He struggled to speak, but felt consciousness slipping away. "Kate.......?"

But there was no reply.

*　*　*

After his rescue, time had no meaning as he lay in a haze of morphia-induced fantasy, drifting from the agonising reality of pain into strange nefarious dreams that left him terrified and near hysteria when he awoke. During brief periods of lucidity his sole mental focus lay on the water pitcher he knew was beside his bed, although bandages prevented him from seeing it. He croaked unintelligible sounds hoping that someone would give him some of its contents and, when they did, he spluttered and gagged as the water washed through his mouth. Then great, jagged, tortuous spasms shot across his face as one nerve ending tossed the pain on to the next. The blessed prick of the needle brought only conditional relief, since it sent him back into the vivid distorted nightmares that waited to torment him.

He vaguely remembered his father's voice telling him that he had been taken to a hospital in Margate from the boat and then to the RAF wing of the Royal Masonic Hospital in London. During one lucid moment he recalled a New Zealand surgeon assuring him that he would be taken to a special place for treatment. Meanwhile, the tannic acid that had been applied to his burns as the preliminary treatment, would have to be removed.

When he was fully conscious, he wondered if perhaps he might be blind. He involuntarily moaned, which brought a nurse to his beside.

"No, Pilot Officer Parke, you're not blind. Your eyes are undamaged, but the skin surrounding the sockets has been badly burned."

Although only a matter of days had passed, time became his enemy as his faculties returned. Unable to see, or use his hands, his irritation grew and fear began to filter into his mind as the German night raids continued. He envisioned himself trapped inside a burning hospital, unable to find his way out if indeed he had the strength to get out of bed. He asked repeatedly when the transfer to the special place would occur, but no one could answer his question.

"Patience," a surgeon told him. "Mr. McIndoe goes to all the military medical establishments selecting the worst burn cases. You're not the only one. He has you at the top of his list which means you could go very soon."

That had been a week ago and before he could vent his irritation on the surgeon again, he was on his way to East Grinstead.

*   *   *

An air raid warning penetrated the kaleidoscopic confusion in his mind as he rose slowly back to consciousness after the operation. The dull ache across his eyes blossomed into full-force pain as he heard the rustle of starched linen beside his bed and smelt the pleasing scent of soap.

"We'll do this as carefully as possible," a nurse said. "But first we'll give you something for pain."

He slurred his thanks; then thought briefly about her first comment.

"Wh.....what're you going to do....... very carefully?" he mouthed, wondering what new sort of pain the medical staff could inflict on him.

"We're going to put you under your bed, Pilot Officer Parke. Enemy bombers have crossed the coast again and are heading in this direction. We haven't time to take any better precautions."

Under other conditions, David felt he might have enjoyed this rendezvous under his bed with a pretty nurse. But as the raid began, the seriousness of its intensity over-rode any attempt at humour. Above the racket of explosions and bomber engines, he could hear plaster showering down from the ceiling, shrapnel clattering down on the concrete path outside his window, and the sound of shattering glass somewhere in another part of the building. While he could not see his under-the-bed fellow, he sensed her fear.

"The radius is widening," he heard Patrick say from under the bed next to him. "It's not just central London now; sounds like they're going for the suburbs, too. Fighter Command hasn't a prayer against this lot."

David turned his head, but said nothing. Rupert had been in to see him briefly two days earlier and had tried to avoid speaking about the squadron and the German blitzkrieg on London. Others in the ward were not so cautious and it became quite obvious that although Fighter Command was building up its strength again, they had little effect on the huge mass of bombers and fighter escorts that operated each night with relative impunity and deadly accuracy.

After the raid, David begged for news of the war in general and was told that news filtering out from occupied Europe reported tyrannical bullying and total suppression by the occupying forces. If the Germans are successful in invading Britain's shores, he thought, what will they do with a half-burned wreck like me? He did not allow himself to consider the possibility of defeat any further.

"All you have to do," Archibald McIndoe told him, "is to concentrate on getting better. Your fretting about things doesn't help in the least."

"He's much admired in the field of reconstructive surgery and something of a pioneer in new procedures," the ward sister told him. "He'll do a great deal for you. He won't allow any self-pity, you understand. But he will encourage self-esteem and camaraderie. You'll soon find out about that when you're stronger."

He heard the rustle of her apron as she left.

"Patrick! Where the hell are you!" He tried to shout, but a could only manage a mere whisper.

"Here, old boy."

"Did they give me eyelids?"

"So I would presume. Can't see anything for bandages at the moment, though."

"Pilot Office Parke! You must learn to lie still!"

"Yes, sister."

"You have prosthetic lids--oversized and under pressure at the moment. But you must realise that you're still weak and need to make allowances. Rest! Just lie still, and rest!"

"Yes, sister."

That night, the raid on London was exceptionally heavy, expanding out toward the southern suburbs. Discomfort and noise contributed to a restless night for David and he lay there wondering what next diabolical move the enemy might make to break the spirit of Great Britain.

CHAPTER TEN

September, 1940

Kate listened with growing consternation as Hugh read from the newspaper each day at breakfast. The radius of devastation extended into the suburbs and beyond as the German blitzkrieg battered London nightly with harsh tenacity. She watched him flag his maps where strategic targets had been selected and systematically destroyed, and saw that the vital docks, still aflame as a result of the continuing bombardments, illuminated the innocent houses unfortunate enough to be in the vicinity, as they crumbled and collapsed from blast or, more often than not, from direct hits. The lists of dead and seriously injured lengthened each night and yet, as a form of defiance she supposed, the newspapers printed pictures of perky London Cockneys who kept the heart of the capital beating with cheeky effrontery toward the enemy. Each morning, after the bombers withdrew, the debris was shoved aside to make room for the kettles to boil water for inevitable cups of hot tea.

After Prime Minister Churchill made a magnificently defiant speech in the House of Commons, the ubiquitous stubbornness continued to spread like wildfire and with one unanimous shrug, people scoffed at Hitler's efforts to break the spirit of London and displayed their indignation with ridicule and laughter.   Yet Kate wondered if they felt the same underlying constant fear that she did beneath this bravado. Each day the results of the night raids were evident along the outer suburban streets where once neat, solid houses had stood surrounded by their lawns and flowers.   As more and more charred breaches in the orderly residential rows reflected the haphazard night targets she knew it would be just a matter of time before flames licked around the splintered timbers of her own home.   Each day familiar faces disappeared as their names were added to the posted casualty lists.

After the initial night raid in early September the Anderson quagmire had been remedied with a thick coating of cement that covered the floor and halfway up the curved walls making it reasonably habitable for safer sleeping.   But in spite of the hurried modifications the place smelt and felt damp, and once the hatch was in place in order to conceal the tiny flame of the night light from the advancing bombers, the air rapidly staled.   True to his word, Hugh refused to enter what he called a "potential tomb" and spent his nights under the stairs in the house, accompanied by BC.   At breakfast he described the way the house rocked as plaster and cement cascaded down beyond the shelter of the stairs raising gray clouds of stifling dust.

"It's still better than the quagmire," he commented.   "At least I'm above ground."

Kate derived little comfort from his remarks since she hated the Anderson, too.   But his descriptions of straining timbers that creaked and cracked against the moving weight of the house and the sound of china, glass, and cookware smashing to the floor, prompted her to choose the lesser of two evils.   Her father argued incessantly with Hugh and once even tried to physically force him into the shelter which caused a dreadful scene.

As the raids continued, Mr. Baxter condescended to join the Hawkins family in their shelter, since he still had none. At dawn, after the All Clear had sounded, he prowled the neighbourhood to assess the damage and returned in time for breakfast over which he gave full account of the devastation and of the dead and injured. Only after a depiction of his observations appeared in the daily papers did the Hawkins family realise that Mr. Baxter was a political cartoonist and artist of some renown.

Kate thought it odd that God would allow His own house of worship to be destroyed as Mr. Baxter talked of the extensive damage to St. Alban's church. She wondered where the old lady of implicit faith was now. As it was, Kate still thought of herself as a skeptic and probably would not miss the place anyway. Two days later the Garage Club's headquarters was destroyed along with the Hamilton's house. Mark and Pamela, who had been in their shelter, retreated to an aunt's home in the country.

"I doubt that even the spider survived in that mess," Peter said as he and Kate dismally surveyed the pile of rubble.

Just after dark on the next night, both Aaron and Wendy were killed after a High Explosive (HE) bomb made a direct hit in an alley between their respective homes and crumpled the buildings like decks of cards. The families had lingered indoors too long after the alert had sounded.

"The Germans got them after all," Peter said, brushing tears away. "I hate the Germans, Kate! I really hate them!"

On the 18th of September, Mr. Baxter did not come to the shelter.

"His lungs are bad," Kate's mother said, tucking the baby into the upper bunk and banking her in with pillows. "All that cigarette smoking can't possibly be good for him!

Perhaps you had better knock on his door to see if he's all right. But do be quick; it's almost dark."

Mr. Baxter's front door was pocked by flying glass and hung on its hinges at an unnatural angle. She selected a reasonably clear spot, since the knocker was gone and, having tapped with her knuckles, stood listening for his footfall in the hallway.

"Mr. Baxter!" she called through the letter slot. "Are you all right?"

She listened again and, at last, heard him shuffling toward the door. It swung drunkenly on its damaged hinges as he released the latch, but he seemed not to notice. Instead he stared over Kate's head at the tree line at the edge of the common. She saw that his eyes were red-rimmed and that his hand shook against the latch as he chewed at his lower lip.

"Are you all right?" she asked again.

"The ship......," he said brokenly. "It was torpedoed by a German U-boat."

Kate suddenly felt ice cold. "R-Ruby's ship?" she stammered.

"The City of Benares. All on board perished except seven. All those children......."

"W-what about Ruby?" Kate shouted. "What about Ruby.....and M-Mrs. Baxter?" She groped for his sleeve. "Tell me! Tell me!"

But Mr. Baxter could not speak. He just shook his head.

Kate found his hand through a haze of tears. "C'mon, Mr. Baxter. Please let's go to the shelter."

The air raid warning began to wail and only then did the distraught man become aware of her. He allowed her to lead him away, following her to the Anderson shelter like a blind man.

A week later, Alfred Hawkins received his call to service from the Royal Navy. Kate watched him walk quickly away and only when he reached the top of the road did he turn to wave goodbye. Perhaps, Kate thought, I won't ever see my father again, either.

Dear David, she wrote. *It has been some time since I've heard from you, but I expect you're quite busy. I do wonder how all those bombers are getting through, though. I hope you'll give George Ravensbrook my regards and also give Charlie a pat the next time you see him. I'm enclosing some of my sketches for you. Everything here is fine.*

As she sealed the envelope she remembered again the comfort of his arms about her in Long Bottom. In the face of overwhelming adversity it seemed to her that her family generally resorted to inner strength rather than to any form of interaction. She supposed that silent mutual support was taken for granted, and that even a brief embrace after a night of terror should not be expected.

*   *   *

October, 1940

"Well," Hugh said from his usual spot behind the newspaper at breakfast. "At least this pasting Jerry's giving London has given the Fighter Command time to dust itself off and get back into business."

Kate's ears still rang from the exceptionally heavy raid the previous night. She looked around the kitchen and wondered how the plaster-less walls managed to hold themselves together. During the daylight hours they tried to live as normally as possible in the shattered shell that had once been their home. But each night the raids grew progressively worse and she wondered where they might go when their house finally collapsed.

Hugh turned the paper over. "They're throwing everything at us," he said. "High explosives, incendiaries, parachuted land mines." He glanced at her over the top of the paper. "Don't pick anything up off the ground, will you. I mean even if it looks innocent. It says here a boy had his hand blown off picking up what he thought was a fountain pen. They're dropping attractive looking lures that are booby trapped. If you see anything, report it to a Warden. Alright?"

Kate wandered outside, kicking aside rubble and picking up familiar bits of patterned china. At least she knew these could not be booby traps as she tried to determine which dish they might have been part of. She held BQ under one arm and watched BC as he gingerly minced over obstacles, shaking each paw daintily after each step. A black tarpaulin that was draped over exposed roof rafters flapped indolently in the breeze and a few deciduous leaves pirouetted upward in a golden cone before floating earthward in a leisurely pas de deaux.

"Oh, Ruby," she whispered. "Perhaps you are better off dead. I don't think anything will ever be the same again."

She looked up at the sky, thinking of Wendy and Aaron. "Perhaps it might be a good idea if you all saved me a place up there."

That night she lay in one upper bunk while Annie slept soundly in another. Kate watched her mother's knitting needles flash in the glow of the night light. A faint smell of whiskey mingled with the waxy scent of the candle as Mr. Baxter breathed heavily on the lower bunk. She shifted her position a little to better see his face and saw that he stared glassily at the bottom of the bunk above him. Since the death of his family he had spoken very little, and every evening Kate knocked on his door to escort him the shelter since he seemed to forget that the air raids began after dark.

The knitting needles stopped and lowered as the enemy aircraft engines throbbed yet again in the distance in unison with the air raid warning.   The airless cocoon shuddered as the planes thundered over causing a fine sprinkling of dry earth to drizzle from a joint in the corrugated iron. Soon the mobile guns ran back and forth along the roads, adding to the din.   Their presence was encouraging, but everyone knew they were rarely successful in bringing down aircraft. She could hear shrapnel clattering and bouncing, red-hot, along the fragmented roofs, some of it penetrating the tarpaulin and setting the rafters smoldering.   Then came the inevitable whistle of the bombs, followed by bone-shaking explosions.   Kate wondered if the rigid muscles in her neck might eventually strangle her as ambulance and fire engine alarms joined in the great crescendo of sound.

An earsplitting scream descanted above the din, followed immediately by another.   A massive explosion violently rocked the shelter and the concrete lining cracked and split from end to end, leaving a wide, muddy fissure along the floor.   Great invisible hands picked Kate up and hurled her savagely from her upper bunk toward the ground below. As she fell, her head crashed against the ledge of concrete reinforcement and she floated into weightless and silent oblivion.

*   *   *

Strange senseless words gradually pierced through the cacophony blasting in her ears and for a moment she wondered if she had been killed and had gone to purgatory. Perhaps that is what happens to skeptics, she mused. But her head throbbed and she surmised that surely death would not be so painful. As she emerged from the mists of unconsciousness she tried to speak, but her voice was lost in the overwhelming noise of the air raid.

"She's coming round," Mr. Baxter said from somewhere very far away. "Don't try to move, Kate."

Instinctively she moved her hand toward the pain in her head and felt the warm stickiness of blood seep between her fingers. I must tell them I'm going to be sick, she thought. But the words stuck like wads of cotton wool in the back of her throat and she choked wretchedly as projectile vomit shot across the shelter and spattered down into the muddy fissure. Annie began to cry and Kate wanted to ask if she were also hurt.

"Annie?" she gasped.

"Shh!" Mr. Baxter said. "Lie still. Annie is fine--just a bit shaken up, that's all."

"Everything has been blown all over the place," Kate heard her mother say. Her voice sounded thin and strained as if she were about to cry. "I can only find bits and pieces of the first aid kit. We'll have to improvise."

Kate heard the sound of water being poured but felt too weak to open her eyes until the cold shock of a wet compress against her skull caused pain to shoot through her head like white hot fire.

"It's all right, Kate," Mr. Baxter said. "You're bleeding a little bit, that's all."

At that moment the All Clear sounded and he reached for the hatch. The cool, fresh air poured into the tiny stagnant cave and Kate felt drunk with relief as she gulped it in. She opened her eyes and blinked at the small rectangle of daylight.

"Now stay here while I go and find some medical help."

Mr. Baxter's grief was deferred in this moment of urgency and his old brisk sense of authority had returned.

"That goes for you too, mate," a voice said through the opening. "There's a UXB (Unexploded Bomb) in your front garden. The Army's on its way to defuse it, so we don't want any movement, see?"

The Air Raid Warden peered into the shelter. "Cor blimey, what a mess," he said. "I'm afraid you'll have to stay there, though." He glanced at Kate. "Er--there was a second bomb. A High Explosive landed in the middle of the road and demolished nearly all the houses, I'm afraid. Kate saw an expression of frozen horror on her mother's face as she peered through the hatch.

"Oh, dear God! Hugh!"

"Are you telling me there's someone in--under--that lot?" the Warden said. His officious attitude quickly melted into concern. "Look, here's the Army now. I'll try to let them know. But you realise you can't hurry these things. Jerry booby traps the fuses sometimes and so the blokes defusing them have to be extra careful."

He tiptoed away leaving the silent group in the shelter to deal with their profound dismay.

Kate felt her injury was secondary compared to the tragedy above ground, but the wet warmth of the pillow under her head began to alarm her and she whimpered, attracting her mother's attention.

Although nothing was said, Kate saw the concern on Mr. Baxter's face as they took away her pillow and hid it from sight. He moved her gently nearer to the hatch which gave her some relief from the stench. She looked up at the remains of the house, its skeletal outline silhouetted against the dark scudding clouds like a naked tree in winter. She listened to the soft hesitant patter of rain drops and smelt the tang of freshly wetted earth. Perhaps, she thought, the world is weeping

Suddenly, something heavy landed on her stomach and BC's furry face loomed into view as he pushed his wet nose against her cheek.

"BC?" Mr. Baxter said, stroking the cat. "Isn't he usually with Hugh?"

* * *

By midmorning the unexploded bomb had been defused and Wardens lifted Kate from the stinking shelter and carried her to the Red Cross mobile station at the top of the road. The deep cut at the back of her skull required eight stitches to close it and she bore the pain with difficulty. Afterwards her anxiety increased, which annoyed the attending nurse.

"We can't do anything else for you. Just don't move about too much, and for heaven's sake, don't go to sleep."

"It isn't that," Kate persisted. "It's my brother, you see."

"He'll have to wait his turn," the nurse said. "We have to see to the worst ones first."

"You don't understand. He's buried."

"Then we'll treat him when they dig him out."

Mr. Baxter peeped around the door. "Don't fret, Kate," he said. "They've started to look for Hugh--with BC's help! I think they're getting rather annoyed with that old cat because he keeps getting in the way." He looked at the nurse and winked. "She's just a little girl, you know. I know you've had a rough night but, well, she is just a little girl."

The nurse nodded and pursed her lips.

"Are you going to send her to hospital?" Mr. Baxter asked.

"They're all overflowing and understaffed," the nurse said, blinking back tears. "She'll get better attention here." She smiled crookedly at Kate. "I'm sorry I snapped. As the gentleman said, I did have rather a rough night. We'll set you up on a chair outside if you like so that you can watch your cat help with the digging."

"Look at that," Mr. Baxter said as he settled Kate on to the promised chair. "Look at that old cat. See what I mean?"

In spite of pain and anxiety, Kate giggled. BC was indeed busily supervising the digging operations and generally getting in the way on top of the debris where the men worked. But she sobered rapidly at the sight of her mother, holding Annie in one arm and accepting support from a Warden with the other at the edge of the rubble.

"Will somebody put that cat in a bag," one of the men shouted. "He's trying to dig a latrine for himself right where I'm working."

In spite of gentle coaxing BC refused to be caught, or to respond, and continued to dig.

"Mr. Baxter," Kate said, wishing she did not feel so ill. "I think BC knows where Hugh is."

Mr. Baxter nodded condescendingly, and continued to watch the digging men.

"Please, Mr. Baxter. Please go and see."

He sighed and patted her shoulder. She watched him from her chair as he walked toward the demolition crew, tripping and stumbling over lumps of wood and mortar. At last, he waved his arms to attract attention to himself.

The rescue crew shook their heads as he spoke to them, glancing skeptically at the cat. At last, one man knelt beside where BC continued to dig and began to move rubble aside with his hands.

"Is anyone there," he shouted, keeping his face close to the ground.

Everyone stood frozen, waiting for some kind of response.

"He's in there!" the man shouted. "Keep still, lad. Don't move a muscle. We'll soon have you out."

Kate saw her mother take a step forward, but the Warden gently took her arm and shook his head.

The waiting became interminable as BC prowled the area, nudging up against legs and generally making his presence known.

"We've broken through!" the man shouted. "Come on, young fellow. Easy does it."

Eager hands reached to help as they brought Hugh up through the hole in the debris. Mr. Baxter put his arm around Kate's mother as two men struggled across the rubble toward the hole with a stretcher. Gray with dust, the boy's body hung limply while his head fell back as they lifted him out. Kate could not bear to look.

"All right, boy. No need to struggle."

Incredibly, Hugh suddenly regained consciousness and insisted on standing by himself, pushing away all offered assistance. He staggered a few steps and looked dazedly down at BC who rubbed against his legs. With some effort he bent down and pick up the cat, looking about him with bewilderment. A Warden held out his arms as Hugh's legs crumpled beneath him, and BC streaked away toward the Anderson shelter.

The men carried the unconscious boy toward the mobile unit, followed by an entourage of concerned neighbours.

"He's just fainted, Kate," Mr. Baxter called, clambering over the rubble. "Probably shock. He'll soon be as right as rain."

"That cat is quite a hero," the Warden said.

"He's gone back to the Anderson," Kate said. "You see, he knows that BQ is still inside."

The Warden turned on his heel. "Why the devil didn't someone tell me there was another child?" he said, hurrying toward the shelter.

He returned quickly, obviously anxious to retreat from the stench, holding BQ under one arm and BC under the other.

"Do you really want……?" He held BQ out to Kate. "I mean, it's a bit of a mess, isn't it?"

Kate held out her arms, ignoring the blood, mud and vomit that had bespattered the harlequin costume.   The Warden's obvious repulsion showed that he had no idea how important both BQ and BC were to her.

*   *   *

Peter came to the ARP station to say goodbye to Kate.

"We lost most of our things during the Croydon bombing," he said. "Now we've lost what was left. It looks like we're both in the same boat except……well….you're wounded." He lifted his hand toward her face and then seemed to change his mind. "Where are you going to go now?"

"I have a grandfather in Kent. What about you?"

"Relatives in Cornwall."

Kate looked into the bright, blue eyes and sighed, acknowledging the end of yet another friendship.   Perhaps it really was just a waste of time to make friends. It seemed to her that life had lost any form of permanency and there was little point in brooding over losses.

"Goodbye, Peter. I enjoyed being your friend for just a little while."

He looked sadly at the bandage around her head. "Goodbye, Kate. I'm sure your wound will heal up quickly." He frowned and looked away. "And I hope Hugh will be able to speak again soon.   I'm sure it's just temporary shock."

"Yes," Kate said. "That, and the fact that he doesn't know any of us…..including himself."

Dear David: I haven't had time to do any sketches I'm afraid. They say that Fighter Command is back on its feet and I'm pleased about that; but that means you'll be very busy again, won't it? Perhaps one day, you'll have time to write to me.

*   *   *

France, November, 1940

In a small villa on the outskirts of Lille Claude sat in front of the fire and shivered in spite of the thick blanket around his shoulders. He knew the hot broth would warm him, yet his stomach still churned from the rough North Sea crossing and the unwelcome swim through the surf for the last one hundred yards in the dark. Even in mild weather, the tidal swells and undertows between the French and English coasts could be unforgiving, and the waters very cold. He pondered over his activities of the past few hours and hoped his plans would proceed with less discomfort.

*   *   *

It had not been easy to arrange a boat since he had always traveled to France by plane with Janine. Obviously he could not expect help from the SIS since he was now operating without orders. Through a series of contacts in England he had

211

been lucky enough to make the trip after dark in a commercial trawler from Shoeburyness in the mouth of the Thames to a point two miles off the coast of Calais. The plan was now to row alone in silent stealth the rest of the way in a small dory. But he lost an oar when a wave hit him broadside and, while struggling to keep the bow pointed shoreward, the outlying surf finally won the battle and capsized him. He knew his excellent physical condition contributed largely to his survival as he swam relentlessly toward Calais in pouring rain.

Although not working as an agent in this instance, he had made his contact with Noe through a British spy who was returning to France from Tangmere. The agent bore a letter addressed to Noe at the university that gave the appearance of having been written prior to the war since the envelope looked old and tattered enough to have been lost in the post en route. It bore a post mark dated July 12th, 1939 and the place of origin was Edinburgh. It had taken several hours to achieve the smudged, worn, and grubby effect and he felt confident that should the note get into the wrong hands it could in no way arouse suspicion. In the letter, Claude expressed pleasure concerning his visit to Paris during the summer of 1939 to discuss a new medical procedure. Aware that it was not a foolproof plan since he had no way of knowing if Noe had received the letter, and that Noe would not have time or contacts in order to reply, he knew his journey to Paris was a risk at best.

He had entrusted two more letters to an American businessman whom he knew through his club in London. While it was known that Americans still hoped to protect their business interests in Europe, this acquaintance had nonetheless indicated that he was ready to pull out due to his observations of German oppression in France. Even so, there was no guarantee that the letters would be delivered.

Since his contact in Calais--an old friend named Jean Decour who had been his French counterpart in intelligence gathering before the war--was not there to meet him, he could only assume that the second letter had not been delivered by the American and there was, in this case, a distinct possibility that the third letter had not reached its destination either. He had addressed it to Noe's younger brother, Lucien, who lived in Lille. When still a boy, Claude met Lucien Marceau who was visiting Paris from Lille with his daughter, Michou. The children had become friends and written to each other for a short while, but once they reached adulthood the correspondence dwindled to a halt. Perhaps Lucien had moved his family away from Lille and the American had not been able to trace them.

In heavy rain, he had dragged himself ashore at Calais and lay quietly for a moment or two to catch his breath. Then he inched slowly up the beach on his belly, thankful that the German guards would have difficulty in seeing him in such low visibility, and carefully cut his way through the barbed wire barricade, expecting any moment to be blown to smithereens by a mine. At last he was safely through and, still slithering like a sidewinder desert snake, he moved slowly toward the concrete sea wall. He lay flat and trembling as a pebble slid from under his foot and clattered toward the sea. After a long wait, he inched forward again and at last reached the deep shadow. Slowly he rose to his feet until the top of the wall was at eyelevel. He saw no one on the rain-swept pavement and no sign of a vehicle on the road. He counted to three and vaulted to street level, running swiftly toward the darkness of a side street where he stood shivering and trying to get his bearings. The failed rendezvous had put him at a serious disadvantage since nothing looked familiar. The areas around the port of Calais had been changed by German fortifications and he no longer knew which way to go. The address of a safe house, although firmly fixed in his mind, could be anywhere. By dodging into doorways and alleys, and by sheer luck, he found it at last; yet he hesitated, wondering if he would be admitted.

His nerves were as taught as piano wire as he waited by the back entrance. Perhaps there had been an arrest which would explain why his contact had not been there. Perhaps, if he tapped on the door, he too would fall into German hands. The words repeated in his head like a sledge hammer....*you are also a Jew.* Perhaps the people in the safe house did not trust him since he was not working with SIS or the Free French. Well, he would just have to risk it. He had come this far. He had no choice but to chance it. He tapped lightly--three short, then a moment's hesitation, then one more. A code used often in the past. He waited, holding his breath, as the door opened and Claude immediately recognised his old associate.

"My God, Claude! We thought you were lost at sea," Jean said, pulling him inside. "You were not at the point of rendezvous. I waited half an hour. The barbed wire was cut and ready for you to get through." He took Claude's hand and shook it warmly.

Claude realised then that he had come ashore in the wrong place. No wonder it had been so difficult to get his bearings.

"You could have been blown up!" Jean said, putting the heel of his hand against his forehead. "It's a miracle you made it."

"You received the letter then?"

"Of course!"

Relief coursed through him. If Jean had received his letter via the American then the third missive would have been delivered in Lille.

"We must go immediately, I'm afraid," Jean said, eyeing the wet clothes. "Your contact in Lille will be wary of you at best and if you don't arrive on time I doubt that he will open the door to you."

In spite of his anxiety, Claude smiled as he was bundled into the cab of a lorry that smelt strongly of fish. "At least I'll blend nicely with the environment," he grinned. "I smell like a fish market myself."

"It might help," Jean said. "But your papers are probably soaked and may cause a problem at the checkpoints."

"I'm wet without doubt. Surely they would believe that I was caught in the rain?"

"They might. Your papers may give you a Christian alias and a remote address near Reims," his driver commented. "But you are still a Jew, and if the Krauts have any reason at all to suspect that, we'll both be in hot water. Try to keep your face in the shadows as much as possible."

In the close quartered confines of the lorry's cab, warmth returned to Claude's chilled body. He studied the inset of Lille on his map and found the name of the street he was looking for. Almost in a state of drowsy euphoria, the first checkpoint came as a shock. He pressed his back against the seat, holding his face away from the light. Every nerve in his body was suddenly alert and tingling. He managed to fake a yawn as the German guard flashed his torch light through the window, and distorted his face into a gaping moue. The young soldier drew back with a look of disgust and waved them on.

"Perhaps I should have offered him a herring or two," Jean chortled. "But I rather got the impression that he wasn't too fond of fish. It always works."

He was true to his word. Although they were stopped several times along the route, they were never delayed.

"Why are you going to Paris without the approval of SIS?" Jean asked as they came to the outskirts of Lille. "It's a true hot spot, you know. Full of Germans."

"My parents were arrested in Austria, but I understand they were brought back to Paris which is where I'll be most likely to get leads on their whereabouts. There is someone there who may be able to help me. An old friend of my father's."

Jean's jaw tightened in the half light. "I wish you luck, but they are intent on seeking out all Jews. Unless you're well-connected, I doubt that anyone will be willing to help for fear of being implicated." He remained silent for a moment. "This Lucien you're to meet in Lille? Who is he?"

"He's the brother of my father's friend in Paris. They're of the Marceau family."

"Lucien Marceau. I don't know him."

"No. You wouldn't. He had nothing to do with any secret organisation that I know of. On the contrary, I'm not even sure what kind of reception there'll be for me. His daughter and I were friends as children and I'm hoping she'll remember that."

"Since my letter was safely delivered, at least you can assume that the letter to this Lucien Marceau reached its destination, too," Jean said. "Let's hope he doesn't have the Gestapo waiting for you." He slowed the lorry and checked the map insert. "You'll understand if I drop you off a block or two away. I have to return to Calais and I'd rather do that without an entourage of Boches on my heels, you understand. There's always the danger that your friend's house might be watched."

Claude nodded. "Of course."

"The other Marceau. The one in Paris. What's his Christian name?"

"Noe."

Jean looked at him sharply. "Doctor Noe Marceau?"

"You know him?"

"I certainly know of him. You'll be in good hands......if you can find him."

"What do you mean?"

"I think you'll find that he's one of us." Jean leaned forward and peered into the darkness. "We're here.....or near enough. Your address, I think, will be about three blocks west from where I drop you off."

As they shook hands Claude saw profound sadness in his friend's eyes. Although gathering intelligence for Britain before the war had always been a cautious operation, he was only now understanding the intense pressure the German presence in France had placed upon the people. During the ride from Calais, Jean described some of the cruel disciplinary punishments the enemy had inflicted upon the French people in order to instill submission and obedience. As a result of underground activities against the enemy, these punishments were becoming more and more frequent.

*   *   *

The Gestapo was not waiting for Claude at Lucien Marceau's house and neither was Michou. Lucien was reluctantly expecting him, and made it quite clear that he was not welcome.

"Your presence here is endangering our safety," he said. "I'm sorry but I have to think of us first. I must ask you to leave as quickly as possible."

"Do you know that I plan to find Noe in Paris?"

"Yes. Michou is also there working at the Sorbonne, but I choose not to be involved in their business. If you don't mind my saying so, I think you're on a fool's errand. How will you get back to England? You can't go back through the forbidden zone. Obviously you had the advantage of bad weather coming in, but the Germans keep a very sharp eye on the coastline under normal circumstances. You'll have to go south to Pau and then to the Spanish border over the Pyrenees, and in order to do that you'll probably have to cross the Somme and the Loire to get to the demarcation line. Even then, Vichy France is full of collaborators who would be willing to turn you in for payment." He shrugged. "I don't envy you. The so-called sanctity of Spain is less than secure, too." He eyed the steaming clothes impatiently.

Claude went over his plans yet again. He could not afford to ponder about the extended future after he left Paris.....if indeed, he left Paris at all. Lucien painted a grim picture which would be better forgotten in the long run. He did not want to lose his nerve now. But first things first. He would leave immediately if only to relieve Lucien's anxiety. Acutely aware of this situation, he donned his still damp clothes as the pale dawn spread along the eastern horizon, and accepted a cloth napkin of food from Lucien's wife, offering them both his gratitude and farewells.

Dubious that the bicycle Lucien had given him would last the approximate one hundred and fifty kilometres to Paris, he hoped his shoes would dry out sufficiently for him to walk with reasonable comfort. When he had struggled to the surface after his dinghy capsized, he tied his shoes around his neck by their laces, almost drowning in the process. But this precaution was merely to enable him to swim and did not prevent the shoes from getting drenched. His stomach had settled a little, but the November chill bit into his fingers and he peddled fast in order to keep warm. He did not find the menacing scrape of the bicycle chain against the cog particularly reassuring although he knew it was better than walking.

He decided to divide the journey into thirty kilometer increments in order to pace himself. He knew his general direction should be due south-south west and had ringed certain villages along the back roads on his rapidly drying Michelin map. His compass would keep him going generally in the proper direction and his labourer's clothing, although still faintly aromatic, plus the old cloth cap Jean had given him, should discourage curiosity. Only his ethnic background and comparative youth could cause problems should he be stopped and questioned. He had quickly learned to keep his head down as much as possible, and he peddled along musing over his Jewish birth. Odd that this issue had never been openly addressed in England--even in the Gentlemen's club in London. With his thoroughly English name, acquired Cambridge articulation, and bogus credentials his true background had gone unchallenged.

He arrived in Arras by nightfall feeling weak and feverish and began to search for a place to spend the night while there was enough light to see by. A small barn stood an approximate quarter kilometer from the road and he wearily pushed the bike toward it across an expanse of rutted ground. A little straw and hay lay about in the loft which made a passable bed when pushed into a pile. The hard cheese and crusty bread that Madam Marceau had given him scratched painfully at his inflamed throat as he swallowed it with difficulty; but he knew he must take nourishment in order to keep up his strength. With the bicycle hidden under some gunny sacks below, Claude burrowed into the hay above praying that he would be better the next morning. But sleep was elusive and it was several hours before he finally fell asleep.

He awoke with a start wondering what had disturbed him, but heard no sound. His clothes felt damp, but the burning in his throat had subsided; perhaps the fever had broken while he slept. Now wide awake, he knew further rest would be pointless and decided to continue the journey. He moved silently down the ladder and uncovered the bicycle below, then crept stealthily to the road knowing that even in winter farmers were up and about before dawn. With sheer determination he peddled southward aiming for Péronne on the west side of the Somme, and stopped only once to drink coffee at dawn in a tiny village a kilometer or so from Arras. By afternoon the weather had worsened as dark, low clouds dimmed the light into an eerie twilight and the temperature began to drop. As least this appeared to discourage outdoor activity to a degree and Claude made excellent time along the almost deserted country roads. Once, he came quickly round a sharp curve and saw, too late, a camouflaged lorry loaded with German soldiers parked by the road side. There was nothing else to do but keep going and he saw with relief that the men were far too preoccupied with relieving themselves into a road side ditch to notice a lone, unobtrusive labourer peddle by. By nightfall he saw an inviting haystack in a small field on the outskirts of Péronne and decided to settle there for the night. Again his strong constitution had pulled him through and although his throat was painful, he felt stronger. The wind had picked up and its chill had already numbed his face and hands before he stopped. Snuggling into the hay, he pulled his cap well down over his ears, and tucked his hands between his thighs for warmth feeling the soft caress of drowsiness already creeping over him. As he drifted into oblivion, he though about Péronne--and Janine.

They were there before the war, having arranged to meet in nearby Albert to exchange written information from headquarters, London. It was a beautiful day and although they were rarely seen in public together, they agreed to picnic near La Porte de Bretagne where there was little chance of them being observed. They wandered down to the Somme and its ponds in the Hardines and enjoyed the quietness of the vegetable gardens in the summer sun. He supposed there might have been opportunities for romance during their peacetime assignments together, yet as attractive as Janine was, she deftly maintained their relationship at a professional level. He remembered thinking that Henry Parke was one lucky devil. Then there was Yvonne. He smiled pleasurably, remembering the chance glimpse of her nakedness in Bayswater and the excitement of his encounter with her in the hotel cloakroom. The chances of it, or any other such experience happening again with her, were as remote as his surviving this present mission.

The next day brought a worrisome turn in events. Approaching the outskirts of Compèign--quietly dignified and steeped in history--he saw German soldiers everywhere. To avoid road blocks it was necessary to push the bicycle through a wide circle of forest land, adding several unwelcome kilometres to his heretofore almost accurate schedule. My papers should pass scrutiny, he thought, but I'm not so sure now that I will. He wondered what he should do to avoid being seen? Should he make yet another detour? Irritated that he should succumb to such intimidation, a quick recollection of past history consoled him. Compeigne had been the scene of Germany's own humiliation when they signed their surrender at the end of the Great War. This thought boosted his confidence a little. But the exact same railway carriage had been used in the local station only five months ago to sign the French armistice. Yet, the Germans did lose the last one. Surely it can happen again. With this encouragement bolstering his confidence, he made a bold decision. Any attempt to conceal himself might, in fact, only draw unwanted attention. Why not openly cross the Oise by the old Louis XV bridge? If he kept his head down, no one would even notice him. After all, a farm labourer would scarcely draw unusual attention. Within ten minutes he was safely across and quickly turned south, seeking a rural route that would take him on the last leg to Paris.

Although luck had prevailed so far, the mood of success that had kept his spirits up during the journey from Lille began to wane. Would Noe feel the same apprehension concerning Jews that his brother had so obviously demonstrated in Lille? Would Noe also consider him a threat to his safety?

"I think you'll find he's one of us" Jean had said.

Best to think along these lines. It would be foolish to be discouraged now.

Approaching Paris, he decided that his appearance should change from that of a peasant to something more urban. While expert in the acquisition of intelligence, there had never been occasion to turn his hand to actual theft; but late that night he broke into a small tailor shop and stole a suit of clothes. The shoes would have to do since another try at breaking and entering may not be so successful. He did, however, take the tailor's glasses from the counter and wore them well down the bridge of his nose since they were so powerful. They contributed admirably to the change in his appearance.

Noe Marceau lived in a large apartment near the Boulevard Saint-Michel in Paris. It was in the same building where Claude had grown up. Many of the intellectuals who were associated with the Sorbonne chose to reside in close proximity to their work and to the excellent libraries they frequented. Bone-weary, Claude approached the outer suburbs of Paris on foot having discarded the dilapidated bicycle at last. Surprisingly, it had served him well.

Although almost dark, the landmarks grew progressively familiar and awakened memories of an unusual and happy childhood. Both parents had been teachers, which largely contributed to his growing up in an atmosphere of higher learning and music. His mother coached members of the Opera and wrote and published accounts of music history, while his father's writings and teaching concerning the many facets of philosophy were highly respected. They were gentle people, never dreaming that they might be marked as a threat to anyone. But as the Teutonic dominance spread across Europe, it became obvious that Adolf Hitler felt that Jews were of a lesser race and a threat to Aryan supremacy. The massive roundups in Poland and Czechoslovakia were stark examples of his determination to be rid of them.

The atmosphere in Paris reflected Jean's observations. Although people seemed to be going about their business, the underlying trepidation seeped through the city like a satanic plague. Claude was immediately affected by it and felt his pulse quicken. As he approached the building he felt sure that someone followed him since he had been aware of the same light footsteps behind him for some time. He knew he was excessively alert and that perhaps his imagination was playing tricks. But the footsteps quickened as he turned the corner and saw to his dismay, two German soldiers coming toward him.

"Monsieur?" a female voice said softly from behind him. "Are you aware you are out after the curfew? Quickly! Pretend you know me very well and put your arms around me like a lover if you don't want to be arrested."

With no other alternative he obeyed, and she quickly urged him to turn away from the soldiers, keeping her arm tightly around his waist and led him back to the corner. Once out of sight from the soldiers, she grabbed his sleeve and pulled him along toward an almost concealed alley way which he immediately recognised as the back entrance to the building where he had once lived.

"In here! I'll take you to Noe."

There had been no time to study her face and although Claude knew she had most likely saved him from arrest, he also knew that following her blindly would be risky.

"Who are you?" he asked when they were well into the alley. "You can't expect me to........"

She turned to face him, putting her finger to her lips. "Shhh. It's been a long time," she said. "But surely you wouldn't forget Michou."

He looked down at the vaguely familiar face, remembering the vibrant brown eyes and ready smile. The shy child had blossomed into an attractive young woman who exuded confidence and a sense of intellect. Before he could speak, she urged him forward.

"Noe received your letter. What an ingenious idea to disguise it as lost mail! The Germans are always on the lookout for anything suspicious--and a British postmark would have certainly alerted them. But the date and the condition of the envelope--plus the innocent message inside if they had chosen

to examine it--must have diverted any reason to confiscate it."
She pointed toward a familiar gateway near the end of the alley.
"Obviously we must go in the back way. Noe's expecting you."

Perhaps he should not have been surprised when she led
him into the basement.

"The Germans have taken over our living quarters," she
said. "We're lucky that we can still use the basement. I have to
cook for them sometimes and Noe and I keep the stairways and
foyer clean. We hate it, but it's a good cover. We're not
allowed to enter any of the apartments, however."

The cellar door flew open as they approached and Noe
hustled them inside without a word. Once the door was safely
shut he embraced Claude, immediately assuring his young
friend of a warm welcome.

"Thank God you made it," he said. "But you should
never have come. Had I been able to respond to your brilliant
letter I could have saved you the trouble. You see, I know
you're here on personal business and can guess what it is." He
gestured to a small table. "Sit down. There's soup. You
should eat first."

Although hungry and desperately weary, Claude needed
a full explanation for Noe's pessimism.

"Paris is the most dangerous place in the country, and
you've come right into the middle of a foul nest of enemy
sadists whose methods of extracting information from suspect
members of the *Résistance* are so despicable they defy even the
most vivid of imaginations. I am speaking of our own
murderous French collaborators as well as the Germans
themselves. Also, my friend, they are purging the city of Jews
and have many ways of seeking them out....mostly by the
treachery of betrayal.....for payment."

"Were my parents betrayed in this manner?" Claude
asked angrily. "Did one of their so-called friends receive
payment for their detection and arrest just because they are
Jews?"

"There's no doubt they were betrayed, but it wouldn't have taken much to find your father, Claude. He's well-known and his lecture in Vienna had been advertised."

"Where are they, Noe? How can I find them and get them to safety?"

The old man looked quickly at Michou who was placing steaming bowls of soup on the table. Claude clenched his fists to stop them from trembling.

"Where are they?" he shouted.

"Be quiet!" Noe hissed. "Do you want to bring the entire German army into this basement?"

Claude fumbled for a chair and collapsed into it, aware that Noe waited for him to regain his composure. He held his face in his hands and took a deep breath.

"Where....are....they?" he whispered.

"We know your father has been taken to Poland. Your mother was in prison at Drancy for a while, but I hear that she too has been moved out of the country--probably to Germany."

Claude looked up into the drawn face and saw lines of grief. "Didn't anyone try to stop them?"

"The students tried, but their efforts resulted in three arrests and one known execution. Yes, Claude. Someone did try."

After a long silence, Claude felt Michou's light touch on his shoulder.

"Eat your soup," she said gently. "We have more to tell you."

Noe leaned forward in his chair. "Aren't you curious about Michou meeting you just now? Don't you want to know how she found you so easily?"

Concern for his parents had prevailed and Noe's question startled him. How had Michou managed to be there at the precise time of his arrival?

"You've been watched since you arrived in Lille," Michou said. "Noe knew you would go first to my father's house in Lille after making contact with Jean Decour."

"How do you know Jean?" Claude asked sharply.

"I'm sure you detected that Lucien did not want you in his house," Noe said, ignoring the question. "You see he does not know....or want to know....of our involvement."

"What involvement?" Even as he asked the question he remembered Jean's comment that Noe was quite likely "one of us". It was obvious now that pockets of resistance were working against the Germans and operating remotely. But it stood to reason that each pod would know certain names associated with the hub of activities in Paris. Jean had known of Noe. Noe, then, must be extremely involved in the cohesion of resistance activities.

A flicker of amusement quirked the side of Noe's mouth as he put down his spoon. "I've always known of your long time involvement with British Intelligence, Claude. I've always known, you see, because I have done similar work for the French service de renseignements. Although I haven't seen you for a long time, I do have this." He held out a recent identification file photograph.

Stunned, Claude stared at his own image. "What else do you know?"

"We know who Dierick is."

Claude waited for a wave of lightheadedness to pass.

"We also know that she was involved in the arrest of your parents," Noe went on.

His mouth twitched downwards at the corners for a brief moment and he took a deep breath. "The Germans pulled out everything your father had ever written and burned it, making him and your mother watch. They did the same thing to six others....all Jews. Then they herded them together and drove them away in the back of a lorry."

"That .....bitch!" Claude staggered to his feet, dashing away hot tears. "She will pay for this?"

Michou took his hand. "Sit down, Claude, and listen. Many Parisians have joined the resistance, among them the students who have gone underground to avoid the German labour camps. They are as angry as you are, and have already demonstrated a degree of defiance. The organisation is growing rapidly and the interference they ran in German operations in the beginning is expanding in both range and importance." She nodded toward Noe, inviting him to continue.

"Our particular headquarters is at the Musée de l'Homme in the Palaise de Chaillot," he said. "A good cover, don't you think?" He grinned impishly. "Now, you could just return to England by continuing south. But there is another alternative. You could join the partisans. We're already receiving a great deal of cooperation from the Free French in England and elsewhere and, thanks to the British Prime Minister, there is also considerable support for more plans and supplies. We are regularly receiving coded messages from the Free French through the British Broadcasting Corporation and know a great deal about the situation in England. You could try to get back, but you could also be a great asset to our cause here in France. We are hoping to accumulate weapons and are readying acts of sabotage and assassination as I speak. If you wish to avenge your parents and, at the same time, help us to prepare an uprising from a quickly growing underground army when the time comes for Britain to invade the European mainland, then join us."

"Britain is on its knees, Noe," Claude said. "The enemy has bombarded the major cities to such a massive extent, incurring hundreds of civilian casualties, I don't know how long the indomitable spirit can keep going. Coventry has been literally burned to the ground, and London is still undergoing a ruthless and seemingly endless blitzkrieg. Convoys bearing food and supplies in the Atlantic are being lost to U-boat attacks at an alarming rate and there is a risk of starvation. The RAF is rallying, but it seems to be a pitiful bleat from the Imperial Lion. I don't know how they can continue, let alone even consider the invasion of France."

"Are you saying we should succumb to this Führer maniac? Are you prepared to live the rest of your life as a slave? In your case, you don't have a chance of surviving at all, Claude."

Burying his face in his hands, Claude pressed his fingers against aching temples. He knew he had no alternative as he thought again of his parents and the crushing presence of the Germans in Europe. Hate rose like black poison within him. If he was destined to be killed anyway, then he would die fighting for release from this tyrannical menace. As well, he could focus upon another diabolical target who was the woman named Beatrix Dierick.

CHAPTER ELEVEN

England, November, 1940

David lay quietly listening to Patrick Kennedy read a letter to him.

"She says everything is fine. Didn't you say she lived somewhere in south London?" Patrick asked. "If everything is really fine, old boy, it must be something of a miracle. That part of the London suburbs has taken a beating, I can tell you."

"What's the post mark?"

"I can't tell--it's smudged." Patrick hesitated. "How old is this girl? I mean, she writes a nice letter, but she seems quite....well....young."

"She must be about ten or eleven," David said.

Patrick whistled through his teeth. "Yet you named your Hurry after her?"

"It's odd, Pat, but she somehow keeps me going. She's had a couple of pretty ghastly experiences and yet seems to cope with them. Sounds inane, but she gives me the courage to go on."

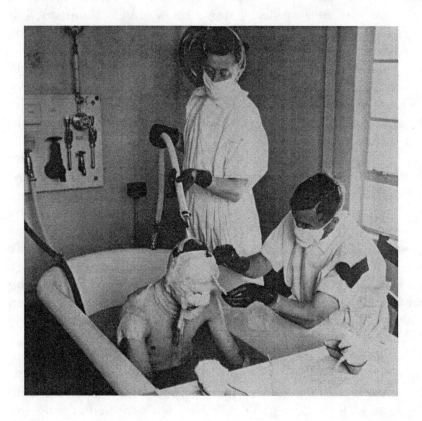

The Saline Bath
(With kind permission of Robert Marchant, The Guinea Pig
Museum, Queen Victoria Hospital, East Grinstead, England)

(iii)

"She sketches very well. When the bandages come off you'll see for yourself. This one is particularly good…..they must be her friends." Patrick laughed. "There's even an excellent one of a spider! I don't know much about art, but she's captured the expressions of the children perfectly and you can almost sense the mood of each child."

Although the incessant bombing of London continued, the constant parade of the young men in Ward III underwent progressive surgery for their hideous injuries. Rallying under the strict nutritious buildup, David began to gain a little weight and certainly felt stronger.

He had heard about the infamous saline bath at the end of the room and wondered about the amount of uninhibited yelling that come from its direction. Yet as he was helped into the soothing warmth of its waters a few days later, he questioned the protests of the others. He felt his limbs relax as tense muscles responded to the soft embrace of the waters. He felt the gentle touch of someone unwinding the bandage around his eyes and hands. That day he learned that yelling helped alleviate pain as dead skin and tannic acid-induced scabs, now well infused into the gauze dressing and stubbornly stuck to the tender pink residue beneath, was bathed away.

After the treatment he was taken back to his bed to await a fresh pressure dressing. He peered across the ward at the bleary outlines of the beds opposite and saw the dim shadows of his fellow patients. Salty tears formed rapidly and began to trickle over the ultra tender skin below his eyes inducing more excruciating pain. He looked down at the blurred raw mass on the back of his hands and fingers and tried to focus.

"I can't see properly," he muttered. "Why can't I see?"

"Your temporary eyelids are oversized, Pilot Officer Parke," the Matron said, approaching him with the dressing trolley. "Hold your head back and look at things from under them. There, that's better, isn't it? Anyway, Mr. McIndoe is on his way and, after he's seen you, we'll redress your eyes and you won't be able to see at all again for awhile."

The young surgeon arrived almost immediately exuding an air of talent, experience, empathy, and efficiency. A stocky man with large, surprisingly gentle hands he made a rapid examination of David's injuries.

"I believe in telling the truth," Archibald McIndoe said. "I'm sure you'd rather I didn't try to skirt the issue." Behind the dark-rimmed spectacles the brown eyes twinkled. "You got off comparatively lightly," he said. "Your plunge into the salt waters of the English Channel could quite likely have served to prevent even worse scarring. The fact that you must have kept your head down after removing the oxygen mask and goggles prevented less severe burns to the lower part of your face. You realise, of course that discarding the mask merely helped to feed oxygen to the flames."

David remembered struggling with the Sutton straps and his subsequent fast exit from the cockpit once he had managed to open the hatch.

"Your helmet buckle obviously became red hot because you have a nasty place on the front of your neck and we may have to patch a section along the right jaw line and certainly a couple of areas on your hands," the surgeon went on. "You'll probably take a smaller glove size after it's all over, and you won't have any identifiable finger prints, but at least you should be able to keep and use all of your fingers. We'll just have to wait and see. I know this sounds discouraging, David, but it could have been so much worse. Look around you. I can't promise to bring you back to the way you looked before; but I think I can make you quite presentable."

"I wish I could look around," David said. "But my eyes keep watering and I can't see under these horse blinkers I have for eyelids."

"Well, we'll do something about that soon. Is there any soreness around the donor area?"

231

David had not given a thought to where his temporary eyelids might have come from. Obviously they must have come from somewhere.

"What?"

"I took skin from the under side of your upper arm."

He remembered then that they had shaved him there and assumed it was merely for hygienic purposes when giving morphia.

"I wish you hadn't mentioned that," he said. "Now it's beginning to hurt."

McIndoe smiled ruefully. "Both upper and lower lids were badly burned," he said. "As the swelling subsided the scarring began to retract. Initially you couldn't blink at all and the major risk then was damage to the eyes themselves. It isn't unusual for the first graftings to also retract and we have to graft on new ones. As before, we have to take skin from a donor section. Perhaps we'll flatten your stomach a bit next time."

David sucked in his already concave abdomen apprehensively.

Archibald McIndoe gestured to a nurse. "Redress the eyes and hands. We'll take him back to surgery in a day or so."

He grinned at David. "Perhaps those brilliant aircraft designers will learn to put a self-sealing auxiliary tank in the Hurricane's nose in future. Why the devil they didn't do it in the first place, I can't even begin to guess."

David wanted this remarkable man to stay with him and keep talking. He found himself clinging to every word and tried desperately to see the stocky figure until the gauze pads and bandages blocked his vision.

"He's quite a man, isn't he?" Patrick said.

David inclined his head toward the voice. "Where have you been? I couldn't see much beyond the end of my bed, but I had hoped you'd be here when he came in. You're right. He is a remarkable man."

"You two have a visitor," Matron said. "He seems like a lively young man, so I've already warned him to keep his hands to himself around the nurses; and that moustache is the most extraordinary thing I've ever seen!"

Rupert needed no introduction. He breezed into the ward exuding his usual panache and dash, plying the nurses with glib and sardonic wit. David heard the footfalls falter as they came toward him.

"Patrick?" Rupert's voice wavered only slightly.

"Yes, old boy. It's me. Look chaps, I'll go and find us some tea. Back in a jiffy."

David felt the weight of Rupert's hands on his bed. "Have you seen him?"

"Who?"

"Patrick."

"No. He's never here when I have to have my eyes re-dressed. Is he.....bad?"

"Yes."

"I don't know what I'd do without him, Rupert. He keeps me up with all the news and reads my letters to me. I didn't know how bad he was. He never complains."

"Extraordinary chap!" Rupert said softly. "We've all been put up for gongs and promotions. All of us. If you ask me, old Pat should get much, much more than that."

"Thank you for letting me know. McIndoe tells me I'm luckier than most."

"Are your eyes all right?"

"They will be when they give me some new eyelids. Not sure about the hands, but I think they'll be fine eventually. Can't wait to get back to flying."

"Right. Well, for your information you are surrounded here by a bevy of beautiful nurses. I shouldn't be in a hurry to get out if I were you."

"What's this I hear about an extraordinary moustache? Why would you want a thing like that crawling along your upper lip?"

"Marvelous lady lure. I was invited in to tea after dropping into someone's back garden cucumber frame on the end of my parachute last week. Having done a hundred percent write-off on the cucumber frame, I doubt very much if the lady would have been half as benevolent if I hadn't had the old mostacho. It's a bit itchy when the insects get in it, but other than that, it's quite the thing."

"I'll take your word for it."

"We've been called The Few, you know," Rupert went on. "Never have so many owed so much…….."

"Yes, I heard about Winnie's speech."

"Well, the old boy is proud of us."

"How are you coping with all the mud at Acklington?"

"Oh, I don't stay up there much. Get into London at any excuse. I suppose you know your mother lent me DDI until you're back on your feet."

"Now there's something that must deter the ladies. I mean, it is rather obvious, isn't it?"

"They love it! You'll see for yourself when you're mobile again."

David felt a stab of pain glance through his bandaged hands. "Not that I'll be attracting the ladies much when all this is over."

"Rot!" Rupert leaned closer. "You look a hell of a lot better than most in here. At least you've got lips. Give it time. By the way, do you have any idea where your mother might be? She told me that DDI would be in front of your place in Bayswater for me to pick up, and it was. I've tried to contact her a few times by telephone, but haven't had any luck."

"She's always busy," David said. "Although, come to think of it, I haven't heard from her lately, either. I'll have to see what my father knows. He's in and out of here all the time."

"Well, I'd just like to thank her properly, that's all."

"How is Treacle…..and I suppose there's still no word of George?"

Rupert remained silent.

"Come on, Rupert. Out with it."

"Well, good old Treacle won't be playing much cricket, I'm afraid. He came a cropper a mile out from Margate shooting down a Dornier 18 Red Cross Flying Boat."

"What? What was he doing shooting down rescue craft?"

"Well, we discovered that the bastards were using them to spy on our shipping. Treacle got back all right. But he nearly bled to death having been hit by a lone wolf Me109. There's a bit missing now, actually…….like his left hand."

David shifted his position slightly. He wondered how Rupert must feel now that all the "old boys" who took part in the deadly battles before the London blitz were in a bad way. All except Rupert. He heard him sigh.

"No word concerning George, I'm afraid. Odd really, because he's not listed as a prisoner. Apparently he didn't go into the drink because his aeroplane was photographed on a French beach by a reconnaissance job……pretty much a wreck, but the identifications were readable. No sign of the pilot, of course."

Approaching footsteps announced Patrick's return.

"Look who I found," he said.

David turned toward the chink of teacups and hoped that Patrick had remembered not to fill his too full.

Rupert whistled softly. "That," he said. "is the most gorgeous woman I've ever set eyes on. Who is she, Pat?"

David heard quick footsteps approaching and grinned to himself as Rupert, for once, was speechless.

"You mean you haven't met the lovely Yvonne?" Patrick said. "Rupert this is David's sister."

Rupert muttered something unintelligible.

"You're looking much better, David," Yvonne said.

"That's a pretty shrewd observation considering you can't see anything for bandages," David laughed. "Actually, I'm due for the chop soon for more new eyelids. What is it, Pat? Ectropic something-or-other?"

"The second set," Patrick said. "They'll keep trying until they get it right. You'll just have to be a patient patient."

The pain in David's hands and across his eyes rapidly increased and he tried desperately to endure it. The tender oozing skin, now exposed to the pressure of gauze and bandages, felt as if nails were being pounded into it. Yet he was loathe to end the visit by asking for morphia. He did not know when he would again hear those familiar voices around him. He tried to keep still, but the white hot searing spasms caused his body to involuntarily jerk and he knew he would not be able to bear it much longer.

"Well," Rupert said. "The Hun undoubtedly will return at dusk, and we should be well on our way by then."

Whether Patrick had given them a signal or they were aware of his agony themselves, he did not know. But now he was most anxious for them to leave.

"See…if you can…track down Mother," he gasped. "Rupert wants to….thank…her."

"Of course, David. I'm sure father knows where she is."

* * *

"I've heard David speak of you often," Yvonne said, as she and Rupert left Ward III.

"Well, he's certainly been hiding you!"

"Not really. I'm very busy. I do, in fact, have to be back at White Waltham this evening, but should go to

Bayswater en route."

Rupert held the car door open for her. "I'm completely at your service," he said, clicking his heels.

She smiled at the highly polished bonnet of the car. Rupert was obviously taking good care of it. At dusk, as they skirted Kensington Gardens, they could hear the faint throb of bomber engines in the distance.

"Here they come again," Rupert sighed.

"Look," Yvonne said. "Perhaps I'd better take my chances and go by train. I'll go to Bayswater another time. Perhaps, if you would drop me off at the railway station......"

"I think it might be too late," Rupert said, peering upwards through the windscreen. "Old Nasty Nazi is almost here."

They could hear the Bofors in the park already putting up a defencive barrage.

"Everyone else is scurrying to shelter," Rupert went on. "Don't you think we should follow suit?"

"But what about you? Aren't you supposed to return to Acklington?"

Rupert shook his head. "Actually, I wasn't going back until tomorrow. Believe it or not, there's still a bit of night life in London and I'd be more than happy to show you some of it.....after this nuisance is over." The moustache tilted suggestively.

Yvonne looked at her watch.

"Perhaps it won't last as long this time," she shouted, as the noise of the aerial armada grew louder. "If we hurry, we could get to Bayswater. At least we could have a cup of tea there."

Rupert pressed his foot down on the accelerator. From the direction of smoke columns they could see the raid had started in the East End, but was rapidly drawing nearer. They ran up the steps of the house, clutching at their tin hats. Inside Yvonne hurried through the blacked out rooms, feeling her way to the lamps and turning them on. The place smelt musty from disuse and she could only assume that Charlie was with Mrs. Dougherty.

She remembered the last air raid she had spent in the company of a man and quickly dashed that memory away. Never at a loss for male company in the past, perhaps the war with all its horror had heightened the importance of special relationships. Yet conversely, she felt that the war also discouraged anything too permanent or binding. But George often came to mind and, in spite of their ongoing verbal battle and his tactless blunders, his ready wit and easy presence created a challenge that excited her. Foolish to dwell on that since he might easily be dead and, if she allowed it, she would grieve for him.

While Ben presented an entirely different image, she felt a certain attraction to him, too. Perhaps this simply stemmed from that brief moment of mutual desire in the hotel. Yet the aura of mystery that surrounded him both baffled and irritated her and she had pointedly dismissed him from her mind. Now this new acquaintance was decidedly attractive, but she had every intention of keeping this friendship on a purely platonic level.

She focused the conversation on the war and things in general.

"David has said very little about the dreadful attrition in the squadron," she said. "I suppose it's a sort of unwritten law not to talk about that."

Rupert nodded. "No point in dwelling on it. If we did, we'd never get back in our aeroplanes."

"I....I suppose there has been no further word concerning George Ravensbrook?"

Rupert glanced quickly at her. "It stands to reason, of course, that you would have known him. Wasn't he at Oxford with David?"

"Yes."

Rupert sighed. "No further word," he said.

With that subject obviously closed, they talked of other things until the mighty mass of bombers withdrew at last.

"It's almost dawn," she said, peering through a chink in the blackout curtain. "Thank heavens I won't be delivering aircraft today. I'd probably fall asleep in the cockpit."

"I've done that before," Rupert said, ruefully. "Sometimes I couldn't remember how I managed to get from the aircraft to the Mess after doing battle with the Hun."

"Thank God for the RAF," Yvonne said. "We'd probably all be in German labour camps by now if it weren't for the likes of you."

Rupert shrugged. "We do our best."

There seemed to be something uncanny about the Daimler and its newly appointed driver. In spite of cascading debris, raining shrapnel, and fallen trees, the car appeared to be unscathed.

But progress toward west London was slow and Yvonne began to wonder if they would ever emerge from the great expanse of utter devastation. The familiar facets of great old building were crumbled, blackened, or completely disintegrated. Wardens diverted pedestrians and traffic in order to avoid areas where men worked in huge craters repairing cables and pipes that were the vital links to power, communication, support and sustenance. Forced to ignore the constant threat of cave-ins that would bury them alive in clay and mud, the unsung heroes of the continued bombings toiled with expedience and skill. Beyond barricaded streets, she saw exhausted firemen who continued to fight massive blazing skeletal infernos that had once been architectural gems. Snake pits of hoses writhed together along puddled streets carrying inadequate streams of water from the River Thames that was unfortunately at its lowest annual tide.

As they passed the intersection of one narrow street, a multistoried building began to collapse, appearing to crumple and topple in slow motion.

"Christ," Rupert shouted, yanking the steering wheel away from the impending cascade. The fiery mass plummeted down in a mass of red-hot mortar and timber with a mighty roar. Several firemen stumbled and tripped over the hoses in their attempt to get clear and were quickly overcome by debris that buried them in a smoldering conclusive grave.

"Oh, dear God!" Yvonne could not stop the uncontrollable shaking of her body as Rupert slammed on the brakes and leapt from the car. She sat paralyzed as he ran toward the devastation.

"Get back!" a Warden shouted brokenly. "There's nothing you can do."

As the dust cleared, she saw one end of a large fire hose protruding from its connection with a half-submerged pump wagon. It lay like a dead serpent with its head buried somewhere in the middle of the gargantuan heap. Beside it lay one solitary Wellington boot.

It was not until they reached the outer borders of Slough that they were able to move faster. Both remained silent, dealing with the horror they had just witnessed. Watching the passing scene from the car window Yvonne's heart went out to the people. Some stood in bewilderment in front of their ruined homes wondering what to do next. Others were busily sweeping debris from their front walks, while still others made obvious efforts to get to their daily place of work, stepping determinedly over rubble and accepting lifts on any form of transportation that was available. A nicely dressed girl climbed gratefully up on a rag and bone cart, now being used for salvage collection. She sat beside the bemused driver and shouted encouraging words to his old horse as he plodded along. Yvonne wondered how long it would take them to get through all the damaged roads and subsequent detours. She tried to remember what part of London the Mallory's evacuees had come from and hoped they were all right. Kate Hawkins had been so instrumental in keeping David's spirits up with her droll letters and clever sketches. She must remember to ask him when he had last heard from her.

"I heard about your Dunkirk escapade," Rupert was saying. "And now here you are facing daily adverse conditions flying aeroplanes all over the place. I do wonder what kind of stuff you Parkes are made of. I understand your mother is a pilot, too."

"A grounded one."

Yvonne wondered if indeed her mother were grounded. She had obviously not been in Bayswater for some time and her father indicated earlier that she had not visited him at his cottage, either. It was evident that Mrs. Dougherty had been told not to bother with cleaning until further notice and must have taken Charlie with her. Since Flint House was virtually shut down, where then, was her mother?

Perhaps, she thought, the Free French was in touch with her, too. She felt a stab of foreboding. Suppose her mother had already gone to France on some kind of secret mission.

"Will you always be flying trainers?" Rupert asked.

"What? Oh, no. I'm due to go to the RAF Central Flying School to qualify for Class Two classification."

The orders had arrived just before she left White Waltham indicating that she should report to Ulsworth this very day. Yet the likelihood of her being whisked into some other kinds of training by the French seemed quite possible, too. She wondered how one entity would tolerate the other if it came to that point and decided that this would be entirely their problem.

"We have to literally "wing" it with all the aircraft we fly for the first time because we are given no notes of instruction," she said. "I've learned to fly certain aircraft while taxi-ing to the runway. It occurs to me that I could probably fly anything they want to hand out, but you know how things have to be done by the book--not to mention they are still not keen to entrust operational aircraft to the female contingency of ATA."

"I haven't heard of too many accidents though," Rupert said.   "I mean, it wouldn't be possible to have a completely clean slate, now would it?"

"Because of male prejudice we have tried that much harder and our safety record is exemplary. Watch out, Rupert Barlow, you might see me delivering a Hurricane or a Spitfire before you know it!"

"Well, although the bombing of London couldn't be more despicable, it has taken the primary emphasis off Fighter Command and given it time to recover.   Perhaps you'll be ferrying one to me one of these days," Rupert said.

"Perhaps I will."

Upon reporting in, she found that her orders for Ulsworth were on track. With no word from her mother, or from the Free French, she decided to focus entirely upon flying. There was little point in agonising over probabilities or possibilities, especially those over which she had little control.

*   *   *

Kent, January, 1941

A miniature cyclone spun over the stubble of the Kentish cornfield across the road, whipping up flurries of chaff as it passed.   The last of the poppies, their black button eyes contrasting with fading red petals, pranced like Spanish dancers for a brief moment and then sank back to the cold earth to finish the business of dying.   As the flurry passed, naked branches rattled a belated accompaniment of castanets and draped a moving mantilla of lacy twigs against the sky.   At the top of the road, Kate could see the woods, austere without their summer finery, yet beckoning to be explored. Perhaps, she thought, I could push Annie in the pram there today.

Her grandfather stirred from his afternoon nap beside the fire and tapped his briar pipe against the hearth.

"A penny for your thoughts," he said, filling the bowl from a soft leather bag.

"I'm not sure they're worth that much," she said. "But I'd give any money to have things back the way they were."

The old man puffed aromatic smoke into the room, squinting his eyes.

"Never mind, Kate. At least we're all still alive."

Since Kent lay directly within the approach of the German bombing routes, Canterbury had been a victim of spontaneous bombings and strafings. While the community feared for their lives, it also looked protectively toward the grand old cathedral that stood steeped in aeons of history. The Stour River ambled its way past the small rural suburb of Thanington where Kate's grandfather lived, and cut a marshy swath through fields dotted with grazing sheep. No doubt a placid and pleasant setting for a child, yet she again felt the deep pangs of loneliness.

She looked at Annie gurgling happily in her pram. How nice it would be, she thought, to be like that again. She isn't aware that our mother has been whisked away to the highlands of Scotland in order to get over a touch of tuberculosis; or that our brother is also institutionalised until he can remember who he is and find his tongue. She doesn't know that censored letters arrive from time to time from our father which give little account of where he is or how he feels.

After all of them had been checked and cleared for tuberculosis since they had been exposed to the virus by their mother, Hugh was immediately taken to the relative quiet and safety of the northwest He had not spoken since being rescued, neither did he appear to recognise any of his family or

friends. The doctor said he was suffering from extreme shock.
His blank look and complete submission had frightened Kate,
and he constantly haunted her thoughts.

With the overcrowding of schools, she attended only
three afternoons a week which left her with a good deal of time
on her hands. Having sketched everything in sight and sent
the drawings off to Tangmere for David, she turned her
attention to the care of her widowed grandfather and her baby
sister. BC had reluctantly made the train journey from London
in a paper carrier bag and had already claimed his territory
around the Kentish house and garden. BQ, bearing the stains
of war, retained his special spot in the middle of Kate's bed.

As she pushed the pram along the lane toward the copse
she realised that her twelfth birthday had passed uncelebrated.
Never mind, she thought, there wasn't much in the way of
celebrations for Christmas, either.

"Hey! You!" someone shouted. "You 'n evacuee?"

Two boys in their early teens approached and barred her
way. She looked at them with distaste, noting the creases of
dirt around their necks and the grime under their fingernails.
Apart from anything else, she did not know the answer to their
question. Was she an evacuee again?

The taller boy grabbed her arm. "Isn't that a London
school uniform? We're from London, too."

Kate did not like the look of them at all. It wasn't just
that they were dirty and, by their strong Cockney accents
obviously from the East End of London, but more because they
were leering at her. Still holding her arm, the boy ogled her
from head to toe.

"She's got bumps under her jumper, Stan. Shall we find
out what else she's got?"

The smaller boy grinned.

Kate eyed her gas mask box laying at the foot of the
pram and wondered how much damage it might do as a
weapon.

"Pretty, ain't she.   Wonder if she's from Wapping?"

"I'm not!" Kate snapped.

The boy's grip tightened, hurting her arm.

"This should be fun," he said.   "We've caught a posh one."

He tried to push her toward the copse, prying her fingers loose from the pram handle.   Kate knew very little about the facts of life, but she did know something frightful was about to happen to her.   The boy ripped her blazer open, tearing the buttons away from the fabric, and pushed his filthy hand under the welt of her pullover.

"Stop it!" she screamed.   "Stop!"

As his other grimy hand went over her mouth she reached frantically for the gas mask box.   Now both vile hands were cold against her ribs as he groped higher.   With strength bolstered by panic, she whipped her meagre weapon down across his back.

"Get away from me!" she yelled, swinging the box above her head, gyro-fashion.   As the boy again lunged for her, the corner of the gas mask box slammed into the side of his head.   Blood oozed from his ear and he stared incredulously at a sampling of it on the end of his finger.   Now obviously seething with anger, he took another step toward her.

"Come on, Stan.   Give me a hand with this little cow."

Kate swung the box again, yelling at the top of her lungs, and successfully delivered both boys direct blows to their heads, one after the other.

"Here, I've had enough of this," Stan said, glancing warily over his shoulder. "Come on, Sid, she's making enough noise to bring out the entire police force."

Still unconvinced that Kate could fend him off, Sid again lunged at her only to receive another direct hit in the face from the corner of the gas mask box.   Now with another freely bleeding wound on his cheek, he hunched his shoulders, glowering with utter venom.   Kate waited, her heart rattling against her ribs.   Suddenly, a ginger streak shot through the air and landed squarely in the middle of Sid's back where it clung with deeply imbedded claws.   Hollering like a frustrated bull, Sid took off at a gallop with BC clinging painfully to his back while Stan scampered off in the other direction.

Although unhurt, Kate looked down at her torn blazer through a haze of tears.   If it's not one thing, she thought, it's another.   The war is ruining my entire life.   Grandpa doesn't seem to know I'm in the house half the time, and Annie is such a big responsibility.   Now I've had to contend with nasty boys who have nastier intentions.   Even growing up is a disappointment with all the strange feelings and changes I don't like or want.   Lately, I feel so confused and mixed up.   I do wish I were a baby again.

As if in response, Annie began to cry.

"Oh, please do shut up," Kate said.   "Can't you see it's my turn to cry?"

Annie cried harder.

"Oh, it's all right!   I said we would go to the woods, and that's exactly what we'll do."

The crying stopped and the wind felt cool and soothing against Kate's cheek as she pushed the pram uphill toward the trees.   Her skin crept as she again felt the impact of Sid's dirty hands against it.   Never doubting that BC would be able to take care of himself, she nonetheless began to worry about him. She was sure the boys would be quite capable of killing him--if they could catch him.

At the edge of the copse, she stopped and looked up, ready to savour the sounds and smells of winter.   The jagged scar from the injury in her scalp still felt sore to the touch and sometimes, when she tilted her head back in this manner, the pain returned.   She half-closed her eyes against the light to better determine the varying shades of the branches.   Some day, she thought, I want to be a real artist.

A strange gap in the topmost branches directly above

puzzled her and she moved to get a different point of view. A blackened tunnel descended from the opening and continued through the trees into the gloom below, ending in the underbrush perhaps a hundred yards from her. She pushed the pram as far as she could and then left it in a clearing while she went on. A single, brief shaft of sunlight dappled the tree trunks ahead and highlighted the unmistakable colours of an RAF roundel dangling in the upper branches. She stood transfixed staring at the half-burned wing section. How stupid I am, she thought. Why has it never occurred to me that there must be a reason for David's silence? Is he dead? Is he badly hurt? Could the Hurricane named Hawkins be in fragments like this one? Had the pilot been carried away in a coffin like Mr. Mallory, or was he safe? The charred channel seemed to spin before her eyes, and the wind in the trees moaned in sympathy.

*   *   *

May, 1941

David talked over the latest war news with other patients in Ward III. Although the intense and continuous blitzing of London temporarily ended on November 13th, it had not marked a complete cessation of the air raids. Yet the bad winter weather, and Hitler's diverted attention toward Russia, North Africa, the Mediterranean and the Middle East had resulted in some relief.

From under his second set of eyelids which were showing signs of complete success, he glanced at Patrick's empty bed and wondered how his friend's operation might be progressing. In making comparisons and evaluations over the long weeks of surgery and recovery, David considered himself fortunate since he had been able to leave the hospital with Rupert once or twice and enjoy a bit of normalcy in the rustic haunts of East Grinstead. Archibald McIndoe had forewarned the townspeople that his patients were brutally disfigured, but he also assured them that beneath the burned skin lived very normal young men. Even so, David had dreaded the first time, knowing that he looked far from presentable.

Just before Christmas, and after the dressings had been removed from his second set of eyelids, he caught sight of his reflection in an aluminium instrument dish.   Allowing for normal distortion due to the bowl's rounded sides, he nonetheless could see the angry concentration of mercurochrome across the upper half of his face, and the odd shaped skin around his eyes as the grafted eyelids began to settle and shrink to a normal size. He could also see the red, ropy scars across his forehead and along the right jaw line which met with a knot of keloid tissue on his neck. Ah yes, he remembered, the red hot buckle on the flying helmet strap. He reasoned with Matron that since he had seen a warped version of himself in the dish, was it not about time that they allowed him a mirror? This usual commodity was discouraged in the wards for obvious reasons. Daily shaving, which would normally require a mirror, was a minimal necessity since most graftings had been taken from hairless donor areas. In any case, new patients were too badly burned to even think about shaving.

In the privacy of Matron's office, he saw his facial injuries for the first time. In retrospect, he understood why mirrors were discouraged. Yet by comparison to others in the ward, he knew that he had been lucky.

"Patience is a good healer," Matron had said. "Those scars will be reduced in time and graftings applied. Instead of the obvious welts you can see now, the scars should be much paler.   Distortion due to atrophy is corrected and.......there you are!"

          After the burns on his hands had been treated in the saline bath and the scabs and blistering reduced, he felt more optimistic about his ability to eventually use them. But Archie had explained that the scar contraction of the dorsal skin and some fixation of the extensor tendons, together with the pull of the flexor tendons would most likely cause his fingers to draw down toward the palm like a claw, as Patrick's had. If this happened, then he would simply do all he could to strengthen them even if the pain might be unbearable. Wasn't he used to pain by now?

          Although the staff of Ward III had excelled in their efforts to make the Christmas season as bright as possible for their patients, the continuing menace of the air raids, shortages of food, cold weather, sober news from the BBC, and an influx of new burn patients contributed to the dampening of any attempted festivities.   Yet the report of alcohol, loud music, and general mayhem in the ward, reached the highest echelons of the RAF medical department and the apparent lack of discipline was subsequently questioned.   Archibald McIndoe however, having refused a commission in that service, was not obliged to adhere to military directions and followed his own highly   successful   programme   of   both   physical   and psychological healing. He allowed no semblance of self-pity to creep into the ward and, if it did, all the patients rebelled against the would-be complainer.   While well aware that they would bear both physical and emotional scars of war in many ways, the camaraderie and mutual empathy, encouraged by their beloved surgeon and his staff, maintained a remarkable level of optimism.   David had returned home to Bayswater for Christmas dinner, and while his family were splendid in their obvious attempts at normalcy, he nonetheless felt relieved when it was time to return to the now-familiar atmosphere and comradeship of Ward III.

A week ago, David underwent his fifteenth operation--
this time on his hands.   He glanced again at Patrick's bed.
Although operations were part of the weekly routine, this one in
particular bore special significance. Braced for his first glimpse
of Patrick's face some months back, he had nonetheless been
shocked. Then the pedicle was in its last stages before being
detached and he had joyfully anticipated the newly formed nose
with his friend.   But in spite of meticulous care and sterile
procedures, a haemolytic streptococcal infection had rampaged
through Ward III causing many of the pedicles and grafts to go
bad. Even though they had heard that a new medical discovery
called Penicillin was in its laboratory state, it was not yet
available. Until it was, no true effective combatant offered itself
against such devastating bacterial infection. After all the long
weeks of waiting and hoping, Patrick's new nose became
infected, along with the pedicle and his new upper lip. Always
cheerful, and the pillar of strength that the others looked
toward, Patrick had wept with angry frustration and, this time,
no one felt inclined to accuse him of self-pity.

David lowered his new eyelids, rejoicing now that he
could completely close his eyes, and tried to think about
something other than Patrick's surgery.

The clear days of May had brought another upsurge of
aerial attacks on all parts of Britain and another exceptionally
heavy nightlong bombing raid on London on the full moon
night of the 11th.   The BBC reported that this raid severely
shocked the true Londoner since Westminster Hall, along with
its famous school and the Abbey and Deanery were badly
damaged as was the British Museum Library, Scotland Yard
and every main line railway station. Sadly, St. Clement Danes'
bells, which prompted the composition of the nursery rhyme
Oranges and Lemons were silenced forever.

David thought often of young Kate Hawkins and eagerly
looked forward to her letters and sketches that continued to
reach him from Canterbury.   Just after Christmas she had

asked pointedly if he were hurt and he wondered how she knew.   He responded in a light-hearted manner, through a First Aid Nursing Yeomanry (FANY) girl who wrote the letter from his dictation, saying that he had been injured a bit, but was rapidly on the mend.   He also told her that Flint House was now a military convalescent home, omitting the fact that the men there were recovering from psychological disorders caused by their war experiences.   The nurse, Philippa, returned often to continue the favour.   To his surprise, she began to show more than just a benevolent interest in him and although he was not similarly attracted, it did convey that he might still be socially acceptable.

"Personality helps," Pat said.   "You're quite a charmer, you know."

"Rubbish!"

Yet in spite of himself, David smiled, remembering Jenny and her obvious attempts to waylay him on the stairs at Flint House.   She came to his bedroom once, and had just begun to make her intentions known when Mrs. Dougherty came in search of her from the kitchen.   There had been parties at Oxford too where young women were readily available. Admittedly, most of those who attended such parties were hardly students of academia. But, David thought, this is all incidental. More important now is that I get well enough to return to my squadron.

Patrick returned to the ward, flat on his back on a stretcher, his face swathed in bandages, and groaning softly as he regained consciousness.

"No pedicle this time, old chap," David said, as Patrick's mumblings became coherent. "That bump under the bandage looks like you might have a nose in the making again."

"Hurts," Patrick whispered.   "Hurts like hell."

Archie had made a point to explain to his patients that he had initiated another method of free grafting derived from

251

an American system. He explained that he used a scalpel with a small drum attached to obtain the donor skin, usually from the abdomen, in paper-thin form. The skin apparently attached easily round the drum where it could be transferred over the wound. Although the method was still in its early stages, there had been far fewer cases of infection.

"I feel like a bloody guinea pig," Patrick grumbled.

David knew exactly what he meant.

Much was done to keep everyone's thoughts away from their injuries and the men themselves, well aware that their treatment was largely experimental, learned the meaning of strength in the face of adversity. Over sherry one day, a group of them swore themselves in as a form of drinking fraternity and called themselves The Guinea Pig Club. The structure was loosely knit since the Secretary had no hands and could not therefore take notes, and the Treasurer's legs were encased in plaster which would prevent him from absconding with the minimal funds. As the weeks passed, the "Club" took on a more structured shape and encouraged others in the ward to join, all of whom were associated with aviation. They made Archibald McIndoe its president and created special categories for the staff.

Apart from the camaraderie of the Club, Yvonne had been splendid about spending her rare free days visiting with him or taking him to lunch in the town. He had asked her repeatedly about their mother and her absence, only to receive vague words of assurance.

"I think she might be traveling about," Yvonne said. "She's very hard to reach these days; you know how difficult the telephone is and I have so little time now to go to London."

He also questioned his father with similar responses. In desperation, he confided his concern to Rupert who had driven him to Shepherd's Market in London to hobnob with many Fighter Command types who sought a welcome break from the rigors of combat flying.

252

"There's so much going on these days," Rupert said. "Judging from her background I should say she's well dug in with some kind of special war effort."

"But there's been no word since Christmas," David insisted. "Even then, she seemed edgy and preoccupied and certainly looked far from well. Thin, you know."

"What does your father say?"

"He feels the same way I do. Whatever it is she's doing, which obviously does include a good deal of traveling, seems to keep her more than normally busy. I've been wondering lately if the Free French have roped her in. Obviously, she wouldn't talk too much about that, would she?"

"And Yvonne?"

"Even vaguer. Have you seen any more of her?"

The moustache drooped sadly. "Unfortunately not. She qualified to fly twin engine aircraft and then went off to train for something else. Like the rest of your family, she's very preoccupied."

David looked upon Rupert as one of his closest friends. He knew that Treacle had returned home to work for his father's company in Yorkshire and that many of Rupert's other chums were either dead or badly injured. The complete antithesis of a coward, Rupert's performance as an RAF officer and fighter pilot was exemplary and yet he had managed to come this far unscathed.

"What about you, Rupert?"

"Oh, me? I'm driving a Spitfire these days out of Duxford. There's still quite a bit going on in the air, you know." Rupert dug his hands in his pockets. "I'm thinking about a complete change of pace, though"

"How will you manage that?"

Rupert pulled at one end of his large moustache. "Well, to start with, I think I might get rid of this thing. I think I need to change my image."

"The moustache doesn't make any difference one way or

the other, you know. It's the personality that counts......they tell me. Anyway, why do you want to change your image?"

"Well, I've been thinking about chucking Fighter Command and going to work for another firm, actually."

David tried to cover his astonishment without success. "But you're everything a fighter pilot should be! You're not going to lumber about in a bomber, are you?"

"Not exactly."

"Then what?"

"I'll let you know."

CHAPTER TWELVE

October, 1941

After some fundamental parachute training in Lincolnshire prior to Janine's departure for France in early September, her drop from a Wellington into the midi sector had gone surprisingly well. Met by two French aviators she had known before the war, they had detected the secret air strips in southern France and the surveys were almost complete. Now alternate auxiliaries, such as farm acreage, and other potential drop zones were under consideration.

She had expected to rotate back to England in approximately three weeks and was surprised when she was told that a Westland Lysander would arrive one night to pick her up near Aude after only ten days of survey work. 'Charles' met her at Tangmere and explained that in view of the fact that she had proven to be exceptionally familiar with the French terrain and had excellent contacts, her assignment there was about to be changed. If she agreed, she would receive further briefings, extensive training, and a code name.

"We're aware," 'Charles' said. "that you've been

concerned about stranded British servicemen in France and have, in fact, become somewhat unofficially involved with guiding them to the Spanish frontier. You've had considerable success in making contacts with French people who are willing to establish and operate relay points along the escape routes."

It was true. Upon making discreet enquiries to people she knew she could trust, she learned that there was a network of routes now in use by British Expeditionary Forces evaders and escapers. Many were soldiers still seeking a way back to England from Dunkirk. Others were downed airmen. Still others were people who had escaped from the clutches of their German captors by executing amazing schemes with fraudulent uniforms and forged papers. The wounded and injured were hidden and nursed in local houses until they were well enough to make the journey.

"However," 'Charles' went on. "None of the various departments concerning intelligence-gathering activities here in London interface in any way and while these escape routes are controlled literally by one man here in London and one in Gibraltar who come under the MI9 umbrella, the physical operation--escorting, hiding, risking lives--is run mostly by the French."

Janine looked at him questioningly.

"Your first assignment concerning documented airstrips is about complete. If you are so inclined, you could return to France and assist your former countrymen with the various escape routes. But be aware that some are also voluntarily involved with sabotage and assassination, and some relay intelligence--such as enemy troop movements, etc.--to the Free French. Such intelligence would also be valuable to the Secret Intelligence Service and the Special Operations Executive. If you remain with us, we'll train you further but you will be obligated to supply information in code to Bletchly Park. In other words, directly to the British."

Again, Janine found herself caught between loyalty to

France and to her adopted country. While well aware of some open animosity between de Gaulle and Churchill, she did not feel inclined to be caught up in it. If she worked for SIS and SOE and at the same time helped send servicemen back to England this, she felt, would be her personal contribution to the war in general. She had made a number of astute observations concerning the German military movements in France and had recognised several high-ranking officers from the prewar social functions. Aware of this attribute, it was clear that she could be of help in this area. As for sabotage and assassination, that might be a different matter. However, for her own well-being, perhaps physical prowess would be advantageous under certain circumstances and the training would be useful.

After the meeting with 'Charles', and by pure manipulation and determination, she managed to bring her family together in Bayswater for dinner and anticipated a pleasant evening of comfortable conversation. But in retrospect the next day, she knew the reunion had failed miserably. Perhaps this opinion might have been prompted by her own guilty conscience. Unable to divulge her activities, her lies and evasive replies sounded spurious and ludicrous to her and she doubted that they entirely believed any of them. It seemed to her that none of them really wanted to be there.

David made a brave pretense at easygoing humour at dinner, but it was evident that he felt uncomfortable away from the septic confines of Ward III and the compatibility of his similarly injured companions.

Yvonne, having passed close examination by the Headquarters chief instructor, had flown her first Hurricane and was extremely busy ferrying aircraft of many categories. Now far less absorbed with her own concerns and more aware of others', in consideration of her brother she had spoken briefly about the pleasure of piloting the fast fighter. She mentioned that only a few of the women so far had been selected for this promotion and that rumour had it that there may even be an all-woman ATA ferry pool created later in the year. Although this had not yet occurred, she was nonetheless in the running to be transferred when it did. Janine sensed that there might be something else lurking in the back of her daughter's mind, but even after extremely cautious and diplomatic prodding, Yvonne confessed to nothing.

Henry, now deeply engrossed with the seriously wounded, had appeared preoccupied at dinner. In fact, it occurred to her that each of them, including herself, seemed distant and anxious to return to their individual environs.

After this difficult experience, Janine completed several weeks of training in Lincolnshire learning, among other things, how to jump out of a moving Lysander at four feet above the ground in the event that a landing site might be bogged down with mud.

"But the parachute entry went beautifully before," Janine reasoned to 'Charles', who had arrived to see how she was faring after a grueling day of training. "Why must I be prepared to enter now in this rather acrobatic manner?"

"Parachuting in is less accurate," 'Charles' said. "Now that you have so much information, and the fact that you will be carrying concealed important maps and other data, it's necessary that you are immediately met and taken into hiding."

Prior to her initial return to Aix, Janine would have argued that surely she could come and go as she pleased without all these extra precautions. But upon her arrival in the south of France, she quickly learned that the Vichy government was ostensibly pro-German. Her "reception committee" in Aix had been through indirect contacts in Marseilles using passwords and points of rendezvous and it was not until after these contacts had been made that she could, at last, visit her parents. They were delighted to see her, but resisted taking her advice.

"If we go about our business and don't antagonise

anyone," her father had insisted, "there is no need for us to leave. We're not in occupied territory and although Pétain and his Vichy government are not what we would ideally want, at least we are reasonably free to carry on normally." He had looked fondly at his daughter. "Your sudden arrival might cause some speculation, but we don't have to tell anyone where you came from, do we?"

Indeed, they did not.

There had been upheavals in French government before the war, and it seemed that the general populace in the south looked toward Pétain now as the military hero who would maintain a fair and comprehensive standard of life from the seat of his "unoccupied" government in Vichy. But it had become increasingly clear that Nazi requirements in the southern sector were accelerating and their financial demands had become crippling. It was obvious that the Parti Populaire Français was structured along fascist lines. The fact that Winston Churchill had seized all French ships in English ports and attacked the French fleet at Mers-el-Kabir in North Africa in July 1940 in order to prevent them from supporting the German cause through the cooperation of the Vichy government, clearly conveyed his distrust.

During that last cocktail party in Paris, Janine had sensed the prevailing mood of the French. That Britain could successfully withstand an inevitable invasion attempt was thought to be entirely unlikely. Yet, ironically, she knew that a Vichy delegate had visited London during the height of the blitz on that city to negotiate for the restoration of French integrity and uninterrupted food supplies from her African colonies should Britain manage to turn the tables and defeat the Axis. In return it was agreed that de Gaulle should retain the African colonies he had claimed. All of this, however, was to remain top secret in order to manufacture an artificial state of tension between the Vichy government and Britain. Their bread, in fact, was to be buttered on both sides and one never knew who to trust.

After she had initiated her primary task of seeking out suitable landing strips, her curiosity concerning stranded servicemen continued to trouble her. She had quickly learned that there were French collaborators and informants working for the Vichy government, and that the people who helped the allied evaders placed themselves in serious jeopardy. Better though, the partisans said, that the men return to fight again to ultimately liberate France than to languish in prisoner of war stalags.

As time would allow and in conjunction with a growing relay network of helpers, she had assisted men in moving from Aix and Marseilles, and even as far east as Pau, to rendezvous points at the foot of the Pyrennese where trusted guides waited to lead them into neutral Spain.

Now, three weeks after her arrival in England and her intensive training completed, she faced 'Charles' across the desk in London. Rising from her chair she began to pace, hardly aware that he patiently watched her. Nebulous segments whirled chaotically in her mind, refusing to settle into any kind of form. How much more would they expect her to do? How could she justify all the training, when within her lay a smoldering ember of fear? She had learned that in September two German officers were murdered by the French Communists in Lille and an ensuing series of random killings were taking place. In retaliation the Germans were executing prisoners in alarming numbers with the threat of raising the number each time the murder of a German officer occurred. This terrorist action was being carried out solely by the Communist group and without sanction from the Résistance. In Vichy, Pétain protested against the Communists and demanded they cease putting fear into the ranks of the occupying German forces. Conversely, de Gaulle in London applauded the acts, seemingly ignoring the vicious retaliatory punishment the Germans were inflicting on innocent prisoners, most of whom were Jews. She learned that Claude's father had been among the last group. Of his mother, she knew nothing. Of Claude, she had no idea where he was or if he were aware of his father's execution.

The extent and ruthlessness of the additional training frightened her. She would be tasked to meet weapons drops from Britain in the middle of the night in order to form a cache in preparation for future invasion. She had learned how to operate each of these deadly weapons. She knew how to blow up a bridge or a railway line. Code, camouflage, stealth, and skullduggery were all now a part of her life. But more frightening to her was the fact that she knew how to kill. Lethal karate blows, piano wire, hat pins and stilettos were only a few of the newly learned diabolical methods. The thought sickened her. Never in her life had she ever felt the need to kill. Ironically she had been given the code name Phalene--a simple, gentle moth--obviously derived from her pre-war aeroplane. What an oxymoron!

Gradually, the confusion in her mind began to settle upon the frightened refugees that had monopolised her time earlier in the war. She had learned that some were now fully occupied training for espionage in selected mansions throughout Britain. She was also aware that tunnels existed in remote villages in England--their existence often unknown by the villagers themselves--for clandestine use in the event of invasion; and that other unexplained and cleverly concealed or disguised facilities had materialised, including an oil-filled pipeline along the southeast coastline which was to be ignited in the event of an attempted invasion by land or sea, and a bogus airfield furnished entirely with inflated aeroplanes and clapboard buildings which appeared genuine from a distance.

Such knowledge must never be revealed to anyone outside the confines of the privileged few who knew about them and, more importantly, to the enemy. What if she should be detected by the Gestapo or SS and attempts made to forcibly make her talk? She thought of the dreaded L Pill--a cyanide capsule with fatal consequences should it be broken while in the mouth--now cleverly concealed in a tiny compartment in the heel of her shoe. The pill could be slipped under the tongue, or even swallowed intact without harm. Obviously, its design enabled an agent under threat of torture to at least resort to escape by biting down on the pill and imposing self-inflicted death. While still a lesser link in the rapidly forming chain of secret activities, Janine was painfully aware that she carried in her mind vital information that would be valuable to the enemy. She looked directly at 'Charles', embarrassed that he still watched her, and smiled ruefully.

"It's all right," he said, offering her a cigarette from a gold case, which she refused. "Everyone has misgivings about themselves. But I must assure you that we consider you one of our best. You always have been."

His remarks brought her to the final elusive conclusion. If she returned to France in this new role, all other facets of her personal life must be dismissed. She doubted that she could function effectively if she gave a single thought to her home and family. The complexity of tasks that loomed ahead and her scope of widening activities would expose her to considerable danger. Yet wouldn't this be all worthwhile if it contributed one small unit of resistance toward the enemy and achieved the ultimate aim of total victory?

"After your return to France," 'Charles' said, returning the case to his inside pocket, "an agent whose network functions from the Paris area will contact you. So far he has succeeded in keeping a step ahead of the Gestapo. He is operating along the escape route, continuously changing his location in order to remain elusive. He is working his way south, but we know that his chances of arrest are extremely high due to paid French informers. We have managed to eliminate some of these betrayers, but there are many more. Although we know him well enough to assume that he would probably not break under torture, he is nonetheless anxious to put into the hands of a trusted agent some photographs and maps relating to his acquired intelligence in the occupied zone. The photographs are of several dangerous moles who have dispersed into Vichy France and England and have disappeared. While we have the reports here, we do not have the photographs. We can only hope that he will get them to you before the enemy catch up with him."

"Why does he not dispatch them to you by Lysander?" Janine asked.

"He can't risk even that. It seems there is a pursuer and they are playing a veritable cat-and-mouse game. It would mean coming out into the open."

"How will I be able to receive the photographs then?"

"He'll find a way I can assure you."

Janine sighed. "Very well. You will, of course, reveal his code name and a pass word."

'Charles' nodded. "He will say 'The blackbird is free'. You will reply 'The water is clear'."

"And the code name?"

"Marcel."

*   *   *

Although psychologically prepared to return to France, further instructions and briefings took place over the next few weeks which afforded Janine another reunion with her family at Christmas. While less tense than before, her anticipation of the coming assignment prevented her from letting down her guard and she was actually relieved when everyone left.

But the new year brought disturbing news. The Paris underground organisation that stemmed from a group of intellectuals at the Musée de l'Homme and was considered the heart of the original resistance, had been betrayed and seven of its original members had been sought out, arrested, and summarily executed on the 23rd. But to counterbalance these setbacks, the first Maquis had been formed near Grenoble and the underground movement was strengthening.   Now all it needed was a form of cohesion.

All of the information network had heretofore functioned by using homing pigeons and without the aid of wireless communication. But now, at last, men and women were being trained as radio operators in England in order to work with the guerrilla groups, which largely consisted of saboteurs and partisans.

Earlier, Janine had attempted to find one of the first operators in Marseilles to contact Paris, only to learn that each network had its own transmitter and code and could only communicate with an assigned controller at the top secret hub of cryptology at Bletchley Park in England--a name and location known only to a very select few. Unfortunately, Headquarters was already painfully aware that the transmitters were easily detected by the enemy and that no mercy had been shown to date to captured operators. They had been arrested, tortured, or shot which gave good reason for the polarisation and exclusiveness of each system.

At the end of January, she prepared to enter this cesspool of treachery and cruelty. She was to rendezvous with her aircraft at Tangmere on the first cloudless night of a full moon. Due to the uncertainty of English weather and potential conditions in France, a waiting station had been set up in a cottage close to the airfield near the village of Shopwyke. The people there provided food and lodging during the waiting periods for both pilots and passengers.

Her flight down from Lincolnshire went smoothly and she watched the shadow of the aircraft, cast by the exceptionally bright moon, dog them across the countryside below.   Although now steeled for the task ahead, her nervous stomach rebelled against the sight of food, and sleep had become entirely elusive.

She waited anxiously in the small cottage lounge and her heart jumped when a sergeant poked his head round the door.

"Your aircraft is here," he said.   He could not address her directly for he had no idea who she was, nor knew her name. "All set?"

She nodded and rose from her chair. Her legs felt like lead and she wondered if she would be able to get herself to the door. The sound of jovial voices in the foyer eased her tension as she entered.

"Excellent conditions," a young pilot was saying. "Perfect night for a spin in the old Lizzie." He turned to face Janine as she came toward him, and his smile melted into an expression of surprise. "My goodness," he said.   "I hadn't expected such a pretty passenger."

Janine said nothing. This was not the pilot she had trained with in Lincolnshire; the pilot who had briefed her so thoroughly about procedures after landing. Why was she to fly with someone with whom she was not familiar? She realised that her expression must have conveyed her dismay.

"We all do the same thing," he said, with a grin. "Sorry Alan isn't here, but I promise to get you in safely."

She let her breath out slowly. "It's all right.   It's just that I was....well....used to......"

As he went over the flight plan and procedures she knew that the pilot really made no difference at all.   Everything was indeed identical.

"There's been a little rain in the Arles area," he said. "But there should be no problem landing. Watch for the flashed code "W" from the ground, which I'll acknowledge.   If it's wrong, we'll hightail it back to England."

Janine knew that should there be no communication, or an incorrect code given from the ground, it would mean the enemy was at hand. Her heart beat faster as she envisioned the significance of these adverse signs.

"We'll be flying very low, all the way to Arles, you understand," he said, flicking back a lock of dark hair. "in order to get in under the limits of early ground detection, you see. As soon as I've landed--it will be quick because as you know the Lysander only needs a few yards--then off you go. We do it all in a matter of three minutes. Your reception committee will get you immediately to a safe house--you'll be an approximate eleven kilometres southeast of Arles--during which time I'll be heading for home."

"Bacon and eggs when you get back, Rupert?" a young aproned woman asked.

He nodded. "Could you throw in a tomato and perhaps a bit of 'shroom?"

Janine felt frozen to the ground. Remembering vague descriptions from both David and Yvonne, and the immediate grasp of his rather unusual Christian name, she quickly recognised Rupert Barlow. Hadn't he mentioned to David that he was changing his image by shaving off an audacious moustache? That he was seeking a change? Suddenly, her spirits soared. Hadn't David also mentioned that this young man's luck was uncannily positive? That he had come heroically through the desperate Battle of Britain air battles unscathed? Unconscious of the uplifting effect he had on his passenger, and that he had no idea in the world who she was, Rupert led the way out into the night, whistling softly.

As Janine followed him across the tarmac, a dark cloud suddenly blotted out the luminescent moonlight that had bathed the aerodrome, casting the well defined outlines of the operations tower into a dim, indistinct silhouette. Rupert slowed his step and looked upward as several large drops of rain splashed on his upturned face. Now primed and eager to go, Janine hurried toward the black gull-winged aircraft waiting on the apron, hoping he would not detain her.

"If the visibility is poor and we can't see the ground over France," he said, catching up with her, "we won't find the signal lights."

"It's just a little cloud," Janine said, one foot the port side ladder. "It'll be fine when you clear the coast. You'll see."

She doubted that she would be able to bear starting all over again, now that every fiber of her being was eager to go. It would mean waiting for another clear, moonlit night.

"We can try," Rupert said.   "You're going to get wet though, if we do run into rain. Although the ladder has been added to make entries and exits easier, the sliding roof from the rear cockpit has been removed for the same reason."

Janine climbed in and pushed her bag well forward and sat down on her parachute. "It doesn't matter. Let's give it a try."

Rupert looked eastward toward an horizon that appeared to be lighter. As they flew out from the shore, Janine realised she had been right.   Although spasmodically cloudy and prone to rain, she could see clearer skies over the French coastline, especially toward the south. They skimmed over the surface of the sea like a pelican in search of food, and were past coastal defences before flak mottled the night sky. Janine had never had the reason or opportunity to navigate by the stars and now cursed her ignorance.   Too dark to read her compass, she could merely guess how far they were into France.   Obviously, there could be no R/T communication between pilot and passenger for fear of detection over enemy territory and she desperately tried to estimate miles traveled versus time.

Remembering that Yvonne had ferried Lysanders and had mentioned its unusual capabilities, Janine tried to bring them to mind. The high, gull-shaped winged monoplane, Yvonne had said, did not have a reputation for speed, but its ability to land and take off in a remarkably short distance gave it a value heretofore not appreciated. Slats in the leading edge of the wing which controlled automatic flaps, gave the aircraft

The Westland Lysander complete
with quick exit ladder used by
secret agents.

the unique ability to slow to almost stalling speed, allowing it to descend at an extremely steep angle and touch down in an astonishingly short distance. Similarly, it could take off in that same distance.

Janine peered over the edge of her cockpit, straining her eyes for the first sign of a flash of light.

Yvonne had been right. The visibility over the side was excellent.

There it was!!

Her pilot quickly acknowledged the code and the Lysander began to descend. Simultaneously, two other lights flicked on forming a faint triangular shape on the ground. She went over the essentials of her instruction in her mind: The flarepath should comprise three electric torches tied to sticks set in the shape of a triangle, pointing downwind. Torch "A" would mark the major point where the escorts and exchange passenger waited; also the point from where the agreed signal-- "W"-- originated. "B" would mark a point one hundred and fifty metres into the wind from "A" while fifty metres to the right of "B", torch "C" would be located. This configuration marked the flarepath.

Three minutes!

She must be ready to leave via the ladder as soon as humanly possible. She felt the wheels touch down and judder over the grass and was standing ready to scramble down the ladder the minute Rupert turned the aircraft into the wind.

"Good luck!" he said, as she ran into the darkness with her French escort.

*   *   *

February, 1942

Kate's mother returned from convalescence in Scotland looking fit and cheerful and more importantly, fully cured and Kate could barely conceal her utter relief.   Annie had started walking three weeks before, and her inquisitive little nose sniffed out all kinds of forbidden interests in the low kitchen cupboards and on Grandfather's special shelf.   Usually even-tempered, the old man had thrown up his hands in agonised exasperation when he found his favourite briar pipe full of soap bubbles in the washing-up water. But in spite of her frustrations and anxieties, Kate defiantly rejected an enquiry from a representative of Doctor Barnardo's Children's Home concerning the lack of a responsible guardian.

"You have no idea how upset my mother would be if you took us away," Kate told the woman.   "She'll be back tomorrow and then you'll be sorry."

Grandfather had concurred although they both knew Kate had lied and it would be almost another month before she returned.

Although the brunt of the German aggression now moved its strategic focus toward Russia, the continual hit-and-run air raids added to the tautness of Kate's already ragged nerves and she reached the point where she was not sure she could go on. With encouragement from her grandfather and the assurance that her mother was recovering nicely and would be home very soon, she did manage to hang on.

"I think it's time," her mother said, after her return, "for you to recapture what's left of your childhood."

Kate thought of the awful boys named Sid and Stan and knew that her mother spoke empty words. While BC had been the victor and had returned home unscathed after the attempted attack, Kate continued to mope over her changing body and quixotic moods.   Now sure that David had been badly injured, she felt her usual optimism slipping into despondency. Because of her preoccupation with her duties at home, she had made few friends during her half days at school. Added to this, Hugh remained in his netherworld of amnesia somewhere near Edinburgh, managing to stammer only a few words on rare occasions. Her solace for the moment were her letters and drawings to David who responded with news of Flint House, currently operating in full swing as a military convalescent home, and the antics of the Guinea Pig Club, although he failed to explain exactly what the Club was.

I've been working hard, he wrote, *to strengthen my hands and it's beginning to show results. I truly want to return to flying and, if I can keep this up, I believe I can do it.....*

*   *   *

It was just an innocent manila envelope that came in the post, but the affect it had on her mother was quite extraordinary. Kate watched her as she stared at the brief, typewritten letter for some time before speaking.

"I don't know what to do," she said at last, showing the paper to her father.

"You should go, of course," Grandfather said, running a pipe cleaner through the briar for the hundredth time.

"But I can't leave you."

"I lived alone before you came," he said, sucking on the stem and grimacing.

Although Grandfather had been the epitome of kindness, Kate knew he longed for the solitude and peace he was accustomed to. She had tried her best to be quiet and helpful, but there were times when she wanted to scream at

Annie, and to throw all the dirty dishes out into the garden.

"How do you feel about returning to Mallory Cottage, Kate?" her mother asked.

For a moment, Kate felt nothing. Then slowly the memory of Toby Mallory's coffin in the front room, and of Mrs. Mallory lying dead by the hedgerow returned. Memories she had tried so hard to forget.

"It isn't Mallory Cottage any more," she said, her voice brittle with renewed bitterness. "How can it be Mallory Cottage when there are no more Mallorys to live in it?"

"Yes," her mother said. "It was awful for you. But, Kate, the cottage belongs to someone named Mr. Boniface now."

Kate glanced toward the letter, but said nothing.

"This is from his solicitors. Before he went away in the middle of the London blitz, he asked them to make inquiries about you. The letter says--in so many words--that should you be in a transitory position because of the bombing (he obviously knew you lived in London) he would be most pleased to put the cottage at your disposal which, of course, would include your family." She folded the letter and waited for Kate to speak.

No doubt BC will love the garden there, Kate thought, and perhaps the Parke family and Charlie will come back to Flint House--even David, when he's finally released from hospital. She moved to the window and looked across the field toward a gun battery on the opposite side. Only last week German Stukas strafed and bombed along the periphery of the field, targeting the gun battery. Perhaps the Stukas might come back and train their guns on more innocent targets. At least the Long Man might remember that he protected us against machine gun fire before and would again. Here, there is nothing to protect us. Well....if Grandfather prefers to live alone--and I don't blame him for that--then there really isn't much choice, is there?

271

* * *

As they prepared for their journey, Kate wondered if Mr. Baxter would come to Long Bottom to see them. While her mother was away in Scotland, he had come several times to Thanington and Kate looked forward to his visits. Since Ruby's death he changed from a rather opinionated boor to a quiet and thoughtful man. She suspected that he had always been that way, and for reasons known only to himself had hidden behind a coarse façade of his own making. He showed considerable interest in Kate's drawings and talked to her at length about pursuing art as a career. It seemed to her that he had become her surrogate father in the absence of her own.

Somehow he found a car and enough petrol to drive them to Sussex. She had not relished the thought of struggling with BC's brown carrier bag on a train again and was grateful for this favour.

Motoring through the Kentish countryside was a privilege indeed. With the soft smell of leather in her nose and the feel of the lap rug tucked snugly about her legs, Kate's spirits began to rise. Yet her heart beat faster as they approached the village although nothing at all had changed and the old houses and cottages still seemed half asleep.

"I'll get the key," Mr. Baxter said, stopping the car in front of Mr. Banberry's stationery shop.

Kate walked across the road to the cottage and found, to her dismay, that the gate refused to open and she wondered if the cottage no longer welcomed her.

"Hinges are a bit rusty," Mr. Banberry said as he crossed the road. "Hello, young Kate." He spoke as if he had seen her only yesterday.

The garden looked sad and overgrown, while the murky windows no longer winked at the post office across the narrow street. The brass fixtures on the front door had turned black and seemed to still be in mourning for the previous dead owners.

"It will need a bit of sprucing up," Mr. Banberry said, unlocking the door. "I've laid a fire in the front room and once we have it going, we'll soon have the place warmed up. Ben hasn't been here for over a year and if Mrs. Dougherty hadn't come down from London a couple of times, you wouldn't have been able to find the furniture for the dust, I'm sure."

Kate smelt the familiar odour of thatch as she went in search of her old bedroom and felt the damp coldness seeping into her bones. The cottage needed the comfort and warmth of people. Through the weather-streaked latticed window, she could see the leafless poplars standing in their prim line at the edge of the village. Squinting against the winter sun, she looked for the Long Man on the hillside beyond and could not find him. Had the grass been allowed to grow high enough around the chalk etching to obliterate it? Had an attempt been made to camouflage him, or was he simply fading back into the past to hide from the atrocities of this modern war?

As the days passed and work was done to clean things up, the cottage took on a friendlier and more habitable appearance. Not yet established in a new school, Kate felt obliged to purchase a newspaper from Mr. Banberry every evening and tried to make sense of the news. Although the Japanese attack on Pearl Harbor in Hawaii on December the 7th was an unprincipled act of savagery, it appeared that at last America would enter the war against both Japan and Germany. Although not mentioned in the article, it was quite obvious that Britain had breathed a sigh of long-awaited relief. An editorial on page three indicated that upper income residents of the Belgravia district in London were somewhat appalled at the number of Americans milling about the United States Embassy in Grosvenor Square. It was no wonder, the article said, that the gum-chewing Military Police had been nicknamed "Snowdrops" because of their gleaming white helmets and spats. She recognised Mr. Baxter's political cartoon by the distinctive art style and signature and pondered the thought that perhaps the nightingale in nearby Berkeley Square should learn to sing the Star Spangled Banner as a gesture of recognition and appreciation.

When Mr. Baxter came down from London for the day with contributions for dinner, Mr. Banberry joined them and enjoyed a rare quiet moment in front of the fire. Before he departed, he handed Kate a bag full of coins as a belated Christmas gift to buy her supply of newspapers for the rest of the year. She suspected they were the very same coins she had given him. Meanwhile, Mr. Baxter studied some of her drawings and commented on their excellence.

"The best art schools in London have disbanded, I'm afraid," he said. "But I'll see what I can do to get you some private tuition. It's a shame to see this kind of talent go to waste."

She read the next day that Hong Kong, which had been surrendered to the Japanese on Christmas day by the British, Canadian, and Indian armies, was suffering under the occupation. Reports from the Sahara ricocheted back and forth as the Axis and Allied troops grappled for territory. German armies were making rapid progress into Russia. But to brighten her day, there was a letter from David.

I've just received the best gift imaginable, he wrote. *They're going to let me try flying again.....something very light and easy at first. I'll be working for Army Cooperation for a while which isn't very exciting, but at least I'll be back in the air. I'll have to return to East Grinstead from time to time for patch-ups, but I can't tell you how encouraged I am now, Kate.*

It had been nineteen months since Kate had seen him

and she had no idea what his appearance might be like. She wrote to him immediately, reminding him to keep her apprised of his new addresses.

*   *   *

Wales in winter could not be bleaker and the long, dull days tweaked at David's patience. He felt his hands were almost normal in strength, and with the issue of special side-zipped gloves, the scars no longer chafed against the softness of the lining. Pulling a drogue, or simply flying up and down at set altitudes in order to train the antiaircraft gun crews, in a poky Lysander or a Miles Master for Army Cooperation target practice was hardly his idea of excitement. The only point of concentration was at take-off when the Cardiff barrage balloons loomed up in front of him.

Aware that his CO watched the first time he entered the cockpit, David deliberately expelled all thoughts of his fiery experience in the Hurricane. His gloved hands functioned well with the minimum of pain and he flew the Miles Master with his usual expertise. Yet he knew that if he allowed himself the luxury of contemplation, he would never get the aircraft off the ground.

Upon reporting in, he expected some covert glances at his facial scars, but was both surprised and relieved when no one stared or commented. Unable to decide if the personnel in the antiaircraft Cooperation Squadron were completely blind, or simply did not care, he found his own reaction confusing. After pondering the situation for a few days, he concluded that in all truthfulness, he wanted them to know that he had been injured while in desperate combat, and certainly had the capability to fly something more challenging than these slow, outdated aircraft. Content now that that psychological dilemma was solved, he knew that he must find something far more satisfying to do.

"Well, you've proved how determination can pay off," Rupert said over a drink at the Shepherd's pub in London one weekend. "I suppose if you really wanted to, you could eventually get back into a fighter squadron. Wing Commander Douglas Bader did it with no legs, didn't he?"

The plucky legless pilot he spoke of had fought his way back into flying after a devastating accident and had become something of a legend, and certainly an example to similarly injured men. If he could do it, so could they. This kind of determination was the strength that had seen David through the long, painful months of surgery and recovery.

"I do, however, have another idea," Rupert went on. "I can't tell you anything personally, but if your interested, I might be able to wangle an interview."

"How do I know if I'm interested, if I don't have a clue what you're talking about?" David said.

Rupert shrugged. "It's up to you."

"Is it something you're involved in?"

"Yes, as a matter of fact, it is."

"Then I'm interested."

*   *   *

May, 1942

The somewhat cautious relaxation of tension in the Spring of '42, did not extend to England's southern coastal towns. Aware of the short distance across the Channel and the obvious ease any potential German attacker would have to reach them, the population remained alert. But even with this kind of vigilance, Eastbourne was taken entirely by surprise on the fourth day of the month.

Kate sat in class feeling drowsy after lunch and desperately tried to pay attention to the teacher. While knowledgeable of her subject, the woman seemed unaware that the monotone in which she delivered her information contributed largely to this somnolent atmosphere.

Suddenly, the sound of low-flying rapidly approaching aircraft penetrated the wearisome drone.

"Get down!" the teacher shouted, startling the lethargic girls.

The young students barely had time to scramble beneath their desks as a series of explosions shook the building. Kate crouched on the floor with her hands clamped over her ears, and felt the vibration shudder through her body. She lifted her aching fingers for a brief moment and heard the rip of machine gun bullets ricocheting along the streets outside and into the roof over her head. She heard screams and whimpers around her and stared at the girl under the next desk who howled hysterically.

"Shut up!" Kate snapped. "Just shut up!"

The roar of engines faded into the distance but the girls remained transfixed beneath their desks. Kate crawled out and stood up, brushing her skirt with the palm of her hand. She looked quizzically at the class mistress who seemed to have become completely paralyzed as she stood gaping with her back to the blackboard. The woman's eyes stood out from her head like marbles and her mouth kept opening and shutting like a goldfish.

"Anyone hurt?" Kate asked. "Come on out. It's all

right, they've gone."

Gradually the terrified girls crept from under their desks checking themselves for injuries. A large window on one side of the room had shattered in spite of the precautionary brown paper reinforcement, and had strewn glass shards on top of the three desks adjacent to it. Two of the girls slowly emerged from beneath these desks, stooping on flat feet like ducks to avoid cutting their bare knees. Kate took a step toward the third desk and saw a limp, blood-covered hand. She spun quickly around to avoid seeing any more and stared at the gibbering, terrified girls around her.

Head Mistress burst into the classroom with her usually immaculate hairdo awry.

"Is everyone all right?" she panted.

The girls nodded dumbly. Kate pointed toward the windows. "One isn't," she said, tersely. "May the rest of us go home?"

As a belated All Clear sounded which had not been preceded by the Warning, no one appeared able to make a decision. The class teacher had only just begun to gather her wits while Head Mistress fumbled with a hairpin. Kate waited.

"Don't you think," she said to the Head Mistress, "that our parents might be worried. Shouldn't you tell us all to go home?"

The woman frowned. "Yes, yes. Of course."

As the girls gathered their belongings together, some glanced mutely toward the third desk. Kate closed her eyes and took a deep breath. With her back ramrod straight, she marched briskly through the door without acknowledging either of the women. She did however overhear a whispered comment between them.

"It isn't natural! That child appears to be completely immune to fear."

*   *   *

August, 1942

Yvonne, now sharing a flat with an ATA colleague in Southampton, sat at the window drying her hair in the sun on her day off.   She waved back to one of the American women pilots who had come to England to assist with the ferrying. Based at Ratcliff, the American had been to visit Hamble for the day and was on her way to join friends in Southampton for lunch.   It had not taken these women long to organise themselves through a well-known aviatrix named Jackie Cochrane, after America entered the war.   Aggressively eager to assist, and all excellent pilots, they tended to awe their more reserved British counterparts. But they were witty and fun, and soon   warm   friendships   blossomed   between   the   two nationalities.

As the American turned the corner, a car drew up in front of the building and a figure Yvonne immediately recognised--and was not at all eager to see again--got out.

She quickly dressed and ran a comb through her still-damp hair just as the French uniformed officer knocked on the door. She offered him tea, which he refused, obviously anxious to get immediately to the business in hand.

"We know of the invaluable service you are giving to ATA.," he said.   "but their ranks have been augmented by the arrival of the American pilots and I really think you might be spared.   Of course, the decision is entirely yours but, as we have discussed before, you speak excellent French and know the country, plus you are a skilled pilot."

If only I weren't so qualified, she thought, then perhaps he would not be so persistent.

"Please think very seriously about it," the Colonel said. "There have been many adverse things going on, and continue to do so, especially concerning the Jews. The Germans have rounded up thousands of them in Paris and shipped them off to Germany. The Vichy government is cooperating in that respect and has arrested over four thousand stateless Jews in the unoccupied zone and handed them over to the Germans. This obvious interaction with the enemy has brought more and more French patriots into the ranks of the Résistance."

He leaned forward and joined the tips of his fingers together.

"Miss Parke, one of my tasks is to deal with any potential betrayals that could disrupt the work and preparation for unity when the Allied invasion comes. While we know there are several extremely clever and elusive German agents that both the British and the French want out of the way, we know one in particular that you may be able to help us track down. She operates on both sides of the Channel, but she's elusive. Part of the reason for our lack of success is that we really don't know what she looks like. She speaks several languages fluently, including perfected English, which makes her difficult to detect, and is adept at changing her appearance which stems, we understand, from theatrical training. She is a woman of many faces and forms."

Yvonne listened patiently, but could not determine why he would confide in her in particular. She knew nothing about this sort of thing.

"Earlier in the war, she was operating very close to where your home is near Eastbourne, obviously due to the fortifications concerning defence in the event of invasion, and the detection device, now named Radar by the Americans," the Colonel went on. "Through knowledgeable scouts who were close to ferreting her out, we believed she actually visited Long Bottom. As I mentioned, she is very clever, and managed to slip through their fingers. Since it is such a small village, and most strangers would be noted, we wondered if perhaps you had seen such a woman."

In spite of her astonishment, Yvonne smiled. How on earth did he expect her to remember something so unremarkable from all those months ago?

"I'm sorry," she said. "I'm afraid I don't recall seeing anyone."

"Well," the Colonel said, rising. "If something should come to mind--even the remotest thing--please contact me at this address, which is at a civilian residence in London. Do not attempt to telephone. I have never introduced myself for obvious reasons, but you should know who you are dealing with. If you decide to help, you will know who I am, of course." He handed her a card. "Please learn this by heart and then burn it. It would be such an advantage if we could recognise at least one of her disguises."

Yvonne saw him to the door, relieved that he was leaving.

"Meanwhile, perhaps you might think about joining us in France," he said.

After watching him drive away, the brunt of his words echoed in her mind. Why should she give up flying, which was the thing she loved the most, for a dangerous mission behind enemy lines? In all honesty, her sympathies lay far closer to England than France.

Yet there had been a photograph in the paper of a pretty young woman with a bullet hole in her temple. A member of the French resistance, she had been caught and publicly shot. Each day, acts of sadistic retaliation performed by the enemy were reported, or rumoured, and the British public was appalled. With empathetic indignation, the people knew that it could quite easily happen in England.

The arrival of the French officer into an otherwise lovely day had ruined Yvonne's happy mood. Not only had he asked her to delve into the past and try to awaken a possibly nonexistent memory, but he had also suggested that she lay her life on the line. The room was suddenly stifling and she felt the need of fresh summer air. Within minutes she found herself in the tranquil woods near Hamble. But the Frenchman's words would not go away. Think hard, Yvonne. Think hard! What was it that lay obscured by time in the back of her mind? Someone's girlfriend. Why could she not remember? Mallory Cottage flashed momentarily to mind and before it faded she tried to grasp it--capture it. Christmas and the evacuees! That was it! It was Kate Hawkins who had said: I even drew a picture of her. It was Kate who had seen the woman talking to someone in the village. It was Kate who had described her as Ben's friend. Could Ben be involved in espionage? Wouldn't that explain all the prolonged disappearances; his unavoidable absence from the Dunkirk affair; his remarkable change of demeanor in London? Stunned, she stood among the trees watching the sunlight send flickering shadows through the underbrush and wondered if she were perhaps asleep and dreaming. But the rustle of the branches and the breeze brushing her cheek, although intangible, were real enough and she knew that her fearful assumptions were true. Ben Boniface was an enemy agent!

After a long while, she walked back into Hamble and sought out the Bugle pub where she ordered something to steady her nerves. Ben Boniface had deceived them all for several years and had even found his way into a small corner of her heart.

If Kate had drawn a picture, perhaps she might still have it--or at least remember what the woman looked like. But Kate was a mere child, and the picture would most likely be a primitive rendition. Anyway, although the London blitz was long over, occasional raids still occurred which demolished homes. Victims of raids had become nomadic in their need for places to live and Kate could quite likely be amongst them. Yet hadn't David continued his strange correspondence with her over these many months?

As Yvonne looked out across the river she felt calmer. Now positive that Kate had mentioned a strange woman in the village, she wondered if this information should go directly to the French Colonel. Yet she quickly recalled the grim interview that took place on the first day of the blitz in the Baker Street basement. The French military men had frightened her and she did not feel that a child should be subjected to such intense interrogation. Now entrusted with this information, Yvonne knew she was involved, albeit reluctantly. Perhaps, in this case, she could soften the approach to Kate by seeking her out and gently questioning her. Only David knew where she was and contacting him would be the first step.

CHAPTER THIRTEEN

September, 1942

"DDI has done us rather proud, you know," Rupert commented from the passenger seat as they bowled along in the green Daimler. "Far better than sitting on a kit bag in some drafty train corridor. I wonder if poor old Rosebud would have repeated his insulting christening ritual if he had known what a talisman this crate has turned out to be?"

He crammed his hand into a brown paper bag and produced a sandwich. "Rather good of your mess sergeant to provide us with sustenance. Especially since you have forsaken the Army Cooperation squadron for good."

How wonderful it is, David thought, to be back to almost normal--especially with Rupert Barlow. What a positive inspiration he is--and has been all along!

"Well, I must say I wasn't particularly impressed with the grub, Rupert, but I suppose, with your appetite, you scarcely notice how bad anything is."

"Damn right. Doesn't do to be fussy these days."

Rupert chuckled, continuing to munch on the nondescript sandwich.

"Tell me what to expect," David said, keeping his eye on the road. "I'm proficient now with the Lysander and I know its capabilities. Because of your insistence I've flown so many night hours in one I'm beginning to feel like a bat, and although aware that I'm not going into actual combat, I know what I'm about to do is certainly not trouble-free. How frequently have you had to abort a mission, or at least make a hasty retreat because of approaching enemy after delivering your passenger. There seems to be a distinct reluctance on your part to pass along that sort of information. What kind of a ratio is there between uneventful runs and.....others?"

Rupert swallowed the rest of the sandwich before speaking. "None, actually. There's always the element of surprise to think about. But isn't that rather a prominent characteristic of war? There isn't any facet of it that is truly predictable, is there?"

"That's true. But isn't this a bit different?"

"Yes, of course. Anything this hush-hush is a 'bit different'. Sometimes one gets shot at, and sometimes one doesn't. But there's no room for error, you know. If you don't get the right signal from the ground, you have to turn around and go back. No question. If that happens, it creates quite an impact on the agent in the rear. Anticlimax might allow them time to think--to face the reality of exactly what they're doing-- which could result in them refusing to try it again. They know the enemy isn't in the least forgiving when they arrest these people. Since you're in with us now, I can tell you that I heard last month that ninety-three 'terrorists' were executed by the Nazis, and this month another one hundred and thirteen. They were most likely innocent people. Dying is one thing, but dying from the agony of torture, which these agents do, and the remorse that one might have revealed vital information, is a completely different aspect. I'll tell you one thing, old friend. I couldn't do it."

"But you are involved. You could get caught, too."

Rupert said nothing.

"Have you thought about that?" David insisted.

"I thought about it once. I've done a lot of missions now which indicates that I obviously haven't thought about it since."

"But things can be accomplished without incident, can't they?"

Rupert smiled. "It happens all the time. The partisans on the ground are brilliant. When everything's pukka, we're in and out in three minutes flat. I've come to the conclusion that the most difficult part is leaving my passenger behind. I understand, though, that they've devised ingenious ways to 'disappear' even in the path of advancing SS patrols. Determination to deliver their country from the Germans is prevalent, as is hate--which is quite justified, of course. They're going through hell. But for us pilots, we simply turn ourselves around, take off into the night and return to a free country, just like that."

"Do you talk to the agents? I mean, do you know any of them?"

"Some don't want to talk.......and by the way they are all fondly known as 'Joes'--even the woman. They get in the back without a word and slip off into the night on the other side like ghosts. Others are quite friendly, although they avoid discussing their missions like the plague. There are a number of women, you know. Some of them damned good-looking. That makes me feel somewhat humble, I can tell you."

"I think you had everyone baffled at first when you said you were posted somewhere near Newmarket," David said. "First speculations were that you'd deserted in order to bet on the horses. Then we realised that there isn't any racing there anymore."

"That's exactly where we were, though--right on the

race track!   Actually, the brass at the top weren't too cooperative at first because they didn't think 161 and 138 Squadrons were proposing a very good idea concerning sneaky tricks like dropping off and picking up agents.   But I have a strong suspicion that the PM was very much behind the concept, and used a bit of personal influence.   Anyway, we moved to Tempsford--Gibraltar Farm to be exact--in Bedfordshire and built a building within a building--actually within the barn which makes excellent camouflage--to use for preparing the agents for departure.   You'd be amazed at the precautions the SOE officers take in order to prevent detection, going as far as ensuring that French labels are in their clothes and that they don't even carry a spent match that was manufactured in England.   Those agents who are going to jump in from Halifaxes are strapped into parachutes that have been checked and rechecked and properly packed, down to the last inch."

"A building within a building," David mused.   "Do we sleep in the.....barn?"

For the first time in months, he thought of Jenny and the Farnsworth's barn.   Flashes of the carefree walks with Charlie on the downs taunted him, and he envisioned Flint House nestled in its collar of lawns and shrubs, and suddenly felt very homesick. Who, he wondered, might be sleeping in his room now?   But this was no time to reminisce about the past.   Things would never be the same again.   He glanced down at his scarred hands on the steering wheel.   Never.

"No," Rupert said, starting on a second sandwich.   "No one really has a room to themselves, but the accommodations aren't bad at all. We're a few miles from the airfield in a manor house, actually."

"How long do you think it will be before I can fly my first mission?"

"You've only just been accepted, old boy.   You'll probably have to get some more night flying hours in first to get

287

as close to the required two hundred and fifty as possible, to be exact. But the fact that you speak fluent French will give you a seventy-five percent boost, I should imagine." He glanced at David's hands. "Are you sure you're up to it, old man? I mean, it's not a case of twenty minutes to get up, twenty in battle and twenty to get down, as it was in Regatta, you know.   They're long hauls into France.   Think the hands are up to it?"

"You have a short memory," David retorted.   "My hands are probably stronger than yours after all the exercising I did." He winced as he remembered the excruciating pain at first, when he began squeezing a squash ball in order to straighten and strengthen his fingers."

"Once a pilot, always a pilot, I suppose," Rupert said. "Well, at least you're back at it. I think Treacle is about to blow his top working in the banking world, in spite of the fact that he's found himself a wonderful woman and is making heaps of money."

RAF Tempsford, ostensibly Gibraltar Farm, was indeed unobtrusive in the Bedfordshire countryside. Well, David thought, here I am setting out in yet another direction and leaving the piloting of Spitfires and Hurricanes to others. Even my sister is flying them now.

*   *   *

Yvonne wondered what kind of Special Operations David might be flying after she ran into him by sheer chance in Tangmere Operations. He had come from the direction of a Lysander and she could only assume that he flew it in, since he would not elaborate on how he happened to be at Tangmere. Thank heavens, she thought, that he did not witness my arrival in a Spit.

His injuries--hideous enough two years ago that one would assume that he would never function as a normal person again--had been considerably reduced. His face was alive with enthusiasm and he stood straight and tall in his uniform. She noticed the grafted upper and lower lids lifted a little at the corners suggesting a hint of the Orient, but that the eyes themselves sparkled with interest and humour. His smile, slightly lopsided due to some retraction of the scars along his jaw, was infectious.

"I still look like a patchwork quilt," he grinned. "And there's more to come--but it all blends together a bit more each day."

She noticed that he kept his hands in his pockets when not using them and did not know if this might be to protect them, or hide them. When he revealed them to sign papers in Operations, she saw that the grafted skin was still a vivid, shiny, and almost transparent pink. What dreadful pain he must have suffered.

"It seems to me," she said, "that you're successfully following the general trend of this family by being elusive. I tried to contact you in Wales and they said you had left and, of course, had no idea where you were. Actually, I really don't think they had a clue what the contents of your orders were. Running into you here has saved me a lot of extra searching, David."

"Sorry. I hadn't realised so much time had passed. I dropped a note in the post to Bayswater, for what it's worth. As you say, both our parents are decidedly difficult to find these days and I should have known that the chance of them returning to the house there and subsequently relaying my new address to you might be remote."

They chatted over coffee and agreed to meet in London when time would allow. She asked after Patrick, still painfully aware of his hideous injuries and the time it would take before he too could be considered an outpatient.

"They wanted to teach him some kind of trade," David told her.   "But he declined. He has a wonderful mind, you know, and has composed some excellent poetry and prose. He and one of the nurses were getting along famously when I left and they were talking about collaborating on a novel--he doing the composition and she the typing. I think there might be romance in the air."

Yvonne remembered how shocked she had been when first seeing Patrick; but then recalled the beautiful, resonant voice that had turned her head. As Archibald McIndoe had so often indicated, beneath the brutal injuries dwelt normal men, and in this case, a man of great perception and empathy. The novel would no doubt be a masterpiece.

"By the way," she said. "Do you still correspond with that little evacuee who stayed at Mallory Cottage at the beginning of the war?"

David nodded. "Odd, isn't it. She's never given up on me--even when I was unable to reply to her letters. She contributes a great deal to keeping my perspective of the war in balance. For a time I thought only of the RAF and what I was doing in a Hurricane. But she conveyed in a subtle way that civilians are suffering too--really in a worse way because they have no personal defence. She rarely complains, but by reading between the lines, and being aware of her address changes, I know that she's had a very difficult time of it."

Yvonne waited, hoping he might reveal the child's current address. David carefully placed his cup into the saucer with both hands and leaned back.

"Have you had any opportunity to return to Long Bottom?" he asked.   "I understand Flint House is full of military unfortunates who are suffering mentally from the affects of war."

Yvonne shook her head, wishing he had not changed the subject.

"The last time I was in Bayswater," David went on. "Mrs. Dougherty was just leaving having gone through the mail for Father.   She mentioned she had been to Mallory Cottage earlier in the week to get it ready for occupancy. It belongs to Ben Boniface now, you know, but I understand that he's never there."

"Then he should lease it out," she said, too abruptly. "There are plenty of bombed-out people who would love to live there."

"Well, apparently, he has.   In fact the last letter I received from Kate bore Mallory Cottage as her return address which is why I came to the conclusion that her home in Streatham had been demolished. It's only an assumption, of course, because she has never mentioned it. But the fact that she was living in the Canterbury area for a while rather confirms it, don't you think?"

Although loathe to end the delightful interlude with her brother, the task set her by the French officer had taken precedent. Again promising a meeting with David in London when time would permit, she signed the chit for her next delivery and left for Southampton.

The next day found her speeding along the south coast road in a secondhand Morris 10 toward Eastbourne, bent on a mission she doubted could possibly come to fruition. If Kate had been bombed out, surely the sketch would have been destroyed and the chances of her remembering such an obscure moment all those months ago in Long Bottom were even more remote. To avoid fretting over what she thought to be time lost on a hopeless errand, Yvonne mused over the current war news.

Much of the focus was now on Japanese activities in Asia, and the continuing battle between Rommel and Montgomery in North Africa. But the signing of the Declaration of the United Nations in January by no less that twenty-six Allied nations offered a small sense of security and hope. U-boat activity had spread as far as the East coast of

America and there was little doubt that the parameters of the initial conflict had widened alarmingly and now affected the entire world. The fact that Britain was still free seemed to Yvonne a miracle. Malta, under cruel siege by the Germans, had been awarded the George Cross by the king, but this recognition of bravery did not fill empty Maltese stomachs. Yvonne herself had ferried some of the Spitfires for transportation to Malta earlier in the year and had later learned that the forty-seven delivered were rendered unserviceable on the ground by German air attacks. How the Maltese must be suffering, she thought.

She stopped for a sandwich at a small country inn and enjoyed the unique smell and atmosphere of an English pub. Perhaps it was the blend of beer, smoke, ancient timbers, brass and furniture polish, and the faithful old sheep dogs who waited patiently under the benches for their masters that contributed to this. For one short interlude, Yvonne almost forgot that England was at war--until the proprietor suggested that they listen to the noon news.

The Vichy Government was suffering intimidation by the Germans. This time they had demanded that a forced labour law be passed to enable the enemy to take all young men over the age of twenty-one to work for them in Germany. It was also believed that another one hundred and thirteen people had been executed in further retaliatory actions.

Having finished her lunch, she returned to her car and continued eastward. While the Sussex countryside showed a few fresh pockmarks from jettisoned bombs and crashed aircraft, nature had taken hold and covered the older scars in a mantle of green. But towns and villages revealed evidence of haphazard devastation which left historic buildings, once in a fair state of conservation, ruined beyond renovation. Surely, Yvonne thought, nothing at all can be gained by this. She took the main street through Brighton, saddened by what she saw and drove along the coast to the lovely little village of

Rottingdean.   Driving along the cliff road, she noted heavy fortifications well to her right on Beachy Head. Eastbourne, bearing similar scars to those of Brighton, spread below her in the intermittent sunshine.   She tried to remember the last time she had been home and she calculated that it had been many months.

Long Bottom appeared unscathed, and her spirits lifted as she passed Mallory Cottage and the Post Office and coasted through the village toward Flint House. Perhaps a glimpse of home might put everything back into the proper perspective and help to dispel the growing seed of uneasiness the Frenchman had so successfully implanted.

She parked opposite the gates and looked in, pleased that the house looked normal enough, although she could see no signs of life.   The grounds, now showing hints of early autumn colours, did not seem entirely unkempt. How long, she wondered, will it be before this conflict ends? We've been at war now for three years and some thought it would only last three weeks. She sighed, turned the car around and drove slowly toward the Post Office.

 Mr. Banberry's greeting was somewhat offhand as she entered and he spoke to her as if continuing a recent conversation instead of initiating one.

"The Hawkins boy isn't back yet, you know," he said, eyeing her uniform with obvious appreciation. "But the others are there."

It seemed to Yvonne that he had no concept of time and that her long absence from the village meant little to him.

"Where has Hugh been that he isn't back yet?" she asked.

"Oh, of course you couldn't possibly know that he was buried in debris during the London blitz and is still in a bit of a mental fog."

"Buried!"

"Yes, it affected his mind. Sort of prolonged shock."

"What about Kate?"   Yvonne wondered who "the others" might be and hoped fervently that Kate was all right.

"She seems to be all right.   But Hugh's in a special boarding school in the north.   I haven't seen him since Kate moved into the cottage, but I understand he's allowed to come home sometimes and is, in fact, due in today.   Nice boy, from what I can remember. I suppose he must be about fifteen or sixteen now."

"Who's actually living in the cottage?" Yvonne asked.

"Mrs. Hawkins with young Kate, and a little one named Annie. Ben Boniface seemed to have had everything arranged in anticipation of Kate being homeless since he had his solicitors keep an eye on her. I understand they had a devil of a job trying to find her after her home was bombed."

How strange, Yvonne thought, that Ben would show this kind of benevolence while spying for the enemy.

"She had a bit of a setback in May, you know."

"As if she hadn't had any before!"

"Well, I suppose this one must have been due to an accumulation of things. After the hit and run raids on Eastbourne she seemed to withdraw behind a barrier of bravado--a sort of defence against fear, if you will. Her brother succumbed to trauma in another way, of course. I do wonder if any of our children will remember how to live without anxiety again."

"Is she......ill?"

"Not in the physical sense of the word. She lost interest in her art studies which were her greatest pleasure. A friend, Clarence Baxter, is trying to get her back on track. He's an artist himself, you know. He does that political cartoon in the Tribune for one thing."

"Then she isn't pursuing art at all?"

Yvonne could see her plans rapidly crumbling.

"Baxter says he has made some progress with her. He's sort of her mentor and surrogate father. The father's away in the Navy, you know."

"What?" Yvonne tried to concentrate on Mr. Banberry's remarks.

"The father. He's away in the Navy. But I go over and help out from time to time. Kate showed me a couple of sketches just the other day of your mother and Mrs. Dougherty she said she had done from memory, so I would say she is getting back into it. They were extraordinarily good."

"Perhaps I should drop by to see how they are getting along."

"Good idea." He began vigorously banging a rubber stamp down on some envelopes. "It will be nice when you can all move back into Flint House," he said, without looking up. "We never see a soul from the hospital out and about, except a couple of nurses once in a while. It's downright spooky, really."

As Yvonne opened the cottage gate, Charlie streaked down the path toward her and leaped around her like a puppet on a pogo stick.

She narrowed her eyes against the sunlight as a girl opened the front door and hurried toward her.

"I'm sorry. He's so full of energy, but he means no harm." The dark eyes flashed as her expression changed from concern to recognition. "It's Yvonne Parke, isn't it?"

Could it be possible, Yvonne thought, that the little pixie of 1939 could have changed so much? Could this vibrant young girl be the once quizzical elf who evaluated George Ravensbrook's black eye all those months ago?

Yvonne recognised the school emblem on the blazer pocket. If the school had maintained its excellence in spite of wartime conditions, then Kate was in good hands. Small in stature, there was a certain intrinsic charm about her as she spoke. Most intriguing were the sloe-shaped eyes that conveyed a myriad of emotions. The stoic cocoon Mr. Banberry had described was not in evidence. Perhaps the child had recovered more than he realised.

"Please come in," Kate was saying. "Mother was just making some tea."   She led Yvonne to the front room and gestured toward an armchair. "It's been quite some time now since we've seen any of the Parke family in Long Bottom," she said. "You may know that I correspond with David, but I haven't seen him since before the London blitz."

"I saw him quite recently actually," Yvonne said. "In fact, it was he who told me you were here."

"I knew he had been injured," Kate said, quietly. "But he never told me how seriously."

"Perhaps he didn't want to worry you."

"In which case, he must have been badly hurt."

Yvonne nodded slowly. "Yes."

"How seriously?"

"He was burned, Kate.   His aeroplane caught fire and.......he was burned."

"He couldn't write his own letters for a while. It must have been his hands--or his eyes."

Yvonne nodded again. "He isn't quite the same any more."

"I'll bring in the tea. Mother will be here in a moment." She hesitated at the door.   "He suffered a great deal, didn't he?"

"Yes. But he's so much better now.   In fact, he's back on active duty."

Kate returned with the tea tray accompanied by her mother whom she quickly introduced.

"Kate has been writing to your brother all along," Mrs. Hawkins said, pouring tea.

"Yes, I know." Yvonne took the cup and saucer offered her. "You have no idea how much he looked forward to your letters, Kate........and the drawings."

Kate smiled.

"Do you still have all the sketches you made when you

were here before?"

"No. They were destroyed in the blitz, except the ones I sent to David. I did leave some here in the cottage when I left, but they're not here anymore."

Yvonne's heart sank. "Do you remember all the things you drew then?"

"I don't want to remember some of the things. But I've redrawn others.....like Charlie and Mr. Banberry."

".........and Mr. Boniface?"

"I haven't seen him for a very long time. I'm not sure I remember how he looks."

"I heard you recently did one of Mrs. Dougherty and my mother. You haven't seen them in a long time either. Didn't you do them from memory?"

"I doubt that they are entirely accurate."

"I would particularly like to have any you could do. Sort of mementos from the beginning of the war."

Kate looked doubtful.

"Perhaps if you manage to recall Ben, you could do others. Didn't you mention once that he had a girl friend?"

Acutely aware that her questions were bordering on invasive, Yvonne wondered how she might continue. She felt uncomfortable as Kate hesitated.

"I don't really know if he did," she said, at last. "I did see him meet someone I didn't know in the village once. But it might have been just somebody asking the way."

"But didn't you draw this person?"

"I think so. I don't really remember."

Yvonne felt perspiration dampening her upper lip.

"Perhaps she may have been a relative, you know. Perhaps she might be able to tell us where Ben is so that you could contact him if you needed anything done here."

"The solicitors do that. They pay my school fees and for any maintenance on the cottage. Miss Parke, I barely saw that woman's face, you know."

297

"Yes, I know, but you drew her before."

Kate frowned as she put down her tea cup. "Yes, perhaps I did."

Mrs. Hawkins offered Yvonne more tea. "Miss Parke," she said. "You couldn't have known this, of course, but my son is due for a visit home this afternoon and we must go to the station to meet him. It's a big occasion for us because it will be his first visit back to Long Bottom since he became…..ill. We must catch the bus to the station."

Yvonne felt tears of frustration sting her eyes. "Oh, my dear. Of course!" she murmured. "Mr. Banberry mentioned it, but I had forgotten. I will be most happy to drive you, and then I'll go so that you can have some time alone with him."

Mrs. Hawkins began to put the tea things back on the tray. She straightened and looked directly at Yvonne.

"We would be grateful for the lift, but I don't think that will be necessary for you to leave," she said. "Kate will think very hard about your suggestion concerning the sketches, won't you Kate?" She stared squarely into Yvonne's eyes and gave a barely perceptible nod. "I'm sure she will think very hard."

* * *

Kate watched the train draw into Eastbourne station and edged nearer to the barrier in order to better see the platform. How would Hugh look? Would he be as strange and uncommunicative as he was six months ago during his last visit home in Canterbury?

"There he is, Kate," her mother said. "You see, he's so very much better now."

A pale young man came through the ticket barrier and

stood looking about him. He looked puzzled as they hurried toward him and seemed bewildered as Kate took his hand.

"Hello, Hugh," she said.

"Hello." His deepened voice astonished her and she felt intimidated by his almost adult height. Although he smiled, she knew he did not recognise her.

As Yvonne drove them all back to Long Bottom, he spoke hesitatingly about recent occurrences at school, choosing his words carefully and often pausing for long moments, never once mentioning the past. When they arrived at the cottage, Kate watched him carefully as he shaded his eyes and looked over the gate into the garden. He commented on a ginger cat skulking under the roses, and once inside the cottage, stooped to pat Charlie, asking his name. He straightened and turned to Kate.

"I'm Hugh, you know."

Lunch was a strained affair of forced conversation, artificial pleasantries and carefully worded questions. Kate longed for it to end.

"Perhaps I could be excused and try to draw that picture for you," she said to Yvonne. It was clear that the woman in the village had suddenly become very important, but Kate doubted that she could remember all the features after so long. Yet the barely perceptible nod and significant eye contact between her mother and Yvonne had not gone unnoticed.

Hugh fidgeted with his serviette. "Could we take that dog for a walk before you do any drawing?" he asked. "I could do with some fresh air."

Doubtless, he too was feeling the strain.

Yvonne looked at her watch.

"It wouldn't take long," Kate said. "Since Charlie isn't allowed to sniff around his old haunts at Flint House any more, perhaps you wouldn't mind if we went as far as the Long Man and gave him a good run instead." All of a sudden the cottage seemed airless and the outdoors beckoned, offering relief.

299

Kate felt guilty as Yvonne suppressed an exasperated sigh and said: "All right. Perhaps I'll go with you. The walk and fresh air will do me good, too." It was obvious that Yvonne Parke had come for something other than a friendly visit and that she was attempting to suppress her impatience.

Again Kate watched Hugh carefully as they tramped up the Wilmington main street toward the church, alert for any signs of recognition. Following the old wall toward the back, she looked up at the faded outline of the Long Man. Mr. Banberry had commented that the lack of maintenance was deliberate in order to prevent his being a navigational aid to the enemy from the air.

The musty fragrance of the old church timbers blended pleasantly with the tangy scent of the hedgerows as they approached the stile. She looked up toward the hill half expecting the stricken Dornier to appear above its crest.

Hugh stood silently staring at the stile, but seemed unperturbed. All at once, he threw back his head and held his arms out toward the hill. His terrible cry echoed across the downs as he leapt over the stile and began to stagger along the hedge line, bleating like a wounded animal.

"Wait!" Kate yelled, lunging over the stile. "Wait, Hugh! It's all right! It's all right!"

Hugh mindlessly careened back and forth into the brambles, oblivious to the raking thorns, and then suddenly he flung himself under the hedgerow.

"Hugh!" Kate screamed as she ran toward him with Yvonne sprinting ahead.

He whimpered with pain as he struggled, entangling himself further, then dropped to his knees, clutching his stomach.

"Oh, God," he sobbed. "Oh, God!"

"I'll take care of him," Yvonne panted. "Go to Flint House and find a doctor.......and for heaven's sake, run like the wind."

With Charlie racing beside her, who obviously thought that it was all a lark, Kate sped through Wilmington and along the Lewes Road. As in a nightmare, her legs felt like lead and her feet sucked into imagined mud as she struggled along. The large gate hasp at Flint House weighed heavily in her trembling hands and the house itself seemed to be a hundred miles away along the driveway.

"Someone!" she cried. "Please, someone! Hurry! I think my brother has gone mad!"

A nurse appeared at the front door and watched her progress along the driveway. Kate pointed frantically toward the downs, unable to catch her breath.

"Please send help," she gasped at last. "Please help my brother."

"If he's hurt, this isn't that kind of hospital," the nurse said.

"You don't understand," Kate shouted. "He's gone mad. Mad!"

A man in military uniform appeared behind the nurse at the door.

"Be quiet, child!" he said. "Don't you know this is a hospital?"

"My brother," Kate said, desperately attempting to calm her voice. "He's been ill for a long time. He was buried, you see. But something up there has terrified him." She pointed behind her toward the Long Man. "He isn't making any sense."

The officer said something quietly to the nurse beside him and reached into his pocket to produce some keys.

"This had better not be a joke," he said. "Our time is very precious here, you know."

"Oh, it isn't a joke," Kate stammered. "You'll see. He's in the brambles with Yvonne."

The man sighed. "All right, but you'll have to show me the way."

The short drive lasted an eternity for Kate as she sensed the man's irritation. She wanted to reassure him that Hugh was genuinely ill, but knew he would be difficult to convince. As they approached the hedgerow, she could see her brother still kneeling amongst the thorns quietly sobbing. Yvonne knelt on the grass beside him, murmuring softly to him. Hugh's face, swollen and tear-streaked, looked deathly pale, and he seemed completely unaware of his surroundings. He moaned from time to time and rocked himself gently back and forth.

"He's calm now," Yvonne said as they approached. "But I believe he's had some kind of a trauma. He's terrified."

The doctor's irritability vanished the moment he saw Hugh. Somehow, among the three of them, they disentangled the boy from the brambles and led him to the churchyard where the car waited.

"I didn't want Kate to see," Hugh said, clearly. "It's not the sort of thing one forgets in a hurry, you know."

"He's in good hands," Yvonne said, putting her arm about Kate's shaking shoulders. "He recalled the whole awful incident when Mrs. Mallory was killed. Every small detail."

Kate preferred to walk home with Charlie while Yvonne accompanied Hugh to Flint House in the doctor's car. The dreadful sound of Hugh's anguished howl still echoed in her mind, and the terror in his eyes would haunt her forever.

Mr. Banberry waited at the cottage gate when she arrived, awkwardly holding Annie in the crook of his arm.

"I hope everything will be for the best," he said. "Sudden recollection like that can often be a shock, you know. He's been in denial for so long. Your mother is over at Flint House."

In a short while Yvonne joined them and made preparations to leave. "I must go," she said. "But will you promise to give me news of Hugh? I truly believe that he's going to get better."

Kate escorted her to her car.

302

"This drawing isn't very good," she said, handing Yvonne a sheet of paper. "But Mother said it was important that you should have it."

*   *   *

November, 1942

Heavy ferrying assignments kept Yvonne busy for two days, but her plans for the third day--her time off--were set. The London address remained clear in her mind and she wondered how well the Frenchman would receive the drawing. She had studied it herself and concluded that the face, although well-drawn, was nondescript. The pale eyes stared like those of an inanimate china doll, but there was a disturbing coldness about them. Heavy pencil strokes suggested dark hair while the mouth, bracketed by creases, lacked any sign of humour.

"The artist is extremely observant," the Frenchman said after he had studied the drawing for some time. "This is almost identical to the composite sketch we have of Dierick on file. Would you be willing to reveal the name of the artist?"

Yvonne shook her head. "No. She's a child. You have your picture. Isn't that enough?"

He turned to view the rooftop scene from his office window and Yvonne followed suit. London as she knew it would never be the same again. Huge gaps between battered buildings had begun to cover their nudity with self-seeded grasses and trees. Shadowy outlines of fireplaces and balustrades were imprinted on surviving flanking walls offering the observer a brief glimpse of the now demolished floor plan.

"I think you should know," he said, at last, "that the

Vichy government approved a Compulsory Labor Law on the fourth which is simply another name for forced labour. I think you'll see that those who are considered eligible will join the resistance and go underground to avoid it; but who knows how many we can trust?"

"Of course," Yvonne murmured, gathering together her gloves and gas mask case. "I'm afraid I must hurry. My continuing lateness for duty won't be tolerated any longer."

As she rose to leave, a young man quietly entered the room and delivered a printed sheet to the Colonel without speaking. He looked unsmilingly at Yvonne as he left the room. She hesitated as the Frenchman read, watching the paper tremble in his fingers. When he looked up, the expression of hate on his face shocked her.

"The Germans now completely occupy France," he said. "There is no doubt that Laval will receive full power. I doubt that Pétain will survive this. He's an old and disillusioned man."

"But the Vichy.....?"

He shook his head. "France is entirely occupied by the enemy. Now we must double our efforts to arm and train the secret army to oppose them from behind the lines."

He opened the door for her. "I believe you have relatives in Aix-en-Provence, do you not?"

Her nod was barely perceptible as she turned to leave.

"Good afternoon, Miss Parke. I imagine we shall be hearing again from you soon?"

CHAPTER FOURTEEN

France, January, 1943

While large attendance meetings were discouraged in the organisation due to the risk of detection by both the French and German adversaries, Janine had agreed this once to meet her group of partisans in a local farm house three kilometers north of Aix-en-Provence. Apart from anything else, mass meetings were forbidden by German law and they would need to be extremely cautious. Some of the younger members were anxious for more aggressive action and wanted to talk about it. It was thus agreed that they would arrive at the farm at staggered intervals within an hour's time to avoid arousing suspicion.

Janine listened now to the murmur of conversation around the fireplace and studied the faces reflected in the flickering light. Some were young and eager, others, older and more cautious, while still others drew upon varying specific talents to assist in the overall secret war of the Résistance. They were partisans who tenaciously prepared for the day when they would assist the allies in liberating their country from the grisly grasp of the hated Germans, and who were willing to die for this cause. All of them were also vital links in the escape routes from the north.

They discussed the invasion of Vichy France by the Germans in November, commenting on the silent swiftness of its execution with little or no resistance from the small French army. The group knew that the military had originally intended to show their disapproval, in spite of orders not to resist from General Bridoux, the Vichy minister of war. With the arrest of only one General who insisted on putting up a fight, the whole affair was quickly over. The French fleet, however, had been scuttled at Toulon as a gesture of refusal to be used against the Allies. This action foiled all negotiable instruments that the Vichy might have held against the Germans.

The group spoke of the treachery and betrayal that had sprung up as a forerunner to the Vichy Milice, now in formation. These adversities were no strangers to the Résistance and no member allowed his or her guard against it to weaken. Yet clever and undetectable plants had become all too common in their ranks causing tension and distrust toward newcomers. In Holland, the entire resistance movement had been blown apart by such betrayal.

It seemed to Janine that the Vichy government had lost sight of its proper focus in France and appeared to be sympathising entirely with German policies versus French interests in North Africa and in France itself. When the Allies invaded North Africa, indignation erupted in some areas of France. Vichy government activist and close admirer of Pétain, Josef Darnand, was most anxious to send his own formation, The Service d'Ordre Légionnaire, to fight against the invaders and thus protect French possessions in North Africa. Conversely, anti-Gaullists in Vichy joined the demand of the German collaborators in Paris had echoed the insistence that France declare war on America and Britain.   But the

Résistance had grown stronger and bolder, keeping in view the overall desire to rid France of its German occupancy.

With such conflict within the country, unrest bubbled to the surface and rumour had it that a growing anxiety hung over the head of the German Führer. Apparently he felt that something had to be done to keep order. Who better than to organise this than the pro-German Pierre Laval?

On this last day of January, Janine knew that the law establishing the Milice Française had been published in the Journal officiel in Vichy. Its voluntary members were non-Jewish and French-born with no affiliation to any secret society whatsoever. *No affiliation with any secret society whatsoever,* she repeated to herself, pulling her anorak tighter around her. Its members, then, would have no loyalty toward the hill-based, and as yet undisciplined and untrained, Maquis, or to any underground partisan activities and would therefore be nothing less than a French SS. She looked at the ring of concerned faces around the fire, studying each one with analytic scrutiny.

While the selection of drop off and pick up zones was still necessary since weaponry supply was also involved as well as agents and important fugitives from the enemy, her participation in the escape routes was running well, too. She had almost lost count of the number of Allied pilots, soldiers and fugitive dignitaries that had been delivered to safety across the mountains into Spain and ultimately to England via Gibraltar. Innumerable safe houses stretched along the routes where people risked their lives daily to help pass along the evaders and escapers. The "O'Leary" escape line, initiated by a Belgian military doctor named Albert-Marie Guérisse and now fondly known as the "Pat" line, had survived the tragic "Comet Line" which had been established and running in Belgium, but betrayed in November. The O'Leary line, then, was vital. Janine mentally ran its course in her mind pinpointing names like Haute Savoie, Annemasse at the

307

frontier, Ugines, Lake Annecy, Chambéry and finally, Marseilles. If only, she thought, we might have combined our efforts enough to rescue those military prisoners held in the fortresses near Nimes and La Turchie so near by at Monte Carlo before they were all taken to Germany for interrogation. But they could only do so much. Instead, she had watched as the enemy advanced into southern France, and noted their dispersal to later relay her observations in code to the Beaconsfield code center near London through a transmitter operator in Marseilles. As yet--and thankfully so--she had not been obliged to use her expertise in other activities. There had been no further word concerning the incoming agent, Marcel, and for security's sake, she had made no enquiries. If he had been caught, they would most certainly know about it.

The mountain guides, arrangers and partisans gathered here were all trusted and familiar to her and had been active within the organization for more than a year. For one brief moment she thought about her parents and desperately hoped there would be no probing of her past activities by the Milice now that the Nazis fully occupied France. Would her frequent presence at significant pre-war social functions where political and international situations were openly discussed, be remembered? Or the unaccountable coincidence of Claude's Simone's presence at the same gatherings? Considering that he was now a known double agent, somebody might conclude that there was some connection. As it was, Dierick was already aware of their association. In all truth, her parents were innocent of any collaboration with covert operations. Obviously they must have suspected her involvement, but when they broached the subject she quickly deterred further questioning. In this way they had, indeed, remained uninformed and ostensibly innocent of any knowledge of her activities. Since they were entirely adamant about staying in France, it was imperative that they knew as little as possible.

Again, she scanned the faces endeavoring to comfort herself with the assurance that each one was loyal. But should any fragment of information slip into the wrong hands, no doubt a rapid inquiry would begin by this new Milice Française and all family connections taken into consideration.

Convinced now that there were enough trained people to safely operate the escape routes and to form the reception committees that met incoming aircraft, she felt that in order to deter any adverse focus on her parents, she must return to England and leave the area embracing Aix-en-Provence. She allowed herself the infrequent luxury of thinking about her husband and children, and longed for them. Twice she had been due to return to London during the past eleven months and twice her pick up had been aborted; firstly due to weather, and secondly because known enemy collaborators were skulking near the arranged area of contact.

But now circumstances had changed and it was imperative that she leave.

One of the younger women was speaking, gesturing widely in her usual manner.

"He is moving southward from midi France," she said.

"Where is he from?" another asked.

"Nobody knows, but he has been operating in a wide radius. It will be good when he arrives since we've anticipated his coming for so long now. He has known so many successes, not only with the escape routes, but also with incidental sabotage activities We can seek advice from him before we help him get to safety. Both the Gestapo and the SS are out looking for him, you know."

They were speaking of the agent named Marcel who had been extremely active in all facets of clandestine operations, which included the escape routes, spanning wide areas from the north.

"Who is his contact?" someone asked.

"He hasn't revealed one. He can't afford to breeze into town with a fanfare, you know." She glanced at Janine. "I should tell you, Phalene, that when he does arrive I want to join up with him."

The girl was young and impressionable and had obviously conjured up some dashing roué in her imagination. Yet for some time now, Janine had suspected that some distrust and dissatisfaction was infusing the integrity of the group. The constant watch for betrayal and treachery was taking its toll.

Janine looked at her watch. A Lysander would be due in less than an hour and the selected field must be ready. Two returning agents would squeeze into the aft cockpit and she must ensure they understood the need for haste. Since her arrival in France, she had seen Rupert several times in the cockpit, but the turnarounds were so fast there was never time for conversation. She felt thankful that he did not know who she was.

"Time enough to prepare for the arrival of Marcel," she said. "We have to leave now for the field."

*   *   *

April, 1943

In spite of the victory at Alamein in North Africa and the subsequent lightening of spirits in England, London nonetheless appeared down-at-heel to Yvonne. Although spasmodic hit-and-run air raids continued, and damaged homes and buildings were systematically shored up or pulled down, older repairs had begun to deteriorate. The inadequate clothes coupon allowance prompted people to clean and brush up their existing wardrobes which were showing the marks of time. Food was scarcer than ever and housewives were concocting strange new dishes from unlikely ingredients. Whale meat and horse flesh were now part of the weekly menu. An air of lethargy hovered over the city and it seemed that it hung in limbo.

"Deladier has been sent to a concentration camp, Miss Parke," the French Colonel said. "And Leval is due to discuss the common defence of Europe with Hitler. Surely you can no longer procrastinate. There is so little going on here for you, and so much is needed in France."

Angry now, Yvonne rose from her chair. "You've hounded me all these months and I thought I had made it quite clear that I wish to continue my duties with ATA."

She sat down quickly, aware that she sounded petulant and childish. True, aircraft deliveries were still very much required and one of the women had been tested for four-engine bombers in February which certainly indicated that even more demanding flying hours lay ahead. Yet conditions in France had certainly worsened and she admitted her conscience bothered her as well as the Frenchman's insinuations. The ranks of ATA had swelled considerably since its onset and, although she now wore the double stripes of a First Officer on her shoulder, she knew that her services were quite likely dispensable.

The Frenchman pressed the tips of his fingers together, watching her.

"One has to be particularly courageous to become involved in something like this," Yvonne said, at last. "I'm not sure that I'm up to that."

When accompanying Hugh to Flint House, the military patients she saw there had left a disturbing impression. While normal in appearance, the doctor explained that their behavior was often unpredictable. One good-looking youth wearing a Naval Lieutenant's uniform had approached her as she left the foyer and asked her when the next train left for Nice. Although strong during past adversities, Yvonne questioned her endurance under direct German oppression.

"What about Dunkirk?" the Colonel asked.

"You know about that?"

"Why do you think I have been so persistent?"

"So you think I could do it?"

"Without question."

He shifted his position, continuing to watch her closely.

"Surely I would require some kind of training."

"Yes, indeed. That would begin immediately."

He leaned forward, eagerly.

She sighed and stood up. "All right."

With a look of triumph, he shook her hand.

"I knew you'd come around in the end," he said. "My name, incidentally, is Andre Chambrun."

"Comte Andre de Chambrun?"

"I'm surprised that you would remember. I met you in Aix-en-Provence when you were a very little girl. I suppose you know that your mother ....well......."

He had no need to complete his sentence. Yvonne knew now that her speculations concerning her mother had all been justified. She also knew that she could not reveal this to anyone.

*   *   *

May, 1943

If the awful clutches of apprehension were not so overwhelming, the soft velvet night might have been quite romantic. The moonlight over Tempsford lent the landscape an aura of fantasy and Yvonne--now code-named Renee-- wished that it was indeed, all a dream. She glanced at the female agent beside her and tried to smile. Since this was Nichole's third jump into France, it stood to reason that she might feel more assured than her less experienced companions, and Yvonne longed for similar confidence.

"An excellent night for it," Nichole said, running her fingers through boyishly cut blonde hair. "I hope the weather holds until after we have shuttled down to Tangmere."

Although all preparations were made at Gibraltar Farm in Tempsford, Lincolnshire, the actual flight to France would leave from Tangmere, primarily because of the shorter flight distance. A cottage near Shopwyke would be their interim place of waiting before embarkation since they were not to be seen by the general staff at the airfield.

When they had met at the last briefing in London, Yvonne thought that Nichole gave the impression of a naïve English school girl with her bobbed hair and rounded, rosy cheeks, rather than a seasoned saboteur. Yet, she had immediately liked the way she adapted to difficult requirements during training, and her quick wit which lent a relaxed atmosphere to an otherwise tense situation. Other than this somewhat superficial friendship, Yvonne knew nothing concerning Nichole's background nor, in fact, her real name. This situation prevailed throughout the group in training and no one knew or asked about Yvonne's connections.

"We have a well-seasoned Halifax pilot who has delivered at our drop zone often," Nichole went on. "It'll be a piece of cake. You'll see."

Their training in secret intelligence activities had been supervised by Free French personnel while the actual parachute jumping and ground exits from aircraft were handled by the pilots themselves, who knew their students only by code names or as potential Joes. It was obvious that General de Gaulle did not favour the existence of British SOE agents in France since he believed they infringed on his own operations. Yvonne was not comfortable with the rift between so-called allies and had experienced second thoughts about her affiliation with the French several times.

She eyed the third member of their party, who sat quietly clutching the handles of a canvas crew bag. Code named Margot, she was dark and withdrawn and seemed unaware of the comments going on around her.

"The first time is always the worst," Nichole continued. "But there's no wind and we should have little trouble hitting the mark. Make sure you move fast and get rid of the parachutes as soon as you land."

Apart from the fear of being met by a unit of German soldiers, the parachute jump itself loomed ahead. Yvonne had managed to get through the training with no mishaps apart from a scraped elbow, and wondered if her luck would continue to hold. I'm supposed to *fly* aeroplanes, for heavens sake, she thought, not *jump* out of them.

For the hundredth time she rehearsed the routine in her mind and fervently hoped that the contact would be there. All semblance of British manufacture identification had been removed from their clothing, even down to the last handkerchief. She and Margot had been issued papers and a letter inviting them to teach at a school near Toulouse in the south. Their credentials stated that they were both from Lyons. Their forged degrees in education, birth certificates, and required German identification documents were included. While Nichole would land with them, her ultimate destination was Paris where a brave leader of the Resistance who worked directly for General de Gaulle, one Jean Moulin, would receive her after she had completed an assignment for him en route from the south. She was, in fact, going into the heart of the organisation where danger lurked at every turn.

Yvonne wished that Margot might be more communicative since they were to work together, but the girl had seemed preoccupied from the start since she obviously knew that her position as a wireless operator was precarious at best. Due to mobile detection units, several operators had already been caught.

"Once we meet our contact," Yvonne said, attempting to sound reassuring, "we'll move quickly southward and keep moving in order to avoid detection."

"Yes, of course."

While no dual briefing had been offered and Margot was not apprised of Yvonne's appointed task, she was nonetheless qualified to relay any message to their interpreter in London in the given code. Once the task was completed, Yvonne was to return to England while Margot would remain in France to await another agent.

Yvonne closed her eyes, remembering the details of Kate's sketch. She knew the face could be deftly altered by expert disguise and had spent hours watching an artist make possible modifications and changes in every detail to copies of the original. She had studied variances in stances and deportment and learned to quickly identify inconsistencies from films and photographs. Expert civil investigators had picked up fragments of Dierick's movements in England, but had been unable to apprehend her. Meanwhile both British and French agents were on the lookout for her in France. They knew of only one person who had actually conversed with her in England and would be the most likely to recognize her. Yet he too was elusive and a known double agent.

Yvonne's initial indignation had softened into sympathy when she learned that Ben had been forced into a dual role. The investigators had informed her that he was operating under the name of Pierre Bonhomme--a gentile name--and were surprised that she knew him only as Ben Boniface and knew nothing about his given name, Claude Simone. She wondered how the FFIC had obtained this information since he was supposedly involved with British Intelligence. They also knew that his erratic movements had puzzled the staff at M16. since he was apparently functioning without orders from either side and there seemed to be no structure to his system. He sometimes disappeared completely during these inconsistent wanderings. Oddly, he had made no effort to contact the enemy, and his spasmodic spurts of sabotage were always beneficial to the French and British operations. He was, nonetheless, a dubious ally and must be returned to England in order to justify his motives. But first, if at all possible, he must be used to identify Dierick. The German woman had been instrumental in the devastating end to the Dutch resistance by use of infiltration and betrayal. At all costs, she must be prevented from inflicting a similar tragedy on the French organisation.

One of only a few who actually knew Ben Boniface of Long Bottom, it seemed that Yvonne was the obvious choice to find him in France. She wondered how much these inquisitive officials really knew of her acquaintance with him.

With flimsy evidence concerning the general area in which he was thought to be currently operating, her task then, was to locate him and immediately contact her code base. If by some stroke of luck he made contact with the German, Beatrix Dierick, while under Yvonne's observation, this would indeed be a bonus. Otherwise, the process might take much longer.

The French pilot signaled that they were ready to leave. Yvonne picked up her gear and followed him out into the night to embark on the first leg of this terrifying errand.

*   *   *

July, 1943

The words Hugh read aloud held no special interest for her. Just to hear his voice again was all that really mattered. Kate cupped her chin in the heels of her hands and listened to him read news items from the newspaper. The initial stutter had almost disappeared, and he no longer fought to find the correct word. Now nearing his sixteenth birthday, his academic achievements were equal to his peers which qualified him to sit for his final secondary exams. If he succeeded, he would most likely leave home again, and she hated that thought. Too many times those near to her had gone away.

"The Americans are calling our RDF (Radio Detection Finding) Radar, you know," Hugh said, eyeing her over the top of the newspaper. "I like that word--R-a-d-a-r." He snapped the paper inside out and carefully folded it back. "Here's something that ought to please David Parke. Someone has come up with some kind of combatant against viral infection and its been called Penicillin."

Kate supposed that David might be very pleased to hear about this because he probably still had friends undergoing surgery.

"David isn't in hospital any more, Hugh. He's been assigned to a Special Duties squadron. I haven't a clue what he's doing, but I can tell you he's really happy to be back flying."

"I should think his injuries were rather bad," Hugh said "when you take into consideration the amount of time he spent in hospital. I shouldn't think he would be doing anything-- well, you know--of much significance."

"Yvonne said he was burned." Kate said. "She also said he was determined to fly again and I suppose that's all that really matters, don't you think?"

317

Hugh nodded absently and continued to scan the newspaper. "There's an article here about the American servicemen we have in England now. There are some new ones billeted at the other end of the village, you know," he said. "I saw some of them in Mr. Banberry's post office the other day when I was picking up the evening paper." He grinned. "There was a girl in there, too, trying to buy some stamps. They weren't half making it difficult for her, flirting and asking her out, you know."

Kate's spirits rose. Could it be possible there might be a local friend for her at last?

"A girl?"

"Well, she was a young woman, actually. She was asking Mr. Banberry if he knew where Ben was."

"Did he know?" Kate's mother interjected from the stove. Her terse tone matched the sudden ramrod straightness of her back.

Hugh shook his head. "He told her that we haven't seen Ben in Long Bottom for months."

"What did she look like?"

Hugh shrugged. "Hard to say, really. Sort of fair I suppose and...... well, you know.......young looking."

"Are you sure she was fair?"

Hugh looked at his mother curiously. "Yes, I'm sure. What's so important about her?"

Although she did not understand why, Kate did not like the way this conversation was progressing. Once again the matter of the strange woman in the village had surfaced, although from Hugh's description she could not have been the same one. Perhaps all his talk of spies had affected their mother, too. Yet, hadn't Yvonne Parke also been interested in the unusual visitor? Had Kate seen and actually sketched a known German spy all that time ago? The thought sickened her. She exchanged a quick look with her mother, who immediately moved toward the door.

"Keep an eye on Annie for a minute, will you Kate? I must run over to the post office for some stamps," she said.

The only functioning telephone in the village was in Mr. Banberry's stationery shop and Kate knew that Hugh had hit a nerve. Now enlightened to Yvonne's urgent need for the sketch, she surmised that perhaps her artistic talent had, in fact, placed her in dire jeopardy.

The balmy summer days and the six week respite from school studies allowed Kate to concentrate entirely on art. With renewed interest, she sometimes worked with an artist friend of Mr. Baxter's who came down from London on occasional weekends. Gaining experience daily, she experimented with pastels and water colours. Always seeking subjects, she wandered along the hedgerows studying flowers and grasses, and often asked the people who lived in the village to momentarily stand still for her while she sketched quickly and accurately. Later she finished the drawings in more detail, adding colour, texture, and shadows.

It seemed to her that these pleasant days in the country belied a world caught up in the turmoil of war, until Hugh apprised her of the daily news. While the tide of battle turned in favour of the Allies as they successfully invaded Sicily on the 9th, innocent people nevertheless died daily in alarming numbers as a result of it. The Fascist leader of Italy, Generalisimo Benito Mussolini, was arrested on the 23rd allowing an anti-Fascist government to form. But six days later the Germans quickly moved into the French zone previously occupied by the Italians. One advancement, she thought, always appears to cause some form of nasty counteraction.

*   *   *

Late August, 1943

Yvonne and Margot's arrival in France had been faultless. Their cover as teachers in a small parochial girls' school near Toulouse was almost too good to be true. Margot taught the gym class with surprising efficiency while Yvonne took an English class. At first her unaccustomed association with little girls had been difficult, but as her students began to show interest, she actually enjoyed her newly found profession.

Success in tracing Ben or Dierick, however, had been elusive. She bicycled about the countryside during her free time simply keeping her eyes and ears open, and made a point to become well-acquainted with shopkeepers and the local farmers and housewives, always careful to keep her enquiries discreet and casual until she had won their confidence. If Ben had been observed in this area before, nobody seemed to know of him. Meanwhile, to justify her presence in France to the Free French, she observed certain German troop movements and occasional unusual occurrences which Margot transmitted to England via wireless.

At last, she made a small breakthrough which produced a new concern. She thought one of the shopkeepers had dropped a vague hint pertaining to some planned sabotage, but could not be absolutely sure. If she made an attempt to pursue the matter further, the risk remained that she might have been mistaken and succeed in only arousing suspicion. On the other hand, if she hesitated, her chances of confirming her assumption would be ruined. The Gestapo were in evidence along with the French Milice and there had been some betrayals and arrests only a week ago near Vichy. The dilemma haunted her for the rest of the day.

The following afternoon brought a surprise solution when a young woman came to the convent looking for work in the kitchens. While Yvonne rarely involved herself with the domestic help, she spoke briefly with the young woman as she was being shown around the kitchen facilities and noted that she seemed too well-educated to work in such a capacity. Yet, she reasoned, people from all backgrounds work in incongruous positions these days. As the woman followed her guide about the kitchen, she glanced several times in Yvonne's direction and appeared anxious to speak further with her.

It was Yvonne's habit to walk through the garden after classes, largely to think and make plans. But the mellowness of late August on this balmy afternoon reminded her so much of home and she allowed herself a rare moment of complete self-indulgence. She lingered for a moment by an ornamental pond where a huge willow draped its fingers into the water, displacing an emerald layer of scum. Deep in thought, she barely heard soft footsteps approaching.

"You are Renee?" the young woman asked as Yvonne spun around to face her.

"Yes, I'm Renee Dubois. I teach English here. I understand you are to work in the kitchens."

The woman looked up at the willow, and smiled. "It is so beautiful here, isn't it?"

"Yes, quite beautiful."

"Your French is excellent for an English woman."

"What do you mean?" The casual comment sent a shiver through Yvonne.

"Oh, don't worry, you haven't given yourself away. Your French is perfect."

"Who are you?"

"I'm a friend; and we have a mutual friend. I believe you know him as Ben Boniface."

The impact of his name stunned her. How must I handle this, she thought frantically? Although this person is obviously French, she could be setting a trap.

"He was as surprised as you now are when he saw you. We were in a book shop in Toulouse and it was an astonishing coincidence that he should look up just as you cycled by."

"Who are you?" Yvonne asked again.

"My name is Michou Marceau. Ben--code name, incidentally, Pierre Bonhomme, and true name Claude Simone --and I knew each other when I was a child visiting Paris. He is a little older than I, but we used to write to one another after I returned to Lille. Professor Noe Marceau, my uncle, knew Claude's father through their work and teachings at the Sorbonne. Claude heard that his Jewish parents had been arrested and came to Paris in order to help them--rescue them I suppose. But it was too late. They were no longer in France. Claude learned that a woman was responsible for their arrest and his entire focus now is to get even with her."

Michou's account corroborated Andre Chambrun's assumptions and certainly accounted for Ben's erratic movements.

Glancing around her to ensure that no one else was near, the young French woman continued. "Yvonne, Ben told me how brave you were at Dunkirk. I know Comte de Chambrun expects you to complete your assignment successfully, but I must put these facts before you. First, I must be sure that you trust me."

It seemed that there were too many truths in Michou's story for it to be fabricated and Yvonne at last acknowledged her authenticity. She nodded briefly.

" I don't blame you for being cautious," Michou went on. "Although Ben is considered a double agent, I can assure you that he has done very little for the Germans. Now that he knows the truth about his parents he has in fact intensified his activities against them."

"I'm sure Ben was surprised to see me, but how does he know why I'm here?"

"Noe was one of the leaders of the underground in Paris and obviously well-informed.   However, he was told of Chambrun's intention after Ben had left Paris in pursuit of Dierick and sent me after him to warn him.   Ben did not know who Renee Dubois was until he saw you from the book shop and put two and two together."

"I've spent many weeks trying to infiltrate the Résistance and I suppose I know now why I haven't been able to do it.   Did your friend Noe alert them?" Yvonne asked.

"While they respect Chambrun's motives, they also know Ben will not rest until he has avenged his parents.   Don't you see?   He'll be doing everyone a favour when he does away with Dierick?   If you run interference, she will be allowed to continue with her diabolical missions.   You have no idea how Claude--Ben--has studied her and has learned all of her disguises and methods of operation.   He is the most valuable key to getting rid of her."

Yvonne could see the point very clearly.   She could not, however, see how she might explain away her failure if she did not complete her assignment.

"If I cooperate with you, how will I justify my mission here in France?"

"I think Chambrun will see our point.   In fact, I'm sure Noe already apprised him of it."

"Then why have I not been recalled?"

"Knowing Chambrun, he will still want to talk to Ben after it's all over and will expect you to report his whereabouts. He's a very exact man and won't tolerate loose ends.   Actually, it wouldn't surprise me if Ben would oblige you by turning himself in if that's what you want.   You can return to England in triumph having used Ben to dispose of Dierick as well as bringing home the wayward double agent."

"If Dierick is so clever with disguises, how will I know that Ben has.....disposed....of the right person?   I think I know what she looks like and could probably detect a disguise."

"I believe you have a sketch. I can tell you now, you would never find her with that."

"Why not?"

"Because you already know her in person and she looks nothing like your sketch."

Yvonne stared unbelievingly as tears sprang to Michou's eyes.

"She has betrayed the entire Résistance organisation in Lyons," Michou said.

"What?"

"You have heard of Jean Moulin, the man who tried to bring all segments of the Résistance together throughout France?"

"Yes. I parachuted in with an agent who had trained to assist him. He is working directly for General de Gaulle."

"Was. He died as a result of torture on June 24th. The core of the Résistance had arranged to meet for a decisive conference and all those of significant importance were trapped and arrested. They were betrayed."

Yvonne desperately tried to absorb the impact of this dreadful news as Michou went on. She spoke of Klaus Barbie, The Butcher, and Yvonne immediately knew that they had all suffered indescribable brutality and torture. This infamous German fiend had caused innumerable agonizing deaths to suspected members of any kind of opposition and his name brought intense fear into the hearts of all who heard it. A woman, Michou said, had played a prevalent part in the betrayal.

"Dierick!" Yvonne said. "You said I have met her? I have no idea……."

"She has even infiltrated the ranks of the Free French successfully. I think you know her as Nichole."

Suddenly faint, Yvonne reached for Michou's support. "B-but she looked nothing like the sketch," She said, regaining her balance with some difficulty.

"Exactly. We heard that it was the work of an English child Ben knew who may have observed her in one of her disguises at the beginning of the war."

"Nichole could not possibly have been in disguise. She looks like a schoolgirl."

"She can also look like a crone if she chooses."

Apparently the tragic news of the mass arrest had immediately traveled through the accessible ranks of the Résistance and Yvonne wondered why she had not been approached. Perhaps she had kept her cover too well. She thought of the derelict potting shed in the corner of the school kitchen garden where Margot's transmitter lay hidden. Perhaps someone *had* tried to contact her and the message had been intercepted! Nichole knew that she and Margot were not destined to travel northward as she did, after they were dropped. In which case, she also knew the general area in which they were now operating. Could this be the reason that no partisan had attempted to approach them? But why, then, had the Gestapo not arrested them?

"I think it's time for you to disappear," Michou said. "Your wireless operator is in even more danger."

It seemed that Michou had read her mind.

"How do you know? Is Ben still in Toulouse?"

"No. He should be on his way to Marseilles. But he wanted to warn you, through me, to leave as quickly as possible. It's quite possible that your messages to Beaconsfield have been intercepted by the Gestapo. You see, we have a mole in the Abwher but, of course, Dierick would have told the Gestapo of your whereabouts."

Yvonne could scarcely believe that all this was truly happening. Could it be possible that she and Margot had been watched by the enemy since their arrival? If Ben had been in Toulouse then Dierick must be in the area, too.

"W-Why has Ben gone to Marseilles?"

"He suspects that Dierick's next assignment is there. Many escapers and evaders accumulate there waiting for escorts to take them over the Pyrenees. Some British agents return to England that way too when the weather is too bad for them to be picked up by aeroplane. She has contacted the Milice and has a list of names. Obviously she is preparing to blow the rest of the Résistance apart in the south."

The shock of Michou's information continued to numb Yvonne's clear thinking. What action should they take now? If messages were being intercepted she dare not try to contact Beaconsfield where all wireless messages were received.

"If she was here, why did she leave Margot and me alone?"

"We believe the Gestapo picked up your code and identification through wireless infiltration and are distorting your messages enough to transmit misinformation."

Knowing that she had been used by the enemy to pass erroneous information to England, plus the added shame that she had completely failed in her mission to locate Ben and ultimately Dierick, Yvonne felt utterly humiliated.

"I can't contact London for a means of transportation if the messages are being intercepted," she said, huskily. "What then, Michou, do you suggest Margot and I do? Vanish into thin air?" She immediately regretted her words. Michou, after all, was her potential benefactor.

"Neither the Germans nor the British know where Ben is," Michou said, ignoring the slight. "Like Dierick, he has functioned in disguise and has avoided contact with anyone other than people he can positively identify in the French underground. We'll join him in Marseilles and try to make it to Spain."

Everything was happening too fast, yet Yvonne dared not think what might have happened if Michou had not warned her.

"You realise, of course, that the detection of the transmitter by the Germans has put everyone in the area under suspicion and you must know the sort of solutions the German pigs have for such situations. They are likely to take everyone out in the entire community, including the children, and machine gun them."

Yvonne reeled away, covering her face with her hands.

"Be careful," Michou warned. "You must behave as if nothing unusual has happened. Someone could be watching us. It isn't your fault. Think of your brilliant performance at Dunkirk and all the useful work you have been doing with ATA.   You will be able to go back to England knowing that your lack of action here has resulted in the death of Dierick. Now you know all the facts, you can see how vital your inaction is."

Yvonne felt her breath coming in rapid gasps. The impact of the situation had finally taken hold, and fear enveloped her.

"I'll go with you and Margot as far as Marseilles," Michou said. "It's easier to make arrangements there for transport to Gibraltar. We'll go south via the escape route with your French papers. You'll be interrogated by the British in Gibraltar, of course, but I'm sure Chambrun will vouch for you in the end."

CHAPTER FIFTEEN

September, 1943

Charlie sat at Kate's feet outside the stationery shop hoping for attention. His wagging tail cleared a space in the fallen poplar leaves that had blown in from the edge of the village, and his sides heaved from exertion. Across the street, BC sat on top of his gatepost, watching them with disdain. Arthur Banberry stuffed his hands into his trousers pockets and rocked back on his heels, pondering Kate's last question concerning the war situation. She did not always understand the newspaper news items and, rather than give Hugh the satisfaction of telling her she was not too bright, she usually prodded Mr. Banberry for his opinion.

"Well, Italy's thrown in the towel," he said. "Talk about fair-weather fighters, but I suppose we should be glad. It's one less enemy to deal with." He sighed and turned to go in. "On the other hand, young Kate, Denmark isn't faring so well. The bl.....er....the Germans are really clamping down on those poor people."

"It's so confusing, Mr. Banberry. The bl...er...Germans are supposed to be occupying Italy, yet Hugh said they rescued Mussolini in the Abruzzi mountains. On the other hand, the

Allies are invading Italy, too."

"Well, Kate," he said, smiling at her audacity. "That's the way war is--up and down; back and forth--until one side ultimately gains the major portion of control."

"Are we winning, or what?"

Mr. Banberry shrugged.   "I wouldn't dare to be that optimistic."

As he went inside, an American jeep cruised through the village and the driver waved to Kate.   They're always so friendly, she thought; although some people don't respond in kind to them.   Like the girl buying stamps that Hugh had told her about.

"Mr. Banberry," she called through the door. "Did that girl ever come back?"

"What girl?"

"The one who didn't like the Americans.   The one who asked after Ben."

"No. Odd really. There was another young woman in the village months ago asking after Ben, but this one was different. Perhaps that cunning blighter has been sowing some wild oats." He winked knowingly at Kate. "Hope he hasn't got her into trouble. Anyway, I couldn't help her. I have no idea where he is."

He looked across the road where BC walked along the top of the wall. Although the cat and Charlie maintained a mutual and distant respect for one another, he did nonetheless prefer to remain out of reach and usually made his way along the tops of fences and walls.

"Every time I look at that cat," Mr. Banberry said. "I get this feeling that he knows something I don't. It's almost as if he's trying to tell me something."

Kate smiled as she crossed the road. "Hello, BC," she said, as he butted his head against her shoulder. "What is it you're trying to tell us? Do you know where Ben is? Do you know where any of them are?"

BC held his silence as he always did. He did not meow or purr like other cats, but simply blinked his big yellow eyes.

Later that afternoon it seemed that Mr. Banberry's suspicions concerning BC's sixth sense were to be corroborated. Since 1939 only one War Office telegram had been delivered to the village. The widow Fordham, who lived six doors down from the stationery shop, had received word that her son had been killed during Operation Dynamo at Dunkirk in 1940. Since her husband had been lost in France in 1916 during the Great War Kate, once again, found cause to question God's apparent injustices.

Now, in 1943 a second telegram came to Long Bottom and was delivered to Mallory Cottage. While no details were offered it was clear that while in the Mediterranean the destroyer *HMS Arrow* was badly damaged by an explosion while alongside and assisting a burning merchantman--the *Fort La Monte*. There were many fatalities and Kate knew that her father would not be coming home again. An uncanny feeling of unreality enveloped her as her mother stood, stricken with shock, with the telegram trembling in her hand. Mr. Banberry, who saw the young female messenger arrive on her bicycle, immediately closed the post office and hurried to Mallory Cottage.

"Tea!" he said, obviously unsure how to offer his sympathies. "I'll make some good strong tea!"

Frightened by her mother's lack of any response, Kate led her to a chair and urged her to sit, taking the telegram gently from her fingers. Then she followed Mr. Banberry to the kitchen and automatically began to set the tray. She knew he was doing his best and felt that she should follow suit. Sugar. Milk. Teaspoons. Tea cozy. Like any man, she supposed, he felt uncomfortable in the presence of grieving females. Yet oddly, she felt nothing. Absolutely nothing. Together they coaxed Mrs. Hawkins to sip the strong tea and gradually she became aware of her surroundings. After a short while, she rose from her chair and smiled at them.

"I believe I would like to be alone for a little while," she said and walked quickly and deliberately toward the stairs."

After Kate had assured Mr. Banberry that they would be all right, he left to re-open the shop. She stood staring after him as BC brushed against her legs.

"You knew, didn't you BC?" she said. "You knew he was dead."

BC circled her legs once more and then walked toward the stairs.

Charlie crept from his basket in the corner now that the coast was clear and quietly sat at her feet.

"Oh, Charlie," she said gathering him up into her arms. "Oh, Charlie. Even the Italians coming on our side didn't make any difference." She buried her face in the rough fur and at last quietly wept.

* * *

October, 1943

Unable to explain fully in code to 'Charles' her reason for wanting to return to England, it took several attempts before Janine eventually made her point. She was asked to stand by and wait for the next moonlit night in order to be airlifted out by Lysander. Her code base was Aude and she had already apprised them of an appropriate landing site. Aware that her position in the south of France entailed a much longer flight from England she knew the probability of her not making it out was quite high. She had already decided that should her pick up again fail, she would make her own way home.

With the loosely formed connective chain of contacts and a reasonably willing and well-paid Basque guide, she could made it through the Pyrenees to Andorra-la-Vella on the Franco-Spanish frontier. But at this time of year her progress would be slowed by altitude and subsequent thin air plus bitterly cold weather and snow. She wondered if she were in good enough physical shape to endure that kind of hardship.

From the beginning her plan had been thwarted by one incident after another, and she wondered if it could possibly have been as long ago as February when she initially made the decision to leave Aix. Gestapo, Milice, weather, suspected betrayals and subsequent wasted days in hiding had tried her patience. In utter exasperation she joined the underground movement in a number of sabotage activities. Never dreaming that she would put to use the lethal techniques taught her in England, detonation, thievery and assassination had become a part of her daily life.

Since her departure from Aix, she had not maintained contact with the partisans there and often wondered if the agent named Marcel had managed to get that far. She continued to keep the passwords in the back of her mind, although she had little hope now that she would ever use them. As a highly sought-after fugitive, he too must have experienced similar delays, or perhaps had been caught by the SS. She had pondered whether to entrust the code to another, but decided against it. 'Charles' had convinced her that this man--if indeed it were a man--was astute and highly experienced and would surely find another way to make contact. Conditions had deteriorated so severely concerning betrayal, she had become something of a cynic, unable to wholly trust anyone.

By the beginning of November the weather had deteriorated and her hopes of getting out by aircraft waned. She decided to return to Aix if only to set her mind at rest that her parents were still safe. Upon her arrival, she saw to her relief that there did not appear to be any unusual German activity at the estate, and immediately contacted her old headquarters.

"We're glad you're back"

Bernard Fabré had been loyal and reliable from the beginning and had taken over the leadership after her departure. He would likely remain with the group until the bitter end. As one of the older men, he made the transition from the domesticity of a daytime baker to the perils of nighttime espionage with absolute ease and Janine trusted him implicitly. With this brief but sincere welcome, she was indeed glad to be back.

"There has been a great deal of sabotage activity along the railway lines in the north, and several bridges have been blown up," Bernard said. "We think there is something brewing in the way of a probable invasion."

His usually somber face brightened with anticipation.

"If this is true," Janine said. "What will happen to the remaining allied airmen who are trying to get back to England?"

He shrugged. "They're as vulnerable as the rest of us, I suppose. As it is, we've lost three of our younger members who've joined the Résistance full time in order to fight. As you know it's what they were waiting for."

"Yes. Of course. But we can't just abandon the escape routes," Janine said.

"Once the battles begin, they won't be able to move very fast anyway," Bernard said.

Surely, Janine thought, the entire system at the southern end can't break down now. She had to think of a way to keep this group on the job.

"What happened to the agent, Marcel? Did you ever hear from him? He was due here before I left."

"He never arrived. The Gestapo is everywhere, although we usually know when an arrest is made."

Deflated, Janine sat down.

"Look, Phalene. We believe the Résistance has been successful in infiltrating the ranks of the Milice. If it isn't the Résistance then there are others who are most effective. Doesn't it occur to you that France could be in the throes of a civil war, in spite of the German occupation? Some of us feel we can't ignore the situation and want to join up with the partisans full time in order to fight. One or two of us is willing to stay and help you with the incoming aircraft, of course, but…………..."

Although she wanted to argue, Janine knew that they had already weighed their priorities, and she even understood them. Having risked their lives for the cause for so long, it made sense that they would want to defend their beliefs.

They made ready to leave and Janine knew that her previously tightly knit group was unraveling. They had worked together with success for many months, and its sudden disintegration saddened her. The room echoed with their voices long after they had left. She stared dejectedly into the fire, knowing now that her return home would have to be delayed indefinitely.

A soft sound behind her brought her quickly to her feet as a figure moved into the flickering light. Terrified, she nonetheless stood her ground as his long, animated shadow danced against the wall behind him. The intermittent half-light deepened the lines of his face and a flesh-coloured patch over one eye added to the insidious effect. He watched her with an almost satanic smirk.

"The blackbird is free," he said in English.

The portentous smirk suddenly broadened into a brilliant smile and Janine reeled back, fumbling for the chair.

"Are you indeed?" she said with difficulty. "And is the water clear?"

Smiling through her tears, she held out her hand.

"We….we all thought you were dead, George Ravensbrook. David thought you had crashed into the sea and

334

drowned. And yet, you were never reported killed in combat."

"There are some who would wish that I was," he said, with a chuckle.

"Why didn't you try to get back to England?"

"At first I was too badly injured to move. The French took care of me very well. After recovery I surmised that a one-eyed pilot wouldn't be much good to anyone and when someone approached me concerning the escape routes, I decided to stay on."

"But the RAF said they had no record of you."

"Of course they would say that. But MI9 knew where I was." He grinned. "I think David would be amazed to think that this boorish old rugger player who always managed to blunder his way out of Yvonne's favour could possibly have become a fairly effective spy."

"Both you and he are older and wiser," Janine said. "I......I suppose you couldn't know that he was badly burned."

George's grin quickly faded. "Yes, I knew. A chap from our squadron was shot down over Dieppe in late '40 and was among a group of five that we moved along the escape route to the Pyrenees. He said it was quite bad. This war is so unfair. Flying was David's great love."

"He's gone back to it in spite of everyone's doubts."

George shook his head. "Surely not a fighter squadron."

"No. I can't elaborate, because I don't know for sure. But it's a Special Operations squadron of some kind. I think you might draw your own conclusions from that. I've watched for him but never seen him. I did, however, fly over here with Rupert Barlow, unbeknown to Rupert himself because, you see, we were never actually introduced."

George gaped with astonishment. "You know, Mrs. Parke, none of us really knew for sure what you were up to. I think both David and Yvonne had some idea, but perhaps didn't want to acknowledge it. This is rather dangerous stuff, you know."

Janine laughed. "Is it?"

"Obviously I made sure none of the Special Operations pilots saw me." George said. "The less known the better. Because I have always delegated the job of getting the passengers off and on board, I've never actually seen any of the pilots. One did get stuck in the mud and had to set fire to his kite, but the group was soon passing him down the escape route and I heard he was back in England within the week and back at it."

"Now, Marcel! I understand we have much work to do." Janine said, her mood greatly lightened by George's devil-may-care presence. "But first, let me see what we can find you to eat."

He nodded as he almost fell into an armchair, obviously near exhaustion.

In a little while, his appetite was adequately sated with weak stew and he lingered afterwards over a mug of coffee.

"I could hardly believe it when I heard you had been involved in British Intelligence all this time," he said. "You've been quite busy one way and another. How on earth do you keep it all from your family?"

"It isn't easy. But you see there is so much top secret activity going on these days in England, and they know I have been involved with Europeans in London from the start. They don't ask questions, even though I know they want to and I appreciate that. Whether or not they suspect, I don't know. But at least they know absolutely nothing for sure."

"You've done an excellent job here," George said. "And we are almost finished. Soon we can both go home."

She looked at him questioningly. "Invasion?"

"It's getting close, I think. But we have the problem of getting the remaining people still in hiding to safety. Most of them are allied airmen. There is a plan for the allied air forces to completely destroy rail communications in northern France and we are already working with the Belgians to get as many of the escapers and evaders away from that battle zone. Because of the number--there are at least four hundred to five hundred involved--it would be impossible to get them out of the country, and so camps are being set up in the forests near Chateaupun and Rennes. An expected outburst of SS activity will obviously make things difficult, but the operation, which is named 'Marathon' is already underway."

"You're aware, of course that the Vichy government held several hundred allied soldiers, sailors and airmen prisoners in fortresses near Nimes and Monte Carlo." Janine said. "In November last year they handed them over to the Gestapo who subjected them to considerable indignities and interrogation."

"It broke my heart," George said. "We tried several ways to intervene which failed, and we lost several of our own people as well. So much for the Geneva Convention. Are you able to pick up the coded messages sent over the BBC by the French? Obviously, I've learned to communicate in the language, but my colleagues tell me my French is dreadful. My Latin master at Eton tore out his hair over my inability to learn the stuff, so I'm not surprised. You would be a great help to me there."

"There were some photographs........?"

"They're already in England. I was able to get them on a Lysander after all. I understand they have dispatched two of their best agents to Tangiers where our main nasty is headed." He shook his head. "It's a woman, you know. Evil as they come. They'll get her, I'm sure. The rest are much easier prey."

George's happy approach had given Janine a greatly needed sense of well-being. As Marcel, he was esteemed in the escape route activities, and as George, he was her friend.

* * *

337

December, 1943.

During pre-war days, Yvonne had visited Marseilles on several occasions in order to board the pleasure steamers bound for Spain. Primarily used as a port for commercial trade, the tramp steamers and merchantmen tended to darken the more glamourous aspect of the docks. Today, since no trace of gay pleasure seekers festooned the wharves, the wet streets seemed sinister and unfriendly and an atmosphere of unsavoury intrigue lurked in every corner. Perhaps she was imagining things, but personal circumstances certainly contributed to her apprehension. She took a sip from her coffee cup and grimaced. It had, after all, been over twenty minutes since they arrived at the waterside café and it stood to reason that the contents would be cold.

"Are you sure he's coming?" she whispered to Michou.

"One can never be sure of anything. But he hasn't let me down yet."

Yvonne shrugged, remembering Ben's sudden disappearance before the Dunkirk venture. She shivered and looked at Margot on the opposite side of the table. While an excellent wireless operator, she had never succeeded in overcoming her constant fear of capture and subsequent torture. The school atmosphere had been reasonably normal and there were times when a good sense of humour shone through. But tonight, Margot's pallor was marked in the dingy light of the café and her fingers trembled around her cup. Quite justified, Yvonne reasoned as she covertly watched three men at a nearby table. While patrons of the café were generally a motley lot, she surmised that these men in particular bore watching. Instinctively she knew they were not French in spite of their workmen's clothes. But their gestures and expressions

338

were too controlled and they were certainly far too observant of others in the room around them. She was sure they were German SS.

They peered through their blue cigarette smoke as the door swung open to admit a bearded debardeur who reeked of sweat and tobacco. Simultaneously, heat, steam and smoke escaped into the damp night like a fading specter and Yvonne felt the cold creep in from the outside and swirl about her legs until the door edged itself slowly shut. She watched the stevedore leer at a couple of prostitutes and noted that his teeth were black with decay and that the dregs of his latest meal still clung to the grizzly beard under his lower lip. The prostitutes turned their backs on him. Who can blame them, Yvonne thought with a shudder? He certainly would not make a desirable bedfellow. The man shrugged and found himself a small table wedged awkwardly in a murky corner toward the back.

Another fifteen minutes passed as the three men watched people come and go and even Michou began to fidget. Suddenly, one of the men rose from his chair, staring fixedly at Margot as he walked toward their table. Yvonne's throat constricted as she tried desperately to appear unperturbed.

The man's mouth stretched into an ugly smile as he stopped beside their table.

"Ça va?" he said, continuing to stare at Margot. Obviously terrified, she whispered something inaudibly.

The man turned his attention to Yvonne.

"My companions and I are quite lonely," he said, his guttural abuse of the French language immediately detectable. "Perhaps you and your friends will join us for a little while."

"We are waiting for our father," Yvonne said, clearly.

The man looked surprised. "You are sisters? You do not bear any resemblance to one another."

He laid the palms of his hands on the table and leaned toward each of them to scrutinise their faces. Yvonne tried not to move as his foul, smoke-laden breath reached her nostrils. Willing her mind to work quickly, she sought desperately for a way to deter the man without making him angry. Her pulse raced as she wondered if he suspected who they really were.

Before she could conjure up some kind of diversion, Margot suddenly slumped in her chair and slid heavily to the floor. One person in the café stood up, scraping his chair back in order to see what was going on while others looked on with blasé disinterest. But the bearded man in the corner sprang across the room in a flash.

"She's fainted," he shouted. "Stand back while I get her outside into the fresh air."

Yvonne immediately recognised Ben's voice and for one brief moment froze.

"Quick!" he hissed.

"Yes, yes," she shouted. "She is pregnant. Oh, dear God. Look! Blood!"

She moved quickly in front of the German primarily to help Ben lift Margot, but also to hide the area where the nonexistent blood might have been. Michou joined in, and the three of them shuffled rapidly through the café to the door carrying the inert body.

"I'm not sure that he's convinced," Ben whispered. "Quick, go through here."

They were through the alley in a flash, still bearing their limp burden, and were soon following him down slippery basement steps into deep shadow. He cautioned them to crouch down in the conduit and stay quiet. After ten agonising minutes they knew their ruse had worked. How clever of Margot to think of such a thing, Yvonne thought. She looked down at the unmoving heap and frowned.

"Come on, Margot. The coast is clear now," she whispered. "It was a wonderful diversion."

There was no response. Michou knelt down and laid two fingers at the side of Margot's neck.

"She's dead."

"*What?*"

"She must have panicked."

The blood in Yvonne's veins seemed to turn to ice as she looked down at the inert figure. "A-are you saying…….Cyanide…….?"

*   *   *

They wrapped Margot in a blanket from Ben's rented room, adding crowbars for weight, stolen from the dockside warehouses. In the dead of night they sadly slid the small bundle into the dark water and watched it rapidly sink. Only because of the need for silence did Yvonne control her tears. Perhaps a time would come when she could cry for her brave friend for as long and as loud as she desired.

They left the city on stolen bicycles and spent the rest of the night in a boat house along the coast toward Aubagne. As Yvonne huddled against a canvas sail bag, she felt Ben move toward her in the darkness.

"There will be a boat tomorrow night," he whispered. "You should be familiar with this coastline."

"Yes. I was here often as a child."

She saw the flash of his teeth in the half-light. "You're not much more than that now, are you?"

The old anger began to rise and he raised both hands in protest.

"You'll not need a map, then," he said. "Go into Aubagne to this address." He slid a small slip of paper into her hand. Somehow the smell of sweat and tobacco had disbursed and she saw in the shadows that he no longer wore the jacket.

The filthy beard and blackened teeth had also miraculously disappeared.

"I can't do that," she said. "I still have a job to do."

He moved closer. "So do I. Did Michou's words mean nothing? Can you not back down just this once?"

"All my work was for nothing," she said, tears springing to her eyes. "I have nothing to show for it except a dead friend."

"You were an unintended decoy," he whispered. "You held the Abwehr's attention while the Résistance got on with a number of very satisfying jobs. Now let me finish what I started which is to put an end to the woman who has been instrumental in killing hundreds."

He wiped away a tear from her cheek with the tip of his finger. She felt the warmth of his body against her and it seemed that it had been a lifetime away when his arms were around her in London. Yet she knew that Michou must be watching.

"Dierick!" she said. "With all her prowess as a spy, surely she must know you are after her."

"Let her know. She is my personal vendetta. I know her well now and it will only be a matter of time before I catch her. I know the time and the place of her next rendezvous where she plans to leave for Tangiers after her next massive betrayal. She will never get there. Her plans to expose certain members of the Maquis and of our own partisans have been ruined because those concerned were warned in time."

He stood up and looked toward the shadows where Michou rested.

"Perhaps your job, as you call it, will not be fulfilled in the way you might have imagined. But it will be fulfilled in that Beatrix Dierick will no longer exist. And neither, my dear, will I."

* * *

January, 1944

"This has been a brilliant season for operations," David said, pulling off his flying boots and flopping back onto his bed. "Can this good weather and smooth operations possibly continue?"

"Things do seem to be taking a turn for the better all over," Rupert said, following suit. "Frankfurt has been taking a licking and the Italians have decided they want to be on our side for a change; and the American, General Eisenhower has been appointed Supreme Commander, Allied Expeditionary Force--whatever that means."

David adjusted his pillow and closed his eyes, pondering the past year with satisfaction. During the nights of the full moon he had flown Lysander missions to various points in northern France picking up and dropping off agents and supplies without serious incident, except once. During a double Lysander pick up when he flew in unison with his commanding officer, the code from the ground had been inaccurate and he and his colleague were forced to turn back. They learned later that turmoil had erupted in the underground movement due to a mass betrayal in Lyons. God, he thought, what a tragedy! He could still see the people on the ground running toward his aircraft on previous flights, eager for news and supplies; anxious to get one or two people away from the awful pressure of German oppression; staunch in their ultimate aim to liberate their country. He knew he would never forget them or cease to admire their incredible courage.

He had returned to East Grinstead for further surgery on his face only twice. His hands had strengthened considerably and the tenderness of the grafted skin had subsided. Each day the scars faded just a little bit more and while Archibald McIndoe deemed it necessary to do further surgery on the deep burn scar on his neck, he had agreed to wait another few months.

After the initial camaraderie of Ward III which stemmed from the mutual involvement of fighter pilot experiences and the formation of the Guinea Pig Club, David had felt rather strange returning to the new Canadian wing of the hospital filled with bomber crew. Even the injuries were of a different nature in some cases. One young navigator bitterly surveyed ten black sticks lying on a pillow in front of him. Ten useless, frostbitten digits that had once been deft and talented fingers would undoubtedly have to be amputated. Bomb bays at high altitudes were frigid, and when gloves were removed to help a wounded comrade, fragile extremities against icy metal paid the price. Another lad, although not air crew, had barely escaped with his life when en route with his unit to join forces in southeast England. His jeep suddenly and inexplicably blew up and a severe blow to the head left him unconscious for days. He awoke to learn that, due to his injuries, his face must now be entirely reconstructed.

David's continuing visits for surgery never seemed to coincide with those of Patrick's, but McIndoe assured him that he had produced three excellent books and a bonny baby boy. The nurse had not only proved to be an excellent typist, but also a perfect wife.

While Lysanders had been David's prime transport for clandestine drop offs and pick ups, on his last mission he co-piloted a Hudson with one of the senior officers into an area west of Lons-le-Saunier to drop off a most important agent and a number of odd-looking packages. Although never briefed on the nature of the missions, he nonetheless knew that all were vitally crucial to the direction of the war. It seemed that the delivery of supplies was picking up and, along with an obvious concentration of American troops along the southwest coast of England, and British and Commonwealth military establishments on the southeast coast, he wondered if the war was at last coming to an end.

A far cry from the excitement of one-to-one air combat, this type of covert operation gave him a much more mature and profound sense of satisfaction. Perhaps the risks and daring that he experienced each time may never be acknowledged by the general public. Yet this did not matter. His glaring glory days had left him scarred and a little bitter. These current experiences gave him food for thought and a source of admiration for the brave men and women who faced a different kind of enemy. An enemy that delighted in sadism. An enemy who had lost all reasoning concerning the survival of true intellect and the appreciation of freedom. There could be no accounting for their satanic aspects on life and thus no hope of retribution. The only course now was to crush this monster by both overt and covert operations and David knew that the latter had already contributed a vast amount to these efforts in lives, plus a complex network of secret activities known only to a very few elite allied statesmen. The whole big picture would probably never be fully revealed and those participating in it, never acknowledged.

With eyes still shut he groped about the surface of his beside table and found the envelope he sought. Her letters to date were always optimistic with understatements concerning adversities. But this time Kate had been less cautious and he immediately detected her anger and deep sorrow. He wondered how to word his next letter to her. While she continued to keep him abreast of occurrences in the civilian world, she also described in poetic detail the countryside when the seasons changed or the types of flowers that clustered under the Sussex hedgerows. Often she included lovely little water colours of the flowers she mentioned. The comic observations and misconstrued facts of childhood had faded in both her writings and drawings and she offered surprisingly sagacious slants on a number of interests, always asking for his opinion. She spoke of the village and the changing aura as Allied military personnel stopped off en route to the coast or to London. She spoke fondly of Charlie, the amazing BC, and of her siblings and often quoted both Mr. Banberry and Mr. Baxter concerning their points of view--just to offer a different aspect.   In short, her letters always gave him considerable pleasure and he found himself happily anticipating   their arrival.

Today she apologised for her sadness and wished she had not written the letter at all.   Yet he remembered the frightened little girl who desperately needed to purge herself of the dreadful memories that lurked beside the Long Man. He could still feel the intense empathy he experienced as he tried to console her.   Although not witness to it this time, she nonetheless deeply mourned the loss of her father at sea.   *It's odd, David, but when he turned to wave at the top of the road in London all that time ago, I wondered then if I would ever see him again.......I truly believe that BC knew it would happen, right from the start.......*

CHAPTER SIXTEEN

January, 1944

Claude leaned forward to better see his image in the spotted mirror while he put the finishing touches to his despicable false beard. Michou stood behind him shaking her head with quizzical amusement.

"You couldn't look more disreputable if you tried," she grinned.

He turned and smiled, giving her the full benefit of his disgusting teeth. "Come 'ere, me beauty," he growled. "and give me a kiss!"

She backed away, laughing. "How do you manage to smell like *pourie pommes de terre?*"

"It isn't easy," Claude said. His smile faded as he glanced at his watch. "Half an hour," he said. "And it will be over at last."

"You're positive that she will be there? She's so slippery and has escaped your grasp before."

"Her mission here failed," Claude said. "We forewarned

everyone.......and she wasn't successful. I doubt that she has ever had to deal with her own incompetence before and perhaps won't know how to cope with it."

Michou looked apprehensive. "But still........."

"She knows she is being hunted by several groups of the FFI (Forces Françaises de l'Intérieur) and has requested her Gestapo boss that she be transferred to Berlin instead of going to Tangiers. For the first time in her life I believe she's scared."

Claude leaned closer to the mirror, seeking defects in his makeup.

"Although I'm not exactly working alone in this any more, at least I'll have the privilege of personally avenging my parents--and Noe--and hundreds of others."

Michou looked at his reflection in the mirror, meeting his eyes.

"This distraction that you've devised with the Résistance is clever," she said. "But we can't underestimate the German pigs. I hope they won't smell a rat."

"Why would they? Because they have commandeered all reasonable transportation, the rattletraps they have left us with often break down. In this case, it will be a burst tyre. Now the first part of the plan will cause only mild interest, but the second phase should certainly get everyone's attention. We were lucky to get hold of that old lorry and it won't take much to shove it over on its side and set fire to it. I'd say those SS gentlemen will be nicely distracted, wouldn't you? I just hope the lorry doesn't blow up too soon, that's all."

Again, he looked at his watch. "This time, stay out of it, Michou. It's imperative that we leave together very quickly afterwards. You must go directly to the arranged place. Do you understand?"

Her look of reluctance might have caused some doubt, but past experiences concerning her obedience and loyalty assured him that she would be there.

Within five minutes, he entered the café in his usual

manner and ogled the same prostitutes as he walked toward his favourite table. He had come at the same time for several nights having learned that the three Germans did the same thing. It was quite usual for the dock workers to stop in after a day of work and his regularity did not arouse any undue suspicion. It was on one of these occasions that he had overheard the plan to transport Dierick to Berlin at her request.

The three Germans were already there and Claude noted a suitcase by one of their chairs. The man seated next to it would be Dierick's escort, no doubt. He had eavesdropped on their conversations long enough now to know that Dierick would be driven to Nice from Marseilles this evening where she would board an aircraft for Berlin with one of the men. Aware that she was being hunted, she would obviously use one of her many disguises. He wondered which one she had adopted this time. Through the grueling months of pursuit, Claude had become familiar with all Dierick's clever ruses. In fact, he was more than merely familiar with them since they had been the cause of his dereliction. He knew what to look for and how she adapted her characters according to the terrain or the environment. He knew the various walks and stances she adopted and often combined. She could be a child or an old woman. She had even become a young man on a few occasions. Several times he had been so close, and she had managed to slip by him. Only in retrospect when reviewing failed entrapments, did he realise how she had done it. Now he was ready for all or any of her clever costumes and transformations. Even if she created yet another, he knew he could detect her. He knew her as well as he knew himself.

The café where Margot had tragically met her demise was a known cesspool of intrigue, betrayal, espionage, and counter-espionage. Prior to Yvonne's arrival in Marseilles, Claude had spent several long evenings at his corner table eavesdropping with a trained ear on the conversations taking place around him. He had easily identified the three SS agents in spite of their French get ups and when they had mentioned the name 'Nichole' a number of times, they confirmed in Claude's mind that this 'Nichole' and Dierick were one and the same. He knew Dierick used the name openly as an English agent and had cleverly retained the same name for her German code, thus eliminating any chance of counter-identification through an intercepted wireless message, or even a mere slip of the tongue. The agents had been careless when mentioning *une vielle laide femme* in their fractured French, giving him the advantage of knowing the current selected disguise Dierick would most likely use. According to their past conversations, she would be due at the café in five minutes.

Claude glanced anxiously toward the steamy window fervently hoping that everything would go according to plan. Suddenly, a loud report from the street brought everyone to their feet, pushing their way to the door, including Claude himself. From the corner of his eye he saw the Germans rising cautiously. The exploding tyre had been exactly on time. Brilliant! He prayed that the three men would be curious enough to go out onto the street to see what was going on. At the intersection fifty metres from the café, the lorry had skidded and overturned. Deliberately set flames were already creeping perilously close to the petrol tank beneath the exposed chassis. He glanced back and, to his relief, saw the Germans standing by the café door, craning their necks toward the intersection. Several partisans were running about wildly shouting that people were inside the lorry. Claude knew this was not true, but the lie certainly created even further concern and drew a distracting crowd. The Germans began to edge slowly toward the lorry and Claude desperately scanned the street behind them.

There she was!

An ugly old woman poised on the curb opposite the café, ignoring the scene of devastation at the intersection. This abnormal unconcern for the so-called victims would be her fatal mistake. It could only be Dierick. With every sinew tensed to its limit, Claude sprang into the road, weaving through people who were running toward the stricken lorry. For a moment he lost sight of Dierick as the crowd thickened. In near panic, he pushed people aside and then saw her again as she prepared to cross. Within seconds he stood at her side.

"Let me help you," he hissed into her ear.

She immediately stiffened, but he was ready for her. He grabbed her arms and forced them behind her immediately feeling the outline of a stiletto concealed in her sleeve. Holding her wrists with one hand he clamped the other over her mouth. Dierick was extremely strong and he remembered her extraordinarily large hands from that first fateful meeting in the warehouse at Lewes. She tried to throw him with an expert twist of her body, but he was ready for her and began to drag her toward an alley a few steps away, lifting her feet from the ground. He heard her gasp as he pressed her arms backward and upward far beyond their normal limits. He knew the deadly stiletto lay in her sleeve and he could not afford to let her reach it. Barely believing that he held her in his power at last, he spun her around to face him and with almost inhuman strength held her two wrists between her shoulder blades with one hand and, lifting his hand from her mouth, quickly grabbed her around her throat with the other before she could cry out. Her eyes mocked him as he began to squeeze with all of his strength. He no longer heard the commotion on the road behind him and could only focus on the evil face in front of him. She tried to break away and he wondered if she had any other weapon concealed about her clothing. He squeezed harder and derived the vindictive pleasure he had so long sought as she began to fight for her life's breath. He could feel the sinews in her neck pressing against his fingers like rope and he watched as her eyes began to bulge. Those pale, cruel eyes that had watched so many others die. Her tongue began to protrude through thin lips and a cotton pad slid down over her teeth like a massive marshmallow. The gray wig slid back to reveal her short, blond hair, and the cleverly applied makeup around her eyes began to run with salt tears. So much, he thought, for this last attempt at disguise. The murderous grasp on her throat tightened even more and she no longer tried to struggle. Even as she sagged against him, he would not let go. She was dying too quickly. He wanted her to die slowly and painfully. Her arms swung loose as he released them and her weapon slid harmlessly to the ground. Now, using two hands, he continued to strangle her. He could not afford to let go. He likened her to the Russian Rasputan who featured so prominently in the death of the Tsar and his family and who had been so difficult to kill. But he had no intention of allowing this German fiend to revive.

A massive explosion from the street told him that the petrol tank must have exploded, and he relaxed his grip at last allowing Beatrix Dierick to drop to the ground like a rag doll. Quickly, he found the stiletto and sought the exact spot below her left breast in which to drive it upwards into her heart. He stabbed the knife blindly into the same general area twice more, then into her throat.

"Get out of here, you idiot! Can't you see she's very dead?"

The young partisan looked panicky.

"The SS are just going back into the café. They expect to find her there and when they don't, they'll set up the alarm and start looking. Get moving--quick!!"

Claude dragged the body behind a few rotting crates that would serve as a temporary screen from the street. He looked once more at the distorted face and felt suddenly sick.

"You get out of here, too," he said, turning to the young man. "Did you all keep your faces covered so that you will not be recognised again? Get away from Marseilles and lie low. There will be reprisals."

With a wave of gratitude toward the agitated youth he

sprinted to the opposite end of the alley and turned toward the old town waterfront.

It was over. After months of hunting down his prey, it was finally over. Yet he felt strangely empty. Her death had not given him the pleasure he might have expected. What had he expected? A feeling of triumph? A sense of victory? Why then did he feel nothing?

He slowed to a walk, now well away from the alley, and looked up at the ridge where the Notre-Dame de la Garde was silhouetted against the rising moon. Uncannily he suddenly thought of a similar scene when he had looked out from the warehouse in Lewes and watched the outline of the castle ruin at the top of the hill slowly fade in the dusk. He wondered if he would ever see it again. He remembered too the reflection of the red sunset on his hands and how he quickly withdrew them. Now he did indeed have blood on his hands. He tried not to think of the retaliatory punishment the Germans would inflict on selected victims after they found Dierick. He concentrated instead on the immense relief her death would give to so many other people.

He walked warily along the wharf peering into the darkness, seeking the bulky outline of a tramp steamer. Once, he heard the brisk clip of heels and dodged quickly behind a mammoth pile of crates. As he hid, he read the lettering on the nearest container and learned that it was incoming German weaponry. Was it for attack, or defence? No doubt the Résistance knew about it and had plans to spirit some of the crates away. How ironic, Claude thought, that both sides will be using the same calibre of weapons and ammunition.

He continued to wait. At last, only the lazy lap of the wavelets against the side of the pier broke the silence. Then he heard another sound. A soft whistle--a monotone. He whistled back acknowledging that the coast was clear. Although he had posed as an aging stevedore without being questioned for some days and there was no apparent reason for him to be apprehended at this moment, he was taking no chances. Even so, how could anyone know that he had just murdered a woman?

Michou crouched on the deck of the tramp steamer peering anxiously into the darkness.

"It's done," he said, coming aboard.

She pulled him into the shadows as the ship's propeller began to turn.

* * *

March, 1944

"The RAF has been truly significant these last few weeks," Janine said, smiling at George over the rim of her cup.

"Bomber Command," he said. "It's their turn now. I don't envy them, though. The chances of coming back in one piece these days is pretty remote. I'd like to be a part of it even so." He looked wistful.

"You did your part," Janine went on. "How would anyone else know the importance of bombing Amiens prison last month? The resulting French escapees have swelled the ranks of the Résistance and at this point every contribution is vital."

"The big day is getting closer," George said. "The RAF had a go at Berlin--the heaviest raid of the war so far. Now this month they've pelted Frankfurt twice."

He studied the frown between her eyes. "Yes, I know," he said. "It hasn't all happened without tremendous losses. The fighters received all the glory in '40. Now there's no doubt the bombers are doing equally as well in '44."

"How far along are the people in Room 900 in London concerning hiding those pilots and crew members that have succeeded in evading capture?" Janine asked.

George shrugged. "Haven't you noticed the increase in German soldiers and equipment on all the roads? We can't very well move four hundred men to the Forêt de Fréteval right under their noses. It's an MI9 decision and all I can do is stand by and see what I can do to help."

"I?"

"When I said we would be going home soon, I didn't say we would necessarily be going together. You're going back now. It's all arranged."

Janine opened her mouth to protest, but George held up his hand.

"There will be fighting in the streets after the invasion," he said. "There will be plenty of people in the underground involved with that, but it's not for you. You're well overdue to go back, you know that. Go home, Janine, and tell that lovely daughter of yours that I'm coming back to marry her. No arguments!"

Not since her latest involvement in extreme skullduggery had Janine allowed herself to think of her family. She had deliberately put them out of her mind in order that she may function without interference. George was right. There would be people fighting the Germans in the streets. Hadn't they been collecting arms specifically for this opportunity?

In all the time she had been in the south of France, she had thought from time to time about Claude. Thoroughly entrenched in her own tasks, she had not had time to make any special enquiries about him. But he came vividly to mind when news of a murder reached the group in Aix. The German agent who had been instrumental in so many betrayals by using ingenious theatrical guises, one Beatrix Dierick, had died in Marseilles. Perhaps this might not have been such startling news since there had been a number of gangster-style drive-by

shootings in Marseilles.   Puzzling disappearances and
mysterious murders happened constantly--not without dire
consequences to innocent victims as random punishment--but
this had obviously been a premeditated murder prompted by
loathing. A killing for vindication perhaps? After the victim's
death from strangulation, why would it be necessary to also
stab her multiple times? This must have been an act entirely
prompted by hate, Janine thought.   Even so, the woman had
been sought by the Allies for months and her unofficial murder
could only be counted as a positive accomplishment.

How would she, Janine, feel if her parents had suffered
in the same manner that Claude's had?   Could she have
resorted to such extreme venomous actions? She shuddered as
she envisioned this scenario. Yes, she thought, indeed I could.
There was little doubt in her mind that Claude Simone had
fulfilled his mission and at the same time had done the Allies a
great favour.   But what of the consequences? He must have
thought of this, too. Where would he go? Spain, perhaps?

"We'll travel together as far as Tours," George was
saying. "To be closer to the forest, you know."

"And then?"

"Someone will meet us there--a Belgian--who will escort
you to Brittany."

"But that's pretty much out of reach, isn't it?" Janine
said. "The Belgian escape route is still functioning, but rather
risky at best, and any attempt at a coastal contact would
be........"

George held up his hand again.

"Trust me. How are your sea legs?"

* * *

Having never visited the town before, Tours was not familiar to Janine. They had arrived at a safe house on the opposite side of the Loire River without incident since all German activity seemed to be preoccupied with a massive movement of men and equipment. This in itself had caused some concern upon their arrival since they were obliged to cross the river by one of the two existing bridges--a bridge for traffic and a suspended pedestrian crossing. How would they cross unobserved?

"I remember there was an institute here," Janine said, attempting to lighten the mood. "For foreigners to study the French language, I think. Perhaps you might want to attend some classes now that I'm leaving!"

George grinned. "Never fear. There are three willing ladies to fill your spot," he said.

"They have a big wine and brandy industry here, too.....or did. We'll all have to come back one day."

George sobered. "Yes, indeed we will. While Tours is a good place to make my contacts, it also has a steel industry which, of course, the Germans have made good use of. Unfortunately, this has attracted quite a concentration of them in this area."

"The bridges," Janine said. "How will we cross?"

"You have no need to worry about them. Your Belgian escort will be here very soon and you'll be off to Benodet."

Although she knew they were nearing the end of their association, she had not realised that it would be so soon.

"How long before you'll be following me home?" Even as she asked the question she knew the answer. He would leave as soon as the movement of the airmen to Le Forêt de Fréteval had been completed. He looked at her and smiled.

After working so successfully together Janine was loathe to leave George behind in this atmosphere of dread and mistrust. Perhaps he had spoken in jest concerning Yvonne.

With silent self-reproach, she cautioned herself not to interfere with matters of the heart. She suspected that Yvonne held a certain attraction toward him, but there had been no real mention of it--just a certain look when his name was mentioned. She glanced at George who waited by the window, the patch over his eye distorting his profile. Surely the experiences and risks he had encountered must account for a number of added years to his actual age. Could he be only twenty-three? Indeed, he had the mind and demeanor of a forty year-old. And Yvonne. Undoubtedly her experiences had changed her outlook entirely--to everyone's advantage. Janine remembered the pre-war selfish dazzle of youth and a craving for adventure, then recalled the last time she had seen her daughter. A different aura had surrounded her and although she still turned heads with her loveliness, there seemed to be an inner beauty and a great sense of empathy. Both she and George had faced their individual ordeals with bravery and determination and this must surely be a common bond.

"Here they are," George said, moving quickly to the door of the tiny house.

There were so many things she wanted to say to him and desperately hoped that the opportunity would be there for her when they were both back in England.

*　　*　　*

April, 1944

In London for a brief respite, both David and Rupert sensed the ubiquitous electric aura of anticipation as they walked toward Henry's club. The concierge greeted them with a respectable salute and assured them that they were expected, and that David should wait for is father in the bar. As they enjoyed the ambiance of luxury, in spite of plasterless ceilings and boarded up windows, they noted that the place was almost empty.   One man left as they entered and after they had ordered their drinks they were left entirely alone. They were in no great hurry for lunch since Henry had said on the telephone that he would try to take a brief break and join them. David hoped very much that he would make it.

Rarely able to speak freely about their secret assignments, the quietness of the club and the absence of others allowed them to converse, albeit in soft tones, away from the confines of Tangmere Cottage and Tempsford.

"I wonder if we'll be pulling more of our agents out of France now?" Rupert said quietly, leaning back in the leather club chair. "I suppose the locations of the invasion landings--if there is going to be an invasion--will decide from where we'll be picking them up. I've heard talk--unfounded, of course--about Norway. Apparently there is a British build-up of troops in Scotland. On the other hand, I've also heard talk of an attack on Pas de Calais in July by the Americans. I suppose the new American Supreme Commander, Allied Expeditionary Force knows what he's doing."

"Well, the Americans do seem to be concentrated in southwest England. But have you noticed that there are British units moving down to the southeast, too? But if such rumours are running so rampant," David said.   "I doubt that any of them hold credence.   I should think anything to do with an all-out invasion would be kept well under wraps."

He glanced toward the door and rose.   "My father's here."

Henry looked tired as he sank gratefully into a leather club chair.   The old waiter knew his preference and immediately served him with whiskey.

"Thank you, Bernard," Henry said, "but I have surgery

this afternoon. A cup of tea would be wonderful."

"What do you hear from Yvonne?" David asked. "I haven't had any contact with her for ages. Mother, either for that matter. What on earth keeps them so preoccupied?"

Even as he spoke, he felt he had known the answer to that question for some time. His mother was French as were his maternal grandparents who were still in France. Perhaps he had suspected some time ago that Janine's magazine travel column could not have taken up quite so much of her time. He had justified her absences then by assuming that her association with European society kept her in demand. Yet, hadn't he wondered why her destinations toward the onset of war with Germany coincided with pertinent political news bulletins from Europe? Didn't he wonder more than once why sometimes her telephone conversations were rapid and monosyllabic, often abruptly terminated if anyone in the family inadvertently entered her sitting room? But the evasive excuses from Yvonne's ATA colleagues when he tried to contact his sister at Ferry Pool 15 in Hamble were equally as baffling. If his mother's equivocal explanations were frustrating, Yvonne's odd disappearances also nudged his curiosity.

"Whatever your mother is doing it's obviously top secret," Henry said. "Of what nature, I honestly don't know. But I can guess. Yvonne 's fluency in French would be put to good use in one of the numerous communications agencies in London, I'm sure. Both she and her mother have made it clear that they can't talk about their work. I suppose that's normal in wartime. I've noticed your answers to my questions aren't too specific either, David." He sighed and took a sip of tea.

"Well, one thing I can talk about is the fact that I'm due to return to East Grinstead next week," David said. "Archie wants to work on this." He pointed to the purple gouge at the side of his neck that had been giving him some trouble. "He's also started to do things with tendons and hopes he can ultimately get my fingers to straighten completely."

360

"As I've said before, David. You couldn't be in better hands."

Rupert was unusually quiet, and David knew that the thought must have entered his mind too that both Yvonne and his mother might have actually been conveyed to France by the Moon Squadron. Often they didn't see the faces of their passengers.

"Do you think the invasion is imminent, sir?" Rupert asked, huskily. "Are you preparing for heavy casualties?" He seemed calm but his voice hinted that he was still in shock concerning Yvonne and Janine.

"Only that I'm soon probably going to be very busy. I understand there has been a movement of German dispositions along the French coast. What else can I say? Shall we go into lunch?"

Henry encouraged the young men to stay on at the club after the meal.   He apologised for his rapid departure, but a telephone call had summoned him back to the hospital.

"Perhaps," David said. "We might check the post at the house in Bayswater. There are probably a few outstanding bills on the doormat. My father appears to spend most of his time in London at the hospital and in his cottage near East Grinstead and often forgets to go by the flat. After that, let's go and sample the fleshpots of Shepherd's Market, shall we?"

"Hardly luxurious," Rupert said. "But we might come across someone we know there." He picked up his hat and studied the RAF emblem on the front. "You know, old boy," he went on.   "I'm beginning to think I should get back into flying fighters again. You know, all this talk of invasion has me wondering if I wouldn't be more useful giving the Hun a run for his money."

"I had thought about the same thing," David said. "But I doubt that the medical board would pass me out for that kind of flying."

As he turned toward the door, Rupert touched his arm

and made a quick cursory check around the empty dining room. "I think we both know what your mother and Yvonne are doing. It troubles me to think that there have been times when our passengers' faces were not visible and that these same passengers declined to speak at all."

David pursed his lips together tightly. "I know," he said at last.

The Bayswater flat smelt musty and damp from neglect. Henry contacted Mrs. Dougherty only when he used the facilities there, and it was obvious that it had been some time since she had been summoned. David felt a twinge of resentment. It seemed that he really did not have a home at all these days; nor a family, for that matter.

Later in the day he and Rupert found their way into the dubious establishments of Shepherd's Market and joined a number of RAF comrades-in-arms in propping up the bar at the local pub. At one end of the room two American airmen chatted amiably with British RAF pilot officers, comparing pre-war life in England with that of America, while two tawdry girls wearing distastefully revealing dresses hovered nearby, obviously attempting to lure the Americans into their grubby boudoirs. The British military were somewhat disgruntled by the Americans' generous pay scale which, in itself, baited certain young women who had been so long deprived of the luxury of a drink, or a pair of nylon stockings. David glanced at the girls with disinterest. He wondered, though, what it might be like to go to bed with the taller one, and quickly averted his eyes as she turned toward him. He glanced at her again and saw that she looked directly at him, staring rudely. Still acutely aware of the stares and covert glances his scarred face drew, he was about to turn away when he suddenly realised that he knew the girl.

He murmured her name in astonishment and raised his hand in recognition.

"Jenny?"

She frowned and took a step backward. Her previous demonstrative interest in him at Flint House had obviously dwindled, or perhaps she simply did not recognise him. Her promiscuity in the Farnsworth's hayloft had undoubtedly expanded to the seamy backstreets of London and perhaps one man looked the same as another. Even as he hoped that this was the situation, her eyes widened in recognition.

"Let's get outta here," he heard her say as she grabbed her companion's sleeve and pulled her toward the door.

"Glad they've gone," the bartender said. "We don't much like that sort in here."

David studied the contents of his glass. Jenny's expression had sent a distinct message and he wondered if his scars would be a permanent deterrent for all women. Most of the men he had met simply stared for only a moment. But what of the women? And the children? Would children turn away from him in fear? He hadn't yet faced that possibility. He felt a pang of foreboding as he thought of young Kate. Would she too turn away from him?

"You knew her, didn't you?" Rupert was saying.

David stirred himself. "What? Oh, yes. She was a maid at Flint House."

"I know what you're thinking," Rupert said. "But has it occurred to you she might just be ashamed of herself. After all, she's obviously a prostitute."

Rupert moved along the bar to chat with a young fellow from Fighter Command.

"What are you flying, these days?" he asked. "Spits? Hurrys? Typhoons?"

*   *   *

May, 1944

Kate could no longer see the aesthetic charm of Mallory Cottage. To her it symbolised mortality. Too many people associated with it, directly or indirectly, had been affected and every second she remained in the cottage it became more unbearable. Ghosts of the past haunted her and she could no longer look up at Windom Hill toward the Long Man. It would be pointless, she thought, to confide in Mother. We couldn't move away since there's nowhere else for us to go.

If these misgivings affected Hugh in any way, he had escaped them since he went away to school at the start of the winter term. Kate's fifteenth birthday was due in the coming December and it would be another year before she could finish school. The thought sickened her. How could she go on living in Mallory Cottage for that much longer?

She looked down at the garden from her latticed window and saw the yellow stream of daffodils and narcissus meandering at random through the shrubs and trees. Along the path the last of the crocuses faded to make way for the awakening summer perennials, and the grass shone like an emerald carpet offering colour contrast. The Mallorys had left a legacy of country loveliness that could go on forever, and for a moment Kate's spirits lifted. As if to jeer at her pleasure, a small dark cloud covered the sun and the brilliant yellow in the garden cowered in its shade.

That's the way it always is, she thought as she turned away from the window.

She sighed and picked up a book, fanning the pages with no inclination to read them. BC stirred and stretched luxuriantly at the bottom of her bed and sauntered up to BQ who lay in all his grubby glory on her pillow. The cat cautiously circled the doll and then sank down beside it with his head in BQ's lap and promptly went back to sleep. Obviously nothing ominous was on his mind today.

At least, she thought, I can look forward to Mr. Baxter's arrival.

He had written that he would be down for the weekend with some news. She did not want him to come if it were not good news.

The year to date had been a disastrous one for Eastbourne and much of the devastation had spilled over into the countryside. The German hit-and-run raids were too numerous to count as were the numbers of killed and injured. With the loss of her father and the constantly decreasing quantities of rationed food, Kate's usual optimism had again begun to waver.

Charlie barked in the foyer below. As Mr. Baxter pushed open the garden gate, he looked up at Kate and waved cheerfully.

"Good news for you," he said, meeting her in the foyer. "Although I don't know how your mother will feel about it."

Enjoying tea in the front room he explained that a friend who had taught advanced art at the Slade school in London, which had sadly been blitzed in September of 1941, had seen some of Kate's work. Recognising remarkable talent he had offered to tutor her in preparation for a scholarship.

"Things are looking much brighter concerning the war," Mr. Baxter said. "It doesn't seem so pointless any more to prepare for the future.   By the time you're ready to leave school, you'll have everything squared away for college. Slade is currently in Oxford, you know so you'll have a foot in the door later on."

Mrs. Hawkins smiled faintly and shook her head. "We couldn't afford it, Clarence."

"He isn't charging his usual tutorial fee," Mr. Baxter said. "He'd only need to be covered for art supplies. They're almost impossible to find, of course. But I have a feeling he has a supply stored away somewhere."

Again Mrs. Hawkins shook her head. "He surely isn't going to come all this way to Long Bottom every day and it would be impossible for Kate to go to London. Where would she live? Apart from anything else, she's too young to be out on her own."

Mr. Baxter looked crestfallen. "There's got to be something we can do." He scratched his head. "I'm renting a single room in Balham, so that wouldn't do."

They sat in silence for a while. Kate prayed that one of them would come up with a solution, but in the end no one could. She watched Mr. Baxter walk slowly back to the garden gate and then hesitate.

"Think I'll just pop over and see old Banberry," he said. "Don't despair, Kate. We'll find a way."

BC rubbed against her legs as she waved goodbye. He continued to circle her even as she tried to walk back to the kitchen. For the rest of the evening he watched her with his yellow eyes.

* * *

June, 1944

As if there weren't enough going on--at least one would assume that something certainly was--the telephone call had been quite astonishing. Yvonne felt positive now that her mother had been involved with operations in France and her telephone conversation that morning gave it away. She had never quite lost her French accent when speaking English but her sentences today were strongly laced with swallowed "r"s and slurred "th"s. It had obviously been some time since she had spoken English at any length.

"I've been doing something in Scotland," she said, lamely.

More astounding was the fact that, quite possibly, they had been in France at the same time.

Since her return from France, the ferrying schedule had kept Yvonne fully occupied. Factories were churning out aircraft at a rate of 2,400 per month which included four engine bombers, fighters, and fighter bombers. Everyone had been talking about the new Allied Commander, Dwight D. Eisenhower, and the obvious preparations for invasion of mainland Europe. Having made deliveries to several airfields within one week, she noticed that ground personnel were occupied with painting the aircraft with black and white stripes. This uniformity obviously meant that these aircraft would be participating in the same mass operation. It did not take much to assume that it would be the coming invasion, given that a considerable concentration of troops and equipment was flooding toward the south coast and that her landings and departures from all airfields were strictly monitored.

*   *   *

During her debriefing in Gibraltar Yvonne was strongly cautioned not to mention her activities in the past months to anyone at any time. But there were so many things she needed to clarify and a sandwich lunch in the now-familiar basement with a French officer in London gave her the opportunity to ask questions. The first one centered upon Comte Andre de

Chambrun, who had not been available to clear her through Gibraltar. The Free French had quickly come forward and within two days she was being flown home in an American Dakota.

It had been easy to explain away her long absence from ATA duties simply by saying she was needed at the War Office in London due to her fluency in French. But why had Colonel de Chambrun not been available?

"He was rarely in London, you know," the young French officer explained. "Chambrun and others were extremely active in Paris until the betrayal. He managed to get away before the mass arrests and was helped down the O'Leary escape route to Lyon where he was picked up by Lysander. He was strongly advised to remain in England but insisted on returning to France, where he is now. You have, of course, heard all the rumours concerning invasion."

Yvonne's second question concerned Dierick.

"Yes, she is dead. Very much so. She was murdered in Marseilles."

"By whom?"

"Nobody knows. But somebody succeeded in getting rid of her."

She wondered if she would ever know for sure.

"But I failed," she said.

"No, Miss Parke. You did not fail. You did exactly what you were sent to do--although perhaps you were never aware of it. You would have been recalled anyway. The invasion is imminent, and the partisans are poised to help. We don't expect you to do that."

He rose and brushed crumbs from his uniform jacket.

"I believe that you will be handling just about anything that can fly when you return to ATA You are an excellent pilot and your work there is extremely vital at this time."

He had thanked her and given her the distinct impression that she would quite likely never see him again.

Apart from this sudden confirmation of past suspicions, Janine's telephone call was quite reassuring.

"I'm giving the flat a thorough clean up with the help of Mrs. Dougherty," she told her.   "There's so much bomb damage, of course, but it's livable. As soon as that's done I'm going to track down David and get you both here for dinner. I've tons of food points saved and somehow I'll get your father to sneak away for a few hours. Heaven knows he's earned at least that. We'll even open some of our champagne reserve."

Her mood was infectious and Yvonne felt a renewed touch of spring in the air. At least the flat would be occupied again, and if the coming invasion was a success, they may even have Flint House back before too long.

With the obvious movement of troops and equipment to the south coast, train transportation for anyone not involved with the preparations was denied. Apart from anything else, most of the seaside towns were closed to incoming traffic other than military. Yvonne did a quick bit of trading and managed to get enough petrol coupons together to give her a round trip between London and Hamble. It seemed odd to her that in spite of huge preparations for invasion of the European mainland, people in London were apparently going about their pursuits of pleasure as if everything were normal.

The newspapers had reported that there were crowds at the horse races at Windsor and plenty of spectators watching the cricket at Lords. As she drove through London she could see queues of people outside the news cinemas and a general throng of amiable souls going in one direction or another, intent on pleasure. Perhaps, she thought, they are trying to disguise their apprehension. Everyone knows that an all-out attack by the Allies will result in thousands of casualties. Husbands and sons had left on secret orders, but everyone knew where they were going. It was something that everyone had wanted......longed for.....dreaded....for years. Now the time was near, and people really did not know what to feel.

As Yvonne ran up the steps leading to the house in Bayswater, she was shocked by the damage the building has sustained. Yet, she supposed, they were lucky. It was still habitable. The pleasant smell of wax polish, soap, and disinfectant reached her nostrils the moment she opened the door and she savoured again the scent of home.

Janine met her at the top of the stairs. This was indeed a wonderful occasion to have the family back together again after so long, but her mother seemed unusually elated. Her blue eyes sparkled and her cheeks were faintly flushed.

"Isn't it marvelous?" she said. "David's here already and so is your father. This is going to be perfect!"

The moment she entered the dining room Yvonne saw the young man leaning nonchalantly against the mantel with a glass of whiskey in his hand. In spite of a white gauze dressing over one eye, and a decided loss of weight, not to mention almost four years of added age, she recognised him immediately.

"Hello," he said, coming toward her. "About those open cockpits we were talking about......"

CHAPTER SEVENTEEN

June, 1944

Claude left the pension quietly to find hot coffee and a newspaper. He glanced back at Michou's peaceful, sleeping face before leaving the room and knew he would have to tell her today.

While avoiding any possible chance of recognition and subsequent arrest in France, they had traveled north from Barcelona after their arrival by boat from Marseilles in December. For five months they operated out of Andorra at Andorra-la-Vella struggling for the full duration with the Spanish Catalan language. As both French and Allied fugitives reached Spain after long and exhausting treks across the Pyrenees, Claude and Michou ensured their safe continuing journeys down to Barcelona and on to Gibraltar. At first the high altitude and bitterly cold weather had been difficult for Michou. As time went on and spring warmed the lengthening days, she began to fully appreciate the breathtaking scenery that surrounded the valleys where sparse vegetation fed mostly sheep and a few horses and goats. The people were poor and largely distrusted intruders, but with the event of war in France had allowed helpers and guides to function there.

Michou worked well and efficiently beside Claude and there were times when he wondered how he could have managed without her.

With rumours becoming stronger concerning the possible invasion of the Normandy coast by the Allies, Claude withdrew to Barcelona to rethink his plans. Still unsure of the kind of reception he would receive in England, he hesitated to return. He was sure that the hue and cry concerning Dierick must have died down by now and felt he should return to France.

They had been in Barcelona for two days, languishing in the Spanish sun and enjoying full and tasty meals. Thanks to Noe's generosity prior to his arrest, they had survived over the months on a small amount of money. But their funds were now running low and, since Claude had been operating independently, he could expect nothing from the SIS or SOE. It would take too long to arrange for money to be sent from his accounts in London, if indeed, that might be possible. But circumstances now rendered this period of relaxation as wasted time anyway. He knew he must return to France.

The newspaper headlines blared that massive Allied landings on the Normandy beaches had begun. The Americans, the following article said, were in the areas of La Madeleine and were moving toward Ste Mere Eglise, St. Marie-du-Mont and Chef du Pont having made their first landing on the Iles-St.-Marcouf, tiny islands three miles off shore. The British and Canadians were coming ashore between Arromanches and St. Aubin and Lion and Sallenelles.

Leaving a full cup of hot coffee under the umbrella, he sped back to his room and awoke Michou.

"It's happening at last," he shouted, laughing at her sleepy face. "It's happened!"

"The invasion?"

"Of course, the invasion."

She sat up, running her fingers through tousled hair. "I suppose I should be as pleased as you are," she said. "But in the face of it, the Germans will put up an intense defence, Claude." She got up and padded to the window. "Also, if they are forced to retreat, the Gestapo will most likely go on a killing spree in the villages and towns. You know them as well as I do."

These remarks were true and had a sobering effect on Claude's elation.

"Then, in the face of it," he said. "We.....I.... can't just sit here while that happens."

She turned from the window and he noticed the sun highlighting her hair like a drift of golden gossamer and perhaps, for the first time, he was truly aware of his need of her. He had taken her loyalty and reliability for granted during their involvement in sabotage and yet he now realised her presence had always been important to him.

"I must go back," he said to her. "But I can't ask you to go, too."

She smiled. "I believe that option is entirely mine," she said.

* * *

London

Deeply absorbed in an extensive report for the SIS, Janine did not welcome the sound of the doorbell interrupting her thoughts.

She was tracing her journey from Tours to Benodet, trying to remember where all the safe houses and escape line contacts were. Upon arrival in Benodet, she was surprised at the warm reception. They had heard a great deal about her, they said, and were impressed with the number of men and women she had helped. After eating some food and encouraged to rest, she was taken to the coast where, to her surprise, a British Motor Torpedo boat waited off shore for herself and three others. Although a German patrol vessel briefly opened fire as they sped away from the shore, they arrived safely at Dartmouth. She later learned that bogus signals tricked the Germans into thinking they were friendly. The crew, she learned, had been operating in this fashion for months and were also making trips between Norway and Aberdeen.

The doorbell rang again and Janine clucked with exasperation. Mrs. Dougherty had gone to the shops and there was no one else in the house. Perhaps she would ignore it. But the bell rang again and she reluctantly laid down her pen and walked to the window in order to look down at the front entrance. A man with thinning hair and a robust build stood patiently on the top step looking anxiously at the front door.

The report isn't due until this afternoon, she thought. Surely they haven't sent somebody to pick it up. It would be most unusual since Baker Street is rarely this obvious.

Although safely back in England, she had grown accustomed to being almost fanatically cautious. Perhaps, she mused, my telephone is being tapped. This would certainly be cause for them to make direct contact like this. She glanced up and down the road to see if anyone else was in evidence and saw no one. The door bell rang yet again.

She walked down the stairs and opened the door, standing close to it on the inside.

"Mrs. Parke?"

This was definitely no one from SIS. They would use her code name, Phalene or another means of identification.

"I'll look and see if she's in," Janine said. "There are three flats here, you know."

"If you find her, will you tell her my name is Clarence Baxter and that I'm a friend of Kate Hawkins and her family?"

Now completely off-guard, Janine caught her breath.

"Oh, I say! Is she all right?"

Without waiting for an answer, she looked closely at him.

"Clarence Baxter did you say? The political cartoonist and artist?"

Mr. Baxter nodded. "And you are, of course, Janine Parke."

"One has to be careful, Mr. Baxter," Janine said, holding the door open and gesturing to him to enter. "I do hope you haven't brought bad news."

Over a cup of tea, Mr. Baxter explained Kate's dilemma and then clasped his hands in his lap and waited.

Without hesitation, Janine stood up. "Well, of course she will stay here."

Mr. Baxter closed his eyes and smiled. "Thank you, Mrs. Parke," he said. "Thank you so very much."

She smiled at his obvious relief and offered him a second cup of tea.

He talked at length about Kate and her trials and tribulations since the beginning of the war. He spoke of the death of his own daughter, Ruby, and the fact that she had been Kate's closest friend."

"No one can ever replace a daughter," he said, rising. "But Kate gives me the incentive to go on. She has lost her father, a normal childhood, and has seen so much adversity for one so young."

Janine watched from the top front step as he quickly walked away with a spring in his step and a smile on his face. She was sure she could hear him humming. For no reason at all, she began to cry.

*   *   *

David looked out across the airfield at Tempsford and tried to put things in order in his mind. Still in blissful shock concerning George's return, he was nonetheless baffled since there seemed to be no official acknowledgment of it. George did condescend to reveal that the French had quickly dragged him from his Hurricane after he crashed on the beach and taken him to a safe house. Ruefully admitting that he hadn't a clue what his rescuers were talking about, he did manage to conclude that he was--in his words--"all broken". Splinted and stitched over various parts of his body by someone who was obviously a doctor, it took several days before he was lucid enough to realise that he could not see out of his left eye.

"They did a marvelous job for me, old boy," he said, enjoying Mrs. Dougherty's specially prepared partridge at dinner. "Unfortunately, there was no morphine or anything so it was bit dodgy for awhile."

Henry had asked what the prognosis was concerning the eye.

"It's hard to say. It's a sliver of shrapnel, they think," George said. "Difficult to get at, you know. I think they're afraid that it might shift." He had shrugged in his usual nonchalant manner. "Just have to wait and see, that's all."

Apart from that, George had been entirely reticent concerning his activities during the following three years after his rescue. David had noticed a quick glance pass between George and his mother which immediately clarified a myriad of possibilities.

David had also taken note of Yvonne that evening. Unusually quiet yet surprisingly elated concerning George's miraculous return, she had made no comment on her long absence, either. The resultant enigma surrounding this reluctance to reveal details was unsettling.

A day or so after the dinner party, David was to suffer a crushing blow concerning his other close friend. Rupert had made the decision to return to combat duty in order to take part in the D-Day invasion over Normandy. David supposed that since Rupert was such a brilliant pilot, his request to be reassigned to Fighter Command was eagerly accepted. For this, and due to his experience, he was promoted to Squadron Leader. However, David had not taken into account that he might not return. Given that his friend had experienced extraordinary luck in the past, he simply assumed that it would continue in the same manner. But Rupert had been put to the task when assigned to a Hurricane which carried a 250-pound bomb attached to the underside of each wing. A later report from the Wing Commander indicated that they were only a few miles out from the French coast, in readiness for their dive-bombing attack on a Panzer convoy near the coastline of Normandy, when a group of Me109s sprung them from the clouds. Rupert went down in flames and, upon impact on the beach, undoubtedly perished as the bombs detonated. How like Rupert not to dither with injuries and a slow death. He succumbed quickly and completely, just as he would have wanted.

This small mercy was no consolation to David. He considered Rupert his best and closest friend after George disappeared, and he would miss him badly. What would he have done without his breezy accounts of life outside Ward III when recovering from his burns? How would he have faced the world afterwards without the reassurance and companionship of his good friend as he ventured back into the "real" world away from Queen Victoria Hospital. Rupert was a rare and loyal friend and when he returned to Fighter Command as a Squadron Leader, David had celebrated his promotion with him. They had been through a great deal together and Rupert's uncanny knack for survival had always been the brunt of many a joke. But, unlike George, there was no spurious report of possible survival. Rupert was positively dead.

David thought of his friend's easygoing approach to life and his willingness to "try anything if it will help" attitude. He had never talked about his private life and when David learned that his next of kin lived in America, he was astounded. He discovered that Rupert had studied at Oxford on a Rhodes scholarship prior to the war and had somehow accomplished the perfect English mien, outlook, and manner of speaking. He was, in fact, an American anglophile.

It seemed that both of David's closest friends held secrets they did not care to share. Yet the covert glance between his mother and George had told him a great deal. If, indeed, they were both involved in undercover work, then he understood that they were not to be questioned. Apart from recovering from intricate surgery on his eye, George seemed to be doing absolutely nothing at the moment. It occurred to David that his own work with the Moon Squadron contributed to this network of intrigue since he never spoke of his experiences either, and this in itself must set the others wondering.

His quiet observance of Yvonne at dinner that night concluded that there was a certain radiance about her. The cause might be the changing winds of war, although this would not account for the soft aura of romance in the presence of George.

Another incident set him wondering after he received word of Rupert's death, concerning Janine. He realised that he must have been distraught when he telephoned her about it and perhaps his personal grief might have affected her. Yet her own shocked reaction had been evident and he wondered about that since she had never met Rupert.

"I'm to go down to Tangmere to pick up the Daimler," he told her. "Rupert truly loved that car and I doubt that I shall ever think of it as mine."

There had been a long silence over the telephone.

"I..... do wish I could have met him when he came to pick it up," she said at last. "I had a train to catch and couldn't wait for him."

Another long silence.

"I'm so very, very sorry, David."

*   *   *

June 13, 1944

There had been little opportunity for Kate to visit London since the Blitz of 1940 and she anticipated spending the summer there with pleasure. But the great gaps in the rows of buildings, the gutted ancient churches and historic towers, and most facades showing evidence of damage, shocked her.

"Well," Mr. Baxter said. "Think of Streatham. It has taken quite a beating, too. The buildings in central London were bigger, that's all."

"There really isn't much left, is there," she said, sadly.

"Oh, there's plenty left. You know the British. They'll have it all built up again in no time now that we've got Jerry on the run."

She liked his cheerful approach, but his cartoons had shown that the fighting in France was at its fiercest. Mr. Baxter was certainly aware that the number of Allied casualties was soaring, but she deeply appreciated his attempt to keep her from fretting. She knew they each shared their own personal sadness of loss.

Mrs. Dougherty gave Kate a hearty welcome when they arrived at the flat in Bayswater.

"My goodness, Kate. I wouldn't have recognised you. It will be so nice to have our chats like we used to in Long Bottom."

Mrs. Parke appeared at the top of the stairs. "Kate, my dear! Let me look at you."

In spite of the damage Kate noted the expanse of the rooms and the quality of the furnishings. She understood then why Mrs. Parke had given Flint House to the military for the duration of the war. This was certainly an adequate alternative.

After Mr. Baxter had left for Balham she felt that the last of her childhood connections had been severed. Here in London she would be expected to behave as an adult in order to be as little trouble as possible, but the anticipation of traveling alone on the underground trains terrified her. Her private tutor, Marcus Bartholomew, lived in Chelsea and she was to go each day to his studio there. But as the days passed, her fears were quickly dispelled and she began to find her way around West and Southwest London with growing confidence. Often she cut her train journey short and walked the rest of the way through Hyde Park, saving a piece of her lunch sandwich to feed the ducks and swans on the Serpentine. She wrote to her mother and Mr. Baxter in the evenings assuring them that she was working hard and had easily adapted to city life.

Due to occasional night bombing raids which had never quite ceased since the Blitz, Mrs. Parke had moved their sleeping quarters to the basement flat since the military officer had been transferred. With her full and interesting days, Kate slept well and was rarely aware of the air raid alert. But on the night of the 15th of June something awoke her with a start. A single aircraft was passing directly overhead, yet the sound of it was not familiar. The harsh grating of its engine might suggest that it was in trouble, yet there was no hesitancy or variation. Suddenly, the sound stopped, leaving an ominous, echoing silence. Within seconds a massive explosion shook the flat, sending a shower of cement dust onto her coverlet. She was out of bed in a flash and almost collided with Mrs. Dougherty in the foyer.

"A plane must have crashed," she gasped.

Mrs. Parke joined them, shaking her head. "I'm afraid," she said, "we have just been attacked with a different kind of weapon. There have been rumours for some time about a bomb operated by remote control. A pilotless plane. I think we have just been introduced to it."

She had scarcely finished speaking when they heard the same menacing sound again followed by another sudden cut in the engine and a loud explosion. Mrs. Dougherty tied her dressing gown cord a little tighter and turned toward the basement kitchen.

"Well," she said. "If this is going to go on all night, we might as well have a cup of tea."

The morning news was devastating. No less than seventy-three of the new weapons had fallen on Greater London during the night. One touch of irony brought a smile to Mrs. Parke's face.

"Would you believe," she said. "The antiaircraft gun batteries thought they were shooting them down and that they had accomplished one hundred percent direct hits! Of course, if they are remotely controlled they simply cut out by themselves and fall to the ground."

In spite of the new missiles, officially named the V1, but unofficially known as the Doodle Bug or Buzz Bomb, London continued to function. The sound of the single ramjet engine constantly hovered over London and southern England. Easily identifiable by the spurt of flame fluttering from the tail end and its unique silhouette, people learned to run to shelter when the engine shut down. After the explosion, a tower of black smoke marked where the deadly weapon had fallen. Although the targets appeared haphazard, they were nonetheless shattering.   Once again the people of England were experiencing the terror of lethal bombardment from the Germans. The antiaircraft guns were moved toward the coast in order to intercept the missiles while they were still out over the water.   Attempting to shoot them down over land accomplished nothing since the bomb still detonated, causing devastation.

One afternoon Kate watched a V1 pass over, waiting for the engine to stop before running for shelter. (This had become something of a general procedure since constant "shelter hopping" was quite simply a nuisance.) It occurred to her that the missile was in the shape of a distinct cross and wondered if the German scientists who had created it realised what a study in contradiction it was.

"Can you imagine," Mrs. Parke said one evening in July. "David tells me that the Hawker Tempest V and Spitfire IX fighter pilots returning from the Normandy operations are flying alongside the Doodle Bugs and tipping the fins with their wings until the missile either turns around and goes back where it came from or plummets harmlessly into the sea. I suppose that would be possible since the wing span is about seventeen feet and the length an approximate twenty-five feet. Even so, I should think that's a rather dangerous solution."

"Why wouldn't they just shoot at them?" Mrs. Dougherty asked.

"If they're returning from Normandy," Kate surmised, "they probably don't have any bullets left."

The two women looked at her in surprise. "Of course," Mrs. Dougherty said. "I didn't think of that."

*   *   *

August, 1944

Since nowhere was safe, Kate continued to walk through Hyde Park on her way home, ignoring the distance between herself and a shelter. Tomorrow she would return to Long Bottom to prepare for the autumn term at school. She had learned a great deal from Marcus although there had been times when she wondered if she should continue. He was a stern and exacting teacher and had not allowed her to breach the student-teacher relationship with general conversation. The concentration of work had been beneficial, if often stressful. She felt more prepared to return to Mallory Cottage since the summer respite from the village had given her renewed courage. Her one regret was that David had not been able to return to London for leave. According to his latest letter, the Special Operations Squadron he was involved with was extremely busy. Neither had Yvonne returned, probably for the same reason. Kate had wanted to ask her about the woman she had sketched. That small mystery still lingered in the back of her mind.

The ducks seemed especially hungry today and she regretted that there was not more bread for them. Looking up at the unusually quiet sky, the afternoon sun felt warm on her face and she felt at peace. A group of students, lolling on the grass, whistled appreciatively as she passed and she quickened her step, flushing with embarrassment.

"Wait!" one of them shouted.

She walked faster, unused to coping with this kind of situation. While her friends at school covertly discussed boys and even touched on the possibilities of sex, Kate had never had the opportunity to indulge in such activities. Nor had she particularly wanted to.

"Wait!" The student was on his feet and running toward her. "Kate! It's me!"

At the sound of her name she stopped.

"It's me," he said again. "Peter."

No one could mistake the startling blue eyes. The shadow of an adolescent moustache followed the line of his upper lip, his voice had changed, and he was considerably taller, but there no doubt that it was indeed Peter Trimble. Knowing him as a twelve-year-old boy had been a natural childhood friendship, but this good-looking young man aroused something within her she had not known before.

"I couldn't believe it," he said. "You're not a bit as I remembered you; and yet there was something there that made me recognise you. That unique smile, I think."

He asked after Hugh and was genuinely delighted to hear of his recovery. Then, smiling quizzically, he said: "You know, even though I recognised you, you've really changed."

"I should hope so," Kate said. "It's been four years for heaven's sake."

"I mean, you were a pretty dogmatic type back in '40. All that skepticism about God, and your absolute devotion to an inanimate puppet and an uncanny cat."

"In one respect, perhaps I have changed," she said. "But I still have the puppet and the cat. And I'm still not too sure about that skepticism either."

He asked what she was doing in London and was not surprised when she told him about her interest in art.

"I'm going to study architecture," he said. "Something tells me there will be a great deal of rebuilding after this lot is over. I live in Hammersmith now and am doing some pre-exam studies in London. At least the Blitz got us out of the suburbs."

"Peter, it's nearly over, isn't it? I mean soon we'll be back to normal....whatever that is....."

"Doesn't it seem to you that we were supposed to meet up again?" he said. "What real chance would there be for me to find you in London, otherwise? We can see each other often now."

His enthusiasm was infectious and for a brief moment she forgot that she was returning to Mallory Cottage the next day.

"Well, at least we know how to keep in touch," he said after she told him. "I don't want to lose you again. You will let me know when you are coming back, won't you?"

His friends were calling to him and he looked at his watch.

"I have a class," he said. "Kate, promise that you'll keep in touch."

Not understanding why, she felt as light as air as she walked back to Bayswater.

*   *   *

September, 1944

Three women in smart ATA uniforms walked through the Savoy foyer drawing stares of admiration and puzzlement. Although uniforms were prevalent in London, the ATA women always drew covert curiosity since the distinct navy blue suits with the gold shoulder tabs depicting rank would suggest Navy; yet the forage cap and full brevet belied that possible association. At this point in time, all three had flown every conceivable type of aircraft from the smallest bi-wing to the heaviest bomber. But how would the general public know that?

Yvonne looked at her watch.

"I'm a little early," she said to her companions. "I'll just wait here in the foyer for George. Enjoy your lunch, and you can tell me all about the film when we're back at Hamble."

They had just visited their assigned tailor in Saville Row, although they had generally wondered if new uniforms would be necessary now that the Normandy invasion had taken place. The old tailor had dithered with embarrassment as he always did when he gingerly took unaccustomed female measurements. Yvonne smiled to herself, remembering the somewhat intimate alterations that had to be made the last time, especially around the seat of the trousers. After their morning appointment, they had planned on lunch and the cinema which Yvonne had looked forward to. Yet, George's later suggestion to meet him that afternoon had been too tempting and she had, in fact, eagerly accepted his invitation. As she watched her colleagues walk away, she sank into an arm chair to wait.

*   *   *

Although tired after long hours of flying, she often lay awake at night thinking about her experiences in France. Where were Ben and Michou now, she wondered? Had Margot's body ever been discovered? What had happened in Toulouse after they had left and abandoned the transmitter. Had the Gestapo taken vengeance on the people? The children? Who had really murdered Dierick? The whole thing seemed like a ghastly dream and sometimes she wondered if it had all really taken place.

But odd and unaccountable things did often happen. Although barely perceptible, the glance between George and her mother at dinner had been full of innuendoes. David was obviously with 161 Squadron at Tempsford and might have easily flown his own mother into France; obviously fate had stepped in there and not allowed that to happen. Odd too, that her mother would suddenly surface in May, just as preparations for D Day were beginning.

It had taken several weeks for Yvonne to completely detach herself from the Free French operations in London, and while David had been delighted to see her afterwards, his lack of inquisitiveness concerning her absence baffled her. Yet perhaps everyone in the military refrained from asking questions these days.

*   *   *

"You're obviously not thinking about me," George said standing directly in front of her to get her attention. "You were miles away somewhere."

Apart from the new dressing over his eye, he looked the complete fighter pilot in his newly pressed uniform.

"There's so much to think about these days, isn't there?"

"Good things, I hope." He held out his hand and helped her to her feet. "Eisenhower has established headquarters in France and the course of liberation is moving fast."

"I suppose after so long, it's difficult to realise that the war could soon end."

"It's just the beginning of the beginning," George said, escorting her to the dining room.

"Tell me about your eye," Yvonne said, carefully placing her wine glass back on its indentation in the tablecloth.

"They've located the shrapnel fragment. I've been given a couple of days to think about alternatives."

"What kind of alternatives?"

"Well, I suppose there's three, to be exact. The bit of metal has been in there so long it's embedded in scar tissue, which is understandable I suppose. If they try to take it out and things go wrong I could lose the eye altogether. If they try to take it out and all goes well, there's a chance that I'll be able to see out of it again. There's accumulated blood in there, they tell me."

"And the third alternative?"

"They can leave it alone, bearing in mind that it might shift either to my advantage or disadvantage."

"Have they made any recommendations?" His decision could make a vast difference to the rest of his life, and she knew he must be suffering.

"Those were they," he said. "But, I don't think I want to make any decisions today." He poured wine for both of them. "I hope you brought your dancing shoes."

Long after they had finished eating, they continued their conversation, and only when Yvonne noticed the hovering, anxious waiter did she realise how late it was. It occurred to her that she and George had not argued even once. They left the hotel intent on walking the weight of the lunch off in the park, and agreed to later try a newly reopened club for dancing. George had taken her hand in the park, and then laughed as they remembered that their uniforms forbade any form of demonstrative affection. But his touch had been pure magic and was a prelude to the excitement of his nearness as they danced at the club.

"I must return to duty tomorrow," she murmured as they moved slowly together on the dance floor.

"Must you?"

The dawn would bring his day of decision and the thought of it must be terrifying. He should not have to face this alone. She knew her mother was staying at the cottage near East Grinstead with her father and since Kate had returned to Mallory Cottage, and David to duty, Mrs. Dougherty would not be at the flat.

"Come to Bayswater now," she said. "We'll talk there."

* * *

He sat in front of the fire on the oversized French sofa looking young and somehow vulnerable. His uniform and ruffled hair lent him the appearance of a schoolboy and the white, gauze dressing might have been covering a black eye acquired on the playing fields instead of a brutal combat injury. If he had been in France all these months, he must have experienced far more than any adolescent could ever imagine and if he had been working for Special Operations there, she knew he could not speak of it.

He took the coffee cup she offered him and smiled.

"I've thought about you a great deal over the past months. When I first met you, I thought of you as a beautiful self-centered shrew. I'm not sure if I've gone a little mad, or if you might have changed, but I don't think about you like that any more. "

"I didn't think about you at all, of course! It's odd that you would have had a black eye the last time I saw you and now there's this......."

She looked briefly at the bandage, and then lowered her eyes to his mouth. His face was thinner than she remembered which was not surprising, and the dressing looked enormous. But she was not thinking of the injury, or of the impending decision concerning it. He carefully placed the cup and saucer on the lamp table and reached for her.

Never in her short life had she experienced such intense feeling toward another human being. His nearness meant far more than any ritualistic flirtation as she spun in a vacuum where no other thought occupied her mind than the wonder of being in love. There was no past; no war; no dissension as they soared in a gossamer world of pure ecstasy.

She awoke in his arms hardly daring to believe that he was really there. Moving cautiously, intent on letting him sleep, she held her wrist watch toward the lamp. Six thirty-five. The fire had died and the room felt chilly. She would have time for a bath before leaving for the station. I'll perk some coffee first, she thought.

If any bombardment had occurred during the night, she doubted very much if she would have heard it. Yet things did seem uncannily quiet as she puttered about the basement kitchen, putting out cups and saucers.

Suddenly, the room swayed and the walls around her creaked and groaned like a falling tree. As she clung to the counter, George rushed into the kitchen.

"That was a close one," he said, his voice thick with sleep. "But at least we're still standing. Why didn't you duck for cover?"

"I--I didn't hear any ramjet engine," Yvonne stammered. "Not even an explosion."

"But it has to be blast to affect a building this solid." He looked at her steadily and held her by her shoulders. "This must go no further, you understand, but there is another missile in existence," he said.   "The launchers were sighted by returning bombers and then photographed by reconnaissance. A complex plan to attempt to destroy them must have failed. This….." He inclined his head toward the window. "This must have been one of the first."

On the verge of asking him how he knew these facts, she suddenly understood why he had not returned from France. Could it be possible that all of them had been involved in secret work? Her brother as a Lysander pilot for the Moon Squadron, her mother working for the British, George doing heaven knows what, and herself working for the French?

He held her close to him. "The government should enlighten everyone now…..I'm sure they hesitated to do so earlier because they hoped the silos could be destroyed. No point in alarming everyone. But now, the public hasn't a clue what to expect…..since the rockets give no warning, perhaps it is better that they don't. How can one prepare for the arrival of such a silent weapon?"

Even as he finished speaking, the building rocked again and this time they heard the thunderous explosion. They clung together, waiting for the ceiling dust to settle.

Oddly enough, George had been wrong. There was not an official announcement concerning the new weapon and people were left wondering for several weeks. Finally, after a number of terrible incidents where the rockets landed on crowded shopping areas, killing hundreds, the government decided to announce that it was indeed a new weapon being launched in Holland and was logically named the V2.

CHAPTER EIGHTEEN

October, 1944

Although Lysander operations to France were now dwindling, David did not want to leave the squadron for another bout in hospital. He tried to ignore the dreaded signs of tendon atrophy in his left hand, but had known for some time that the fingers were obviously drawing down into the typical claw. With Rupert gone, he felt that he and George should continue the quality service that they and the other "old boys" of Regatta squadron had rendered in the RAF. Yet they were both incapacitated.

So much had happened in the past few months that it all seemed somehow unreal. In July the Allies broke out of the Normandy beachhead and the United States had recognised de Gaulle's French Provisional Government in all liberated areas, which must have been exhilarating for a population that had suffered under so much suppression for so long. August, too, was full of encouraging news as the Allied forces reclaimed for France its capital and all cities, towns and villages in between.

Of special significance was the entry of American forces into Nice and David wondered how much this had affected his grandparents only a few miles to the west. Also in that month everyone menaced by the V1s in England breathed a sight of relief as the launching sites were being over run at Pas de Calais. Little did they know that the V2, a worse and entirely unstoppable weapon, would follow. That September they learned how damaging this silent and diabolical missile could be. Apparently the government had opted not to warn the public that the V2 was forthcoming although much later information indicated that they had knowledge of it through aerial reconnaissance and agent feedback. Perhaps, David thought, public morale was a more important factor since the people of London and its surrounds had just about had enough.

In September too, the Free French troops from the south had made contact with United States troops near Dijon. What an event that must have been! After the victories of August, David's squadron moved its forward base to RAF Winleigh in Essex since Tangmere was too near to the beachhead operations. With the Moon Squadron aircraft operating virtually unarmed, the sense of this location change was obvious.

Now, only in the past week the wily Desert Fox, Field Marshal Erwin Rommel, was reportedly dead by his own hand.

David returned to the Queen Victoria Hospital reluctantly aware that he could not function as a pilot with a weakened left hand. As a form of consolation, Patrick met him in the foyer, his own hands again swathed in bandages.

"Just like old times," he said.

David was surprised to see the VAD volunteer, who had previously helped him with his letter writing, at his bedside when he came round after the surgery the next day. Many of the volunteers had gone on to other things and it was a surprising coincidence that Philippa should be still there.

The scars on Patrick's face had settled down considerably and while he was still undoubtedly disfigured, no one could describe him as hideous. In any case, the aura of contentment and happiness detracted from his physical appearance and he eagerly offered photographs of his wife (who David immediately recognised as a nurse from his initial introduction to Ward III) and two children. Sales of his novels were doing very well and he had been asked to convert one into a screen play.

"What are you going to do after it's all over?" he asked.

The question stunned David. He had not given his future any thought at all. Obviously he could not pursue his father's preference for medicine because of his hands, unless he went into the quiet privacy of laboratory research. He cringed at that since, unlike his father, he did not have the patience for tenacious systematic investigation nor was he inclined toward study and deep analyses. Flying was still a great pleasure and always would be, but it did take a toll on his hands after long periods.

"I'll find a wealthy heiress, I suppose," he said, facetiously. "Get married and spend long idle days on the French Riviera." In all honesty, that thought appalled him even more.

"What about that one?" Patrick said, nodding toward Philippa as she entered the ward. "Did you know she asked to be told when you might be returning? She hasn't worked here for some time."

David felt a pang of guilt. She had written to him at Tangmere in 1941 and he had never answered. A girl of breeding, intelligent humour, and good looks, he wondered why he had not pursued a closer relationship. In retrospect he realised that he had never really given her much thought and in any case assumed that his disfigurement might promote sympathy rather than romance. He watched her approach and saw for the first time how very attractive she was.

With his hand supported by a long splint and masses of bandages he knew there was little he could do while in hospital to enhance any kind of relationship. But Philippa was obviously not content to wait for a better opportunity and solved the problem by suggesting that she might drive them both to London for the evening. While pain was still a major factor, David nonetheless accepted, and suggested they go to the newly reopened Hungaria restaurant, to which she readily agreed.

In spite of drastic food shortages and the early threat of a frigid winter in the making, red, white and blue bunting in the shop windows displayed a cautious optimism. With the war going so well, victory must be imminent, he thought. Philippa talked of her home and family in Wiltshire subtly hinting at titles and wealth as they drove toward the restaurant. Her interest in him was baffling and again he thought of Patrick's remark years ago concerning his charm and personality. Even so, there were plenty of others who displayed prolific wit and who were interesting company and would be far more deserving of such an eligible young woman. Why would she be attracted to a scarred wreck like himself?

After a pleasant dinner he anticipated further, less public, pleasures in her company. But pain took precedence once more and he knew he must ask her to return to the hospital He doubted that her interest in him would continue after such an anticlimax to an evening that bore so much promise, and he cursed his bad luck.

She smiled. "You're still a patient," she said. "and you've been a very good one. I've watched you try to cope with pain in the past and I've always thought you were very brave."

As they drove back to East Grinstead, he experienced the familiar malaise of fever. Although he wanted to know more about Philippa he could only truly concentrate on his own hospital bed and something to kill the infernal fiery stabs that were coursing through his left arm.

Archibald McIndoe was not pleased the next day. An infection had taken hold, streaking the arm with angry welts and causing the axillary lymph glands to swell in the arm pit.

"The dorsal skin on your hands is paper thin," McIndoe said. "The new incisions have become infected and caused boils to erupt on your forearm." He looked at David closely. "Did you leave the hospital? Did you forget that I told you to wait a couple more days?"

David felt cheated, but he knew that Archie McIndoe was right.

"I-I suppose now that I'm back flying again, I thought I was invulnerable. I didn't think anything could go wrong any more."

The doctor's expression softened. "Well, you've been through the mill and, up until now, an obedient patient. I suppose when the juices rise………." He grinned. "Take your medicine like a man and you'll be back on track before you know it."

All the patients knew that under the crusty facade, Archibald McIndoe had a heart of gold. But it had been an evening of pleasant anticipation and because nothing at all had come of it, an anticlimax. Through no fault of his own, he was undoubtedly paying for it. When his anger subsided, he knew he was wrong. He should have waited for a more appropriate time to indulge in such activities. He lay back on his pillow feeling foolish and remorseful. The last thing on earth he wanted to do was to upset Archibald McIndoe.

"Sorry, old chap," Patrick said, approaching his bed. "I was part of the ruse, I'm afraid."

"What ruse?"

"Well, it was me who let her know you were coming back. I knew months ago that she was interested. I'm surprised you didn't notice."

"Well she's set me back another week," David snapped.

"Wasn't intended. Truly. Come on, David. It isn't all bad. Christmas is coming and with it the end of the war we hope, and you've been recommended for a DSO (Distinguished Service Order) to add to your DFC (Distinguished Flying Cross)."

"What for? Indulging in intended debauchery?"

Patrick shook his head. "The pros far outweigh the cons. Think about it."

David did think about it and found sleep elusive that night. He envisioned how it would be if things progressed further with Philippa and could not understand this unfamiliar concern. There had been plenty of female companionship during his sojourns into London with Rupert although none had ever had any substance. Why should this one make any difference? Since it was making a difference, why was he so reluctant to admit it?

*   *   *

When he returned to duty at Winleigh in November, two letters waited for him. The first--from Kate--offered him a form of relief from the awkward relationship with Philippa. Kate seemed in excellent spirits and mentioned her delight in having found an old friend, Peter, in London who had already been to Long Bottom to see her. Her schooling was going well and the tiny water colour she enclosed showed the positive results of her special tutoring in Chelsea. How like her not to brood too long over the excruciating loss of her father.

The second letter was from his mother. This too was full of optimism which was plainly due to the liberation of southern France and the fact that she had received the first letter from her parents since the occupation. She spoke of Kate's stay in London and mentioned how nice it had been to have a young person about the house for the summer. But the most startling news was her reference to his own future. Her uncanny premonition was even more amazing since he had only recently wondered about that dilemma himself.

Come to Bayswater when you can, she wrote. *We need to talk.*

* * *

December 1944

Claude waited quietly as Lucien Marceau wept and knew there was nothing he could do to console him. He had suffered through a similar sorrow years before and had learned to live with it, as would Lucien. Although the Gestapo had fled from Paris in a hail of Allied--including the Free French--and French Resistance bullets, they had done their worst before leaving. Perhaps, Claude thought, the eradication of any familiar evidence of Noe's existence might be a blessing since mementos and memories of happy boyhood days could quite likely make the loss even more painful. The destruction of inanimate and impersonal furniture and furnishings was not that devastating. But books and photographs were a different matter. Nothing had been left for Lucien to brood over.

Michou tried to comfort her father by taking his hand and holding it against her cheek.

"Your brother--Uncle Noe--died valiantly and for a great cause," she said softly. "Without him and his colleagues we would never have been able to fight as we did."

Claude stared unseeingly at the city beyond the window and listened to the sound of her voice. Throughout the entire war she had fought for freedom and had never taken or expected any credit. "It is a job that has to be done," she once said; "and I'm doing it."

* * *

There had been a call from the Résistance in August that help was needed somewhere near the Forêt de Fréteval. The Germans were rapidly retreating in that direction and it appeared that there was a large encampment of Allied airmen there. Incredibly, these men had been evading capture for months and an operation, headquartered in London, had made it their business to move them away from the initial impact of the Normandy invasion. Claude and Michou joined up with the Résistance and spent the fine, hot days of August sniping at the retreating German forces and throwing petrol bombs into their tanks in an attempt to divert them from the encampment. At night, they mined the retreat route all the way to the Seine. Several times they heard the name Marcel mentioned and learned that he was an Englishman of some renown who had been working along the escape routes with extraordinary success.

The airmen were to be moved again out of the line of German retreat, but a lack of transportation and drivers posed another problem. Some of the airmen, impatient to be away from the approaching enemy, followed the escape routes south and took the grueling trek across the Pyrenees. But soon, several grey-painted abandoned German buses were accumulated and the next task was to find people to drive them

399

to the encampment. Since there were several hundred evaders and enough buses to accommodate them, the problem seemed to be solved--until it was discovered that there was, indeed, a lack of drivers. All the young men in the area were in labour camps in Germany and few of the women knew how to drive. Michou and Claude made their way to Le Mans to volunteer their services and were highly amused to find that the buses had been bedecked with flowers and French flags. Since there were still Germans along the roads toward Chartres, they felt that this jubilation was perhaps a little premature, but set out in a convoy on the road to Vendome accompanied by groups of SAS (Special Air Service) guards. These men went ahead to ensure the villages were cleared of Germans and often appeared at the road side with groups of grubby and demoralised prisoners.

Having completed this task and learned that nearly all of the rescued men returned safely to their squadrons and immediately went back to flying, Michou and Claude traveled back to Paris and fought with the Freedom Fighters against the Germans in the streets as the Allied armies drew nearer. They regularly listened to messages from London via the BBC and the introduction always served to keep their spirits high--*"Ici Londres.....V-dot, dot, dot, dash"* (the code for victory). The messages were directed not only toward France, but to Norway, Belgium, Holland, Czechoslovakia, Poland, and Denmark. The fight for freedom was indeed far-reaching. His thoughts drifted back to October when Maquis and Résistance courts martial were dealing so ruthlessly with the French Vichy officials that those remaining were taken to Sigmaringen in Germany for "safety". However, they continued to live in fear of retribution since the Free French also considered them to be traitors. With the daily execution of French prisoners by Canaris' SS (the SS had now completely disencumbered itself from the more lenient Abwehr by abolition) and the vindictive determination of the Free French to punish the French Vichy collaborators, even General de Gaulle himself felt the need to intervene.

While the liberation of France continued, hunger still prevailed. Parisians went into the countryside in order to barter for crops in exchange for soap and shoes and Claude wondered how much longer France could endure this grave shortage of food. While his own stomach cramped, his compassion focused on the children. But even as he pondered the problem, the Maquis were welcoming American Dakotas into the liberated sections, and supplies of food began to arrive at last.

After Claude and Michou returned to Paris, Lucien arrived from Lille in order to help with Noe's personal papers. As they approached the Boulevard Saint-Michel together, they shared mutual apprehension. Perhaps the rooms would no longer be familiar; perhaps treasured pictures and furniture might have been stolen. They stood silently in front of the building loathe to enter.

Now, as Lucien wept, Claude grieved over news from the Underground that the Germans had launched a massive desperate offensive in the Ardennes. Why, he thought, would they see the need to kill and be killed when their situation is virtually hopeless? Adolf Hitler, the grapevine reported, continued to command his war from his headquarters near Rostenburg in East Prussia and was reported to be going completely mad. Old in appearance, and surrounded by his fanatical SS guards, he worked and lived in an impenetrable fortification. He seemed neither to know nor care how many men he had sent to their deaths.

Claude knew he could no longer delay entering his old apartment. Ironically, he had faced enormous adversities throughout the war, yet now this simple task made him feel incredibly afraid to go back in time. Would he be overwhelmed by the ghosts of the past? Would all the bitterness and hate return to such an extent that he would not be able to deal with it?

Leaving Michou to console her father, he trod the debris-strewn carpet along the hallway toward the last door. Perhaps it might be locked and he would not be able to enter after all; but it swung easily open under only light pressure and he found himself on the threshold of his boyhood home. He immediately saw his mother's piano standing in its old place by the window and he walked hesitatingly toward it to run his fingers over the keys. Surprisingly, the piano was well tuned and in good condition. Then he hastily withdrew his hand as he imagined some vile German soldier playing a bawdy beer hall waltz.

"Maman," he whispered as he turned away.

He moved into his father's study and saw that every last book had been taken from the surrounding library shelves. The desk, also empty of paper and writing materials, seemed to be unharmed, and the lack of dust implied that it must have been used by a German officer. He looked toward the fireplace where his father's chair backed against the adjacent window for better light to read by. He could almost see the long sensitive fingers laying gently on the ends of the brocade arms now shabby and darkened from years of wear.

In the kitchen he found several cups, some half filled with cold, congealing coffee. Angrily, he picked one up and dashed it against a wall--and then another. He watched the dregs trickle in large drops down the tiles and likened it to blood. Not knowing how long he stood there, he started at the sound of Michou's voice.

"It's over, Claude," she said. "Now we have to think about the future."

He allowed her to take his hand to lead him away. "I thought I might wait until tomorrow to scrub away the foul traces of German existence," he said, suddenly halting. "But I think I'll begin immediately. The sooner I can make this my home again, the better; and the sooner I can get to work, the less I'll be likely to brood."

"Work?"

"My father must have kept some notes at the university. I mean to find them. Somehow I hope to reconstruct some of his theories and restore them for publication. I'm no philosopher, but I know the basics of his way of thinking."

"But the Nazis purged the archives and destroyed everything. They might easily return. Haven't you heard that they are advancing again?"

Claude shrugged. "Nevertheless, I'm going to try."

He walked quickly back into the kitchen and began to fill a bowl with water. "But first I must remove the Nazi poison that has contaminated my father's home."

Michou pushed up her sleeves. "Yes," she said. "We have much work to do."

While she worked in the kitchen, Claude cleaned away any trace of German presence, first from his mother's piano and then from the furniture in his father's study. The 19th century cylinder top writing-table that had always been cluttered with papers and books used for research, now looked unfamiliar in its current pristine state. His father rarely used it to write at, preferring to sit at the library table and spread things out around him. Claude had often wondered if his father knew the true value of the lovely piece, and as he opened and closed each marquetry inlaid drawer to ensure its emptiness he remembered how he had often hidden odd things in the false bottom of the small one on the top of the console. It had been many years since he had thought about his fascination for old coins and hoped that the Germans had not found his small, childhood collection. His hand was larger now and he groped awkwardly toward the back, seeking the tiny lever. Suddenly, the panel snapped open and to his delight he saw that the coins were still there. He stared at them for a moment, gently moving them about with the tip of his forefinger. If only there could have been such a compartment to conceal his father's manuscripts. He sighed and began to push the panel back in place when he saw a small slip of paper at the back of the drawer. He recognised his father's handwriting immediately and had difficulty in reading the words through a mist of tears.

Académie de Musique. Archives. Bizet.

Obviously, it has something to do with my mother, he thought. She often taught there. As he stood deep in thought, the significance of the note slowly dawned on him. Why would his father have written a note concerning his mother's field of interest?

"Come on, Michou!" he shouted. "We have an errand to run"

Oh God, he thought as he hurried her along the corridor, please let this be what I think it is. He remembered how impatient he had been when his father did not appear to understand the gravity of the approaching German occupational armies. He had wondered at his lack of awareness and stubborn refusal to leave. Perhaps he had known all along that his fate was doomed where ever he went in occupied Europe simply because he was a hated Jew. With this knowledge, he must have also known that his books would be destroyed. Yes, the books were gone. But if the manuscripts had been hidden amongst the volumes of music scored at the Academy, they could be republished. The books were gone, but their content may have survived. If this were so, the enormous task that he had envisioned would be radically reduced.

The startled Doyen shouted after them as they raced up the stairs of the Music Academy.

"It's all right," Claude shouted back. "I am Claude Simone. My father.....my mother was......."

The Doyen followed him up the stairs. "Yes. Yes. I had forgotten the boxes in the archives. Your mother brought them here before the occupation. I believe they might be in "B" section. Was it "B" for Bizet? I never knew exactly what was in them, but wondered at the time that she would want to store so many music scores."

Claude's joyous laugh echoed down the stairs. "Yes. "B" for Bizet!"

The manuscripts were indeed there in their entirety, concealed behind vast volumes of music. "Imagine," Claude whispered. "They could have lain here for years if I hadn't remembered my boyhood coin collection." Conscious of Michou's hand on his shoulder, he quickly grasped it. "How does life in the musty realms of academia appeal to you?" he said.

"In England? I shall have to brush up on the language."

He shook his head. "You can brush up on the English language all you like, but we'll work here, in France--at the Sorbonne. My father's writings will eventually be available again for all to read in order to see the fine points of his philosophies. How could he have known that his beliefs in the importance of universal alliance could be so pertinent to today's needs in order to rebuild, go forward, and must be instilled into those who will be eventually taking on the mammoth task. I intend to teach the values of international policies and procedures. I believe my father would have wanted that."

There might have been a problem in getting the manuscripts back to the apartment if a young American sergeant had not heard of their plight. A man whose knowledge and appreciation of music seemed to predominate over his military mien, he had come to ask permission to play one of the pianos at the Academy.

"I should think," he said, "my jeep would take most of the boxes, leaving room for the driver of course." He studied the pile thoughtfully. "But I'm afraid you'll have to walk."

With the manuscripts safely in the apartment, Claude suddenly felt the dreadful onus of the past few years lift from his shoulders. He was free. He had regained his own identity.

He had avenged his parents. And he was truly happy. He stood up and looked around the large room.

"I think my father wanted me to continue on here." He looked intently at Michou's upturned face. "Will you help me?"

"Do you really need to ask?" she said.

* * *

January, 1945

Although no relief from the icy clutches of the worst winter on record appeared to be forthcoming, the ATA pilots nonetheless reported for duty hoping for even a brief rise in the frigid temperatures. Since September, aircraft were being ferried to the Continent by the male pilots and in October the first woman flew a Spitfire to France, in spite of continuing pockets of German resistance. Now the women were regularly flying operational aircraft to France to areas as close to the front line as possible, and bringing those in need of repair back to England.

Yvonne leaned close to the window in the Mess at Hamble and peered out across the field where a low fog was threatening to envelop it. Perhaps, she thought, this mist might indicate a change in temperature and Operations may allow an aircraft or two to take off. It had been strange to fly back into France after so long and the devastation from the recent battles saddened her. She sighed and picked up a sock she had been trying to knit for several months and held it up for inspection. There was little doubt that it was not going to match its mate which had turned out to be two sizes too small. Well, she thought, my talents obviously lie elsewhere and the war's nearly over anyway. The soldier the socks might have been destined for would probably not be needing them now.

The telephone rang suddenly and everyone in the room looked expectantly toward it as the nearest woman picked it up.

"There's a senior military officer needs to be taken to Brussels," she said, putting her hand over the mouthpiece. "Who's willing to fly when even the birds are walking?"

"I'll go," Yvonne said, throwing her knitting aside.

"You'll have to fly up to Smiths Lawn in Great Windsor Park first where you'll receive further orders. There's a Spit available to get you there, provided you can see to get it off the ground."

Yvonne thankfully grabbed her gear and headed for the door. Inactivity was not her most favourite pastime and she was grateful for anything. The Spitfire did indeed make it off the ground and she landed near Great Windsor Park without incident. Within half a day Yvonne had been briefed for the flight to Brussels. Even though she was to navigate a specially equipped Anson for one of the senior ATA male pilots, she was glad to be going somewhere.

"I'm taking the Anson on to another assignment after this," the pilot told her. "Evasive action might be necessary on this leg since it's likely to get a bit hot over Belgium, which is why I need you. But the second leg will take me south over liberated territory so extra navigational assistance won't be required. There'll be something for you to ferry back, I'm sure."

Yvonne settled down to her charts, checking the best route to Brussels and the possible alternatives. If they did run into hostile action, then they would have to go south toward Paris. The pockets of continuing German resistance moved about the countryside erratically and were unpredictable. One simply had to be prepared to take evasive action.

They crossed the Channel in spasmodic fog and drizzle and assumed that they might get through undetected since the weather was less than ideal. Yvonne knew that their passenger was a high-ranking American, but his identity had not been revealed for security purposes. There had been no introductions, neither had any names been listed, but she instinctively knew that this man must be delivered to his destination safely. The responsibility of this task quickened her pulse and she prayed that nothing adverse would happen.

As they approached Ostende, she looked southward envisioning the evacuation scene at Dunkirk over four years ago. She wondered if those rescued soldiers might have gone back into battle and perhaps not have survived this time. Yet perhaps she had been instrumental in giving them a little more time to live.

Suddenly, the plane jolted. Black puffs of flak quickly surrounded them, some perilously close, and Yvonne knew that their chances of getting through now were extremely slim.

"Hang on!" the pilot shouted. "We're going south." He quickly banked the Anson and pulled back on the stick. "We're also going up," he muttered.

Unarmed and thus most vulnerable, it was obvious that they could not continue on to Brussels.

"We'll have to make for Paris," he said. "We'll refuel and go north from there."

Yvonne plotted their course into Le Bourget with trembling fingers. How ironic it would be if she should die now that the end of the war was in sight. By the time they landed, she felt calmer. Perhaps, after all, the need for dash and excitement was beginning to fade. Was it just the war, or was she simply getting older and wiser?

By coincidence, an American aircraft had landed at Le Bourget en route to Brussels and their very important passenger changed planes. Yvonne watched the strange looking craft take off and wondered if she would ever have the opportunity to fly a B-25 Mitchell. Heaven knows, she thought, I've flown just about everything else. Fascinated, she watched the great war machine gradually disappear into the clouds as its main wheels retracted rearwards and its mass of cockpit Perspex glinted just once as it reached for the sun.

The Anson pilot had already picked up his flight plan. "I'm on my way to Naples," he said. "Freight's being loaded now. There should be something for you to take back to England by this afternoon. Ops suggests going into Tangmere to avoid the east coast as much as possible. There's weather closing in, so be careful." He hesitated for a moment. "You girls are doing a grand job, you know," he said awkwardly.

Although the compliment appeared to be an afterthought, she nonetheless appreciated it. Such observations were quite rare.

An RAF Flight Lieutenant approached her as she lingered over a cup of tea in the snack bar. "Ever flown a Lancaster?" he asked, dubiously.

She and a co-pilot had delivered a two-engine Bristol Blenheim to the north only last week and a Lancaster the week before; both within the borders of the British Isles. She smiled confidently. "Of course."

"I thought you might have," the young man said. "This time you'll be copilot, though. We'll also have an SIS type passenger."

Although willing to try anything, full responsibility for the big bomber over hostile territory might have been somewhat overwhelming. Having completed the check list with the Flight Lieutenant, she looked around for the passenger he had mentioned.

"You have a choice," a voice said from behind her. "You can fly me as Ben Boniface, or Pierre Bonhomme, or Claude Simon. It's up to you."

He had changed considerably. Much too thin and with hair rapidly graying at the temples, he looked ten years older than when she had last seen him. She stared, unable to think of anything to say.

409

"Y-you made it," she said at last.

"What?"

"Dierick!" she whispered, leaning closer.

"Who?"

She smiled. "Are you ready to go home?"

"Not home for me any more, Yvonne. But I am going back to tie up a few loose ends. I have many responsibilities in France, but feel the need to clear the air in England first."

"I'm so sorry about your parents."

He looked away. "Yes. Thank you. I believe there were millions of victims like them. Time will tell, I'm sure."

The noise of the Lancaster's four 1,390 horsepower engines made further conversation impossible. Claude sat behind the copilot's seat and watched her, with unbridled admiration, help fly the great aeroplane. In spite of the weather, they landed at Manston on the east coast due to the longer runway there. Before Claude left for London, he agreed to join her in the American cafeteria at the air field for some coffee.

"When I returned," she told him. "There was so much going on in the Southampton area. The town was jammed with invasion equipment, although we weren't supposed to know what it was. The jetty outside the Hamble Yacht Club was awash with landing craft and the water was so choppy it looked like there had been an underwater earthquake! In just a few hours, it had all gone and we knew the invasion had begun. I somehow knew you and Michou would return to Paris to fight in the streets. That is what you did, isn't it?"

He nodded. "That, and more. Afterwards I had a compulsion to try and restore my father's work."

"But wasn't it destroyed?"

"The books, yes. But I found the manuscripts. Michou and I are going to publish them again."

"Ah, yes. Michou. She's a remarkable woman."

"The war has revealed that there are many remarkable women who have shown great dedication and bravery." Their eyes met for a brief moment. "Most will not expect any kind of acknowledgment, but that doesn't make them any less significant."

He rose and held out his hand and as she bade him farewell she knew that it would be a very long time before she would see him again.

CHAPTER NINETEEN

Long Bottom, February, 1945

Mr. Banberry appeared deflated, and he had looked that way since the beginning of December--the 3rd, to be exact. True, the winter weather was enough to make anyone depressed, and the lack of simply everything made things even worse. But the war was obviously coming to an end--albeit a slow end since the fighting continued both in Europe and Asia and there had not been an air attack by German bombers in quite some time. Although Kate could find all these logical reasons for happiness she did, in fact, understand Mr. Banberry's problem. The Government had seen fit to demobilise the Home Guard which had left him with nothing to do toward the war effort. His role as an observer had diminished, too, and it was obvious that his job in the post office had become mundane to him. He missed all the excitement.

"I suppose," he said, gloomily, "things will never really be the same again. All the lads coming back from the war will find it difficult to settle down to a routine peacetime sort of life, too."

"From what I can gather," Kate said, "they'll be jolly glad to come home. The fighting in Europe is worse than ever, even though they say the war is ending."

"Ah, yes. But there really is an end in sight now."

If things were not going so well for her at this time, she might have been able to sympathise even more with Mr. Banberry. Christmas had been another bleak celebration knowing that her father would never share another one with them, but she had rallied her optimism and encouraged her family to do the same. Somehow she and her mother had found odds and ends to fill Annie's Christmas stocking and Kate made a doll for her out of an old sock which Annie had promptly named Toots. Hugh, now looking forward to university where he planned to read History joined in the general congenial mood. There had been river trout for Christmas dinner (caught, they learned to some degree of chagrin, by a local poacher) and Mr. Baxter brought some vegetables from somebody's victory garden for which he had traded soap and jam rations. It might have been the turning point of the war, but food scarcities and the continuing lack of luxuries like turkeys, wine, clothes, and toys would tend to contradict that. The weather had aligned itself with the adverse conditions by bringing grippingly frigid days. Buildings devastated by V2 rockets became ice palaces as water from the fire hoses froze and draped them in sparkling icicles. Even the inkwells in school solidified overnight, and bottles of milk that had been delivered in the early hours popped their caps as the frozen cream pushed upward.

But none of these adversities could dampen Kate's spirits for long, for she had won a scholarship and the necessity for Ben's generous contributions toward her education could now cease. To add to her elation, Peter Trimble had shown more than a casual interest in her and had, in fact, kissed her goodbye when he caught the train from Eastbourne only last weekend.

A letter, addressed to Mrs. Hawkins from Ben's London solicitors, arrived in the afternoon post. Under normal circumstances this would have been of little significance since they regularly communicated in this manner, but the contents of the letter proved to be quite surprising. Kate watched as the expression on her mother's face blossomed from casual interest to pure delight.

"It appears that Mr. Boniface is liquidating his holdings in England, Kate," she said. "He's offering me the cottage for a ridiculously small sum. According to the solicitors it's only a token amount in order to make it a legal transaction." She glanced at Kate over the top of the letter. "I know you have disturbing memories of this place but you'll be leaving for college soon. It would make a perfect home for Annie and myself--and, of course, BC."

Kate felt a pang of remorse. It had not occurred to her that her mother might have detected her aversion to Mallory Cottage. Perhaps in time she would see it from a different aspect. It was, after all, a pretty place and the environment was both friendly and tranquil. Of course her mother should take it.

"Mr. Boniface has seen you through the vital years of your schooling Kate, and has been most generous in respect to Mallory Cottage. I must admit that because of that strange woman in the village, I thought he was up to something rather devious. But I don't think anyone evil would be so considerate of another. I honestly don't know what we would have done without him. I must find a way to make personal contact with him, where ever he is."

"I remember Yvonne Parke being interested in his whereabouts, too," Kate said. "She seemed most anxious to find him when she was here last."

"I think we must be patient, Kate. I'm sure the puzzle will all come together after the war is over. Right now I must make an appointment with his solicitors in order to buy the cottage."

As Kate toasted bread for tea in front of the fire she could hear her mother humming in the kitchen. It had been so long since she had seen her really smile. How odd that a strange man like Ben Boniface could have extended so much happiness.

* * *

London, March, 1945

The smell of carbolic and the rustle of starched linen are the two main symbols of a large and bustling hospital, Janine thought as she hurried along the corridor. Such a far cry from the stench of Ward III in 1940. She was on her way to see George who had just undergone the last and most crucial operation on his eye. With Yvonne busier that ever with ATA assignments and David going through the required administrative process of leaving the RAF at last, she felt the need to be at George's side when he regained consciousness. Deep in thought, she barely noticed her surroundings, or the people going to and fro around her.

There had been pictures of the Auschwitz concentration camp liberation in several publications last month and the dreadful evidence of extreme Nazi cruelty was exposed for the world to see. Shocked and sickened, Janine had spent sleepless nights since, and wondered if she would ever be able to obliterate those pitiful images from her mind. Would she and others have all died in this manner if Hitler had been allowed to continue?

415

Even now, the Germans were putting up an offensive in Hungary in order to protect the oil fields there. This all seemed so futile since the lack of fuel had been their main setback as the battles continued to rage. Did they really believe that they could hold out against the entire Allied forces? She remembered their supercilious arrogance as they strutted through the streets of occupied France and could envision the terror they must have inflicted on the people confined in the concentration camps. There were others yet to be liberated and she could not bear to think what this might reveal.

She stood aside to allow a nurse who pushed a wheelchair to pass, barely noticing them. Yet something caused her to pause--something familiar.

"Mrs. Parke? It is Mrs. Parke, isn't it?"

The nurse turned the wheelchair around and Janine looked hard at the wizened, stooped figure who smiled at her from its depths.

"I don't blame you for not recognising me," the woman said, huskily. She smiled again and the emaciated face rippled with a myriad of wrinkles and deep creases. "I'm glad I have this opportunity to tell you that you were right, after all. I should have left Paris as you suggested."

Astounded, Janine could barely believe her eyes.

"Mrs. Clyde-Pruitt?"

"I was a fool, Mrs. Parke. I was arrested as a suspected spy, but was spared because they could find no solid evidence that I was. How inane of them to think that I could possibly know anything, or anyone, associated with espionage."

"Y-yes. How silly of them," Janine stammered.

"It took a very long time for them to release me." The emaciated woman closed her eyes for a moment. "I think I would have preferred to have been executed after all." She paused, obviously short of breath. " I understand you left for England the following morning."

A victim of mere misdirected speculation, it was obvious that this poor innocent woman had suffered indescribable indignities in the hands of her captors. Promising to visit her soon, Janine continued along the corridor with yet another mental demon to fight. The proud Mrs. Clyde-Pruitt had been reduced to a mere shadow of her former self.

George lay flat on his back with his bandaged head encased in rigid pillows with orders not to move a muscle.

"Well," he said, cautiously. "This is it. Either I have an eye, or I don't."

She carefully took his hand in both of hers. "Should I try to contact your parents?"

"No! Absolutely not. You see, Phalene, they really wouldn't be interested. I'm supposed to have disappointed them deeply by opting for law at Oxford instead of pursuing the field of Diplomatic Service like my father. Unlike your husband, my father could not tolerate his son's independence-- defiance, he called it."

She smiled at his use of her code name but felt she should caution him. "First of all, you must stay calm, George. Secondly, habits can be difficult to break and I think you'd better drop the 'Phalene'."

"Yes, yes, of course. I didn't go through all that intensive training as you did and I suppose my mind isn't as alert to such things. You'll have to keep an eye on me, won't you?"

"I intend to do that, anyway," she said.

"Whatever happens," he went on, "I'm going back to finish at Oxford. I don't have to rely on my parent's financial support, you see. A legacy from my grandfather has seen to that. The most important thing now, other than my sight, is Yvonne."

"I don't think you have to worry about her," Janine said. "I don't see much of her these days, but when I do you're all she talks about."

Again he tried to smile. "What? She doesn't go on about aeroplanes any more?"

"You know she doesn't!"

"To change the subject--albeit reluctantly--I've heard that almost all of the men rescued from the Forêt de Fréteval have gone back to flying. Remarkable isn't it?" George said.

"Everyone wants to see a rapid end to this wretched war, and the more people involved, the quicker it will end. By the way, did they ever learn who finished off that menace Dierick?"

George smiled with difficulty because of the bandages across his cheek. "No, but I can guess. It's better that we leave it at that, don't you think?" The smile faded. "There was a ghastly incident afterwards that might have been an act of revenge by the Germans. The town of Oradour-sur-Glane was completely wiped out. I'm sorry, Janine, but I think we all need to know this. The 2nd Panzer Division, while moving from the town of Montauban just after D-Day, took all the women and children of Oradour into the town church and machine gunned them. The men were also executed and the town set on fire. There was a similar incident in Tulle about the same time. The evil Dierick might be one less to deal with, but doesn't it occur to you that there are many more like her? It's unlikely that the world will ever be rid of them all."

*   *   *

London, April, 1945

At last the frigid clutch of winter began to slacken and with it the doubts concerning imminent victory. The lethal and silent bombardment of V2s had ceased, and trees and shrubs in

Hyde Park were cautiously budding, seemingly convinced that they would not be destroyed again by war.

David passed the Queen Victoria Memorial in front of Buckingham Palace and looked down The Mall toward Admiralty Arch. As he walked slowly along the periphery of St. Jame's Park he savoured the spring air and the gentle warmth of a hesitant sun. But he was not at peace. Not sure if the irritation nagging at his conscience was one of guilt or misgiving, he tried to analyse his true priorities. For the past few weeks he had enjoyed Philippa's company and he supposed that their relationship had transitioned from companionship to love. But had it? She obviously thought so, since her conversation had lately focused on a future together.

He wondered how well she would adjust to life in the south of France. The problem of his future livelihood had been solved by his grandparents since the war had taken its toll on their health and they had asked if David might be willing to help manage the estate in Aix. With weakened hands and a reluctance to continue his university studies, this seemed to be a perfect solution. True he would have to set about learning the quality of wines and the maintenance of the vineyards. There were orchards and cultivated flowers to oversee, and the property itself. In this environment he would be able to fly a light plane occasionally which would certainly complete the promise of an idyllic way of life. But where would Philippa fit in? She was a society girl used to the social life of London. He glanced down at the ribbons on his uniform jacket which served to remind him of his wartime performance. He had achieved rank, the coveted distinction of being an ace Battle of Britain pilot, plus a DSO and a DFC for his efforts. Would he be able return to a quiet and tranquil life. If only he could return to Flint House in order to put himself through a period of transition. He wondered when the property in Long Bottom might be returned to the family.

Treading the grass in deep thought, he almost tripped over a young couple on the ground locked in a passionate embrace. Embarrassed, he turned away, thinking of Philippa and hurried on, urging his thoughts back to Long Bottom and his mother.

She had been particularly disturbed by the photographs of Auschwhitz and he knew she would be devastated by those of Belsen and Buchenwald. It seemed so ironic that the sadistic fiend who had created this gruesome situation would have celebrated his birthday only eight days after the death of the United States' President. How sad, he thought, that the man who had been responsible for the turning point in the war would not live to see the end of it. The newspaper and magazine media had reveled in yet more horrendous photographs of Mussolini who had been executed by Italian partisans near Lake Como and strung his upside down from a lamp post. David wondered how little children must react when seeing such pictures of his mutilated body blazoned across the front pages. While he knew he could not ignore these things, he desperately wanted to be somewhere where the news media was not so evident. Somewhere tranquil and quiet.

He sighed, realising that he could not solve all of his problems at once. The return to Flint House had become more of a need than a notion now and he decided to ask one of his parents when this might be possible.

*   *   *

The Long Man   Pauline Furey

London, May, 1945

"Please let the results be positive," Yvonne muttered as she hurried along. "Please let them be positive."

In spite of her punctual, if breathless, arrival at the hospital, she was asked to wait. Don't they know, she thought, what agony this is? Don't they understand the vital importance of it all? She paced about, agitated and angry, decrying the inane hospital rules under her breath. After fifteen minutes of forced detainment she sat down.

In a moment of speculation she saw the situation in a different light. If the operation had not been a success and George was destined to be blind in one eye, what real difference would it make to her? She had been in love with him from the beginning and any affliction could not change that. Obviously, she would share his disappointment, but they had already made plans that would apply to their future either way.

Yvonne had not been idle since her return from France. When opportunities for further aviation-related qualifications were offered, she grasped them and had endorsed her commercial "B" license for civil passenger conveyance. She had attended courses for navigational competence and passed all the required exams. George intended to accomplish his law degree one way or another and she would continue to fly--one way or another--until he had.

A nurse called her name and pointed to a door. "You may go in now," she said.

Calmer now, Yvonne braced herself for the results of the surgery as her eyes accustomed themselves to dim light.

"Where are you?" she said, softly.

"I'm over here in the armchair."

He did not rise to meet her and that, along with the darkened room, did not bode well. She moved quietly toward the chair.

Suddenly, he was on his feet, gathering her into his arms and showering her face with multitudes of kisses.

"How many eyes do we have between us?" she gasped.

"Two for you and....well....two for me. Doesn't that make four?"

* * *

Bayswater

"I'm led to believe," Janine said, "that there are still a few diehard Nazis willing to prolong the war in spite of Hitler's apparent suicide."

She looked at the two war-scarred young men seated at the breakfast table in Bayswater.

"Have you seen today's paper?" George said. "They're surrendering all over the place....Italy, northwest Europe....and today they have accepted the Allied terms of unconditional general surrender in Rheims. I don't think those diehards you mention have much choice."

Janine suddenly felt very tired. Could the war really be over?

"We'll be hanging up our uniforms for good now," David said. "My squadron is disbanding this month, anyway."

"I suppose it is difficult to realise that it's over," Janine said. "I should have accepted that when Yvonne mentioned that Fighter Command Headquarters had dissolved the Balloon Command in February. But after so long........."

"Care to join us in a celebratory drink at the Shepherd's?" David asked.

"I wouldn't go near that dreadful place," Janine laughed. "But you two should join up with your RAF chaps, and if you tie one on don't slam the door when you come in."

* * *

London, May 8th and 9th, 1945

Although the official recognition of Victory in Europe did not occur until the following day, London was alive with relieved and jubilant citizens through the night. Two weary and blissfully happy young men watched the dawn come up as they sat on the steps in front of the Bayswater house. They had toasted their lost comrades throughout the night and at one point, when they were in their old haunt in Shepherd's Market, David thought he could even feel Rupert's presence beside him. He had turned his head, half expecting to see his good friend standing there, and saw instead another familiar face.

"Well, I see you two made it through--although not exactly unscathed."

Donald Moore walked stiffly toward them, leaning heavily on a cane.

"I thought I'd come in to London to see if any of you might be here," he said, shaking their hands. He looked briefly at David's hands and face and shook his head. "Cockpit burns, they're calling your type of injury. They don't have a name for mine.....although I can tell you, I do! You've come through pretty well though, David. I've seen Patrick and he's coping admirably."

He turned his attention to George. "I heard you disappeared for three years. How did you manage that?"

423

George put his finger to his lips. "Sh-h-h. I'm incognito, you know. Hence the dark glasses."

Donald nodded knowingly and smiled.

They talked for awhile about the war and their peacetime plans. Donald and his wife had bought some acreage in Kent and were embarking on a market garden business.

"The tin legs aren't that incapacitating," he said. "My wife can always use me as a scarecrow! We're expecting, you know."

"Expecting?"

David nudged George. "They're going to have a baby, idiot!"

"Oh, right. Well, congratulations, sir."

"Keep in touch, chaps," Donald said, turning to leave. "We'll have a squadron reunion one of these days."

David watched him move toward the door, and felt a lump rise in his throat as he remembered his last drink at Tangmere with Donald. There had been a deep sense of understanding between them and David knew he would never forget him. He vowed then that there would indeed be many reunions. He had ambled home beside George sobered by the memories of war, reliving again the fierce determination to kill or be killed, and the dreadful fear that he had so desperately tried to ignore. Yet they had come through it all, albeit battered and scarred. There would always be memories--some even pleasurable. Soon, they would cease to mourn their dead and simply remember them as the close and courageous friends that they were. The survivors were ready now to take their places in a world at peace. They shared this time of celebration with the happy crowd as they made their way through a city aglow with street lights and blatantly glaring windows. Tomorrow would be time enough to turn toward the mammoth task of rebuilding their lives, their homes, and their places of work. On this memorable night, no amount of dull and drizzly weather could

possibly succeed in dampening the overwhelming feeling of joy
and relief.

CHAPTER TWENTY

Flint House, August, 1945

At the shimmering start of the month, Janine felt sad. Prime Minister Winston Churchill had seen them through the most devastating war imaginable and yet the people of Britain had opted not to keep him in office when the election results were announced on July 26th. What unmitigated ingratitude, she thought. But she knew that with the relief of victory in Europe the working people had shrugged off the need for protection and demonstrated their preference for a new leader. A new beginning.

She walked through the rooms of Flint House and decided that the entire place needed a cosmetic lift. Considering it had been a hospital for over four years it had fared well. Upon noticing small areas of damage, she wondered to what extent the young men who might have caused them would recover. The cure of mental anguish had to be an elusive thing and she wondered if their phobias, anger, and frustrations might ever be banished.

David had asked to come home for awhile. She knew he had much on his mind--decisions to make, his future to think of--and what better place to get things into perspective than the peaceful countryside of East Sussex. Her children were no longer in need of her parental protection, but she hoped they would always consider Flint House as their home.

Although the war had come to an end, the wounded and maimed would need treatment for years to come and Janine knew that Henry would continue to be occupied with his practice, and at the military and civilian hospitals. But any physician worth his salt would always be busy, and she had known this from the beginning. Bayswater and Flint House would continue to function and she would continue to work. Already there was talk that the United Nations coalition would be headquartered in New York and she had been approached to consider a position as a delegate, or at the very least, an interpreter. There were so many loose ends to be tied all over the world. Pétain had been sentenced to death for treason and she wondered if they would really snuff out the life of an already old and tired man. The evil Laval had been extradited from Spain and handed over to the French Provisional Government. Conversely, Janine hoped that he *would* be executed. A new and devastating weapon had been used against the Japanese that had brought the war in Asia to an end. Again the media had enjoyed publishing photographs of the horribly burned victims, the carnage, and the complete obliteration of Hiroshima and Nagasaki caused by the Atomic Bomb.

As she looked out from her sitting room window, the ancient beech shading the lawn seemed to rustle its leaves to welcome her home and the poplars beyond the wall quivered in the August sun. She suddenly thought of Charlie. Kate would be living in the Bayswater house with Mrs. Dougherty until she finished college. Perhaps the little dog would want to come home. But that could all wait until the rest of the furniture arrived from storage. Her immediate task was to find the crate with the linens and make up a couple of beds. John Farnsworth at the farm had sold her a small chicken and she planned to then put together a meal for herself and David. When buying the chicken, she had asked after Jenny.

"She married one of those American chaps and is off to the United States," he said with a shrug. "The last time I saw her she was as big as a house. Hope she gets to America before that baby's born." He had shaken his head. "Worse Land Girl in the whole Land Army. But she certainly knew how to climb up into a hay loft!" He had kicked at a clod of earth. "I suppose she felt life might be short and decided to live it while she could."

Thank heavens everyone didn't think that way, Janine thought. As she puttered about the kitchen she allowed her thoughts to travel back in time to the first day of the war when her friend and colleague, Claude Simone, had justifiably fretted over his Jewish parents in Paris. An absolute victim of circumstances, he had somehow untangled himself from the subsequent mess his ethnic background had created. Whether his anger and deep sorrow had been the cause of Dierick's demise no one would ever really know; in fact, it no longer mattered. It appeared that the SIS had no quarrel with Claude Simone and had unofficially praised his significant contribution to the French Underground activities. Perhaps, one day in the far future, they would be able meet again and reminisce about their work together.

She thought of David and his eagerness to fly a fighter plane. His face had been flushed with enthusiasm. She doubted that he had the slightest inkling of her concern for him then. She glanced at the armchair where he had stretched out his long legs and blocked Jenny's way. Of all ridiculous things, she suddenly remembered that inevitable hole in his sock.

If the war has changed anyone for the better it must certainly be Yvonne, she thought. Still young and beautiful, her emergence from the self indulgent focus of youth has been quite remarkable. Her dedication and exemplary record with ATA came as quite a pleasant surprise. Janine wondered how her daughter might adjust to civilian life, for surely the women of ATA would not be asked to continue their services in peacetime conditions; if indeed ATA would exist at all. Perhaps next month she, Janine, would see if either of the Fox Moths might be released back to them. The one thing that neither she nor Yvonne would ever abandon was their mutual love of flying. In any case, now that George's eyesight was restored they would all most likely continue to pursue that pleasure.

The crunch of tyres on the gravel announced David's arrival in the Green Daimler. What had Rupert called it.....DDI? One day, perhaps she would be able to tell her children how Rupert flew her on a mission to France, never knowing who she was. Thank heavens, Janine thought, that I was the only one in the family to become involved in that sort of thing!

*   *   *

Mallory Cottage

"Don't go," Annie said. "I don't want you to go."

She sat in the middle of the bed hugging BQ to her chest, watching her sister pack a suitcase. It seemed to Kate that it was only yesterday when she pushed Annie about in her pram. Now at five years old, her little sister had already begun to attend preliminary school.

"I'll only be in London," Kate assured her. "That's not very far away at all. Besides, you're going to be busy now,

Annie. You have school to think about and you'll make lots of friends."

Even as she spoke, Kate knew how her sister felt. Hadn't she known this apprehension often herself? But time has a way of eliminating fear of the unknown, she thought. I suppose there really isn't anything that could be more frightening than war. Yet, although it was she who was leaving, she still empathised with Annie's anxiety since she herself still had difficulty with good-byes. Hadn't she felt the same when Hugh left--when her father left?

"I'll come home every weekend," she said, assuredly. "I promise."

BC, stretched out in a most ungainly position on the rocking chair, opened one eye and seemed to be weighing the situation. He sat up and yawned, revealing every one of his sharp teeth, and jumped onto the bed, leaving the chair rocking back and forth.

Kate smiled as he nosed BQ over and tried to sit on Annie's small lap. She was about to speak when the cat suddenly meowed and began to purr.

"He's never done that before," Annie said, staring.

"I didn't know he could," Kate gasped. "All this time I thought he was mute. How very strange."

She looked at her watch. Her mother would be back from the post office soon and there would be just enough time to take Charlie for one last walk up to the Long Man. She knew Mrs. Parke had arrived at Flint House that morning and that it would be just a matter of time before Charlie would have to go home. Perhaps Annie might be allowed to take him for walks when she was old enough.

"When is Mr. Baxter coming?" Annie asked.

"As soon as Mr. Banberry leaves for Canada. Not long now."

Arthur Banberry had not spoken empty words when he lamented the disbandment of the Home Guard. Although an

430

old bachelor who was very set in his ways, he had nonetheless decided to seek new horizons in Toronto where there were relatives. After his announcement, the villagers wondered who would run the shop and post office, until Mrs. Hawkins quietly offered to take over the position. Now in training for Post Mistress, she was also learning the intricacies of retail sales.

"A bit of paint and some summer-time spring cleaning should spruce it up quite a bit," she had said, well out of Mr. Banberry's hearing. "I think it just needs a woman's touch."

With Mr. Banberry's departure, the flat above the shop would become vacant. As it was, the entire structure was for sale and Kate had hoped that whoever bought it would allow her mother to make the changes she planned. Meanwhile, the village waited and watched. Within the week, Mr. Banberry announced that he had a buyer and assured everyone in the village they would be pleased.

It so happened that the house in Balham in which Mr. Baxter still rented a dismal room, had been condemned since a V2 landed close by, and was due to be pulled down. Trying to find somewhere else to live had become frustrating since there was nothing available. Then he heard of Arthur's plans. What better solution to his problem than the accommodation above the post office in Long Bottom? The attic under the deep roof would make an ideal studio for him once a skylight had been installed and some cheerful decoration in the living area would brighten the place no end.

*   *   *

Flint House

How odd to feel like a stranger in ones own home, David thought. The house looked the same from the outside and although the grounds were somewhat overgrown it would not take long to get them back in shape. But he had been away for so long and things were so very different for him before that. The village remained unchanged and, when driving though, he had thought about stopping at Mallory Cottage. But Kate mentioned in her last letter that she would be leaving for London and it occurred to him then that she may have already gone. He would have to seek her out in the city before he left for France. Although never having quite faced up to it, he dreaded the thought of seeing her. He was no longer a dashing young pilot in the RAF but a disfigured civilian who could not fly an airplane without pain. He had never told her the extent of his injuries and regretted that now. It might have prepared her.

He found his mother making up beds and they talked for awhile about Aix and what his life would be like there. He made no mention of Philippa but knew that his mother waited to hear their plans. How like her not to probe. He left her preparing the chicken in the kitchen, suggesting that he might go and say goodbye to Arthur Banberry.

As he strolled through the village his unease began to lessen. The familiar cottages, the soft green curve of the downs beyond where the outline of the Long Man was now barely visible, the row of poplars, the uneven pavement, and the old stationery shop, all served to calm him.

He found Arthur putting the last pieces of mail in order ready for delivery.

"Hello, young David," he said. "Nice to see you back." He looked at the letters in his hand, and sighed. "Won't be doing this much longer, will I?"

As usual, the old Post Master appeared to be oblivious to the passing of time and the arrangement of his shop reflected this. No one ever needed to ask where anything was since each category of merchandise had been displayed in the same place for twenty years. Mr. Banberry had conducted his business in the same manner without deviation, and for a brief moment David suddenly felt like school boy again. But the war had changed all that. Mr. Banberry was bored and ready to seek new interests away from the village.

"What are you going to do in Canada, Mr. Banberry?"

"Retire!"

"But I thought you missed all the activity."

"Well, a change is as good as a rest. Think I'll do some traveling. Perhaps I'll be a lumberjack or a Mountie. Maybe I'll even get married."

David laughed. "That'll be the day. But I wish you luck. They say it's a good institution."

He left the shop and stood on the edge of the curb. His stomach tightened as he looked at Mallory Cottage, again dreading the thought of a child's reaction to his appearance. I can't do it, he thought. I'll write to her from France.

Feeling like a criminal, he hurried away. At the end of the road, he broke into a run. The openness of the downs drew him like a magnet, and he ran blindly up the Wilmington Road as tears misted his vision. Oh, God, he thought. How could I pretend everything would be all right. How can I expect others to accept me, if I can't accept myself. Half way through Wilmington Village he stopped to catch his breath. Although he wanted his life to be productive and interesting, he suddenly felt things were changing and moving too fast. Positive now that he wanted to go to Aix, he was equally sure he wanted to go alone, at least for the time being.

He ran his fingers along the top of the church wall and looked up, seeking the outline of the Long Man. Barely visible in its deliberately obliterated state, he could just make out the perpendicular shape of a pole. Perhaps he would go up and try to follow the entire outline as he had done before the war. As he moved toward the stile he could see a figure walking beside the hedgerow. A slight, dark-haired girl. A black dog darted in and out of the wild flowers, and he heard the girl laugh.

He stood transfixed for a moment and quickly turned to leave, but the dog had seen him and came to him whimpering and yelping and leaping about like a wild thing.

"Charlie!" the girl cried. "Come here!"

"I-it's all right," David stammered.

She was there beside him and he knew he could not escape.

"David!" Her unique ponderous smile embraced him in all its candid warmth.

"It's Kate," she said, holding out her hands to him. "I heard you were coming home."

All his apprehension melted as he took her hands and looked down at her lovely, young face. He thought of the hundreds of words she had written to him over the years and how he had always envisioned her as the little girl in Mallory Cottage when he read them. He remembered the many times she had made him laugh and how often he reread her letters when she wrote about her war. He had lost count of the times she had come to him in his delirium and pulled him through. How many times, when pain had relentlessly stalked him, had her sketches and water colours soothed him?

She looked down at his hands holding hers and gently ran her fingers over the scars.

"It was a dreadful war, David. But it's all over now and we can get on with our lives."

"Yes," he said, suddenly feeling the burden of indecision drifting away. "We *can* get on with our lives. We can go in any direction we choose, and we can think about our future without any interference. Nothing can change that now, can it?"

His sudden enthusiasm was infectious and Kate began to laugh. Filled with uninhibited joy and relief, he ran up along the path of the Long Man's supporting pole.

"Come on, Kate. I'll race you to the top."

And the sound of their laughter echoed around the hills.

Exhibitions, Clubs and Memorials Today

There are several societies and clubs in England that continue to commemorate the Battle of Britain. Memorials exist at Biggin Hill in Kent, and the Battle of Britain Memorial statue is aptly situated on the cliffs near Folkstone. St. Clement Dane's in London is now the official RAF church and lists all squadrons.

The Guinea Pig Club still exists with HRH Prince Philip of England as its patron. The numbers have dwindled, but the reunions each year in East Grinstead continue with enthusiasm. Sir Archibald McIndoe's ashes are interned at St. Clement Dane's.

The ATA flag can be viewed at the White Waltham parish church. The flag was retired at White Waltham Airfield on November 30th, 1945. In the crypt of St. Paul's cathedral a plaque commemorates those men and women who died whilst serving with ATA.

Other exhibitions around England highlight the homefront during the war and several depict the civilian gas masks, the tiny food rations, the Anderson air raid shelter, and much more.

Special Acknowlegements

Special thanks is directed to the following people who were so very helpful in my research:

The late Wing Commander
      Alan Geoffrey Page,
         DSO, DFC and Bar, OBE.
Richard Wallington
George Holloway
Jack Alloway
Sam Gallop, OBE
Dennis Smith
The late Frank Dean
The late Percy Jays
Thomas Brandon,
Leslie Syrett
John Higden
Bill Foxley
Diana Barnarto-Walker
Maureen Dunlop Popp
Philippa Bennett Booth
Isobel Davidson
Dr. James Davidson
June Heaslip
Joyce Bobby
Cherry Benzman
Robin Brooks
Betty Winder
William Allchorn

Roy Davis
Cdr. John Devereaux, USN (ret)
Lt.Col. Keith Baker, USA reserve
Gordon Wheeler
The late C.A.L. Hurry
Wing Commander Stan Hubbard
Wing Commander Tim Elkington
Pat Fry
John Southwell
Tom Potter
Peter Mailing
Heather Symes
Len TellingGeoffrey Nutkins

ISBN 155395306-1

9 781553 953067